From the
Fifteenth
D·i·s·t·r·i·c·t

Other titles available from G. K. Hall by Mavis Gallant:

A Fairly Good Time
The Other Paris

From the Fifteenth District

Mavis Gallant

G. K. HALL & CO.
Boston, Massachusetts
1986

This G. K. Hall paperback edition is reprinted by arrangement
with the author.

First G. K. Hall printing, 1986.

Library of Congress Cataloging-in-Publication Data

Gallant, Mavis.
  From the Fifteenth District.

  "All of the stories in this book originally appeared in the New
Yorker"—T.p. verso.
  I. Title.
[PR9199.3.G26F7   1986]   813'.54   85-24909
ISBN 0-8398-2897-7 (pbk.)

To H. T.

CONTENTS

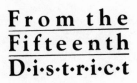

From the
Fifteenth
D·i·s·t·r·i·c·t

THE
FOUR SEASONS

I

THE SCHOOL Carmela attended for much of six years was founded by Dr. Barnes, a foreigner who had no better use for his money. It had two classrooms, with varnished desks nailed to the floor, and steel lockers imported from England, and a playing field in which stray dogs collected. A sepia picture of the founder reading a book hung near a likeness of Mussolini. The two frames were identical, which showed the importance of Dr. Barnes—at least in Castel Vittorio. Over their heads the King rode horseback, wearing all his medals. To one side, somewhat adrift on the same wall, was the Sacred Heart. After Carmela was twelve and too old to bother with school anymore, she forgot all the history and geography she'd learned, but she remembered the men in their brown frames, and Jesus with His heart on fire. She left home that year, just after Easter, and came down to the Ligurian coast between Ventimiglia and Bordighera. She was to live with Mr. and Mrs. Unwin now, to cook and clean and take care of their twin daughters. Tessa and Clare were the children's names;

Carmela pronounced them easily. The Unwins owned a small printing press, and as there was a large Anglo-American colony in that part of the world they never lacked for trade. They furnished letterhead stationery, circulars, and announcements for libraries, consulates, Anglican churches, and the British Legion—some printed, some run off the mimeograph machine. Mr. Unwin was also a part-time real-estate agent. They lived in a villa on top of a bald hill. Because of a chronic water shortage, nothing would grow except cactus. An electric pump would have helped the matter, but the Unwins were too poor to have one put in. Mrs. Unwin worked with her husband in the printing office when she felt well enough. She was the victim of fierce headaches caused by pollen, sunshine, and strong perfumes. The Unwins had had a cook, a char, and a nanny for the children, but when Carmela joined the household they dismissed the last of the three; the first two had been gone for over a year now. From the kitchen one could look down a slope into a garden where flowering trees and shrubs sent gusts of scent across to torment Mrs. Unwin, and leaves and petals to litter her cactus bed. An American woman called "the Marchesa" lived there. Mrs. Unwin thought of her as an enemy—someone who deliberately grew flowers for the discomfort they created.

Carmela had never been anywhere except her own village and this house, but Mrs. Unwin had no way of knowing that. She pressed a cracked black change purse in Carmela's hand and sent her down the hill to the local market to fetch carrots and not over a pound of the cheapest stewing beef. Carmela saw walled villas, and a clinic with a windbreak of cypress trees and ochre walls and black licorice balconies. Near the shore, work had stopped on some new houses. One could look through them, where windows were still holes in the walls, and catch a glimpse of the sea. She heard someone comment in an Italian more precious than her own, "Hideous. I hope they fall down on top of the builder. Unwin put money in it, too, but he's bankrupt." The woman who made these remarks was sitting under the pale-blue awning of a café so splendid that Carmela felt bound to look the other way. She caught, like her flash of the sea, small round tables and colored ices in silver dishes. All at once she recognized a chauffeur in uniform leaning with his back to a speckless motorcar. He was from Castel Vittorio. He gave no sign that he knew Carmela. Her real life was beginning now, and she never doubted its meaning. Among the powerful and the strange she would be mute and watchful. She would swim like a little fish, and learn to breathe under water.

At the beginning, she did not always understand what was said, or what Mrs. Unwin expected. When Mrs. Unwin remarked, "The chestnut trees flower beautifully up where you come from, though, of course, the blossoms are death for *me*," Carmela stopped peeling vegetables for the English stew Mrs. Unwin was showing her how to make and waited for something more. "What have I said now to startle you?" said Mrs. Unwin. "You're like a little sparrow!" Carmela still waited, glancing sidelong, hair cut unevenly and pushed behind her ears. She wore a grey skirt, a cotton blouse, and sandals. A limp black cardigan hung on her shoulders. She did not own stockings, shoes, a change of underwear, a dressing gown, or a coat, but she had a medal on a chain, an inheritance from a Sicilian grandmother—the grandmother from whom she had her southern name. Mrs. Unwin had already examined Carmela's ears to see if the lobes were pierced. She couldn't stand that—the vanity of it, and the mutilation. Letting Carmela's ears go, she had said to her husband, "Good. Mussolini is getting rid of most of that. All but the medals."

"Have I pronounced 'chestnut' in some peculiar way? My Italian can't be that bad." She got a little green dictionary out of the pocket of her smock and ruffled its pages. She had to tilt her head and close an eye because of the cigarette she kept in her mouth. "I don't mean horse chestnuts," she said, the cigarette waving. "How very funny that is in Italian, by the way. I mean the Spanish chestnuts. They flower late in the season, I believe."

"Every flower has its season," said the child.

Carmela believed this conversation to have a malignant intent she could not yet perceive. The mixture of English and unstressed Italian was virtually impossible for her to follow. She had never seen a woman smoking until now.

"But your family *are* up the Nervia Valley?" Mrs. Unwin insisted. "Your father, your mother, your sisters and your cousins and your aunts?" She became jocular, therefore terrifying. "Maria, Liliana, Ignazio, Francamaria . . ." The names of remembered servants ran out.

"I think so," said Carmela.

Her mother had come down to Bordighera to work in the laundry room of a large hotel. Her little brother had been apprenticed to a stonemason. Her father was dead, perhaps. The black and the grey she wore were half-mourning.

"Mussolini is trying to get away from those oversized families," said Mrs. Unwin with confidence. She sat on a high stool, arranging flowers in a copper bowl. She squashed her cigarette suddenly and drank out of a teacup. She seemed to Carmela unnaturally tall. Her hands were stained, freckled, *old,* but she was the mother of Tessa and Clare, who were under three and still called "the babies." The white roses she was stabbing onto something cruel and spiked had been brought to the kitchen door by the chauffeur from Castel Vittorio. This time he had given Carmela a diffident nod.

"Do you know him?" said Mrs. Unwin instantly.

"I think I saw him in the town," said Carmela.

"Now, that is deceitful," said Mrs. Unwin, though without reproach. "He knows who *you* are, because he vouched for your whole family. 'Hard-working, sober, the pride of the Nervia Valley.' I hope there is to be none of that," she added, in another voice. "You know what I mean. Men, giggling, chatting men up in the doorway, long telephone calls."

The white roses were a peace offering: a dog belonging to the next-door neighbor had torn up something precious in the Unwins' garden. Mrs. Unwin suddenly said that *she* had no time to stroll out in pink chiffon, wearing a floppy hat and carrying a sprinkling can; no time to hire jazz bands for parties or send shuttlecocks flying over the hedge and then a servant to retrieve them; less time still to have a chauffeur as a lover. Carmela could not get the drift of this. She felt accused.

"I don't know, Signora," she said, as though some yes-or-no answer had been required point-blank.

Where the roses had come from everything was white, green, lavish, sweet-smelling. Plants Carmela could not have put a name to bent over with the weight of their blooms. She could faintly hear a radio. All of that belonged to the Marchesa. She was the one who had said, "Hideous."

Pollen carried on the wind from the Marchesa's garden felled Mrs. Unwin in May. She was also assaulted by a large tree-like shrub on the Marchesa's side called a datura; some of its bell-like creamy flowers hung over the cactus patch. Their scent, stronger than jasmine, was poison to Mrs. Unwin's nervous system. From her darkened room she sent for Carmela. She opened a leather box with a little key and showed her a sapphire set in diamonds and a loose emerald. She told Carmela the names of the stones and said, "I do not believe in hiding. I am telling you where they are and that the key is in my handkerchief case." Again Carmela felt she had been accused.

The babies sat on their mother's bed meanwhile. They were placid, sleepy children with yellow hair Carmela enjoyed brushing; only one thing was tiring about them—they were too lazy to walk. One or the other had to be carried by Carmela, hooked like a little monkey above her left hip. She began to stand with her spine slightly bent to one side, as a habit. What she remembered of that spring was the weight of Clare or Tessa pulling her shoulder down, and that she was always hungry. Carmela had never known people to eat so little as the Unwins, not even among the poor. They shared a thin cutlet for lunch, or the vegetable remains of a stew, or had an egg apiece or a bit of cooked ham. The children's food and Carmela's was hardly more abundant. Mrs. Unwin did not mean to undernourish her own children; she sincerely believed that very little was enough. Also, meat was expensive. Fruit was expensive. So were cheese, butter, coffee, milk, and bread. The Unwins were pinched for money. They had a house, a printing establishment, furniture, a garden, a car, and they had Carmela, but they had nothing to spend. The drawing-room carpet was scuffed and torn, and the wine-red wallpaper displayed peony-shaped stains of paler dampmold. Mrs. Unwin counted out the coins she gave Carmela for shopping, and she counted the change.

On Fridays the Unwins would send Carmela across to France, where a few things, such as chocolate and bananas, were cheaper. That was not the only reason; it seemed that vegetables grown in Italy gave one typhoid fever. Carmela rode in a bus to within a few yards of the border, walked over (the customs men on both sides came to know her), and took a narrow road downhill to an avenue along the sea. She went as far as the marketplace, never beyond it. She always brought back a loaf of French bread, because it was one of the few things Mr. Unwin could eat with any pleasure. His chronically poor appetite was one of the reasons so little food came into the house. Carmela would break off one end of the loaf to eat on the spot. Then she would break off the other end, to make the loaf symmetrical, but she always kept that crust for later.

Carmela had two other reasons to be anxious that spring. One had to do with the room she slept in; the other was the sea. Although she had spent her life not many miles from the sea, it made her uneasy to be so close to it. At night she heard great waves knock against the foundations of the town. She dreamed of being engulfed, of seeking refuge on rooftops. Within the dream her death seemed inevitable. In the garden, coaxing the twins to walk, she said to the chauffeur from Castel Vittorio, "What happens when the sea comes out?"

In his shirtsleeves, walking the Marchesa's dogs on the road outside, he stopped and laughed at Carmela. "What do you mean, 'out'?"

"Out, up," said Carmela. "Up out of where it is now."

"It doesn't come up *or* out," he said. "It stays where it is."

"What is there where we can't see?"

"More water," he said. "Then Africa."

Carmela crossed herself—not out of a more ample fear but for the sake of her father, who had probably died there. He had been conscripted for a war and had never come back. There had been no word, no telegram, no congratulations from Mussolini, and of course no pension.

As for her room, it was off the pantry, almost higher than long, with a tiled floor and a good view, if one wanted that. Someone had died there—a relative of Mrs. Unwin's; he had come for a long visit and had been found on the tiles with an electric bell switch in his hand.

"A peaceful death," said Mrs. Unwin, utterly calmly, talking as if Carmela would need to know the history of the place. "Not even time to ring."

The old man's heart was delicate; he could not climb stairs. Who would have heard the bell? It rang somewhere in the passage. The servants they'd kept in those days slept out, and the Unwins took sleeping draughts, yellow and green, prepared in the kitchen and carried up to bed. Carmela felt the sad presence of the poor relation who had come ailing to a good climate and had been put in the meanest room; who had choked, panicked, grabbed for the bell, and fallen on it. The chauffeur from Castel Vittorio had still another version: this house had belonged to the old man. The Unwins had promised to look after him in his lifetime in exchange for the property. But so many debts had come with it that they could not raise any money on it. They were the next thing to paupers, and were known along the coast more or less as steady defaulters.

The chauffeur had often seen the uncle's ghost walking to and fro in the garden, and Carmela herself was often to hear the thud as his body fell between her bed and the door. Under the bed—as beneath any bed that she knew of—was a devil, or a demon, waiting to catch her. Not for a fortune would she have sat on the edge of the bed with her feet dangling. At night she burrowed beneath the bedclothes with a mole tunnel left for breathing. She made sure that every strand of hair was tucked out of sight.

Mornings were tender—first pink, then pearl, then blue. The house was quiet, the twins were awake and smiling. From their upstairs window the sea was a silken cushion. White sails floated— feathers. The breeze that came in was a friendly presence and the fragrance of the Marchesa's garden an extra gift. After a time Carmela's phantoms were stilled. The softness of that June lulled them. The uncle slept peacefully somewhere, and the devil under the bed became too drowsy to stretch out his hand.

II

LATE IN JUNE, Carmela's little brother ran away from the stonemason and came to the kitchen door. His blond hair was dark with sweat and dirt and his face streaked with it. She gave him a piece of bread she had saved from a French loaf, and a cup of the children's milk out of the icebox. The larder was padlocked; Mrs. Unwin would be along to open it before teatime. Just as Carmela was rinsing the cup she heard, "Who is that, Carmela?" It was Mr., thank God, not Mrs.

"A beggar," said Carmela.

The babies' father was nearsighted. He wore thick glasses, never shouted, seldom smiled. He looked down at the boy in the doorway and said to him, "Why do you beg? Who sends you to do this?" The child's hand was clenched on something, perhaps a stolen something. Mr. Unwin was not unkind; he was firm. The small fist turned this and that way in his grasp, but he managed to straighten the fingers; all that he revealed was a squashed crust and a filthy palm. "Why do you beg?" he repeated. "No one needs to beg in modern Italy. Who sends you? Your father? Your mother? Do they sit idly at home and tell you to ask for money?" It was clear that he would never have put up with an injustice of that kind. The child remained silent, and soon Mr. Unwin found himself holding a hand he did not know what to do with. He read its lines, caked with dirt and marked clearly in an M-shape of blackness. "Where do you live?" he said, letting go. "You can't wander around up here. Someone will tell the police." He did not mean that he would.

"He is going back where he came from," said Carmela. The child looked at her with such adult sadness, and she turned away so gravely as she dried the cup and put it on a shelf, that Mr. Unwin would tell his wife later, in Carmela's hearing, "They were like lovers."

"Give him something," he said to Carmela, who replied that she would, without mentioning that the larder was padlocked; for surely he knew?

Carmela could understand English now, but nobody guessed that. When she heard the Unwins saying some time after this that they wanted a stonemason because the zoning laws obliged them to grow a hedge or build a wall to replace the sagging wire that surrounded their garden, she kept still; and when they asked each other if it would be worthwhile speaking to Carmela, who might know of someone reliable and cheap, she wore the lightest, vaguest of looks on her face, which meant "No." It was the Marchesa who had lodged a complaint about the Unwins' wire. The unsightliness of it lowered the value of her own property. Mrs. Unwin promised her husband she would carry the bitterness of this to her grave.

The light that had sent the house ghosts to sleep brought Mrs. Unwin nothing but despair. She remained in her curtained bedroom and often forgot even to count the change Carmela returned in the black purse. Dr. Chaffee, of the clinic down the hill, called to see Mrs. Unwin. He wanted to look at the children, too; their father had told him how Tessa and Clare were too lazy to walk. Dr. Chaffee was not Italian and not English. The English physician who had been so good with children and so tactful with their parents had gone away. He was afraid of war. Mrs. Unwin thought this was poor of him. Mussolini did not want war. Neither did Hitler, surely? What did Dr. Chaffee think? He had lived in Berlin.

"I think that you must not feel anxious about a situation you can't change," he said. He still wore the strange dark clothes that must have been proper in another climate.

"I do not feel anxious," she said, her hands to her face.

Carmela parted the curtains a little so that the doctor could examine the twins by light of day. They were not lazy, he said. They had rickets. Carmela could have told him that. She also knew there was no cure for it.

Mrs. Unwin seemed offended. "Our English doctor called it softening of the bone."

"They must have milk," said Dr. Chaffee. "Not the skimmed stuff. Fresh fruit, cod-liver oil." He wrote on a pad as he spoke. "And in August you must get them away from the coast."

Mrs. Unwin's hands slid forward until they covered her face. "I was too old," she said. "I had no right to bring these maimed infants into the world."

Dr. Chaffee did not seem to be alarmed at this. He drew Carmela near, saying, "What about this child? How old is she?"

Carmela remembered she knew no English; she looked dumbly from one to the other. Dr. Chaffee repeated the question in Italian, straight to Carmela, and calling her "little girl."

"Nearly thirteen," said Carmela.

"Good God, she looks nine."

Mrs. Unwin's hands parted. She wore the grimace that was one of her ways of smiling. "I am remiss about everything, then? I didn't create her. Tell me how to make her look nearly thirteen."

"Partly heredity," he said.

They began to chat, and Mrs. Unwin to smile widely.

"I shall do whatever you say," said Mrs. Unwin.

After the doctor had departed—Carmela saw him in his dark suit pausing to look at the datura tree—Mrs. Unwin sent for her again. "The doctor says that part of your trouble must be spaghetti," she said seriously, as if she did not know to a crumb what Carmela was given at meals. "You are to eat meat, fresh vegetables. And take these. Now don't forget. Dr. Chaffee went to some trouble." She gave Carmela a small amber bottle of dark pills, which were said to be iron. Carmela never tasted any, of course. For one thing, she mistrusted medicines; but the bottle remained among her belongings for many years, and had the rank of a personal possession.

Another thing happened about that time: Mrs. Unwin paid Carmela the first installment of her wages.

Mrs. unwin said that the doves in the Marchesa's garden made more noise than was required of birds. By seven in the morning, the sky was heavy and held the afternoon's thundershower. Carmela, rushing outside to bring in washing dried on the line, felt on her face a breeze that was like warm water. She moved through heat and housework that seemed like a long dream. Someone had placed an order with Mr. Unwin to have poems printed. Mrs. Unwin parted the curtains in her bedroom and in spite of her headaches, which nearly blinded her, stitched one hundred and fifty booklets by hand. One Friday, after shopping in the French market, Carmela went to see a marvel she had been told about—two rows of plane trees whose branches met to form a tunnel. The trunks of these trees turned out to be thick and awkward-looking; they blocked Carmela's view of shops from one sidewalk to the next. Like most trees, they simply stood in the way of anything interesting. She mentioned this to Mrs. Unwin, who walked to and fro in the kitchen, drinking out of a teacup, with a straw sun hat on her head.

"Where there are no trees there are no nightingales," said Mrs. Unwin. "When I am feeling well I like to hear them."

"What, those things that make a noise at night?"

"Not noise but song," said Mrs. Unwin, cradling her teacup.

"Every creature has its moment," said Carmela.

"What a prim creature *you* are," cried Mrs. Unwin, flinging her head back, showing her teeth. Carmela was glad she had made her laugh, but she resolved to be more careful than ever: this was as far as an exchange between them need ever go.

BECAUSE OF WHAT Dr. Chaffee had said, the Unwins rented an apartment in a village away from the coast for the month of August. They squeezed into the car with the tv ins and Carmela and much luggage, drove past the road leading to the Nervia Valley, and climbed back into hills Carmela had never seen.

"Weren't you born around here," said Mrs. Unwin, without desiring an answer.

Carmela, who thought she knew all Mrs. Unwin's voices now, did not reply, but Mr. Unwin said, "You know perfectly well it was that other road." It seemed to matter to him that his wife should have made a mistake.

The twins were shared by Mrs. Unwin and Carmela. Both of them wanted to sit on Carmela's lap. Mrs. Unwin was not at all jealous; some serious matters she found extremely comic. The girls slept, and when they woke and began to fret, Mr. Unwin stopped the car so they could both be moved to the back with Carmela. There was scarcely room even for her, small though Dr. Chaffee had said she was, for the back was piled with bedsheets and blankets and even saucepans. After four hours they came to a village that had grass everywhere, and wooden houses that were painted a soft brown. Their summer flat was half a house, with a long carved balcony, and mats instead of carpets, and red curtains on brass rings. It contained an exciting smell of varnish and fresh soap. The Unwins piled all the luggage in a heap on the floor and unpacked nothing to start with but a kettle and teapot and three pottery mugs. Carmela heard Mr. Unwin talking to the owner of this house in his strange nasal Italian and mentioning her, Carmela, as "the young lady who would be in charge." They drank tea meanwhile, Mrs. Unwin sitting on a bare mattress stuffed with horsehair, Carmela standing with her back to a wall. Mrs. Unwin talked to her as she had never done before and would never again. She still seemed to Carmela very large and ugly, but her face was smooth and she kept her voice low, and Carmela thought that perhaps she was not so old after all. She said, "If there is a war, we may not be able to get money out of England, such as there is. We shall never leave Italy. I have faith in the Movement. The Italians know they can trust us. The Germans are, well, as they have always been, and I'm afraid we British have made no effort to meet them halfway. Dr. Chaffee tells me you are as reliable as an adult, Carmela. I am going to believe him. I would like you to teach the twins the alphabet. Will you do that? Don't forget that the English alphabet has a 'W.' Somewhere near the end. Teach them Italian poems and songs. Dr. Chaffee thinks I should have as few worries as possible just now. There will be a course of treatment at the clinic. Baths. Wet sheets. I suppose I must believe in magic." She went on like this, perched on the edge of the bare mattress, staring out over her tea mug, all knees and elbows, and Carmela did not move or answer or even sip her tea. She wanted to make the bed and put the twins in it, because they had missed their afternoon sleep—unless one counted the fitful dozing in the automobile. Mrs. Unwin said, "I had expected a better south than this one. First we went to Amalfi. I had left my son in England. A little boy. When I was allowed to visit him he said, 'How do you do?' No one would speak to me. We came back to Italy. The moonlight glittered on his eyes. Before the twins came. 'Do not think, but feel,' he said to me. Or the opposite. But it was only being tied again—this time with poverty, and the chatter of ill-bred people. No escape from it—marriage, childbirth, patriotism, the dark. The same circle—baptism, confirmation, prayers for the dead. Or else, silence."

From the doorway Mr. Unwin said, *"Ellen."* He came along with a walk Carmela had not seen before, slightly shambling. "What is in the cup?" he said.

She smiled at him and said, "Tea."

He took it, sniffed it. "So it is." He helped her up.

Unpacking, making beds, Carmela experienced a soft, exultant happiness. The Unwins were going back home early the next morning. Mr. Unwin gave Carmela a handful of money—pulled it out of his wallet without counting—said, "That has got to last you, eh?" with an upward lift that denied this was an order. The money was more than she had ever been trusted with on the coast and actually more than she had seen at any one time. She put the twins to sleep with nightgowns round their pillows (she and Mrs. Unwin between them had forgotten to pack cases) and then shared the Unwins' picnic supper. New people in a new place, they told Carmela to go to bed without bothering about the dishes.

She was pulled out of a deep sleep by a thunderstorm. Her heart squeezed tight in uncontrollable terror. Through the beating of horses' hooves she heard Mr. Unwin speaking quietly. When the storm stopped, the house was perfectly still. She became prey to a hawkmoth and a mosquito. She pulled the sheet up over her head as she had against ghosts, and fell asleep and had the sea dream. She woke up still hearing a thin mosquito song nearby. Along the wall was a white ladder of slatted light that she took to be the light of morning. In her half-sleep she rose and unclasped the shutters and, looking out, saw a track of moon over the village as on the sea, and one pale street lamp, and a cat curled up on the road. The cat, wakened by being seen by Carmela, walked off lashing its tail. She had the true feeling that she was in a real place. She did not dream the sea dream again.

The next thing Carmela heard was the twins bouncing a ball and stumbling after it, still in their nightclothes. The Unwins, up even earlier, had made breakfast. They greeted Carmela as if she were one of their own. The storm had swept the sky clean. Oh, such happiness! Never before, never again. Soon after breakfast they went away, having plotted first with Carmela to distract the twins. In the late afternoon a mist came down so thick and low that Carmela, who had never seen anything like it before, thought it must be the smoke of trees on fire.

WITHOUT ANY WARNING, the Unwins drove up from the coast one Saturday with Mrs. Unwin's son, Douglas, who lived in England. He was taller even than the Unwins, and had a long face, dark straight hair, and horn-rimmed spectacles. With him was a girl he thought he might marry. "Don't be such a fool," Carmela heard Mrs. Unwin telling Douglas in the kitchen. No one suspected how much Carmela now understood. The girl had a reddish sunburn on her cheeks and nose. Her hair was cut rather like Carmela's, but held with metal grips. She unpacked a flimsy embroidery pattern and a large canvas and began stabbing at it with a flat needle. She was making a cushion. Carmela did not care for the colors, which were dark greens and browns. The girl shifted her gaze from the pattern to the canvas, back and forth. Her sunburn made her too cross to speak. Douglas told his mother she wasn't always quite so unfriendly. Carmela thought that to be as large and as ugly as these people was to be cursed.

They all crowded into the flat for one night. Mrs. Unwin went over Carmela's accounts, but did not ask how much money she had been given in the first place. The next day the parents departed, leaving Douglas and his irritable girl, whom Carmela had been told to call "Miss Hermione"—but of course she could not pronounce it. Miss Hermione took the Unwins' bedroom, Douglas was given Carmela's, and Carmela slept on a cot next to the twins. Every night, Miss Hermione said "No, I said *no*" to Douglas and slammed her door. Carmela supposed she sat behind the door embroidering. She also ate things she had brought in her suitcase. Carmela, who made Miss Hermione's bed every day, discovered chocolate crumbs. One night, when Miss Hermione had retired and was eating stale chocolate and embroidering a cushion, Douglas came into the kitchen where Carmela was washing up at the stone sink.

"Like some help?" he said. She knew no English, of course; did not even turn. He leaned against the drainboard, where she had to see him. He folded his arms and looked at Carmela. Then he began to whistle through his teeth as people do when they are bored, and then he must have reached up and tapped the light bulb that hung on a cord. It was only the gesture of someone bored again, but the rocking shadows and the tall ugly boy whistling were like Carmela's sea dream. She dropped her little string dishmop and ran out. She thought she heard herself screaming. "Oh, don't pretend!" he called after her, as mysterious as his mother had once seemed.

He *was* bored; he said so the next day. There was not a thing to do here except stare out at mountains. He went downstairs to where the owner of the house lived, and together they listened to bad news over the radio. He could not understand much of the Italian, but sometimes they caught the BBC broadcasts, and when Douglas did understand something it made the situation seem worse.

"Oh, let's leave, then, for God's sake," Miss Hermione said, folding her canvas neatly twice.

Douglas pressed his hands to his head, for all the world like his mother. He said, "I don't want to be caught up in it."

"Military life won't hurt you," Miss Hermione answered. Without embroidery to keep her hands busy, she kept shifting and changing position; now she had her hands clasped round a knee, and she swung a long foot and played at pointing her toes.

The day they went off, there was a loud windstorm. They paid the landlord to drive them as far as a bus station; Carmela never saw them again. Miss Hermione left a green hair ribbon behind. Carmela kept it for years.

As soon as these two had vanished, the wind dropped. Carmela and the twins climbed a little way out of the village and sat in deep grass. The sky held one small creamy cloud. At eye level were lacy grasses and, behind them, blue-black mountains. She tried to teach the twins the alphabet, but she was not certain where to put the "W," and the girls were silly and would not listen; she did teach them songs.

III

IN SEPTEMBER she slipped back to a life she was sure of. She had taken its color. The sea was greener than anything except Mrs. Unwin's emerald, bluer than her sapphire, more transparent than blue, white, transparent glass. Wading with a twin at each hand, she saw their six feet underwater like sea creatures. The sun became as white as a stone; something stung in its heat, like fine, hard, invisible rain. War was somewhere, but not in Italy. Besides, something much more important than a war had taken place. It was this: a new English clergyman had arrived. Now that England was at war he did not know if he should stay. He told someone, who told the Unwins, that he would remain as long as he had a flock to protect. The Unwins, who were agnostics, wondered how to address him. His name was Dunn, but that was not the point. He was not the vicar, only a substitute.

They had called his predecessor "Ted," straight out, but they did not propose to call Mr. Dunn "Horace." They decided to make it "Padre." "Padre" was not solemn, and marked an ironic distance they meant to keep with the Church; and it was not rude, either.

CARMELA UNDERSTOOD that the Unwins' relations with the rest of the foreign colony were endlessly complicated. There were two layers of English, like sea shelves. Near the bottom was a shelf of hotelkeepers, dentists, people who dealt in fruit and in wine—not for amusement but for a living. Nearer the light dwelt the American Marchesa, and people like Miss Barnes and her companion, Miss Lewis. These two lived in mean rooms almost in the attic of a hotel whose owner did not ask them to pay very much, because Miss Barnes was considered someone important—it was her father who had founded village schools and made a present of them to the Italian government. Between the two shelves the Unwins floated, bumping against the one or the other as social currents flung them upward or let them sink. Still lower than any of the English were Russians, Austrians, or Hungarians, rich and poor alike, whose preoccupation was said to be gaining British passports for their children. As passports could be had by marriage—or so the belief ran—the British colony kept a grip on its sons. Mrs. Unwin was heard by Carmela to remark that Hermione had this to be said for her—she was English to the core.

Mrs. Unwin still smiled sometimes, but not as she had in August. She showed a death grin now. When she was excited her skin became a mottled brick-and-white. Carmela had never seen Mrs. Unwin as smiling and as dappled as the afternoon Miss Barnes and Miss Lewis came to tea. Actually, Miss Barnes had called to see about having still more of her late father's poems printed.

"Carmela! Tea!" cried Mrs. Unwin.

Having been often told not to touch the good china, Carmela brought their tea in pottery mugs, already poured in the kitchen.

"Stupid!" said Mrs. Unwin.

"That is something of an insult," Miss Lewis remarked.

"Carmela knows I am more bark than bite," said Mrs. Unwin, with another of her smiles—a twitchy grimace.

But Miss Lewis went on, "You have been down here long enough to know the things one can and can't say to them."

Mrs. Unwin's face, no longer mottled, had gone the solid shade the English called Egyptian red. Carmela saw the room through Mrs. Unwin's eyes: it seemed to move and crawl, with its copper bowl, and novels from England, and faded cretonne-covered chairs, and stained wallpaper. All these dead things seemed to be on the move, because of the way Miss Lewis had spoken to Mrs. Unwin. Mrs. Unwin smiled unceasingly, with her upper lip drawn back.

Miss Barnes, in a wheelchair because she had sprained a knee, reached across and patted her companion's hand. "Charlotte is ever so bolshie," she remarked, taking on a voice and an accent that were obviously meant to make a joke of it. Her eyes went smoothly around the room, but all *she* chose to see or to speak of was the copper bowl, with dahlias in it this time.

"From the Marchesa. Such a pet. Always popping in with flowers!" Mrs. Unwin cried.

"Frances is a dear," said Miss Barnes.

"Ask Mr. Unwin to join us, Carmela," said Mrs. Unwin, trembling a little. After that she referred to the Marchesa as "Frances."

The pity was that this visit was spoiled by the arrival of the new clergyman. It was his first official parish call. He could not have been less welcome. He was a young man with a complexion as changeable as Mrs. Unwin's. He settled unshyly into one of the faded armchairs and said he had been busy clearing empty bottles out of the rectory. Not gin bottles, as they would have been in England, but green bottles with a sediment of red wine, like red dust. The whole place was a shambles, he added, though without complaining; no, it was as if this were a joke they were all young enough to share.

In the general shock Miss Barnes took over: Ted—Dr. Edward Stonehouse, rather—had been repatriated at the expense of his flock, with nothing left for doing up the rectory. He had already cost them a sum—the flock had twice sent him on a cure up to the mountains for his asthma. Everyone had loved Ted; no one was likely to care about the asthma or the anything else of those who came after. Miss Barnes made that plain.

"He left a fair library," said the young man, after a silence. "Though rather dirty."

"I should never have thought that of *Hymns Ancient and Modern*," said bolshie Miss Lewis.

"Dusty, I meant," said the clergyman vaguely. At a signal from Mrs. Unwin, Carmela, whose hands were steady, poured the clergyman's tea. "The changes I shall make won't cost any money," he said, pursuing some thought of his own. He came to and scanned their stunned faces. "Why, I was thinking of the notice outside, 'Evensong Every Day at Noon.' "

"Why change it?" said Miss Barnes in her wheelchair. "I admit it was an innovation of poor old Dr. Stonehouse's, but we are so used to it now."

"And *was* Evensong every day at noon?"

"No," said Miss Barnes, "because that is an hour when most people are beginning to think about lunch."

"More bread and butter, Carmela," said Mrs. Unwin.

Returning, Carmela walked into "The other thing I thought I might . . . do something about"—as if he were avoiding the word "change"—"is the church clock."

"The clock was a gift," said Miss Barnes, losing her firmness, looking to the others for support. "The money was collected. It was inaugurated by the Duke of Connaught."

"Surely not Connaught," murmured the clergyman, sounding to Carmela not quarrelsome but pleasantly determined. He might have been teasing them; or else he thought the entire conversation was a tease. Carmela peeped sideways at the strange man who did not realize how very serious they all were.

"My father was present," said Miss Barnes. "There is a plaque."

"Yes, I have seen it," he said. "No mention of Connaught. It may have been an oversight"—finally responding to the blinks and frowns of Miss Barnes's companion, Miss Lewis. "All I had hoped to alter was . . . I had thought I might have the time put right."

"What is wrong with the time?" said Mrs. Unwin, letting Miss Barnes have a rest.

"It is slow."

"It has always been slow," said Miss Barnes. "If you will look more carefully than you looked at the plaque, you will see a rectangle of cardboard upon which your predecessor printed in large capital letters the word 'SLOW'; he placed it beneath the clock. In this way the clock, which has historical associations for some of us—my father was at its inauguration—in this way the works of the clock need not be tampered with."

"Perhaps I might be permitted to alter the sign and add the word 'slow' in Italian." He *still* thought this was a game, Carmela could see. She stood nearby, keeping an eye on the plate of bread and butter and listening for the twins, who would be waking at any moment from their afternoon sleep.

"No Italian would be bothered looking at an English church clock," said Miss Barnes. "And none of us has ever missed a train. Mr. Dunn—let me give you some advice. Do not become involved with anything. We are a flock in need of a shepherd; nothing more."

"Right!" screamed Mrs. Unwin, white-and-brick-mottled again. "For God's sake, Padre . . . no involvement!"

The clergyman looked as though he had been blindfolded and turned about in a game and suddenly had the blindfold whipped off. Mr. Unwin had not spoken until now. He said deliberately, "I hope you are not a scholar, Padre. Your predecessor was, and his sermons were a great bore."

"Stonehouse a scholar?" said Mr. Dunn.

"Yes, I'm sorry to say. I might have brought my wife back to the fold, so to speak, but his sermons were tiresome—all about the Hebrews and the Greeks."

The clergyman caught Carmela staring at him, and noticed her. He smiled. The smile fixed his face in her memory for all time. It was not to her an attractive face—it was too fair-skinned for a man's; it had color that came and ebbed too easily. "Perhaps there won't be time for the Greeks and the Hebrews now," he said gently. "We *are* at war, aren't we?"

"We?" said Miss Barnes.

"Nonsense, Padre," said Mrs. Unwin briskly. "Read the newspapers."

"England," said the clergyman, and stopped.

Mr. Unwin was the calmest man in the world, but he could be as wild-looking as his wife sometimes. At the word "England" he got up out of his chair and went to fetch the Union Jack on a metal standard that stood out in the hall, leaning into a corner. The staff was too long to go through the door upright; Mr. Unwin advanced as if he were attacking someone with a long spear. "Well, Padre, what about this?" he said. The clergyman stared as if he had never seen any flag before, ever; as if it were a new kind of leaf, or pudding, or perhaps a skeleton. "Will the flag have to be dipped at the church door on Armistice Day?" said Mr. Unwin. "It can't be got through the door without being dipped. I have had the honor of carrying this flag for the British Legion at memorial services. But I shall no longer carry a flag that needs to be lowered now that England is at war. For I do agree with you, Padre, on that one matter. I agree that England *is* at war, rightly or wrongly. The lintel of the church door must be raised. You do see that? Your predecessor refused to have the door changed. I can't think why. It is worthless as architecture."

"You don't mean that," said Miss Barnes. "The door is as important to us as the time of Evensong."

"Then I shall say no more," said Mr. Unwin. He stood the flag in a corner and became his old self in a moment. He said to Carmela, "The Padre has had enough tea. Bring us some glasses, will you?" On which the three women chorused together, "Not for me!"

"Well, I expect you'll not forget your first visit," said Mr. Unwin.

"I am not likely to," said the young man.

B Y OCTOBER the beach was windy and alien, with brown seaweed-laden waves breaking far inshore. A few stragglers sat out of reach of the icy spray. They were foreigners; most of the English visitors had vanished. Mrs. Unwin invented a rule that the little girls must bathe until October the fifteenth. Carmela felt pity for their blue, chattering lips; she wrapped towels around their bodies and held them in her arms. Then October the fifteenth came and the beach torment was over. She scarcely remembered that she had lived any life but this. She could now read in English and was adept at flickering her eyes over a letter left loose without picking it up. As for the Unwins, they were as used to Carmela as to the carpet, whose tears must have seemed part of the original pattern by now. In November Miss Barnes sent Mrs. Unwin into a paroxysm of red-and-white coloration by accepting an invitation to lunch. Carmela rehearsed serving and clearing for two days. The meal went off without any major upset, though Carmela did stand staring when Miss Barnes suddenly began to scream, "Chicken! Chicken! How wonderful! Chicken!" Miss Barnes did not seem to know why she was saying this; she finally became conscious that her hands were in the air and brought them down. After that, Carmela thought of her as "Miss Chicken." That day Carmela heard, from Miss Chicken, "Hitler will never make the Italians race-minded. They haven't it in them." Then, "Of course, Italian men are not to be taken seriously," from Miss Lewis, fanning herself absently with her little beaded handbag, and smiling at some past secret experience. Still later, Carmela heard Miss Barnes saying firmly, "Charlotte is mistaken. Latins talk, but they would never hurt a fly."

Carmela also learned, that day, that the first sermon the new clergyman had preached was about chastity, the second on duty, the third on self-discipline. But the fourth sermon was on tolerance—"slippery ground," in Mrs. Unwin's opinion. And on the eleventh of November, at a special service sparsely attended, flag and all, by such members of the British Legion as had not fled, he had preached pacifism. Well—Italy was at peace, so it was all right. But there had been two policemen in mufti, posing as Anglican parishioners. Luckily they did not seem to understand any English.

"The Padre was trying to make a fool of me with that sermon," said Mrs. Unwin.

"Why you, Ellen?" said her husband.

"Because he knows my views," said Mrs. Unwin. "I've had courage enough to voice them."

Miss Lewis looked as if she had better say nothing; then she decided to remark, in a distant, squeaky voice, "I don't see why an agnostic ever goes to church at all."

"To see what he is up to," said Mrs. Unwin.

"Surely the police were there for that?"

Mr. Unwin said he had refused to attend the Armistice Day service; the matter of flag dipping had never been settled.

"I have written the Padre a letter," said Mrs. Unwin. "What do we care about the Greek this and the Hebrew that? We are all living on dwindled incomes and wondering how to survive. Mussolini has brought order and peace to this country, whether Mr. Dunn likes it or not."

"Hear, hear," said Miss Chicken. Mr. Unwin nodded in slow agreement. Miss Lewis looked into space and pursed her lips, like someone counting the chimes of a clock.

IV

In spite of the electricity rates, the kitchen light had to go on at four o'clock. Carmela, lifting her hand to the shelf of tea mugs, cast a shadow. At night she slept with her black cardigan round her legs. When she put a foot on the tiled floor she trembled with cold and with fear. She was afraid of the war and of the ghost of the uncle, which, encouraged by early darkness, could be seen in the garden again. Half the villas along the hill were shuttered. She looked at a faraway sea, lighted by a sun twice as far off as it had ever been before. The Marchesa was having a bomb shelter built in her garden. To make way for it, her rose garden had been torn out by the roots. So far only a muddy oblong shape, like the start of a large grave, could be seen from the Unwins' kitchen. Progress on it was by inches only; the men could not work in the rain, and this was a wet winter. Mrs. Unwin, who had now instigated a lawsuit over the datura tree, as the unique cause of her uneven health, stood on her terrace and shouted remarks—threats, perhaps—to the workmen on the far side of the Marchesa's hedge. She wore boots and a brown fur coat like a kimono. Among the men were Carmela's little brother and his employer. The employer, whose name was Lucio, walked slowly as far as the hedge.

"How would you like to do some really important work for us?" cried Mrs. Unwin.

Mr. Unwin would come out and look at his wife and go in the house again. He spoke gently to Carmela and the twins, but not often. There were now only two or three things he would eat—Carmela's vegetable soup, Carmela's rice and cheese, and French bread. Mrs. Unwin no longer spoke of the Marchesa as "Frances," and the chauffeur had given up coming round to the kitchen door. There was bad feeling over the lawsuit, which, as a civil case, could easily drag on for the next ten years. Then one day the digging ceased. The villa was boarded over. The Marchesa had taken her dogs to America, leaving everything, even the chauffeur, behind. Soon after Christmas, the garden began to bloom in waves of narcissi, anemones, irises, daffodils; then came the great white daisies and the mimosa; and then all the geraniums that had not been uprooted with the rosebushes flowered at once—white, salmon-pink, scarlet, peppermint-striped. The tide of color continued to run as long as the rains lasted. After that the flowers died off and the garden became a desert.

Mrs. Unwin said the Marchesa had bolted like a frightened hare. She, though untitled, though poor, would now show confidence in Mussolini and his wish for peace by having a stone wall built round her property. Lucio was employed. Mrs. Unwin called him "a dear old rogue." She was on tiptoe between headaches. The climate was right for her just now: no pollen. Darkness. Not too much sun. Long cold evenings. For a time she blossomed like the next-door garden, until she made a discovery that felled her again.

She and Mr. Unwin together summoned Carmela; together they pointed to a fair-haired boy carrying stones. Mr. Unwin said, "Who is he?"

"He is my brother," Carmela said.

"I have seen him before," said Mr. Unwin.

"He once visited me."

"But Carmela," said Mr. Unwin, as always softly. You knew that we were looking about for a stonemason. Your own brother was apprenticed to Lucio. You never said a word. Why, Carmela? It is the same thing as lying."

Mrs. Unwin's voice had a different pitch: "You admit he is your brother?"

"Yes."

"You heard me saying I needed someone for the walls?"

"Yes."

"It means you don't trust me." All the joyous fever had left her.

She was soon back in her brown kimono coat out on the terrace, ready to insult strangers again. There was only Lucio. No longer her "dear old rogue," he spat in her direction and shook his fist and called her a name for which Carmela did not have the English.

THE ITALIANS began to expel foreign-born Jews. The Unwins were astonished to learn who some of them were: they had realized about the Blums and the Wiesels, for that was evident, but it was a shock to have to see Mrs. Teodoris and the Delaroses in another light, or to think of dear Dr. Chaffee as someone in trouble. The Unwins were proud that this had not taken place in their country—at least not since the Middle Ages—but it might not be desirable if all these good people were to go to England now. Miss Barnes had also said she hoped some other solution could be found. They were all of them certainly scrambling after visas, but were not likely to obtain any by marriage; the English sons and daughters had left for home.

Carmela still went over to France every Friday. The frontier was open; there were buses and trains, though Dr. Chaffee and the others were prevented from using them. Sometimes little groups of foreign-born Jews were rounded up and sent across to France, where the French sent them back again, like the Marchesa's shuttlecocks. Jews waiting to be expelled from France to Italy were kept in the grounds of the technical school for boys; they sat there on their luggage, and people came to look at them through the fence. Carmela saw a straggling cluster of refugees—a new word—being marched at gunpoint up the winding street to the frontier on the French side. Among them, wearing his dark suit, was Dr. Chaffee. She remembered how she had not taken the pills he had given her—had not so much as unscrewed the metal cap of the bottle. Wondering if he knew, she looked at him with shame and apology before turning her head away. As though he had seen on her face an expression he wanted, he halted, smiled, shook his head. He was saying "No" to something. Terrified, she peeped again, and this time he lifted his hand, palm outward, in a curious greeting that was not a salute. He was pushed on. She never saw him again.

Wнат *IS* ALL this talk?" said Mrs. Unwin. "Miss Lewis is full of it. Have you seen anything around the frontier, Carmela?"

"No, never," she said.

"I'm sure it is the Padre's doing," said Mrs. Unwin. "He preached about tolerance once too often. It worked the Italians up." She repeated to her husband Miss Barnes's opinion, which was that Mussolini did not know what was going on.

IN MARCH the wind blew as it had in the autumn. The east wind seemed to have a dark color to it. Twice on the same March night, Carmela was wakened by the beating of waves. At the market, people seemed to be picking their feet out of something grey and adhesive —their own shadows. The Italians began to change; even the clerks in the post office were cheeky with foreigners now. Mrs. Unwin believed the Padre was to blame. She went to listen to his Lenten sermons, and of course caught him out. He preached five Lenten messages, and with each the season advanced and the sea became light, then deep blue, and the Marchesa's garden brighter and sweet-er-smelling. As he had in the autumn, the Padre started off carefully, choosing as his subjects patience, abstinence, and kindness. So far so good, said Mrs. Unwin. But the fourth sermon was on courage, the fifth on tyranny, on Palm Sunday he spoke about justice, and on Good Friday he took his text from Job: "Behold I cry out of wrong, but I am not heard: I cry aloud, but there is no judgment." On Easter Sunday he mentioned Hitler by name.

Mrs. Unwin looked up the Good Friday text and found at the top of the page "Job complaineth of his friends' cruelty." She read it out to her husband, adding, "That was meant for me."

"Why you?"

"Because I have hit, and where I hit I hit hard," she cried.

"What have you been up to?" His voice rose as much as ever it could or would. He noticed Carmela and fell silent.

Late in May, Mrs. Unwin won her case against the Marchesa. There was no precedent for the speed of the decision. Mr. Unwin thought the courts were bored with the case, but his wife took it to mean compensation for the Unwins' having not run away. All the datura branches overhanging the Unwins' garden were to be lopped off, and if Mrs. Unwin's headaches persisted the tree was to be cut down. The Unwins hired a man to do the pruning, but it was a small triumph, for the Marchesa was not there to watch.

The night before the man arrived to prune the tree, a warship sent playful searchlights over the hills and the town. The shore was lit as if with strings of yellow lanterns. The scent of the datura rose in the air like a bonfire. Mrs. Unwin suddenly said, "Oh, what does it matter now?" Perhaps it was not the datura that was responsible after all. But in the morning, when the man came with an axe and a saw, he would not be dismissed. He said, "You sent for me and I am here." Carmela had never seen him before. He told her she had no business to be working for foreigners and that soon there would be none left. He hacked a hole through the hedge and began to saw at the base of the datura.

"That's not our property!" Mrs. Unwin cried.

The man said, "You hired me and I am here," and kept on sawing.

On the road where the chauffeur had walked the Marchesa's dogs, a convoy of army lorries moved like crabs on the floor of the sea.

V

THE FRONTIER was tightened on both sides for Jews—even those who were not refugees. Some of the refugees set off for Monaco by fishing boat; there was a rumor that from Monaco no one was turned back to Italy. They paid sums of money to local fishermen, who smuggled them along the coast by night and very often left them stranded on a French beach, and the game of battledore and shuttlecock began again. Carmela heard that one woman flung herself over the edge of the bridge into the gorge with the dried riverbed at the bottom that marked the line between Italy and France. Lucio gave up being a stonemason and bought a part interest in a fishing boat. He took Carmela's brother along.

Carmela's mother was given notice that the hotel where she worked was to close. She sent a message to Carmela telling her to stay where she was for as long as the Unwins could keep her, for at home they would be sorely in need of money now. Carmela's brother was perhaps earning something with the boat traffic of Jews, but how long could it last? And what was the little boy's share?

Carmela heard from someone in the local market that all foreigners were to be interned—even Miss Barnes. She gave a hint about it, because her own situation depended on the Unwins' now. Mrs. Unwin scolded Carmela for spreading rumors. That very day, the Unwins' mimeograph machine was seized and carried away, though whether for debts or politics Carmela could not be sure. Along with the machine the provincial police confiscated a pile of tracts that had been ordered by the British Legion and had to do with a garden party on the twenty-fourth of May, the birthday of Queen Victoria. The deepest official suspicion now surrounded this celebration, although in the past the Italian military commander of the region had always attended with his wife and daughters. Then the printing shop was suddenly padlocked and sealed. Mr. Unwin was obliged to go to the police station and explain that he had paid his taxes and had not printed anything that was illegal or opposed to Mussolini. While he was away, a carload of civil guards arrived and pounded on the door.

"They don't even speak good Italian," said Mrs. Unwin. "Here, Carmela—find out what they want." But they were Calabrians and quite foreign to Carmela, in spite of her Sicilian grandmother. She told Mrs. Unwin she did not know what they were saying, either. At the same time, she decided to ask for her wages. She had not been paid after the first three months.

Mr. Unwin returned from the police station, but nothing was said in front of Carmela. The frontier was now closed to everyone. Carmela would never go shopping on the French side again. When she mentioned her wages Mrs. Unwin said, "But Carmela, you seemed so fond of the children!"

Early one afternoon, Mrs. Unwin burst into the kitchen. Her hair was wild, as if she had been pulling at it. She said, "It has happened, Carmela. Can you understand? Can you understand the horror of our situation? We can't get any money from England, and we can't draw anything out of the bank here. You must go home now, back to your family. We are leaving for England, on a coal boat. I am leaving with the children. Mr. Unwin will try to come later. You must go home now, today. Why are you crying?" she said, and now she really did tug her hair. "We'll pay you in full and with interest when it is all over."

Carmela had her head down on the kitchen table. Pains like wings pressed on her shoulders until her sobs tore them apart.

"Why are you crying?" said Mrs. Unwin again. "Nothing can happen to you. You'll be thankful to have the money after Mussolini has lost his war." She patted the child between her fragile shoulders. "And yet, how can he lose, eh? Even I don't see how. Perhaps we'll all laugh—oh, I don't know what I'm saying. Carmela, please. Don't alarm the children."

For the last time in her life, Carmela went into the room she had shared with a ghost and a demon. She knew that her mother would never believe her story and that she would beat her. "Goodbye, little girls," she said, though they were out of earshot. In this way she took leave without alarming them. She packed and went back to the kitchen, for want of knowing where to go. All this had happened while Carmela was clearing away after lunch. The larder was still unlocked. She took a loaf of bread and cut it in three pieces and hid the pieces in her case. Many years later, it came to her that in lieu of wages she should have taken a stone from the leather box. Only fear would have kept her from doing it, if she had thought of it. For the last time, she looked out over the Marchesa's shuttered villa. It had already been looted twice. Each time, the police had come and walked around and gone away again. The deep pit of the unfinished bomb shelter was used by all the neighborhood as a dump for unwanted litters of kittens. The chauffeur had prowled for a bit, himself something of a cat, and then he vanished, too.

When Mrs. Unwin searched Carmela's case—Carmela expected that; everyone did it with servants—she found the bread, looked at it without understanding, and closed the lid. Carmela waited to be told more. Mrs. Unwin kissed her forehead and said, "Best of luck. We are all going to need it. The children will miss you."

Now that the worst was over, Mr. Unwin appeared on the scene; he would drive Carmela as far as the Nervia Valley bus stop. He could not take her all the way home, because he had only so much petrol, and because of everything else he had to do before evening. This was without any doubt the worst day of the Unwins' lives.

"Is it wise of you to drive about so openly?" said his wife.

"You don't expect to hide and cringe? As long as I am free I shall use my freedom."

"So you said to me years ago," said his wife. This time Carmela did not consider the meaning of her smile. It had lost its importance.

Mr. Unwin carried Carmela's case to the car and stowed it in the luggage compartment. She sat up front in Mrs. Unwin's usual place. Mr. Unwin explained again that he would drive as far as the Nervia Valley road, where she could then continue by bus. He did not ask if there was any connection to Castel Vittorio or, should there be one, its frequency. They drove down the hill where Carmela had walked to the local market that first day. Most of the beautiful villas were abandoned now, which made them look incomplete. The Marchesa's word came back to her: "Hideous." They passed Dr. Chaffee's clinic and turned off on the sea road. Here was the stop where Carmela had waited for a bus to the frontier every Friday—every Friday of her life, it seemed. There was the café with the pale-blue awning. Only one person, a man, sat underneath it today.

"*Ha*llo," said Mr. Unwin. He braked suddenly and got out of the car. "Fond of ices, Padre?" he said.

"I've spent two nights talking to the police," said the clergyman. "I very much want to be seen."

"You, too, eh?" Mr. Unwin said. He seemed to forget how much he still had to do before evening, and that he and the Padre had ever disagreed about tolerance or Hitler or dipping the flag. "Come along, Carmela," he called over his shoulder. "These young things are always hungry," he said lightly, as though Carmela had been eating him out of house and home.

"My party," said the Padre. Mr. Unwin did not contradict. There they were, police or not, war or not. It was one of the astonishing things that Carmela remembered later on. When an ice was brought and set before her she was afraid to eat it. First, it was too beautiful —pistachio, vanilla, tangerine, three colors in a long-stemmed silver dish that sat in turn upon a lace napkin and a glass plate. Carmela was further given cold water in a tall frosted glass, a long-handled delicate spoon with a flat bowl, and yet another plate containing three overlapping wafer bisquits. Her tears had weakened her; it was almost with sadness that she touched the spoon.

"I won't have it said that I ran away," said the clergyman. "One almost *would* like to run. I wasn't prepared for anonymous letters." The soft complexion that was like a girl's flushed. Carmela noticed that he had not shaved; she could not have imagined him bearded.

"Anonymous letters to the police?" said Mr. Unwin. "And in English?"

"First one. Then there were others."

"In *English?*"

"Oh, in English. They'd got the schoolmaster to translate them."

"Not even to my worst enemy—" Mr. Unwin began.

"No, I'm sure of that. But if I have inspired hatred, then I've failed. Some of the letters came to me. I never spoke of them. When there was no reaction then—I suppose it must have been interesting to try the police."

"Those you had—were they by hand?" said Mr. Unwin. "Let me see one. I shan't read it."

"I'm sorry, I've destroyed them."

Carmela looked across at the houses on which work had been suspended for more than a year—a monument to Mr. Unwin's qualifications as an investor of funds, she now understood; behind them was the sea that no longer could frighten her. She let a spoonful of pistachio melt in her mouth and swallowed regretfully.

"Of course you know the story," said Mr. Unwin. "You have heard the gossip."

"I don't listen to gossip," said the clergyman. They had no use for each other, and might never meet again. Carmela sensed that, if Mr. Unwin did not. "Nothing needs to be explained. What matters is, how we all come out of it. I've been told I may leave. My instructions *are* to leave. Hang them. They can intern me or do whatever they like. I won't have them believing that we can be bullied."

Mr. Unwin was speaking quietly; their words overlapped. He was going to explain, even if it was to no purpose now, whether the clergyman had any use for him or not. ". . . When we did finally marry we were so far apart that she hardly had a claim. I made her see a neurologist. He asked her if she was afraid of me." The lines of age around his eyes made him seem furtive. He had the look of someone impartial, but stubborn, too. "Having children was supposed to be good. To remove the guilt. To make her live in the present." They had come here, where there was a famous clinic and an excellent doctor—poor Dr. Chaffee. Gone now. Between her second breakdown and the birth of the twins, somewhere in that cleared-out period, they married. The Church of England did not always allow it. Old Ted Stonehouse had been lenient. For years they'd had nothing but holidays, a holiday life, always with the puritan belief that they would have to pay up. They had paid, he assured the younger man, for a look at their past—a wrecked past, a crippling accident. At times, he could see the debris along the road —a woman's shoe, a charred map. And they married, and had the twins, and the holiday came to an end. And she was beginning to be odd, cruel, drinking stuff out of teacups. She kept away from the babies. Was afraid of herself. Knew she was cruel. Cruel to her own great-uncle. Never once looked at his grave. Mr. Unwin had been to the grave not long ago, had stung his hands on nettles.

"Oh, I'd never weed a grave," said the clergyman. "I am like that, too."

"Well, Padre, we choose our lives," said Mr. Unwin. "I gave up believing in mine."

"Forget about believing in your life," said the younger man. "Think about the sacraments—whether you believe in them or not. You might arrive in a roundabout way. Do you see?"

"Arrive where?" said Mr. Unwin. "Arrive at what? I never get up in the morning without forcing myself to get out of bed, and without tears in my eyes. I have had to stop shaving sometimes because I could not see for tears. I've watched the sun rising through the tears of a child left in his first school. If ever I had taken a day in bed nothing would have made me get up again. Not my children, not my life, not my country. How I have envied Carmela, here—hearing her singing at her work."

"Well, and how about you, Carmela?" said the clergyman, quite glad to turn his attention to her, it seemed.

Carmela put her spoon down and said simply, "I have just eaten my way into heaven."

"Then I haven't entirely failed," the clergyman said.

Mr. Unwin laughed, then blew his nose. "Let me give you a lift, Padre," he said. "Think twice about staying. If I were you I would get on that coal boat with the others."

THEY LEFT Carmela at what they both seemed to think was a bus stop. Mr. Unwin set her case down and pressed money into her hand without counting it, as he had done last August.

"The children will miss you," he said, which must have been the Unwins' way of saying goodbye.

As soon as the car was out of sight she began to walk. There *was* a bus, but it was not here that it stopped for passengers. In any case it would not be along until late afternoon, and it did not go as far as Castel Vittorio. Within half an hour she was in a different landscape—isolated, lonely, and densely green. A farmer gave her a ride on a cart as far as Dolceacqua. She passed a stucco hotel where people sometimes came up from the coast in August to get away from the heat. It was boarded up like the villas she had left behind. After Dolceacqua she had to walk again. The villages along the valley were just as they'd been a year ago. She had forgotten about them. She did not want to lose the taste of the ices, but all she had kept was the look of them—the pink-orange, the pale green, the white with flecks of vanilla, like pepper. She shifted her cardboard suitcase with its rope strap from hand to hand. It was not heavy but cumbersome; certainly much lighter than one of the twins. Sometimes she stopped and crouched beside it in a position of repose she had also forgotten but now assumed naturally. This was a warm clear June day, with towering clouds that seemed like cream piled on a glass plate. She looked up through invisible glass to a fantastic tower of cream. The palms of the coast had given way to scrub and vineyards, then to oaks and beeches and Spanish chestnut trees in flower. She remembered the two men and their strange conversation; they were already the far past. A closer memory was the schoolhouse, and Dr. Barnes and Mussolini and the King in wooden frames. Mr. Unwin weeping at sunrise had never been vivid. He faded first. His tears died with him. The clergyman blushed like a girl and wished Mr. Unwin would stop talking. Both then were lost behind Dr. Chaffee in his dark suit stumbling up the hill. He lifted his hand. What she retained, for the present, was one smile, one gesture, one man's calm blessing.

THE
MOSLEM WIFE

IN THE SOUTH of France, in the business room of a hotel quite near
to the house where Katherine Mansfield (whom no one in this hotel
had ever heard of) was writing "The Daughters of the Late Colonel,"
Netta Asher's father announced that there would never be a man-
made catastrophe in Europe again. The dead of that recent war, the
doomed nonsense of the Russian Bolsheviks had finally knocked sense
into European heads. What people wanted now was to get on with
life. When he said "life," he meant its commercial business.

Who would have contradicted Mr. Asher? Certainly not Netta.
She did not understand what he meant quite so well as his French
solicitor seemed to, but she did listen with interest and respect, and
then watched him signing papers that, she knew, concerned her for
life. He was renewing the long lease her family held on the Hotel
Prince Albert and Albion. Netta was then eleven. One hundred years
should at least see her through the prime of life, said Mr. Asher, only
half jokingly, for of course he thought his seed was immortal.

Netta supposed she might easily live to be more than a hundred
—at any rate, for years and years. She knew that her father did not

want her to marry until she was twenty-six and that she was then
supposed to have a pair of children, the elder a boy. Netta and her
father and the French lawyer shook hands on the lease, and she was
given her first glass of champagne. The date on the bottle was 1909,
for the year of her birth. Netta bravely pronounced the wine delicious, but her father said she would know much better vintages before
she was through.

Netta remembered the handshake but perhaps not the terms.
When the lease had eighty-eight years to run, she married her first
cousin, Jack Ross, which was not at all what her father had had in
mind. Nor would there be the useful pair of children—Jack couldn't
abide them. Like Netta he came from a hotelkeeping family where
the young were like blight. Netta had up to now never shown a scrap
of maternal feeling over anything, but Mr. Asher thought Jack might
have made an amiable parent—a kind one, at least. She consoled Mr.
Asher on one count, by taking the hotel over in his lifetime. The hotel
was, to Netta, a natural life; and so when Mr. Asher, dying, said, "She
behaves as I wanted her to," he was right as far as the drift of Netta's
behavior was concerned but wrong about its course.

The Ashers' hotel was not down on the seafront, though boats and
sea could be had from the south-facing rooms.

Across a road nearly empty of traffic were handsome villas, and
behind and to either side stood healthy olive trees and a large lemon
grove. The hotel was painted a deep ochre with white trim. It had
white awnings and green shutters and black iron balconies as lacquered and shiny as Chinese boxes. It possessed two tennis courts,
a lily pond, a sheltered winter garden, a formal rose garden, and trees
full of nightingales. In the summer dark, *belles-de-nuit* glowed pink,
lemon, white, and after their evening watering they gave off a perfume that varied from plant to plant and seemed to match the petals'
coloration. In May the nights were dense with stars and fireflies.
From the rose garden one might have seen the twin pulse of cigarettes on a balcony, where Jack and Netta sat drinking a last brandy-
and-soda before turning in. Most of the rooms were shuttered by
then, for no traveller would have dreamed of being south except in
winter. Jack and Netta and a few servants had the whole place to
themselves. Netta would hire workmen and have the rooms that

needed it repainted—the blue cardroom, and the red-walled bar, and the white dining room, where Victorian mirrors gave back glossy walls and blown curtains and nineteenth-century views of the Ligurian coast, the work of an Asher great-uncle. Everything upstairs and down was soaked and wiped and polished, and even the pictures were relentlessly washed with soft cloths and ordinary laundry soap. Netta also had the boiler overhauled and the linen mended and new monograms embroidered and the looking glasses resilvered and the shutters taken off their hinges and scraped and made spruce green again for next year's sun to fade, while Jack talked about decorators and expert gardeners and even wrote to some, and banged tennis balls against the large new garage. He also read books and translated poetry for its own sake and practiced playing the clarinet. He had studied music once, and still thought that an important life, a musical life, was there in the middle distance. One summer, just to see if he could, he translated pages of St. John Perse, which were as blank as the garage wall to Netta, in any tongue.

Netta adored every minute of her life, and she thought Jack had a good life too, with nearly half the year for the pleasures that suited him. As soon as the grounds and rooms and cellar and roof had been put to rights, she and Jack packed and went travelling somewhere. Jack made the plans. He was never so cheerful as when buying Baedekers and dragging out their stickered trunks. But Netta was nothing of a traveller. She would have been glad to see the same sun rising out of the same sea from the window every day until she died. She loved Jack, and what she liked best after him was the hotel. It was a place where, once, people had come to die of tuberculosis, yet it held no trace or feeling of danger. When Netta walked with her workmen through sheeted summer rooms, hearing the cicadas and hearing Jack start, stop, start some deeply alien music (alien even when her memory automatically gave her a composer's name), she was reminded that here the dead had never been allowed to corrupt the living; the dead had been dressed for an outing and removed as soon as their first muscular stiffness relaxed. Some were wheeled out in chairs, sitting, and some reclined on portable cots, as if merely resting.

That is why there is no bad atmosphere here, she would say to herself. Death has been swept away, discarded. When the shutters are closed on a room, it is for sleep or for love. Netta could think this easily because neither she nor Jack was ever sick. They knew nothing about insomnia, and they made love every day of their lives—they had married in order to be able to.

Spring had been the season for dying in the old days. Invalids who had struggled through the dark comfort of winter took fright as the night receded. They felt without protection. Netta knew about this, and about the difference between darkness and brightness, but neither affected her. She was not afraid of death or of the dead—they were nothing but cold, heavy furniture. She could have tied jaws shut and weighted eyelids with native instinctiveness, as other women were born knowing the temperature for an infant's milk.

"There are no ghosts," she could say, entering the room where her mother, then her father had died. "If there were, I would know."

Netta took it for granted, now she was married, that Jack felt as she did about light, dark, death, and love. They were as alike in some ways (none of them physical) as a couple of twins, spoke much the same language in the same accents, had the same jokes—mostly about other people—and had been together as much as their families would let them for most of their lives. Other men seemed dull to Netta—slower, perhaps, lacking the spoken shorthand she had with Jack. She never mentioned this. For one thing, both of them had the idea that, being English, one must not say too much. Born abroad, they worked hard at an Englishness that was innocently inaccurate, rooted mostly in attitudes. Their families had been innkeepers along this coast for a century, even before Dr. James Henry Bennet had discovered "the Genoese Rivieras." In one of his guides to the region, a "Mr. Ross" is mentioned as a hotel owner who will accept English bank checks, and there is a "Mr. Asher," reliable purveyor of English groceries. The most trustworthy shipping agents in 1860 are the Montale brothers, converts to the Anglican Church, possessors of a British *laissez-passer* to Malta and Egypt. These families, by now plaited like hair, were connections of Netta's and Jack's and still in business from beyond Marseilles to Genoa. No wonder that other men bored her, and that each thought the other both familiar and unique. But of course they were unalike too. When once someone asked them, "Are you related to Montale, the poet?" Netta answered, "What poet?" and Jack said, "I wish we were."

There were no poets in the family. Apart from the great-uncle who had painted landscapes, the only person to try anything peculiar had been Jack, with his music. He had been allowed to study, up to a point; his father had been no good with hotels—had been a failure, in fact, bailed out four times by his cousins, and it had been thought, for a time, that Jack Ross might be a dunderhead too. Music might do him; he might not be fit for anything else.

Information of this kind about the meaning of failure had been gleaned by Netta years before, when she first became aware of her little cousin. Jack's father and mother—the commercial blunderers —had come to the Prince Albert and Albion to ride out a crisis. They were somewhere between undischarged bankruptcy and annihilation, but one was polite: Netta curtsied to her aunt and uncle. Her eyes were on Jack. She could not read yet, though she could sift and classify attitudes. She drew near him, sucking her lower lip, her hands behind her back. For the first time she was conscious of the beauty of another child. He was younger than Netta, imprisoned in a porta-ble-fence arrangement in which he moved tirelessly, crabwise, hang-ing on a barrier he could easily have climbed. He was as fair as his Irish mother and sunburned a deep brown. His blue gaze was not a baby's—it was too challenging. He was naked except for shorts that were large and seemed about to fall down. The sunburn, the undress were because his mother was reckless and rather odd. Netta—whose mother was perfect—wore boots, stockings, a longsleeved frock, and a white sun hat. She heard the adults laugh and say that Jack looked like a prizefighter. She walked around his prison, staring, and the blue-eyed fighter stared back.

The Rosses stayed for a long time, while the family sent telegrams and tried to rise money for them. No one looked after Jack much. He would lie on a marble step of the staircase watching the hotel guests going into the cardroom or the dining room. One night, for a reason that remorse was to wipe out in a minute, Netta gave him such a savage kick (though he was not really in her way) that one of his legs remained paralyzed for a long time.

"*Why* did you do it?" her father asked her—this in the room where she was shut up on bread and water. Netta didn't know. She loved Jack, but who would believe it now? Jack learned to walk, then to run, and in time to ski and play tennis; but her lifelong gift to him was a loss of balance, a sudden lopsided bend of a knee. Jack's parents had meantime been given a small hotel to run at Bandol. Mr. Asher, responsible for a bank loan, kept an eye on the place. He went often, in a hotel car with a chauffeur, Netta perched beside him. When, years later, the families found out that the devoted young cousins had become lovers, they separated them without saying much. Netta was too independent to be dealt with. Besides, her father did not want a rift; his wife had died, and he needed Netta. Jack, whose claim on music had been the subject of teasing until now, was suddenly sent to study in England. Netta saw that he was secretly dismayed. He wanted to be almost anything as long as it was impossible, and then only as an act of grace. Netta's father did think it was his duty to tell her that marriage was, at its best, a parched arrangement, intolerable without a flow of golden guineas and fresh blood. As cousins, Jack and Netta could not bring each other anything except stale money. Nothing stopped them: they were married four months after Jack became twenty-one. Netta heard someone remark at her wedding, "She doesn't need a husband," meaning perhaps the practical, matter-of-fact person she now seemed to be. She did have the dry, burned-out look of someone turned inward. Her dark eyes glowed out of a thin face. She had the shape of a girl of fourteen. Jack, who was large, and fair, and who might be stout at forty if he wasn't careful, looked exactly his age, and seemed quite ready to be married.

Netta could not understand why, loving Jack as she did, she did not look more like him. It had troubled her in the past when they did not think exactly the same thing at almost the same time. During the secret meetings of their long engagement she had noticed how even before a parting they were nearly apart—they had begun to "unmesh," as she called it. Drinking a last drink, usually in the buffet of a railway station, she would see that Jack was somewhere else, thinking about the next-best thing to Netta. The next-best thing might only be a book he wanted to finish reading, but it was enough to make her feel exiled. He often told Netta, "I'm not holding on to you. You're free," because he thought it needed saying, and of course he wanted freedom for himself. But to Netta "freedom" had a cold sound. Is that what I do want, she would wonder. Is that what I think he should offer? Their partings were often on the edge of parting forever, not just because Jack had said or done or thought the wrong thing but because between them they generated the high sexual tension that leads to quarrels. Barely ten minutes after agreeing that no one in the world could possibly know what they knew, one of them, either one, could curse the other out over something trivial. Yet they were, and remained, much in love, and when they were apart Netta sent him letters that were almost despairing with enchantment.

Jack answered, of course, but his letters were cautious. Her exploration of feeling was part of an unlimited capacity she seemed to have for passionate behavior, so at odds with her appearance, which had been dry and sardonic even in childhood. Save for an erotic sentence or two near the end (which Netta read first) Jack's messages might have been meant for any girl cousin he particularly liked. Love was memory, and he was no good at the memory game; he needed Netta there. The instant he saw her he knew all he had missed. But Netta, by then, felt forgotten, and she came to each new meeting aggressive and hurt, afflicted with the physical signs of her doubts and injuries —cold sores, rashes, erratic periods, mysterious temperatures. If she tried to discuss it he would say, "We aren't going over all that again, are we?" Where Netta was concerned he had settled for the established faith, but Netta, who had a wilder, more secret God, wanted a prayer a minute, not to speak of unending miracles and revelations.

When they finally married, both were relieved that the strain of partings and of tense disputes in railway stations would come to a stop. Each privately blamed the other for past violence, and both believed that once they could live openly, without interference, they would never have a disagreement again. Netta did not want Jack to regret the cold freedom he had vainly tried to offer her. He must have his liberty, and his music, and other people, and, oh, anything he wanted—whatever would stop him from saying he was ready to let her go free. The first thing Netta did was to make certain they had the best room in the hotel. She had never actually owned a room until now. The private apartments of her family had always been surren-

dered in a crisis: everyone had packed up and moved as beds were
required. She and Jack were hopelessly untidy, because both had
spent their early years moving down hotel corridors, trailing belts and
raincoats, with tennis shoes hanging from knotted strings over their
shoulders, their arms around books and sweaters and gray flannel
bundles. Both had done lessons in the corners of lounges, with cups
and glasses rattling, and other children running, and English voices
louder than anything. Jack, who had been vaguely educated, remembered his boarding schools as places where one had a permanent bed.
Netta chose for her marriage a south-facing room with a large balcony
and an awning of dazzling white. It was furnished with lemonwood
that had been brought to the Riviera by Russians for their own villas
long before. To the lemonwood Netta's mother had added English
chintzes; the result, in Netta's eyes, was not bizarre but charming.
The room was deeply mirrored; when the shutters were closed on hot
afternoons a play of light became as green as a forest on the walls,
and as blue as seawater in the glass. A quality of suspension, of
disbelief in gravity, now belonged to Netta. She became tidy, silent,
less introspective, as watchful and as reflective as her bedroom mirrors. Jack stayed as he was, luckily; any alteration would have worried
her, just as a change in an often-read story will trouble a small child.
She was intensely, almost unnaturally happy.

One day she overheard an English doctor, whose wife played
bridge every afternoon at the hotel, refer to her, to Netta, as "the
little Moslem wife." It was said affectionately, for the doctor liked
her. She wondered if he had seen through walls and had watched her
picking up the clothing and the wet towels Jack left strewn like clues
to his presence. The phrase was collected and passed from mouth to
mouth in the idle English colony. Netta, the last person in the world
deliberately to eavesdrop (she lacked that sort of interest in other
people), was sharp of hearing where her marriage was concerned. She
had a special antenna for Jack, for his shades of meaning, secret
intentions, for his innocent contradictions. Perhaps "Moslem wife"
meant several things, and possibly it was plain to anyone with eyes
that Jack, without meaning a bit of harm by it, had a way with
women. Those he attracted were a puzzling lot, to Netta. She had
already catalogued them—elegant elderly parties with tongues like

carving knives; gentle, clever girls who flourished on the unattainable; untouchable-daughter types, canny about their virginity, wondering if Jack would be father enough to justify the sacrifice. There was still another kind—tough, sunburned, clad in dark colors—who made Netta think in the vocabulary of horoscopes: Her gem—diamonds. Her color—black. Her language—worse than Netta's. She noticed that even when Jack had no real use for a woman he never made it apparent; he adopted anyone who took a liking to him. He assumed —Netta thought—a tribal, paternal air that was curious in so young a man. The plot of attraction interested him, no matter how it turned out. He was like someone reading several novels at once, or like someone playing simultaneous chess.

Netta did not want her marriage to become a world of stone. She said nothing except, "Listen, Jack, I've been at this hotel business longer than you have. It's wiser not to be too pally with the guests." At Christmas the older women gave him boxes of expensive soap. "They must think someone around here wants a good wash," Netta remarked. Outside their fenced area of private jokes and private love was a landscape too open, too light-drenched, for serious talk. And then, when? Jack woke up quickly and early in the morning and smiled as naturally as children do. He knew where he was and the day of the week and the hour. The best moment of the day was the first cigarette. When something bloody happened, it was never before six in the evening. At night he had a dark look that went with a dark mood, sometimes. Netta would tell him that she could see a cruise ship floating on the black horizon like a piece of the Milky Way, and she would get that look for an answer. But it never lasted. His memory was too short to let him sulk, no matter what fragment of night had crossed his mind. She knew, having heard other couples all her life, that at least she and Jack never made the conjugal sounds that passed for conversation and that might as well have been bow-wow and quack quack.

If, by chance, Jack found himself drawn to another woman, if the tide of attraction suddenly ran the other way, then he would discover in himself a great need to talk to his wife. They sat out on their balcony for much of one long night and he told her about his Irish mother. His mother's eccentricity—"Vera's dottiness," where the family was concerned—had kept Jack from taking anything seriously. He had been afraid of pulling her mad attention in his direction. Countless times she had faked tuberculosis and cancer and announced her own imminent death. A telephone call from a hospital had once declared her lost in a car crash. "It's a new life, a new life," her husband had babbled, coming away from the phone. Jack saw his father then as beautiful. Women are beautiful when they fall in love, said Jack; sometimes the glow will last a few hours, sometimes even a day or two.

"You know," said Jack, as if Netta knew, "the look of amazement on a girl's face . . ."

Well, that same incandescence had suffused Jack's father when he thought his wife had died, and it continued to shine until a taxi deposited dotty Vera with her cheerful announcement that she had certainly brought off a successful April Fool. After Jack's father died she became violent. "Getting away from her was a form of violence in me," Jack said. "But I did it." That was why he was secretive; that was why he was independent. He had never wanted any woman to get her hands on his life.

Netta heard this out calmly. Where his own feelings were concerned she thought he was making them up as he went along. The garden smelled coolly of jasmine and mimosa. She wondered who his new girl was, and if he was likely to blurt out a name. But all he had been working up to was that his mother—mad, spoiled, devilish, whatever she was—would need to live with Jack and Netta, unless Netta agreed to giving her an income. An income would let her remain where she was—at the moment, in a Rudolf Steiner community in Switzerland, devoted to medieval gardening and to getting the best out of Goethe. Netta's father's training prevented even the thought of spending the money in such a manner.

"You won't regret all you've told me, will you?" she asked. She saw that the new situation would be her burden, her chain, her mean little joke sometimes. Jack scarcely hesitated before saying that where Netta mattered he could never regret anything. But what really interested him now was his mother.

"Lifts give her claustrophobia," he said. "She mustn't be higher than the second floor." He sounded like a man bringing a legal concubine into his household, scrupulously anxious to give all his women equal rights. "And I hope she will make friends," he said. "It won't be easy, at her age. One can't live without them." He probably meant that he had none. Netta had been raised not to expect to have friends: you could not run a hotel and have scores of personal ties. She expected people to be polite and punctual and to mean what they said, and that was the end of it. Jack gave his friendship easily, but he expected considerable diversion in return.

Netta said dryly, "If she plays bridge, she can play with Mrs. Blackley." This was the wife of the doctor who had first said "Moslem wife." He had come down here to the Riviera for his wife's health; the two belonged to a subcolony of flat-dwelling expatriates. His medical practice was limited to hypochondriacs and rheumatic patients. He had time on his hands: Netta often saw him in the hotel reading room, standing, leafing—he took pleasure in handling books. Netta, no reader, did not like touching a book unless it was new. The doctor had a trick of speech Jack loved to imitate: he would break up his words with an extra syllable, some words only, and at that not every time. "It is all a matter of stu-hyle," he said, for "style," or, Jack's favorite, "Oh, well, in the end it all comes down to su-hex." "Uh-hebb and flo-ho of hormones" was the way he once described the behavior of saints—Netta had looked twice at him over that. He was a firm agnostic and the first person from whom Netta heard there existed a magical Dr. Freud. When Netta's father had died of pneumonia, the doctor's "I'm su-horry, Netta" had been so heartfelt she could not have wished it said another way.

His wife, Georgina, could lower her blood pressure or stop her heartbeat nearly at will. Netta sometimes wondered why Dr. Blackley had brought her to a soft climate rather than to the man at Vienna he so admired. Georgina was well enough to play fierce bridge, with Jack and anyone good enough. Her husband usually came to fetch her at the end of the afternoon when the players stopped for tea. Once, because he was obliged to return at once to a patient who needed him, she said, "Can't you be competent about anything?" Netta thought she understood, then, his resigned repetition of "It's all su-hex." "Oh, don't explain. You bore me," said his wife, turning her back.

Netta followed him out to his car. She wore an India shawl that had been her mother's. The wind blew her hair; she had to hold it back. She said, "Why don't you kill her?"

"I am not a desperate person," he said. He looked at Netta, she looking up at him because she had to look up to nearly everyone except children, and he said, "I've wondered why we haven't been to bed."

"Who?" said Netta. "You and your wife? Oh. You mean me." She was not offended, she just gave the shawl a brusque tug and said, "Not a hope. Never with a guest," though of course that was not the reason.

"You might have to, if the guest were a maharaja," he said, to make it all harmless. "I am told it is pu-hart of the courtesy they expect."

"We don't get their trade," said Netta. This had not stopped her liking the doctor. She pitied him, rather, because of his wife, and because he wasn't Jack and could not have Netta.

"I do love you," said the doctor, deciding finally to sit down in his car. "Ee-nee-ormously." She watched him drive away as if she loved him too, and might never see him again. It never crossed her mind to mention any of this conversation to Jack.

THAT VERY SPRING, perhaps because of the doctor's words, the hotel did get some maharaja trade—three little sisters with ebony curls, men's eyebrows, large heads, and delicate hands and feet. They had four rooms, one for their governess. A chauffeur on permanent call lodged elsewhere. The governess, who was Dutch, had a perfect triangle of a nose and said "whom" for "who," pronouncing it "whum." The girls were to learn French, tennis, and swimming. The chauffeur arrived with a hairdresser, who cut their long hair; it lay on the governess's carpet, enough to fill a large pillow. Their toe- and fingernails were filed to points and looked like a kitten's teeth. They came smiling down the marble staircase, carrying new tennis racquets, wearing blue linen skirts and navy blazers. Mrs. Blackley glanced up from the bridge game as they went by the cardroom. She had been one of those opposed to their having lessons at the English Lawn Tennis Club, for reasons that were, to her, perfectly evident.

She said, loudly, "They'll have to be in white."

"End whay, pray?" cried the governess, pointing her triangle nose.

"They can't go on the courts except in white. It is a private club. Entirely white."

"Whum do they all think they are?" the governess asked, prepared to stalk on. But the girls, with their newly cropped heads, and their vulnerable necks showing, caught the drift and refused to go.

"Whom indeed," said Georgina Blackley, fiddling with her bridge hand and looking happy.

"My wife's seamstress could run up white frocks for them in a minute," said Jack. Perhaps he did not dislike children all that much.

"Whom could," muttered Georgina.

But it turned out that the governess was not allowed to choose their clothes, and so Jack gave the children lessons at the hotel. For six weeks they trotted around the courts looking angelic in blue, or hopelessly foreign, depending upon who saw them. Of course they fell in love with Jack, offering him a passionate loyalty they had nowhere else to place. Netta watched the transfer of this gentle, anxious gift. After they departed, Jack was bad-tempered for several evenings and then never spoke of them again; they, needless to say, had been dragged from him weeping.

When this happened the Rosses had been married nearly five years. Being childless but still very loving, they had trouble deciding which of the two would be the child. Netta overheard "He's a darling, but she's a sergeant major and no mistake. And so *mean.*" She also heard "He's a lazy bastard. He bullies her. She's a fool." She searched her heart again about children. Was it Jack or had it been Netta who had first said no? The only child she had ever admired was Jack, and not as a child but as a fighter, defying her. She and Jack were not the sort to have animal children, and Jack's dotty mother would probably soon be child enough for any couple to handle. Jack still seemed to adopt, in a tribal sense of his, half the women who fell in love with him. The only woman who resisted adoption was Netta—still burned-out, still ardent, in a manner of speaking still fourteen. His mother had turned up meanwhile, getting down from a train wearing a sly air of enjoying her own jokes, just as she must have looked on the day of the April Fool. At first she was no great trouble, though she did complain about an ulcerated leg. After years of pretending, she at last had something real. Netta's policy of silence made Jack's mother confident. She began to make a mockery of his music: "All that money gone for nothing!" Or else, "The amount we wasted on schools! The hours he's thrown away with his nose in a book. All that reading—if at least it had got him somewhere." Netta noticed that he spent more time playing bridge and chatting to cronies in the bar now. She thought hard, and decided not to make it her business. His mother had once been pretty; perhaps he still saw her that way. She came of a ramshackle family with a usable past; she spoke of the Ashers and the Rosses as if she had known them when they were tinkers. English residents who had a low but solid barrier with Jack and Netta were fences-down with his mad mother: they seemed to take her at her own word when it was about herself. She began then to behave like a superior sort of guest, inviting large parties to her table for meals, ordering special wines and dishes at inconvenient hours, standing endless rounds of drinks in the bar.

Netta told herself, Jack wants it this way. It is his home too. She began to live a life apart, leaving Jack to his mother. She sat wearing her own mother's shawl, hunched over a new, modern adding machine, punching out accounts. "Funny couple," she heard now. She frowned, smiling in her mind; none of these people knew what bound them, or how tied they were. She had the habit of dodging out of her mother-in-law's parties by saying, "I've got such an awful lot to do." It made them laugh, because they thought this was Netta's term for slave-driving the servants. They thought the staff did the work, and that Netta counted the profits and was too busy with bookkeeping to keep an eye on Jack—who now, at twenty-six, was as attractive as he ever would be.

A woman named Iris Cordier was one of Jack's mother's new friends. Tall, loud, in winter dully pale, she reminded Netta of a blond penguin. Her voice moved between a squeak and a moo, and was a mark of the distinguished literary family to which her father belonged. Her mother, a Frenchwoman, had been in and out of nursing homes for years. The Cordiers haunted the Riviera, with Iris looking after her parents and watching their diets. Now she lived in a flat somewhere in Roquebrune with the survivor of the pair—the mother, Netta believed. Iris paused and glanced in the business room where Mr. Asher had signed the hundred-year lease. She was on her way to lunch—Jack's mother's guest, of course.

"I say, aren't you Miss Asher?"

"I was." Iris, like Dr. Blackley, was probably younger than she looked. Out of her own childhood Netta recalled a desperate adolescent Iris with middle-aged parents clamped like handcuffs on her life. "How is your mother?" Netta had been about to say "How is Mrs. Cordier?" but it sounded servile.

"I didn't know you knew her."

"I remember her well. Your father too. He was a nice person."

"And still is," said Iris, sharply. "He lives with me, and he always will. French daughters don't abandon their parents." No one had ever sounded more English to Netta. "And your father and mother?"

"Both dead now. I'm married to Jack Ross."

"Nobody told me," said Iris, in a way that made Netta think, Good Lord, Iris too? Jack could not possibly seem like a patriarchal figure where she was concerned; perhaps this time the game was reversed and Iris played at being tribal and maternal. The idea of Jack, or of any man, flinging himself on that iron bosom made Netta smile. As if startled, Iris covered her mouth. She seemed to be frightened of smiling back.

Oh, well, and what of it, Iris too, said Netta to herself, suddenly turning back to her accounts. As it happened, Netta was mistaken (as she never would have been with a bill). That day Jack was meeting Iris for the first time.

The upshot of these errors and encounters was an invitation to Roquebrune to visit Iris's father. Jack's mother was ruthlessly excluded, even though Iris probably owed her a return engagement because of the lunch. Netta supposed that Iris had decided one had to get past Netta to reach Jack—an inexactness if ever there was one. Or perhaps it was Netta Iris wanted. In that case the error became a farce. Netta had almost no knowledge of private houses. She looked around at something that did not much interest her, for she hated to leave her own home, and saw Iris's father, apparently too old and shaky to get out of his armchair. He smiled and he nodded, meanwhile stroking an aged cat. He said to Netta, "You resemble your mother. A sweet woman. Obliging and quiet. I used to tell her that I longed to live in her hotel and be looked after."

Not by me, thought Netta.

Iris's amber bracelets rattled as she pushed and pulled everyone through introductions. Jack and Netta had been asked to meet a young American Netta had often seen in her own bar, and a couple named Sandy and Sandra Braunsweg, who turned out to be Anglo-Swiss and twins. Iris's long arms were around them as she cried to Netta, "Don't you know these babies?" They were, like the Rosses, somewhere in their twenties. Jack looked on, blue-eyed, interested, smiling at everything new. Netta supposed that she was now seeing some of the rather hard-up snobbish—snobbish what? "Intelligum-hen-sia," she imagined Dr. Blackley supplying. Having arrived at a word, Netta was ready to go home; but they had only just arrived. The American turned to Netta. He looked bored, and astonished by it. He needs the word for "bored," she decided. Then he can go home, too. The Riviera was no place for Americans. They could not sit all day waiting for mail and the daily papers and for the clock to show a respectable drinking time. They made the best of things when they were caught with a house they'd been rash enough to rent unseen. Netta often had them then *en pension* for meals: a hotel dining room was one way of meeting people. They paid a fee to use the tennis courts, and they liked the bar. Netta would notice then how Jack picked up any accent within hearing.

Jack was now being attentive to the old man, Iris's father. Though this was none of Mr. Cordier's business, Jack said, "My wife and I are first cousins, as well as second cousins twice over."

"You don't look it."

Everyone began to speak at once, and it was a minute or two before Netta heard Jack again. This time he said, "We are from a family of great . . ." It was lost. What now? Great innkeepers? Worriers? Skinflints? Whatever it was, old Mr. Cordier kept nodding to show he approved.

"We don't see nearly enough of young men like you," he said.

"True!" said Iris loudly. "We live in a dreary world of ill women down here." Netta thought this hard on the American, on Mr. Cordier, and on the male Braunsweg twin, but none of them looked offended. "I've got no time for women," said Iris. She slapped down a glass of whiskey so that it splashed, and rapped on a table with her knuckles. "Shall I tell you why? Because women don't tick over. They just simply don't tick over." No one disputed this. Iris went on: Women were underinformed. One could have virile conversations only with men. Women were attached to the past through fear, whereas men had a fearless sense of history. "Men tick," she said, glaring at Jack.

"I am not attached to a past," said Netta, slowly. "The past holds no attractions." She was not used to general conversation. She thought that every word called for consideration and for an answer. "Nothing could be worse than the way we children were dressed. And our mothers—the hard waves of their hair, the white lips. I think of those pale profiles and I wonder if those women were ever young."

Poor Netta, who saw herself as profoundly English, spread consternation by being suddenly foreign and gassy. She talked the English of expatriate children, as if reading aloud. The twins looked shocked. But she had appealed to the American. He sat beside her on a scuffed velvet sofa. He was so large that she slid an inch or so in his direction when he sat down. He was Sandra Braunsweg's special friend: they had been in London together. He was trying to write.

"What do you mean?" said Netta. "Write what?"

"Well—a novel, to start," he said. His father had staked him to one year, then another. He mentioned all that Sandra had borne with, how she had actually kicked and punched him to keep him from being too American. He had embarrassed her to death in London by asking a waitress, "Miss, where's the toilet?"

Netta said, "Didn't you mind being corrected?"

"Oh, no. It was just friendly."

Jack meanwhile was listening to Sandra telling about her English forebears and her English education. "I had many years of undeniably excellent schooling," she said. "Mitten Todd."

"What's that?" said Jack.

"It's near Bristol. I met excellent girls from Italy, Spain. I took *him* there to visit," she said, generously including the American. "I said, 'Get a yellow necktie.' He went straight out and bought one. I wore a little Schiaparelli. Bought in Geneva but still a real . . . A yellow jacket over a gray . . . Well, we arrived at my excellent old school, and even though the day was drizzly I said, 'Put the top of the car back.' He did so at once, and then he understood. The interior of the car harmonized perfectly with the yellow and gray." The twins were orphaned. Iris was like a mother.

"When Mummy died we didn't know where to put all the Chippendale," said Sandra, "Iris took a lot of it."

Netta thought, She is so silly. How can he respond? The girl's dimples and freckles and soft little hands were nothing Netta could have ever described: she had never in her life thought a word like "pretty." People were beautiful or they were not. Her happiness had always been great enough to allow for despair. She knew that some people thought Jack was happy and she was not.

"And what made you marry your young cousin?" the old man boomed at Netta. Perhaps his background allowed him to ask impertinent questions; he must have been doing so nearly forever. He stroked his cat; he was confident. He was spokesman for a roomful of wondering people.

"Jack was a moody child and I promised his mother I would look after him," said Netta. In her hopelessly un-English way she believed she had said something funny.

AT ELEVEN O'CLOCK the hotel car expected to fetch the Rosses was nowhere. They trudged home by moonlight. For the last hour of the evening Jack had been skewered on virile conversations, first with Iris, then with Sandra, to whom Netta had already given "Chippendale" as a private name. It proved that Iris was right about concentrating on men and their ticking—Jack even thought Sandra rather pretty.

"Prettier than me?" said Netta, without the faintest idea what she meant, but aware she had said something stupid.

"Not so attractive," said Jack. His slight limp returned straight out of childhood. *She* had caused his accident.

"But she's not always clear," said Netta. "Mitten Todd, for example."

"Who're you talking about?"

"Who are *you*?"

"Iris, of course."

As if they had suddenly quarrelled they fell silent. In silence they entered their room and prepared for bed. Jack poured a whiskey, walked on the clothes he had dropped, carried his drink to the bathroom. Through the half-shut door he called suddenly, "Why did you say that asinine thing about promising to look after me?"

"It seemed so unlikely, I thought they'd laugh." She had a glimpse of herself in the mirrors picking up his shed clothes.

He said, "Well, is it true?"

She was quiet for such a long time that he came to see if she was still in the room. She said, "No, your mother never said that or anything like it."

"We shouldn't have gone to Roquebrune," said Jack. "I think those bloody people are going to be a nuisance. Iris wants her father to stay here, with the cat, while she goes to England for a month. How do we get out of that?"

"By saying no."

"I'm rotten at no."

"I told you not to be too pally with women," she said, as a joke again, but jokes were her way of having floods of tears.

Before this had a chance to heal, Iris's father moved in, bringing his cat in a basket. He looked at his room and said, "Medium large." He looked at his bed and said, "Reasonably long." He was, in short, daft about measurements. When he took books out of the reading room, he was apt to return them with "This volume contains about 70,000 words" written inside the back cover.

Netta had not wanted Iris's father, but Jack had said yes to it. She had not wanted the sick cat, but Jack had said yes to that too. The old man, who was lost without Iris, lived for his meals. He would appear at the shut doors of the dining room an hour too early, waiting for the menu to be typed and posted. In a voice that matched Iris's for carrying power, he read aloud, alone: "Consommé. Good Lord, again? Is there a choice between the fish and the cutlet? I can't possibly eat all of that. A bit of salad and a boiled egg. That's all I could possibly want." That was rubbish, because Mr. Cordier ate the menu and more, and if there were two puddings, or a pudding and ice cream, he ate both and asked for pastry, fruit, and cheese to follow. One day, after Dr. Blackley had attended him for faintness, Netta passed a message on to Iris, who had been back from England for a fortnight now but seemed in no hurry to take her father away.

"Keith Blackley thinks your father should go on a diet."

"He can't," said Iris. "Our other doctor says dieting causes cancer."

"You can't have heard that properly," Netta said.

"It is like those silly people who smoke to keep their figures," said Iris. "Dieting."

"Blackley hasn't said he should smoke, just that he should eat less of everything."

"My father has never smoked in his life," Iris cried. "As for his diet, I weighed his food out for years. He's not here forever. I'll take him back as soon as he's had enough of hotels."

He stayed for a long time, and the cat did too, and a nuisance they both were to the servants. When the cat was too ailing to walk, the old man carried it to a path behind the tennis courts and put it down on the gravel to die. Netta came out with the old man's tea on a tray (not done for everyone, but having him out of the way was a relief) and she saw the cat lying on its side, eyes wide, as if profoundly thinking. She saw unlicked dirt on its coat and ants exploring its paws. The old man sat in a garden chair, wearing a panama hat, his hands clasped on a stick. He called, "Oh, Netta, take her away. I am too old to watch anything die. I know what she'll do," he said, indifferently, his voice falling as she came near. "Oh, I know that. Turn on her back and give a shriek. I've heard it often."

Netta disburdened her tray onto a garden table and pulled the tray cloth under the cat. She was angered at the haste and indecency of the ants. "It would be polite to leave her," she said. "She doesn't want to be watched."

"I always sit here," said the old man.

Jack, making for the courts with Chippendale, looked as if the sight of the two conversing amused him. Then he understood and scooped up the cat and tray cloth and went away with the cat over his shoulder. He laid it in the shade of a Judas tree, and within an hour it was dead. Iris's father said, "I've got no one to talk to here. That's my trouble. That shroud was too small for my poor Polly. Ask my daughter to fetch me."

Jack's mother said that night, "I'm sure you wish that I had a devoted daughter to take me away too." Because of the attention given the cat she seemed to feel she had not been nuisance enough. She had taken to saying, "My leg is dying before I am," and imploring Jack to preserve her leg, should it be amputated, and make certain it was buried with her. She wanted Jack to be close by at nearly any hour now, so that she could lean on him. After sitting for hours at bridge she had trouble climbing two flights of stairs; nothing would induce her to use the lift.

"Nothing ever came of your music," she would say, leaning on him. "Of course, you have a wife to distract you now. I needed a daughter. Every woman does." Netta managed to trap her alone, and forced her to sit while she stood over her. Netta said, "Look, Aunt Vera, I forbid you, I absolutely forbid you, do you hear, to make a nurse of Jack, and I shall strangle you with my own hands if you go on saying nothing came of his music. You are not to say it in my hearing or out of it. Is that plain?"

Jack's mother got up to her room without assistance. About an hour later the gardener found her on a soft bed of wallflowers. "An inch to the left and she'd have landed on a rake," he said to Netta. She was still alive when Netta knelt down. In her fall she had crushed the plants, the yellow minted *giroflées de Nice*. Netta thought that she was now, at last, for the first time, inhaling one of the smells of death. Her aunt's arms and legs were turned and twisted; her skirt was pulled so that her swollen leg showed. It seemed that she had jumped carrying her walking stick—it lay across the path. She often slept in an armchair, afternoons, with one eye slightly open. She opened that eye now and, seeing she had Netta, said, "My son." Netta was thinking, I have never known her. And if I knew her, then it was Jack or myself I could not understand. Netta was afraid of giving orders, and of telling people not to touch her aunt before Dr. Blackley could be summoned, because she knew that she had always been mistaken. Now Jack was there, propping his mother up, brushing leaves and earth out of her hair. Her head dropped on his shoulder. Netta thought from the sudden heaviness that her aunt had died, but she sighed and opened that one eye again, saying this time, "Doctor?" Netta left everyone doing the wrong things to her dying —no, her murdered—aunt. She said quite calmly into a telephone, "I am afraid that my aunt must have jumped or fallen from the second floor."

Jack found a letter on his mother's night table that began, "Why blame Netta? I forgive." At dawn he and Netta sat at a card table with yesterday's cigarettes still not cleaned out of the ashtray, and he did not ask what Netta had said or done that called for forgiveness. They kept pushing the letter back and forth. He would read it and then Netta would. It seemed natural for them to be silent. Jack had sat beside his mother for much of the night. Each of them then went to sleep for an hour, apart, in one of the empty rooms, just as they had done in the old days when their parents were juggling beds and guests and double and single quarters. By the time the doctor returned for his second visit Jack was neatly dressed and seemed wide awake. He sat in the bar drinking black coffee and reading a travel book of Evelyn Waugh's called *Labels*. Netta, who looked far more untidy and underslept, wondered if Jack wished he might leave now, and sail from Monte Carlo on the Stella Polaris.

Dr. Blackley said, "Well, you are a dim pair. She is not in pu-hain, you know." Netta supposed this was the roundabout way doctors have of announcing death, very like "Her sufferings have ended." But Jack, looking hard at the doctor, had heard another meaning. "Jumped or fell," said Dr. Blackley. "She neither fell nor jumped. She is up there enjoying a damned good thu-hing."

Netta went out and through the lounge and up the marble steps. She sat down in the shaded room on the chair where Jack had spent most of the night. Her aunt did not look like anyone Netta knew, not even like Jack. She stared at the alien face and said, "Aunt Vera, Keith Blackley says there is nothing really the matter. You must have made a mistake. Perhaps you fainted on the path, overcome by the scent of wallflowers. What would you like me to tell Jack?"

Jack's mother turned on her side and slowly, tenderly, raised herself on an elbow. "Well, Netta," she said, "I daresay the fool is right. But as I've been given quite a lot of sleeping stuff, I'd as soon stay here for now."

Netta said, "Are you hungry?"

"I should very much like a ham sandwich on English bread, and about that much gin with a lump of ice."

SHE BEGAN coming down for meals a few days later. They knew she had crept down the stairs and flung her walking stick over the path and let herself fall hard on a bed of wallflowers—had even plucked her skirt up for a bit of accuracy; but she was also someone returned from beyond the limits, from the other side of the wall. Once she said, "It was like diving and suddenly realizing there was no water in the sea." Again, "It is not true that your life rushes before your eyes. You can see the flowers floating up to you. Even a short fall takes a long time."

Everyone was deeply changed by this incident. The effect on the victim herself was that she got religion hard.

"We are all hopeless nonbelievers!" shouted Iris, drinking in the bar one afternoon. "At least, I hope we are. But when I see you, Vera, I feel there might be something in religion. You look positively temperate."

"I am allowed to love God, I hope," said Jack's mother.

Jack never saw or heard his mother anymore. He leaned against the bar, reading. It was his favorite place. Even on the sunniest of afternoons he read by the red-shaded light. Netta was present only because she had supplies to check. Knowing she ought to keep out of this, she still said, "Religion is more than love. It is supposed to tell you why you exist and what you are expected to do about it."

"You have no religious feelings at all?" This was the only serious and almost the only friendly question Iris was ever to ask Netta.

"None," said Netta. "I'm running a business."

"I love God as Jack used to love music," said his mother. "At least he said he did when we were paying for lessons."

"Adam and Eve had God," said Netta. "They had nobody *but* God. A fat lot of good that did them." This was as far as their dialectic went. Jack had not moved once except to turn pages. He read steadily but cautiously now, as if every author had a design on him. That was one effect of his mother's incident. The other was that he gave up bridge and went back to playing the clarinet. Iris hammered out an accompaniment on the upright piano in the old music room, mostly used for listening to radio broadcasts. She was the only person Netta had ever heard who could make Mozart sound like an Irish jig. Presently Iris began to say that it was time Jack gave a concert. Before this could turn into a crisis Iris changed her mind and said what he wanted was a holiday. Netta thought he needed something: he seemed to be exhausted by love, friendship, by being a husband, someone's son, by trying to make a world out of reading and sense out of life. A visit to England to meet some stimulating people, said Iris. To help Iris with her tiresome father during the journey. To visit art galleries and bookshops and go to concerts. To meet people. To talk.

This was a hot, troubled season, and many persons were planning journeys—not to meet other people but for fear of a war. The hotel had emptied out by the end of March. Netta, whose father had known there would never be another catastrophe, had her workmen come in, as usual. She could hear the radiators being drained and got ready for painting as she packed Jack's clothes. They had never been separated before. They kept telling each other that it was only for a short holiday—for three or four weeks. She was surprised at how neat marriage was, at how many years and feelings could be folded and put under a lid. Once, she went to the window so that he would not see her tears and think she was trying to blackmail him. Looking out, she noticed the American, Chippendale's lover, idly knocking a tennis ball against the garage, as Jack had done in the early summers of their life; he had come round to the hotel looking for a partner, but that season there were none. She suddenly knew to a certainty that if Jack were to die she would search the crowd of mourners for a man she could live with. She would not return from the funeral alone.

Grief and memory, yes, she said to herself, but what about three o'clock in the morning?

By june nearly everyone Netta knew had vanished, or, like the Blackleys, had started to pack. Netta had new tablecloths made, and ordered new white awnings, and two dozen rosebushes from the nursery at Cap Ferrat. The American came over every day and followed her from room to room, talking. He had nothing better to do. The Swiss twins were in England. His father, who had been backing his writing career until now, had suddenly changed his mind about it—now, when he needed money to get out of Europe. He had projects for living on his own, but they required a dose of funds. He wanted to open a restaurant on the Riviera where nothing but chicken pie would be served. Or else a vast and expensive café where people would pay to make their own sandwiches. He said that he was seeing the food of the future, but all that Netta could see was customers asking for their money back. He trapped her behind the bar and said he loved her; Netta made other women look like stuffed dolls. He could still remember the shock of meeting her, the attraction, the brilliant answer she had made to Iris about attachments to the past.

Netta let him rave until he asked for a loan. She laughed and wondered if it was for the chicken-pie restaurant. No—he wanted to get on a boat sailing from Cannes. She said, quite cheerfully, "I can't be Venus and Barclays Bank. You have to choose."

He said, "Can't Venus ever turn up with a letter of credit?"

She shook her head. "Not a hope."

But when it was July and Jack hadn't come back, he cornered her again. Money wasn't in it now: his father had not only relented but had virtually ordered him home. He was about twenty-two, she guessed. He could still plead successfully for parental help and for indulgence from women. She said, no more than affectionately, "I'm going to show you a very pretty room."

A few days later Dr. Blackley came alone to say goodbye.

"Are you really staying?" he asked.

"I am responsible for the last eighty-one years of this lease," said Netta. "I'm going to be thirty. It's a long tenure. Besides, I've got Jack's mother and she won't leave. Jack has a chance now to visit America. It doesn't sound sensible to me, but she writes encouraging him. She imagines him suddenly very rich and sending for her. I've discovered the limit of what you can feel about people. I've discovered something else," she said abruptly. "It is that sex and love have nothing in common. Only a coincidence, sometimes. You think the coincidence will go on and so you get married. I suppose that is what men are born knowing and women learn by accident."

"I'm su-horry."

"For God's sake, don't be. It's a relief."

She had no feeling of guilt, only of amazement. Jack, as a memory, was in a restricted area—the tennis courts, the cardroom, the bar. She saw him at bridge with Mrs. Blackley and pouring drinks for temporary friends. He crossed the lounge jauntily with a cluster of little dark-haired girls wearing blue. In the mirrored bedroom there was only Netta. Her dreams were cleansed of him. The looking glasses still held their blue-and-silver-water shadows, but they lost the habit of giving back the moods and gestures of a Moslem wife.

ABOUT FIVE YEARS after this, Netta wrote to Jack. The war had caught him in America, during the voyage his mother had so wanted him to have. His limp had kept him out of the Army. As his mother (now dead) might have put it, all that reading had finally got him somewhere: he had spent the last years putting out a two-pager on aspects of European culture—part of a scrupulous effort Britain was making for the West. That was nearly all Netta knew. A Belgian Red Cross official had arrived, apparently in Jack's name, to see if she was still alive. She sat in her father's business room, wearing a coat and a shawl because there was no way of heating any part of the hotel now, and she tried to get on with the letter she had been writing in her head, on and off, for many years.

"In June, 1940, we were evacuated," she started, for the tenth or eleventh time. "I was back by October. Italians had taken over the hotel. They used the mirror behind the bar for target practice. Oddly enough it was not smashed. It is covered with spiderwebs, and the bullet hole is the spider. I had great trouble over Aunt Vera, who disappeared and was found finally in one of the attic rooms.

"The Italians made a pet of her. Took her picture. She enjoyed that. Everyone who became thin had a desire to be photographed, as if knowing they would use this intimidating evidence against those loved ones who had missed being starved. Guilt for life. After an initial period of hardship, during which she often had her picture taken at her request, the Italians brought food and looked after her, more than anyone. She was their mama. We were annexed territory and in time we had the same food as the Italians. The thin pictures of your mother are here on my desk.

"She buried her British passport and would never say where. Perhaps under the Judas tree with Mr. Cordier's cat, Polly. She remained just as mad and just as spoiled, and that became dangerous when life stopped being ordinary. She complained about me to the Italians. At that time a complaint was a matter of prison and of death if it was made to the wrong person. Luckily for me, there was also the right person to take the message.

"A couple of years after that, the Germans and certain French took over and the Italians were shut up in another hotel without food or water, and some people risked their well-being to take water to them (for not everyone preferred the new situation, you can believe me). When she was dying I asked her if she had a message for one Italian officer who had made such a pet of her and she said, 'No, why?' She died without a word for anybody. She was buried as 'Rossini,' because the Italians had changed people's names. She had said she was French, a Frenchwoman named Ross, and so some peculiar civil status was created for us—the two Mrs. Rossinis.

"The records were topsy-turvy; it would have meant going to the Germans and explaining my dead aunt was British, and of course I thought I would not. The death certificate and permission to bury are for a Vera Rossini. I have them here on my desk for you with her pictures.

"You are probably wondering where I have found all this writing paper. The Germans left it behind. When we were being shelled I took what few books were left in the reading room down to what used to be the wine cellar and read by candlelight. You are probably wondering where the candles came from. A long story. I even have paint for the radiators, large buckets that have never been opened.

"I live in one room, my mother's old sitting room. The business room can be used but the files have gone. When the Italians were here your mother was their mother, but I was not their Moslem wife, although I still had respect for men. One yelled 'Luce, luce,' because your mother was showing a light. She said, 'Bugger you, you little toad.' He said, 'Granny, I said *"luce,"* not *"Duce."* '

"Not long ago we crept out of our shelled homes, looking like cave dwellers. When you see the hotel again, it will be functioning. I shall have painted the radiators. Long shoots of bramble come in through the cardroom windows. There are drifts of leaves in the old music room and I saw scorpions and heard their rustling like the rustle of death. Everything that could have been looted has gone. Sheets, bedding, mattresses. The neighbors did quite a lot of that. At the risk of their lives. When the Italians were here we had rice and oil. Your mother, who was crazy, used to put out grains to feed the mice.

"When the Germans came we had to live under Vichy law, which meant each region lived on what it could produce. As ours produces nothing, we got quite thin again. Aunt Vera died plump. Do you know what it means when I say she used to complain about me?

"Send me some books. As long as they are in English. I am quite sick of the three other languages in which I've heard so many threats, such boasting, such a lot of lying.

"For a time I thought people would like to know how the Italians left and the Germans came in. It was like this: They came in with the first car moving slowly, flying the French flag. The highest-ranking French official in the region. Not a German. No, just a chap getting his job back. The Belgian Red Cross people were completely uninterested and warned me that no one would ever want to hear.

"I suppose that you already have the fiction of all this. The fiction must be different, oh very different, from Italians sobbing with homesickness in the night. The Germans were not real, they were specially got up for the events of the time. Sat in the white dining room, eating with whatever plates and spoons were not broken or looted, ate soups that were mostly water, were forbidden to complain. Only in retreat did they develop faces and I noticed then that some were terrified and many were old. A radio broadcast from some untouched area advised the local population not to attack them as they retreated, it would make wild animals of them. But they were attacked by some young boys shooting out of a window and eight hostages were taken, including the son of the man who cut the maharaja's daughters' black hair, and they were shot and left along the wall of a café on the more or less Italian side of the border. And the man who owned the café was killed too, but later, by civilians—he had given names to the Gestapo once, or perhaps it was something else. He got on the wrong side of the right side at the wrong time, and he was thrown down the deep gorge between the two frontiers.

"Up in one of the hill villages Germans stayed till no one was alive. I was at that time in the former wine cellar, reading books by candle-light.

"The Belgian Red Cross team found the skeleton of a German deserter in a cave and took back the helmet and skull to Knokke-le-Zoute as souvenirs.

"My war has ended. Our family held together almost from the Napoleonic adventures. It is shattered now. Sentiment does not keep families whole—only mutual pride and mutual money."

THIS TRUE STORY sounded so implausible that she decided never to send it. She wrote a sensible letter asking for sugar and rice and for new books; nothing must be older than 1940.

Jack answered at once: there were no new authors (he had been asking people). Sugar was unobtainable, and there were queues for rice. Shoes had been rationed. There were no women's stockings but lisle, and the famous American legs looked terrible. You could not find butter or meat or tinned pineapple. In restaurants, instead of butter you were given miniature golf balls of cream cheese. He supposed that all this must sound like small beer to Netta.

A notice arrived that a CARE package awaited her at the post office. It meant that Jack had added his name and his money to a mailing list. She refused to sign for it; then she changed her mind and discovered it was not from Jack but from the American she had once taken to such a pretty room. Jack did send rice and sugar and delicious coffee but he forgot about books. His letters followed; sometimes three arrived in a morning. She left them sealed for days. When she sat down to answer, all she could remember were implausible things.

Iris came back. She was the first. She had grown puffy in England —the result of drinking whatever alcohol she could get her hands on and grimly eating her sweets allowance: there would be that much less gin and chocolate for the Germans if ever they landed. She put her now wide bottom on a comfortable armchair—one of the few chairs the first wave of Italians had not burned with cigarettes or idly hacked at with daggers—and said Jack had been living with a woman in America and to spare the gossip had let her be known as his wife. Another Mrs. Ross? When Netta discovered it was dimpled Chippendale, she laughed aloud.

"I've seen them," said Iris. "I mean I saw them together. King Charles and a spaniel. Jack wiped his feet on her."

Netta's feelings were of lightness, relief. She would not have to tell Jack about the partisans hanging by the neck in the arches of the Place Masséna at Nice. When Iris had finished talking, Netta said, "What about his music?"

"I don't know."

"How can you not know something so important?"

"Jack had a good chance at things, but he made a mess of everything," said Iris. "My father is still living. Life really is too incredible for some of us."

A dark girl of about twenty turned up soon after. Her costume, a gray dress buttoned to the neck, gave her the appearance of being in uniform. She unzipped a military-looking bag and cried, in an unplaceable accent, "Hallo, hallo, Mrs. Ross? A few small gifts for you," and unpacked a bottle of Haig, four tins of corned beef, a jar of honey, and six pairs of American nylon stockings, which Netta had never seen before, and were as good to have under a mattress as gold. Netta looked up at the tall girl.

"Remember? I was the middle sister. With," she said gravely, "the typical middle-sister problems." She scarcely recalled Jack, her beloved. The memory of Netta had grown up with her. "I remember you laughing," she said, without loving that memory. She was a severe, tragic girl. "You were the first adult I ever heard laughing. At night in bed I could hear it from your balcony. You sat smoking with, I suppose, your handsome husband. I used to laugh just to hear you."

She had married an Iranian journalist. He had discovered that political prisoners in the United States were working under lamentable conditions in tin mines. President Truman had sent them there. People from all over the world planned to unite to get them out. The girl said she had been to Germany and to Austria, she had visited camps, they were all alike, and that was already the past, and the future was the prisoners in the tin mines.

Netta said, "In what part of the country are these mines?"

The middle sister looked at her sadly and said, "Is there more than one part?"

For the first time in years, Netta could see Jack clearly. They were silently sharing a joke; he had caught it too. She and the girl lunched in a corner of the battered dining room. The tables were scarred with initials. There were no tablecloths. One of the great-uncle's paintings still hung on a wall. It showed the Quai Laurenti, a country road alongside the sea. Netta, who had no use for the past, was discovering a past she could regret. Out of a dark, gentle silence—silence imposed by the impossibility of telling anything real—she counted the cracks in the walls. When silence failed she heard power saws ripping into olive trees and a lemon grove. With a sense of deliverance she understood that soon there would be nothing left to spoil. Her great-uncle's picture, which ought to have changed out of sympathetic magic, remained faithful. She regretted everything now, even the three anxious little girls in blue linen. Every calamitous season between then and now seemed to descend directly from Georgina Blackley's having said "white" just to keep three children in their place. Clad in buttoned-up gray, the middle sister now picked at corned beef and said she had hated her father, her mother, her sisters, and most of all the Dutch governess.

"Where is she now?" said Netta.

"Dead, I hope." This was from someone who had visited camps. Netta sat listening, her cheek on her hand. Death made death casual: she had always known. Neither the vanquished in their flight nor the victors returning to pick over rubble seemed half so vindictive as a tragic girl who had disliked her governess.

DR. BLACKLEY came back looking positively cheerful. In those days men still liked soldiering. It made them feel young, if they needed to feel it, and it got them away from home. War made the break few men could make on their own. The doctor looked years younger, too, and very fit. His wife was not with him. She had survived everything, and the hardships she had undergone had completely restored her to health—which had made it easy for her husband to leave her. Actually, he had never gone back, except to wind up the matter.

"There are things about Georgina I respect and admire," he said, as husbands will say from a distance. His war had been in Malta. He had come here, as soon as he could, to the shelled, gnawed, tarnished coast (as if he had not seen enough at Malta) to ask Netta to divorce Jack and to marry him, or live with him—anything she wanted, on any terms.

But she wanted nothing—at least, not from him.

"Well, one can't defeat a memory," he said. "I always thought it was mostly su-hex between the two of you."

"So it was," said Netta. "So far as I remember."

"Everyone noticed. You would vanish at odd hours. Dis-huppear."

"Yes, we did."

"You can't live on memories," he objected. "Though I respect you for being faithful, of course."

"What you are talking about is something of which one has no specific memory," said Netta. "Only of seasons. Places. Rooms. It is as abstract to remember as to read about. That is why it is boring in talk except as a joke, and boring in books except for poetry."

"You never read poetry."

"I do now."

"I guessed that," he said.

"That lack of memory is why people are unfaithful, as it is so curiously called. When I see closed shutters I know there are lovers behind them. That is how the memory works. The rest is just convention and small talk."

"Why lovers? Why not someone sleeping off the wine he had for lunch?"

"No. Lovers."

"A middle-aged man cutting his toenails in the bathtub," he said with unexpected feeling. "Wearing bifocal lenses so that he can see his own feet."

"No, lovers. Always."

He said, "Have you missed him?"

"Missed who?"

"Who the bloody hell are we talking about?"

"The Italian commander billeted here. He was not a guest. He was here by force. I was not breaking a rule. Without him I'd have perished in every way. He may be home with his wife now. Or in that fortress near Turin where he sent other men. Or dead." She looked at the doctor and said, "Well, what would you like me to do? Sit here and cry?"

"I can't imagine you with a brute."

"I never said that."

"Do you miss him still?"

"The absence of Jack was like a cancer which I am sure has taken root, and of which I am bound to die," said Netta.

"You'll bu-hury us all," he said, as doctors tell the condemned.

"I haven't said I won't." She rose suddenly and straightened her skirt, as she used to do when hotel guests became pally. "Conversation over," it meant.

"Don't be too hard on Jack," he said.

"I am hard on myself," she replied.

After he had gone he sent her a parcel of books, printed on grayish paper, in warped wartime covers. All of the titles were, to Netta, unknown. There was *Fireman Flower* and *The Horse's Mouth* and *Four Quartets* and *The Stuff to Give the Troops* and *Better Than a Kick in the Pants* and *Put Out More Flags*. A note added that the next package would contain Henry Green and Dylan Thomas. She guessed he would not want to be thanked, but she did so anyway. At the end of her letter was "Please remember, if you mind too much, that I said no to you once before." Leaning on the bar, exactly as Jack used to, with a glass of the middle sister's drink at hand, she opened *Better Than a Kick in the Pants* and read, ". . . two Fascists came in, one of them tall and thin and tough looking; the other smaller, with only one arm and an empty sleeve pinned up to his shoulder. Both of them were quite young and wore black shirts."

Oh, thought Netta, I am the only one who knows all this. No one will ever realize how much I know of the truth, the truth, the truth, and she put her head on her hands, her elbows on the scarred bar, and let the first tears of her after-war run down her wrists.

THE LAST TO RETURN was the one who should have been first. Jack wrote that he was coming down from the north as far as Nice by bus. It was a common way of travelling and much cheaper than by train. Netta guessed that he was mildly hard up and that he had saved nothing from his war job. The bus came in at six, at the foot of the Place Masséna. There was a deep-blue late-afternoon sky and pale sunlight. She could hear birds from the public gardens nearby. The Place was as she had always seen it, like an elegant drawing room with a blue ceiling. It was nearly empty. Jack looked out on this sunlighted, handsome space and said, "Well, I'll just leave my stuff at the bus office, for the moment"—perhaps noticing that Netta had not invited him anywhere. He placed his ticket on the counter, and she saw that he had not come from far away: he must have been moving south by stages. He carried an aura of London pub life; he had been in London for weeks.

A frowning man hurrying to wind things up so he could have his first drink of the evening said, "The office is closing and we don't keep baggage here."

"People used to be nice," Jack said.

"Bus people?"

"Just people."

She was hit by the sharp change in his accent. As for the way of speaking, which is something else again, he was like the heir to great estates back home after a Grand Tour. Perhaps the estates had run down in his absence. She slipped the frowning man a thousand francs, a new pastel-tinted bill, on which the face of a calm girl glowed like an opal. She said, "We shan't be long."

She set off over the Place, walking diagonally—Jack beside her, of course. He did not ask where they were headed, though he did make her smile by saying, "Did you bring a car?," expecting one of the hotel cars to be parked nearby, perhaps with a driver to open the door; perhaps with cold chicken and wine in a hamper, too. He said, "I'd forgotten about having to tip for every little thing." He did not question his destination, which was no farther than a café at the far end of the square. What she felt at that instant was intense revulsion. She thought, I don't want him, and pushed away some invisible flying thing—a bat or a blown paper. He looked at her with surprise. He must have been wondering if hardship had taught Netta to talk in her mind.

This is it, the freedom he was always offering me, she said to herself, smiling up at the beautiful sky.

They moved slowly along the nearly empty square, pausing only when some worn-out Peugeot or an old bicycle, finding no other target, made a swing in their direction. Safely on the pavement, they walked under the arches where partisans had been hanged. It seemed to Netta the bodies had been taken down only a day or so before. Jack, who knew about this way of dying from hearsay, chose a café table nearly under a poor lad's bound, dangling feet.

"I had a woman next to me on the bus who kept a hedgehog all winter in a basketful of shavings," he said. "He can drink milk out of a wineglass." He hesitated. "I'm sorry about the books you asked for. I was sick of books by then. I was sick of rhetoric and culture and patriotic crap."

"I suppose it is all very different over there," said Netta.

"God, yes."

He seemed to expect her to ask questions, so she said, "What kind of clothes do they wear?"

"They wear quite a lot of plaids and tartans. They eat at peculiar hours. You'll see them eating strawberries and cream just when you're thinking of having a drink."

She said, "Did you visit the tin mines, where Truman sends his political prisoners?"

"*Tin* mines?" said Jack. "No."

"Remember the three little girls from the maharaja trade?"

Neither could quite hear what the other had to say. They were partially deaf to each other.

Netta continued softly, "Now, as I understand it, she first brought an American to London, and then she took an Englishman to America."

He had too much the habit of women, he was playing too close a game, to waste points saying, "Who? What?"

"It was over as fast as it started," he said. "But then the war came and we were stuck. She became a friend," he said. "I'm quite fond of her"—which Netta translated as, "It is a subterranean river that may yet come to light." "You wouldn't know her," he said. "She's very different now. I talked so much about the south, down here, she finally found some land going dirt cheap at Bandol. The mayor arranged for her to have an orchard next to her property, so she won't have neighbors. It hardly cost her anything. He said to her, 'You're very pretty.' "

"No one ever had a bargain in property because of a pretty face," said Netta.

"Wasn't it lucky," said Jack. He could no longer hear himself, let alone Netta. "The war was unsettling, being in America. She minded not being active. Actually she was using the Swiss passport, which made it worse. Her brother was killed over Bremen. She needs security now. In a way it was sorcerer and apprentice between us, and she suddenly grew up. She'll be better off with a roof over her head. She writes a little now. Her poetry isn't bad," he said, as if Netta had challenged its quality.

"Is she at Bandol now, writing poetry?"

"Well, no." He laughed suddenly. "There isn't a roof yet. And, you know, people don't sit writing that way. They just think they're going to."

"Who has replaced you?" said Netta. "Another sorcerer?"

"Oh, he . . . he looks like George II in a strong light. Or like Queen Anne. Queen Anne and Lady Mary, somebody called them." Iris, that must have been. Queen Anne and Lady Mary wasn't bad—better than King Charles and his spaniel. She was beginning to enjoy his story. He saw it, and said lightly, "I was too preoccupied with you to manage another life. I couldn't see myself going on and on away from you. I didn't want to grow middle-aged at odds with myself."

But he had lost her; she was enjoying a reverie about Jack now, wearing one of those purple sunburns people acquire at golf. She saw him driving an open car, with large soft freckles on his purple skull. She saw his mistress's dog on the front seat and the dog's ears flying like pennants. The revulsion she felt did not lend distance but brought a dreamy reality closer still. He must be thirty-four now, she said to herself. A terrible age for a man who has never imagined thirty-four.

"Well, perhaps you have made a mess of it," she said, quoting Iris.

"What mess? I'm here. *He*—"

"Queen Anne?"

"Yes, well, actually Gerald is his name; he wears nothing but brown. Brown suit, brown tie, brown shoes. I said, *'He* can't go to Mitten Todd. He won't match.'"

"Harmonize," she said.

"That's it. Harmonize with the—"

"What about Gerald's wife? I'm sure he has one."

"Lucretia."

"No, really?"

"On my honor. When I last saw them they were all together, talking."

Netta was remembering what the middle sister had said about laughter on the balcony. She couldn't look at him. The merest crossing of glances made her start laughing rather wildly into her hands. The hysterical quality of her own laughter caught her in midair. What were they talking about? He hitched his chair nearer and dared to take her wrist.

"Tell me, now," he said, as if they were to be two old confidence men getting their stories straight. "What about you? Was there ever . . ." The glaze of laughter had not left his face and voice. She saw that he would make her his business, if she let him. Pulling back, she felt another clasp, through a wall of fog. She groped for this other, invisible hand, but it dissolved. It was a lost, indifferent hand; it no longer recognized her warmth. She understood: He is dead . . . Jack, closed to ghosts, deaf to their voices, was spared this. He would be spared everything, she saw. She envied him his imperviousness, his true unhysterical laughter.

Perhaps that's why I kicked him, she said. I was always jealous. Not of women. Of his short memory, his comfortable imagination. And I am going to be thirty-seven and I have a dark, an accurate, a deadly memory.

He still held her wrist and turned it another way, saying, "Look, there's paint on it."

"Oh, God, where is the waiter?" she cried, as if that were the one important thing. Jack looked his age, exactly. She looked like a burned-out child who had been told a ghost story. Desperately seeking the waiter, she turned to the café behind them and saw the last light of the long afternoon strike the mirror above the bar—a flash in a tunnel; hands juggling with fire. That unexpected play, at a remove, borne indoors, displayed to anyone who could stare without blinking, was a complete story. It was the brightness on the looking glass, the only part of a life, or a love, or a promise, that could never be concealed, changed, or corrupted.

Not a hope, she was trying to tell him. He could read her face now. She reminded herself, If I say it, I am free. I can finish painting the radiators in peace. I can read every book in the world. If I had relied on my memory for guidance, I would never have crept out of the wine cellar. Memory is what ought to prevent you from buying a dog after the first dog dies, but it never does. It should at least keep you from saying yes twice to the same person.

"I've always loved you," he chose to announce—it really was an announcement, in a new voice that stated nothing except facts.

The dark, the ghosts, the candlelight, her tears on the scarred bar —*they* were real. And still, whether she wanted to see it or not, the light of imagination danced all over the square. She did not dare to turn again to the mirror, lest she confuse the two and forget which light was real. A pure white awning on a cross street seemed to her to be of indestructible beauty. The window it sheltered was hollowed with sadness and shadow. She said with the same deep sadness, "I believe you." The wave of revulsion receded, sucked back under another wave—a powerful adolescent craving for something simple, such as true love.

Her face did not show this. It was set in adolescent stubbornness, and this was one of their old, secret meetings when, sullen and hurt, she had to be coaxed into life as Jack wanted it lived. It was the same voyage, at the same rate of speed. The Place seemed to her to be full of invisible traffic—first a whisper of tires, then a faint, high screeching, then a steady roar. If Jack heard anything, it could be only the blood in the veins and his loud, happy thought. To a practical romantic like Jack, dying to get Netta to bed right away, what she was hearing was only the uh-hebb and flo-ho of hormones, as Dr. Blackley said. She caught a look of amazement on his face: *Now* he knew what he had been deprived of. *Now* he remembered. It had been Netta, all along.

Their evening shadows accompanied them over the long square. "I still have a car," she remarked. "But no petrol. There's a train." She did keep on hearing a noise, as of heavy traffic rushing near and tearing away. Her own quiet voice carried across it, saying, "Not a hope." He must have heard that. Why, it was as loud as a shout. He held her arm lightly. He was as buoyant as morning. This *was* his morning—the first light on the mirror, the first cigarette. He pulled her into an archway where no one could see. What could I do, she asked her ghosts, but let my arm be held, my steps be guided?

Later, Jack said that the walk with Netta back across the Place Masséna was the happiest event of his life. Having no reliable counter-event to put in its place, she let the memory stand.

THE
REMISSION

Wʜᴇɴ ɪᴛ ʙᴇᴄᴀᴍᴇ clear that Alec Webb was far more ill than
anyone had cared to tell him, he tore up his English life and came
down to die on the Riviera. The time was early in the reign of the
new Elizabeth, and people were still doing this—migrating with no
other purpose than the hope of a merciful sky. The alternative (Alec
said to his only sister) meant queueing for death on the National
Health Service, lying on a regulation mattress and rubber sheet,
hearing the breath of other men dying.

Alec—as obituaries would have it later—was husband to Barbara,
father to Will, Molly, and James. It did not occur to him or to anyone
else that the removal from England was an act of unusual force that
could rend and lacerate his children's lives as well as his own. The
difference was that their lives were barely above ground and not yet
in flower.

The five Webbs arrived at a property called Lou Mas in the course
of a particularly hot September. Mysterious Lou Mas, until now a
name on a deed of sale, materialized as a pink house wedged in the
side of a hill between a motor road and the sea. Alec identified its

style as Edwardian-Riviera. Barbara supposed he must mean the profusion of balconies and parapets, and the slender pillars in the garden holding up nothing. In the new southern light everything looked to her brilliant and moist, like color straight from a paintbox. One of Alec's first gestures was to raise his arm and shield his eyes against this brightness. The journey had exhausted him, she thought. She had received notice in dreams that their change of climates was irreversible; not just Alec but none of them could go back. She did not tell him so, though in better times it might have interested that part of his mind he kept fallow: being entirely rational, he had a prudent respect for second sight.

The children had never been in a house this size. They chased each other and slid along the floors until Alec asked, politely, if they wouldn't mind playing outside, though one of the reasons he had wanted to come here was to be with them for the time remaining. Dispatched to a flagged patio in front of the house, the children looked down on terraces bearing olive trees, then a railway line, then the sea. Among the trees was a cottage standing empty which Barbara had forbidden them to explore. The children were ten, eleven, and twelve, with the girl in the middle. Since they had no school to attend, and did not know any of the people living around them, and as their mother was too busy to invent something interesting for them to do, they hung over a stone balustrade waving and calling to trains, hoping to see an answering wave and perhaps a decapitation. They had often been warned about foolish passengers and the worst that could happen. Their mother came out and put her arms around Will, the eldest. She kissed the top of his head. "Do look at that sea," she said. "Aren't we lucky?" They looked, but the vast, flat sea was a line any of them could have drawn on a sheet of paper. It was there, but no more than there; trains were better—so was the ruined cottage. Within a week James had cut his hand on glass breaking into it, but by then Barbara had forgotten her injunction.

The sun Alec had wanted turned out to be without compassion, and he spent most of the day indoors, moving from room to room, searching for some gray, dim English cave in which to take cover. Often he sat without reading, doing nothing, in a room whose one window, none too clean, looked straight into the blank hill behind the house. Seepage and a residue of winter rainstorms had traced calm yellowed patterns on its walls. He guessed it had once been assigned to someone's hapless, helpless paid companion, who would have marvelled at the thought of its lending shelter to a dying man. In the late afternoon he would return to his bedroom, where, out on the balcony, an angular roof shadow slowly replaced the sun. Barbara unfolded his deck chair on the still burning tiles. He stretched out, opened a book, found the page he wanted, at once closed his eyes. Barbara knelt in a corner, in a triangle of light. She had taken her clothes off, all but a sunhat; bougainvillea grew so thick no one could see. She said, "Would you like me to read to you?" No; he did everything alone, or nearly. He was—always—bathed, shaved, combed, and dressed. His children would not remember him unkempt or dishevelled, though it might not have mattered to them. He did not smell of sweat or sickness or medicine or fear.

When it began to rain, later in the autumn, the children played indoors. Barbara tried to keep them quiet. There was a French school up in the town, but neither Alec nor Barbara knew much about it; and, besides, there was no use settling them in. He heard the children asking for bicycles so they could ride along the motor road, and he heard Barbara saying no, the road was dangerous. She must have changed her mind, for he next heard them discussing the drawbacks and advantages of French bikes. One of the children—James, it was —asked some question about the cost.

"You're not to mention things like that," said Barbara. "You're not to speak of money."

Alec was leaving no money and three children—four, if you counted his wife. Barbara often said she had no use for money, no head for it. "Thank God I'm Irish," she said. "I haven't got rates of interest on the brain." She read Irishness into her nature as an explanation for it, the way some people attributed their gifts and failings to a sign of the zodiac. Anything natively Irish had dissolved long before, leaving only a family custom of Catholicism and another habit, fervent in Barbara's case, of anticlerical passion. Alec supposed she was getting her own back, for a mysterious reason, on ancestors she would not have recognized in Heaven. Her family, the Laceys, had been in Wales for generations. Her brothers considered themselves Welsh.

It was Barbara's three Welsh brothers who had put up the funds for Lou Mas. Houses like this were to be had nearly for the asking, then. They stood moldering at the unfashionable end of the coast, damaged sometimes by casual shellfire, difficult to heat, costly to renovate. What the brothers had seen as valuable in Lou Mas was not the villa, which they had no use for, but the undeveloped seafront around it, for which each of them had a different plan. The eldest brother was a partner in a firm of civil engineers; another managed a resort hotel and had vague thoughts about building one of his own. The youngest, Mike, who was Barbara's favorite, had converted from the R.A.F. to commercial flying. Like Alec, he had been a prisoner of war. The two men had that, but nothing else, in common. Mike was the best travelled of the three. He could see, in place of the pink house with its thick walls and high ceilings, one of the frail, domino-shaped blocks that were starting to rise around the Mediterranean basin, creating a vise of white plaster at the rim of the sea.

Because of United Kingdom income-tax laws, which made it awkward for the Laceys to have holdings abroad, Alec and Barbara had been registered as owners of Lou Mas, with Desmond, the engineer, given power of attorney. This was a manageable operation because Alec was entirely honorable, while Barbara did not know a legal document from the ace of diamonds. So that when the first scouts came round from the local British colony to find out what the Webbs were like and Barbara told them Lou Mas belonged to her family she was speaking the truth. Her visitors murmured that they had been very fond of the Vaughan-Thorpes and had been sorry to see them go—a reference to the previous owners, whose grandparents had built Lou Mas. Barbara did not suppose this to be a snub: she simply wondered why it was that a war out of which her brothers had emerged so splendidly should have left Alec, his sister, and the unknown Vaughan-Thorpes worse off than before.

The scouts reported that Mr. Webb was an invalid, that the children were not going to school, that Mrs. Webb must at one time have been pretty, and that she seemed to be spending a good deal of money, either her husband's or her own. When no improvements

were seen in the house, the grounds, or the cottage, it began to be
taken for granted that she had been squandering, on trifles, rather
more than she had.

Her visitors were mistaken: Barbara never spent more than she
had, but only the total of all she could see. What she saw now was
a lump of money like a great block of marble, from which she could
chip as much as she liked. It had come by way of Alec's sister. Alec's
obstinate refusal to die on National Health had meant that his death
had somehow to be paid for. Principle was a fine thing, one of
Barbara's brothers remarked, but it came high. Alec's earning days
were done for. He had come from a long line of medium-rank civil
servants who had never owned anything except the cottages to which
they had eventually retired, and which their heirs inevitably sold.
Money earned, such as there was, disappeared in the sands of their
male progeny's education. Girls were expected to get married. Alec's
sister, now forty-four, had not done so, though she was no poorer or
plainer than most. "I am better off like this," she had told Alec,
perhaps once too often. She was untrained, unready, unfitted for any
life save that of a woman civilian's in wartime; peace had no use for
her, just as the postwar seemed too fast, too hard, and too crowded
to allow for Alec. Her only asset was material: a modest, cautiously
invested sum of money settled on her by a godparent, the income
from which she tried to add to by sewing. Christening robes had been
her special joy, but fewer babies were being baptized with pomp,
while nylon was gradually replacing the silks and lawns she worked
with such care. Nobody wanted the bother of ironing flounces and
tucks in a world without servants.

Barbara called her sister-in-law "the mouse." She had small brown
eyes; was vegetarian; prayed every night of her life for Alec and for
the parents who had not much loved her. "If they would just listen
to me," she was in the habit of saying—about Alec and Barbara, for
instance. She never complained about her compressed existence,
which seemed to her the only competent one at times; at least it was
quiet. When Alec told her that he was about to die, and wanted to
emigrate, and had been provided with a house but with nothing to
run it on, she immediately offered him half her capital. He accepted
in the same flat way he had talked about death—out of his driving

need, she supposed, or because he still held the old belief that women never need much. She knew she had made an impulsive gesture, perhaps a disastrous one, but she loved Alec and did not want to add to her own grief. She was assured that anything left at the end would be returned enriched and amplified by some sort of nimble investment, but as Alec and his family intended to live on the capital she did not see how this could be done.

Alec knew that his sister had been sacrificed. It was merely another of the lights going out. Detachment had overtaken him even before the journey south. Mind and body floated on any current that chose to bear them.

For the first time in her life Barbara had enough money, and no one to plague her with useless instructions. While Alec slept, or seemed to, she knelt in the last triangle of sun on the balcony reading the spread-out pages of the *Continental Daily Mail*. It had been one thing to have no head for money when there was none to speak of; the present situation called for percipience and wit. Her reading informed her that dollars were still stronger than pounds. (Pounds were the decaying cottage, dollars the Edwardian house.) Alec's background and training made him find the word "dollars" not overnice, perhaps alarming, but Barbara had no class prejudice to hinder her. She had already bought dollars for pounds, at giddy loss, feeling each time she had put it over on banks and nations, on snobs, on the financial correspondent of the *Mail*, on her own clever brothers. (One of the Webbs' neighbors, a retired Army officer, had confided to Alec that he was expecting the Russians to land in the bay below their villas at any time. He intended to die fighting on his doorstep; however, should anything happen to prevent his doing so, he had kept a clutch of dollars tucked in the pocket of an old dressing gown so that he and his mother could buy their way out.)

In Alec's darkened bedroom she combed her hair with his comb. Even if he survived he would have no foothold on the nineteen-fifties. She, Barbara, had been made for her time. This did not mean she wanted to live without him. Writing to one of her brothers, she advised him to open a hotel down here. Servants were cheap—twenty or thirty cents an hour, depending on whether you worked the official or the free-market rate. In this letter her brother heard Barbara's

voice, which had stayed high and breathless though she must have
been thirty-four. He wondered if this was the sort of prattle poor
dying old Alec had to listen to there in the south.

"SOUTH" WAS TO Alec a place of the mind. He had not deserted
England, as his sad sister thought, but moved into one of its oldest
literary legends, the Mediterranean. His part of this legend was called
Rivabella. Actually, "Rivebelle" was written on maps and road signs,
for the area belonged to France—at least, for the present. It had been
tugged between France and Italy so often that it now had a diverse,
undefinable character and seemed to be remote from any central
authority unless there were elections or wars. At its heart was a town
sprawled on the hill behind Lou Mas and above the motor road. Its
inhabitants said "Rivabella;" they spoke, among themselves, a
Ligurian dialect with some Spanish and Arabic expressions mixed in,
though their children went to school and learned French and that
they descended from a race with blue eyes. What had remained
constant to Rivabella was its poverty, and the groves of ancient olive
trees that only the strictest of laws kept the natives from cutting
down, and the look and character of the people. Confined by his
illness, Alec would never meet more of these than about a dozen; they
bore out the expectation set alight by his reading, seeming to him
classless and pagan, poetic and wise, imbued with an instinctive
understanding of light, darkness, and immortality. Barbara expected
them to be cunning and droll, which they were, and to steal from her,
which they did, and to love her, which they seemed to. Only the
children were made uneasy by these strange new adults, so squat and
ill-favored, so quarrelsome and sly, so destructive of nature and point-
lessly cruel to animals. But, then, the children had not read much,
were unfamiliar with films, and had no legends to guide them.

Barbara climbed up to the town quite often during the first weeks,
looking for a doctor for Alec, for a cook and maid, for someone to
give lessons to the children. There was nothing much to see except
a Baroque church from which everything removable had long been
sold to antiquarians, and a crumbling palace along the very dull main
street. In one of the palace rooms she was given leave to examine

some patches of peach-colored smudge she was told were early Renaissance frescoes. Some guidebooks referred to these, with the result that a number of the new, hardworking breed of postwar traveller panted up a steep road not open to motor traffic only to find that the palace belonged to a cranky French countess who lived alone with her niece and would not let anyone in. (Barbara, interviewing the niece for the post of governess, had been admitted but was kept standing until the countess left the room.) Behind the palace she discovered a town hall with a post office and a school attached, a charming small hospital—where a doctor was obtained for Alec—and a walled graveyard. Only the graveyard was worth exploring; it contained Victorian English poets who had probably died of tuberculosis in the days when an enervating climate was thought to be good for phthisis, and Russian aristocrats who had owned some of the English houses, and Garibaldian adventurers who, like Alec, had never owned a thing. Most of these graves were overgrown and neglected, with the headstones all to one side, and wild grasses grown taller than roses. The more recent dead seemed to be commemorated by marble plaques on a high concrete wall; these she did not examine. What struck her about this place was its splendid view: she could see Lou Mas, and quite far into Italy, and of course over a vast stretch of the sea. How silly of all those rich foreigners to crowd down by the shore, with the crashing noise of the railway. I would have built up here in a minute, she thought.

Alec's new doctor was young and ugly and bit his nails. He spoke good English, and knew most of the British colony, to whose colds, allergies, and perpetually upset stomachs he ministered. British ailments were nursery ailments; what his patients really wanted was to be tucked up next to a nursery fire and fed warm bread-and-milk. He had taken her to be something like himself—an accomplice. "My husband is anything but childish," she said gently. She hesitated before trotting out her usual Irish claim, for she was not quite certain what he meant.

"Rivabella has only two points of cultural interest," he said. "One is the market on the church square. The other is the patron saint, St. Damian. He appears on the church roof, dressed in armor, holding a flaming sword in the air. He does this when someone in Rivabella seems to be in danger." She saw, in the way he looked at her, that she had begun her journey south a wife and mother whose looks were fading, and arrived at a place where her face seemed exotic. Until now she had thought only that a normal English family had taken the train, and the caricature of one had descended. It amounted to the same thing—the eye of the beholder.

From his balcony Alec saw the hill as a rough triangle, with a few straggling farms beneath the gray and umber town (all he could discern was its color) and the apex of graveyard. This, in its chalky whiteness, looked like an Andalusian or a North African village washed up on the wrong part of the coast. It was alien to the lush English gardens and the foreign villas, which tended to pinks, and beiges, and to a deep shade known as Egyptian red. Within those houses was a way of being he sensed and understood, for it was a smaller, paler version of colonial life, with chattering foreign servants who might have been budgerigars, and hot puddings consumed under brilliant sunlight. Rules of speech and regulations for conduct were probably observed, as in the last days of the dissolving Empire. Barbara had told him of one: it was bad form to say "Rivebelle" for "Rivabella," for it showed one hadn't known about the place in its rich old days, or even that Queen Victoria had mentioned *"pretty little Rivabella"* to the Crown Princess of Prussia in one of her affectionate letters.

"All snobs," said Barbara. "Thank God I'm Irish," though there was something she did in a way mind: saying "Rivebelle" had been one of her first mistakes. Another had been hiring a staff without taking advice. She was also suspected of paying twice the going rate, which was not so much an economic blunder as a social affront. "All snobs" was not much in the way of ammunition, but, then, none of the other villas could claim a cook, a maid, a laundress, a gardener, and a governess marching down from Rivabella, all of them loyal, devoted, cheerful, hardworking, and kind.

She wrote to her pilot brother, the one she loved, telling him how self-reliant people seemed to be here, what pride they took in their jobs, how their philosophy was completely alien to the modern British idea of strife and grab. "I would love it if you would come and stay for a while. We have more rooms than we know what to do with. You and I could talk." But no one came. None of them wanted to have to watch poor old Alec dying.

The children would recall later on that their cook had worn a straw hat in the kitchen, so that steam condensing on the ceiling would not drop on her head, and that she wore the same hat to their father's funeral. Barbara would remind them about the food. She had been barely twenty at the beginning of the war, and there were meals for which she had never stopped feeling hungry. Three times a day, now, she sat down to cream and butter and fresh bread, new-laid eggs, jam you could stand a spoon in: breakfasts out of a storybook from before the war. As she preferred looking at food to eating it, it must have been the *idea* of her table spread that restored richness to her skin, lustre to her hair. She had been all cream and gold, once, but war and marriage and Alec's illness and being hard up and some other indefinable disappointment had skimmed and darkened her. And yet she felt shot through with happiness sometimes, or at least by a piercing clue as to what bliss might be. This sensation, which she might have controlled more easily in another climate, became so natural, so insistent, that she feared sometimes that its source might be religious and that she would need to reject—out of principle—the felicity it promised. But no; she was, luckily, too earthbound for such nonsense. She could experience sudden felicity merely seeing her cook arrive with laden baskets, or the gardener crossing the terrace with a crate of flowering plants. (He would bed these out under the olive trees, where they perished rapidly.) Lou Mas at such times seemed to shrink to a toy house she might lift and carry; she would remember what it had been like when the children were babies still, and hers alone.

Carrying Alec's breakfast tray, she came in wearing the white dressing gown that had been his sister's parting gift to her. Her hair, which she now kept thick and loose, was shades lighter than it had been in England. He seemed barely to see her. But, then, everything dazzled him now. She buttered toast for him, and spread it with jam, saying, "Do try it, darling. You will never taste jam like this again." Of course, it thundered with prophecy. Her vision blurred—not because of tears, for she did not cry easily. It was as if a sheet of pure water had come down with an enormous crashing sound, cutting her off from Alec.

Now that winter was here, he moved with the sun instead of away from it. Shuffling to the balcony, he leaned on her shoulder. She covered him with blanket, gave him a book to read, combed his hair. He had all but stopped speaking, though he made an effort for strangers. She thought, What would it be like to be shot dead? Only the lingering question contained in a nightmare could account for this, but her visionary dreams had left her, probably because Alec's fate, and so to some measure her own, had been decided once and for all. Between house and sea the gardener crouched with a trowel in his hand. His work consisted of bedding-out, and his imagination stopped at salvia: the ground beneath the olive trees was dark red with them. She leaned against the warm parapet and thought of what he might see should he look up—herself, in white, with her hair blazing in the sun. But when he lifted his face it was only to wipe sweat from it with the shirt he had taken off. A dream of loss came back: she had been ordered to find new names for refugee children whose names had been forgotten. In real life, she had wanted her children to be called Giles, Nigel, and Samantha, but Alec had interfered. All three had been conceived on his wartime leaves, before he was taken prisoner. The children had her gray eyes, her skin that freckled, her small bones and delicate features (though Molly showed signs of belonging to a darker, sturdier race), but none of them had her richness, her shine. They seemed to her and perhaps to each other thin and dry, like Alec.

Everything Mademoiselle said was useless or repetitive. She explained, " 'Lou Mas' means 'the farm,' " which the children knew. When they looked out the dining-room window she remarked, "You can see Italy." She came early in order to share their breakfast; the aunt she lived with, the aunt with the frescoes, kept all the food in their palace locked up. "What do you take me for?" she sometimes asked them, tragically, of some small thing, such as their not paying intense attention. She was not teaching them much, only some French, and they were picking this up faster now than she could instruct. Her great-grandfather had been a French volunteer against Garibaldi (an Italian bandit, she explained); her grandfather was founder of a nationalist movement; her father had been murdered on the steps of his house at the end of the war. She was afraid of

Freemasons, Socialists, Protestants, and Jews, but not of drowning or falling from a height or being attacked by a mad dog. When she discovered that the children had been christened (Alec having considered baptism a rational start to agnostic life), she undertook their religious education, which was not at all what Barbara was paying for.

After lunch, they went upstairs to visit Alec. He lay on his deck chair, tucked into blankets, as pale as clouds. James suddenly wailed out, believing he was singing, "We'll ring all the bells and kill all the Protestants." Silence, then James said, "Are there any left? Any Protestants?"

"I am left, for one," said his father.

"It's a good thing we came down here, then," said the child calmly. "They couldn't get at you."

Mademoiselle said, looking terrified, "It refers to old events in France."

"It wouldn't have mattered." His belief had gone to earth as soon as he had realized that the men he admired were in doubt. His conversation, like his reading, was increasingly simple. He was reading a book about gardening. He held it close to his face. Daylight tired him; it was like an intruder between memory and the eye. He read, "Nerine. Guernsey Lily. Ord. Amaryllidacae. First introduced, 1680." Introduced into England, that meant. "Oleander, 1596. East Indian Rose Bay, 1770. Tamarind Tree, 1633. Chrysanthemum, 1764." So England had flowered, become bedecked, been bedded-out.

The book had been given him by a neighbor. The Webbs not only had people working for them, and delicious nursery food to eat, and a garden running down to the sea, but distinguished people living on either side—Mr. Edmund Cranefield of Villa Osiris to the right, and Mrs. Massie at Casa Scotia on the left. To reach their houses you had to climb thirty steps to the road then descend more stairs on their land. Mr. Cranefield had a lift, which looked like a large crate stood on its side. Within it was a kitchen chair. He sat on the chair and was borne up to the road on an electric rail. No one had ever seen him doing this. When he went to Morocco during the worst of the winter, he had the lift disconnected and covered with rugs, the pond drained and the fish put in tanks, and his two peacocks, who screamed every dawn as if a fox were at them, boarded for a high fee with a private zoo. Casa Scotia belonged to Mrs. Massie, who was lame, wore a tweed cape, never went out without a hat, walked with a stick, and took a good twenty minutes to climb her steps.

Mr. Cranefield was a novelist, Mrs. Massie the author of a whole shelf of gardening books. Mr. Cranefield never spoke of his novels or offered to lend them; he did not even say what their titles were. "You must tell me every one!" Barbara cried, as if she were about to rush out and return with a wheelbarrow full of books by Mr. Cranefield.

He sat upstairs with Alec, and they talked about different things, quite often about the war. Just as Barbara was beginning to imagine Mr. Cranefield did not like her, he invited her to tea. She brought Molly along for protection, but soon saw he was not drawn to women —at least, not in the way she supposed men to be. She wondered then if she should keep Will and James away from him. He showed Barbara and Molly the loggia where he worked on windless mornings; a strong mistral had once blown one hundred and forty pages across three gardens—some were even found in a hedge at Casa Scotia. On a table were oval picture frames holding the likeness of a fair girl and a fair young man. Looking more closely, Barbara saw they were illustrations cut out of magazines. Mr. Cranefield said, "They are the pair I write about. I keep them there so that I never make a mistake."

"Don't they bore you?" said Barbara.

"Look at all they have given me." But the most dispossessed peasant, the filthiest housemaid, the seediest nail-biting doctor in Rivabella had what he was pointing out—the view, the sea. Of course, a wave of the hand cannot take in everything; he probably had more than this in reserve. He turned to Molly and said kindly, "When you are a little older you can do some typing for me," because it was his experience that girls liked doing that—typing for Mr. Cranefield while waiting for someone to marry. Girls were fond of him: he gave sound advice about love affairs, could read the future in handwriting. Molly knew nothing about him, then, but she would recall later on how Mr. Cranefield, who had invented women deep-sea divers, women test pilots, could not imagine—in his innocence, in his manhood—anything more thrilling to offer a girl when he met one than "You can type."

Barbara broke in, laughing: "She is only eleven."

This was true, but it seemed to Molly a terrible thing to say.

Mrs. Massie was not shy about bringing *her* books around. She gave several to Alec, among them *Flora's Gardening Encyclopaedia*, seventeenth edition, considered her masterpiece. All her books were signed "Flora," though it was not her name. She said about Mr. Cranefield, "Edmund is a great, pampered child. Spoiled by adoring women all his life. Not by me." She sat straight on the straightest chair, her hands clasped on her stick. "I do my own typing. My own gardening, too," though she did say to James and Will, "You can help in the garden for pocket money, if you like."

In the spring, the second Elizabeth was crowned. Barbara ordered a television set from a shop in Nice. It was the first the children had seen. Two men carried it with difficulty down the steps from the road, and soon became tired of lifting it from room to room while Barbara decided where she wanted it. She finally chose a room they kept shut usually; it had a raised platform at one end and until the war had been the site of amateur theatricals. The men set the box down on the stage and began fiddling with antennae and power points, while the children ran about arranging rows of chairs. One of the men said they might not have a perfect view of the Queen the next day, the day of the Coronation, because of Alps standing in the way. The children sat down and stared at the screen. Horizontal lightning streaked across its face. The men described implosion, which had killed any number of persons all over the world. They said that should the socket and plug begin to smoke, Barbara was to make a dash for the meter box and pull out the appropriate fuse.

"The appropriate fuse?" said Barbara. The children minded sometimes about the way she laughed at everything.

When the men had gone, they trooped upstairs to tell Alec about the Alps and implosion. He was resting in preparation for tomorrow's ceremony, which he would attend. It was clear to Molly that her father would not be able to get up and run if there was an accident. Kneeling on the warm tiles (this was in June) she pressed her face to his hand. Presently he slipped the hand away to turn a page. He was reading more of the book Mrs. Massie had pounded out on her 1929 Underwood—four carbons, single-spaced, no corrections, every page typed clean: "Brussels Sprouts—see Brassica." Brassica must be English, Alec thought. That was why he withdrew his hand—to see about Brassica. What use was his hand to Molly or her anxiety to him now? Why hold her? Why draw her into his pale world? She was a difficult, dull, clumsy child, something of a moper when her brothers teased her but sulky and tough when it came to Barbara. He had watched Barbara, goaded by Molly, lose control of herself and slap the girl's face, and he had heard Molly's pitiful credo: "You can't hurt me. My vaccination hurt worse than that." "Hurt more," Alec in silence had amended. "Hurt me *more* than that."

He found Brassica. It was Borecole, Broccoli, Cabbage, Cauliflower. His eyes slid over the rest of what it was until, "Native to Europe—BRITAIN," which Mrs. Massie had typed in capital letters during the war, with a rug around her legs in unheated Casa Scotia, waiting for the Italians or the Germans or the French to take her away to internment in a lorry. He was closer in temper to Mrs. Massie than to anyone else except his sister, though he had given up priorities. His blood was white (that was how he saw it), and his lungs and heart were bleached, too, and starting to disintegrate like snowflakes. He was a pale giant, a drained Gulliver, cast up on the beach, open territory for invaders. (Barbara and Will were sharing a paperback about flying saucers, whose occupants had built Stonehenge.) Alec's intrepid immigrants, his microscopic colonial settlers had taken over. He had been easy to subdue, being courteous by nature, diffident by choice. He had been a civil servant then a soldier; had expected the best, relied on good behavior; had taken to prison camp thin books about Calabria and Greece; had been evasive, secretive, brave, unscrupulous only sometimes—had been English and middle class, in short.

That night Alec had what the doctor called "a crisis" and Alec termed "a bad patch." There was no question of his coming down for Coronation the next day. The children thought of taking the television set up to him, but it was too heavy, and Molly burst into tears thinking of implosion and accidents and Alec trapped. In the end the Queen was crowned in the little theatre, as Barbara had planned, in the presence of Barbara and the children, Mr. Cranefield and Mrs. Massie, the doctor from Rivabella, a neighbor called Major Lamprey and his old mother, Mrs. Massie's housekeeper, Barbara's cook and two of her grandchildren, and Mademoiselle. One after the other these people turned their heads to look at Alec, gasping in the doorway, holding on to the frame. His hair was carefully combed and parted low on one side, like Mr. Cranefield's, and he had dressed completely, though he had a scarf around his neck instead of a tie. He was the last, the very last, of a kind. Not British but English. Not Christian so much as Anglican. Not Anglican but giving the benefit of the doubt. His children would never feel what he had felt, suffer what he had suffered, relinquish what he had done without so that this sacrament could take place. The new Queen's voice flowed easily over the Alps—thin, bored, ironed flat by the weight of what she had to remember—and came as far as Alec, to whom she owed her crown. He did not think that, precisely, but what had pulled him to his feet, made him stand panting for life in the doorway, would not occur to James or Will or Molly—not then, or ever.

He watched the rest of it from a chair. His breathing bothered the others: it made their own seem too quiet. He ought to have died that night. It would have made a reasonable ending. This was not a question of getting rid of Alec (no one wanted that) but of being able to say later, "He got up and dressed to see the Coronation." However, he went on living.

A nurse came every day, the doctor almost as often. He talked quietly to Barbara in the garden. A remission as long as this was unknown to him; it smacked of miracles. When Barbara would not hear of that, he said that Alec was holding on through willpower. But Alec was not holding on. His invaders had pushed him off the beach and into a boat. The stream was white and the shoreline, too. Everything was white, and he moved peacefully. He had glimpses of his destination—a room where the hems of thin curtains swept back and forth on a bare floor. His vision gave him green bronze doors sometimes; he supposed they were part of the same room.

He could see his children, but only barely. He had guessed what the boys might become—one a rebel, one turned inward. The girl was a question mark. She was stoic and sentimental, indifferent sometimes to pleasure and pain. Whatever she was or could be or might be, he had left her behind. The boys placed a row of bricks down the middle of the room they shared. In the large house they fought for space. They were restless and noisy, untutored and bored. "I'll always have a packet of love from my children," Barbara had said to a man once (not Alec).

At the start of their second winter one of the Laceys came down to investigate. This was Ron, the hotelkeeper. He had dark hair and was thin and pale and walked softly. When he understood that what Barbara had written about servants and dollars was true, he asked to see the accounts. There were none. He talked to Barbara without raising his voice; that day she let everyone working for her go with the exception of the cook, whom Ron had said she was to keep because of Alec. He seemed to feel he was in a position of trust, for he ordered her—there was no other word for it—to place the children at once in the Rivabella town school: Lou Mas was costing the Lacey brothers enough in local taxes—they might as well feel they were getting something back. He called his sister "Bab" and Alec "Al." The children's parents suddenly seemed to them strangers.

When Ron left, Barbara marched the children up to Rivabella and made them look at the church. They had seen it, but she made them look again. She held the mistaken belief that religion was taught in French state schools, and she wanted to arm them. The children knew by now that what their mother called "France" was not really France down here but a set of rules, a code for doing things, such as how to recite the multiplication table or label a wine. Instead of the northern saints she remembered, with their sorrowful preaching, there was a southern St. Damian holding up a blazing sword. Any number of persons had seen him; Mademoiselle had, more than once.

"I want you to understand what superstition is," said Barbara, in clear, carrying English. "Superstition is what is wrong with Uncle Ron. He believes what he can't see, and what he sees he can't believe in. Now, imagine intelligent people saying they've seen this—this apparition. This St. George, or whatever." The church had two pink towers, one bearing a cross and the other a weather vane. St. Damian usually hovered between them. "In armor," said Barbara.

To all three children occurred "Why not?" Protect me, prayed the girl. Vanquish, said Will. Lead, ordered the youngest, seeing only himself in command. He looked around the square and said to his mother, "Could we go, soon, please? Because people are looking."

That winter Molly grew breasts; she thought them enormous, though each could have been contained easily in a small teacup. Her brothers teased her. She went about with her arms crossed. She was tall for her age, and up in the town there was always some man staring. Elderly neighbors pressed her close. Major Lamprey, calling on Alec, kissed her on the mouth. He smelled of gin and pipe smoke. She scrubbed her teeth for minutes afterward. When she began to menstruate, Barbara said, "Now, Molly, you are to keep away from men," as if she weren't trying to.

The boys took their bicycles and went anywhere they wanted. In the evening they wheeled round and round the church square. Above them were swallows, on the edge of the square men and boys. Both were starting to speak better French than English, and James spoke dialect better than French. Molly disliked going up to Rivabella, unless she had to. She helped Barbara make the beds and wash the dishes and she did her homework and then very often went over to talk to Mr. Cranefield. She discovered, by chance, that he had another name—E. C. Arden. As E. C. Arden he was the author of a series of thumbed, comfortable novels (it was Mrs. Massie who lent Molly these), one of which, called *Belinda at Sea,* was Molly's favorite book of any kind. It was about a girl who joined the crew of a submarine, disguised as a naval rating, and kept her identity a secret all the way to Hong Kong. In the end, she married the submarine commander, who apparently had loved her all along. Molly read *Belinda at Sea* three or four times without ever mentioning to Mr. Cranefield she knew he was E. C. Arden. She thought it was a matter of deep privacy and that it was up to him to speak of it first. She did, however, ask what he thought of the saint on the church roof, using the name Barbara had, which was St. George.

"What," said Mr. Cranefield. "That Ethiopian?"

The girl looked frightened—not of Ethiopians, certainly, but of confusion as to person, the adult world of muddle. Even Mr. Crane-field was *also* E. C. Arden, creator of Belinda.

Mr. Cranefield explained, kindly, that up at Rivabella they had made a patron saint out of a mixture of St. Damian, who was an intellectual, and St. Michael, who was not, and probably a local pagan deity as well. St. Michael accounted for the sword, the pagan for the fire. Reliable witnesses had seen the result, though none of these witnesses were British. "We aren't awfully good at seeing saints," he said. "Though we do have an eye for ghosts."

Another thing still troubled Molly, but it was not a matter she could mention: she did not know what to do about her bosom—whether to try to hold it up in some way or, on the contrary, bind it flat. She had been granted, by the mistake of a door's swinging wide, an upsetting glimpse of Mrs. Massie changing out of a bathing suit, and she had been worried about the future shape of her own body ever since. She pored over reproductions of statues and paint-ings in books belonging to Mr. Cranefield. The Eves and Venuses represented were not reassuring—they often seemed to be made of India rubber. There was no one she could ask. Barbara was too dangerous; the mention of a subject such as this always made her go too far and say things Molly found unpleasant.

She did remark to both Mrs. Massie and Mr. Cranefield that she hated the Rivabella school. She said, "I would give anything to be sent home to England, but I can't leave my father."

After a long conversation with Mrs. Massie, Mr. Cranefield agreed to speak to Alec. Interfering with other people was not his way, but Molly struck him as being pathetic. Something told him that Molly was not useful leverage with either parent and so he mentioned Will first: Will would soon be fourteen, too old for the school at Rivabella. Unless the Webb children were enrolled, and quickly, in good French establishments—say, in lycées at Nice—they would become unfit for anything save menial work in a foreign language they could not speak in an educated way. Of course, the ideal solution would be England, if Alec felt he could manage that.

Alec listened, sitting not quite straight in his chair, wearing a dressing gown, his back to a window. He found all light intolerable now. Several times he lifted his hand as if he were trying to see through it. No one knew why Alec made these odd gestures; some people thought he had gone slightly mad because death was too long in coming. He parted his lips and whispered, "French school . . . If you would look after it," and then, "I would be grateful."

Mr. Cranefield dropped his voice too, as if the gray of the room called for hush. He asked if Alec had thought of appointing a guardian for them. The hand Alec seemed to want transparent waved back and forth, stiffly, like a shut ivory fan.

All that Barbara said to Mr. Cranefield was "Good idea," once he had assured her French high schools were not priest-ridden.

"It might have occurred to *her* to have done something about it," said Mrs. Massie, when this was repeated.

"Things do occur to Barbara," said Mr. Cranefield. "But she doesn't herself get the drift of them."

The only disturbing part of the new arrangement was that the children had been assigned to separate establishments, whose schedules did not coincide; this meant they would not necessarily travel in the same bus. Molly had shot up as tall as Will now. Her hair was dark and curled all over her head. Her bones and her hands and feet were going to be larger, stronger, than her mother's and brothers'. She looked, already, considerably older than her age. She was obstinately innocent, turning her face away when Barbara, for her own good, tried to tell her something about men.

Barbara imagined her willful, ignorant daughter being enticed, trapped, molested, impregnated, and disgraced. *And* ending up wondering how it happened, Barbara thought. She saw Molly's seducer, brutish and dull. I'd get him by the throat, she said to herself. She imagined the man's strong neck and her own small hands, her brittle bird-bones. She said, "You are never, ever to speak to a stranger on the bus. You're not to get in a car with a man—not even if you know him."

"I don't know any man with a car."

"You could be waiting for a bus on a dark afternoon," said Barbara. "A car might pull up. Would you like a lift? No, you must answer. No and no and no. It is different for the boys. There are the two of them. They could put up a fight."

"Nobody bothers boys," said Molly.

Barbara drew breath but for once in her life said nothing.

Alec's remission was no longer just miraculous—it had become unreasonable. Barbara's oldest brother hinted that Alec might be better off in England, cared for on National Health: they were paying unholy taxes for just such a privilege. Barbara replied that Alec had no use for England, where the Labour government had sapped everyone's self-reliance. He believed in having exactly the amount of suffering you could pay for, no less and no more. She knew this theory did not hold water, because the Laceys and Alec's own sister had done the paying. It was too late now; they should have thought a bit sooner; and Alec was too ravaged to make a new move.

THE CAR THAT, inevitably, pulled up to a bus stop in Nice was driven by a Mr. Wilkinson. He had just taken Major Lamprey and the Major's old mother to the airport. He rolled his window down and called to Molly, through pouring rain, "I say, aren't you from Lou Mas?"

If he sounded like a foreigner's Englishman, like a man in a British joke, it was probably because he had said so many British-sounding lines in films set on the Riviera. Eric Wilkinson was the chap with the strong blue eyes and ginger mustache, never younger than thirty-four, never as much as forty, who flashed on for a second, just long enough to show there was an Englishman in the room. He could handle a uniform, a dinner jacket, tails, a monocle, a cigarette holder, a swagger stick, a polo mallet, could open a cigarette case without looking like a gigolo, could say without being an ass about it, "Bless my soul, wasn't that the little Maharani?" or even, "Come along, old boy—fair play with Monica, now!" Foreigners meeting him often said, "That is what the British used to be like, when they were still all right, when the Riviera was still fit to live in." But the British who knew him were apt to glaze over: "You mean Wilkinson?" Mrs. Massie and Mr. Cranefield said, "Well, Wilkinson, what are you up to now?" There was no harm to him: his one-line roles did not support him, but he could do anything, even cook. He used his car as a private taxi, driving people to airports, meeting them when they came off cruise ships. He was not a chauffeur, never said "sir," and at the same time kept a certain distance, was not shy about money changing hands—no fake pride, no petit-bourgeois demand for a slipped envelope. Good-natured. Navy blazer. Summer whites in August. Wore a tie that carried a message. What did it stand for? A third-rate school? A disgraced, disbanded regiment? A club raided by the police? No one knew. Perhaps it was the symbol of something new altogether. "Still playing in those films of yours, Wilkinson?" He would flash on and off—British gent at roulette, British Army officer, British diplomat, British political agent, British anything. Spoke his line, fitted his monocle, pressed the catch on his cigarette case. His ease with other people was genuine, his financial predicament unfeigned. He had never been married, and had no children that he knew of.

"By Jove, it's nippy," said Wilkinson, when Molly had settled beside him, her books on her lap.

What made her do this—accept a lift from a murderer of schoolgirls? First, she had seen him somewhere safe once—at Mr. Cranefield's. Also, she was wet through, and chilled to the heart. Barbara kept refusing or neglecting or forgetting to buy her the things she needed: a lined raincoat, a jersey the right size. (The boys were wearing hand-me-down clothes from England now, but no one Barbara knew of seemed to have a daughter.) The sleeves of her old jacket were so short that she put her hands in her pockets, so that Mr. Wilkinson would not despise her. He talked to Molly as he did to everyone, as if they were of an age, informing her that Major Lamprey and his mother were flying to Malta to look at a house. A number of people were getting ready to leave the South of France now; it had become so seedy and expensive, and all the wrong people were starting to move in.

"What kind of wrong people?" She sat tense beside him until he said, "Why, like Eric Wilkinson, I should think," and she laughed when his own laugh said she was meant to. He was nice to her; even later, when she thought she had reason to hate him, she would remember that Wilkinson had been nice. He drove beyond his destination—a block of flats that he waved at in passing and that Molly in a confused way supposed he owned. They stopped in the road behind Lou Mas; she thanked him fervently, and then, struck with something, sat staring at him: "Mr. Wilkinson," she said. "Please—

I am not allowed to be in cars with men alone. In case someone happened to see us, would you mind just coming and meeting my mother? Just so she can see who you are?"

"God bless my soul," said Wilkinson, sincerely.

Once, Alec had believed that Barbara was not frightened by anything, and that this absence of fear was her principal weakness. It was true that she had begun drifting out of her old life now, as calmly as Alec drifted away from life altogether. Her mock phrase for each additional Lou Mas catastrophe had become "the usual daily developments." The usual developments over seven rainy days had been the departure of the cook, who took with her all she could lay her hands on, and a French social-security fine that had come down hard on the remains of her marble block of money, reducing it to pebbles and dust. She had never filled out employer's forms for the people she had hired, because she had not known she was supposed to and none of them had suggested it; for a number of reasons having to do with government offices and tax files, none of them had wanted even this modest income to be registered anywhere. As it turned out, the gardener had also been receiving unemployment benefits, which, unfairly, had increased the amount of the fine Barbara had to pay. Rivabella turned out to be just as grim and bossy as England—worse, even, for it kept up a camouflage of wine and sunshine and olive trees and of amiable southern idiots who, if sacked, thought nothing of informing on one.

She sat at the dining-room table, wearing around her shoulders a red cardigan Molly had outgrown. On the table were the Sunday papers Alec's sister continued to send faithfully from England, and Alec's lunch tray, exactly as she had taken it up to him except that everything on it was now cold. She glanced up and saw the two of them enter—one stricken and guilty-looking, the other male, confident, smiling. The recognition that leaped between Barbara and Wilkinson was the last thing that Wilkinson in his right mind should have wanted, and absolutely everything Barbara now desired and craved. Neither of them heard Molly saying, "Mummy, this is Mr. Wilkinson. Mr. Wilkinson wants to tell you how he came to drive me home."

I̲ᴛ ʜᴀᴘᴘᴇɴᴇᴅ at last that Alec had to be taken to the Rivabella hospital, where the local poor went when it was not feasible to let them die at home. Eric Wilkinson, new family friend, drove his car as far as it could go along a winding track, after which they placed Alec on a stretcher; and Wilkinson, Mr. Cranefield, Will, and the doctor carried him the rest of the way. A soft April rain was falling, from which they protected Alec as they could. In the rain the doctor wept unnoticed. The others were silent and absorbed. The hospital stood near the graveyard—shamefully near, Wilkinson finally remarked, to Mr. Cranefield. Will could see the cemetery from his father's new window, though to do so he had to lean out, as he'd imagined passengers doing and having their heads cut off in the train game long ago. A concession was made to Alec's status as owner of a large villa, and he was given a private room. It was not a real sickroom but the place where the staff went to eat and drink when they took time off. They cleared away the plates and empty wine bottles and swept up most of the crumbs and wheeled a bed in.

The building was small for a hospital, large for a house. It had been the winter home of a Moscow family, none of whom had come back after 1917. Alec lay flat and still. Under a drift of soot on the ceiling he could make out a wreath of nasturtiums and a bluebird with a ribbon in its beak.

At the window, Will said to Mr. Cranefield, "We can see Lou Mas from here, and even your peacocks."

Mr. Cranefield fretted, "They shouldn't be in the rain."

Alec's neighbors came to visit. Mrs. Massie, not caring who heard her (one of the children did), said to someone she met on the hospital staircase, "Alec is a gentleman and always will be, but Barbara . . . Barbara." She took a rise of the curved marble stairs at a time. "If the boys were girls they'd be sluts. As it is, they are ruffians. Their old cook saw one of them stoning a cat to death. And now there is Wilkinson. Wilkinson." She moved on alone, repeating his name.

Everyone was saying "Wilkinson" now. Along with "Wilkinson" they said "Barbara." You would think that having been married to one man who was leaving her with nothing, leaving her dependent on family charity, she would have looked around, been more careful, picked a reliable kind of person. "A foreigner, say," said Major Lamprey's mother, who had not cared for Malta. Italians love children, even other people's. She might have chosen—you know—one of the cheerful sort, with a clean shirt and a clean white handkerchief, proprietor of a linen shop. The shop would have kept Barbara out of mischief.

No one could blame Wilkinson, who had his reasons. Also, he had said all those British-sounding lines in films, which in a way made him all right. Barbara had probably said she was Irish once too often. "What can you expect?" said Mrs. Massie. "Think how they were in the war. They keep order when there is someone to bully them. Otherwise . . ." The worst she had to say about Wilkinson was that he was preparing to flash on as the colonel of a regiment in a film about desert warfare; it had been made in the hilly country up behind Monte Carlo.

"Not a grain of sand up there," said Major Lamprey. He said he wondered what foreigners thought they meant by "desert."

"A colonel!" said Mrs. Massie.

"Why not?" said Mr. Cranefield.

'They must think he looks it," said Major Lamprey. "Gets a fiver a day, I'm told, and an extra fiver when he speaks his line. He says, 'Don't underestimate Rommel.' For a fiver I'd say it," though he would rather have died.

The conversation veered to Wilkinson's favor. Wilkinson was merry; told irresistible stories about directors, unmalicious ones about film stars; repeated comic anecdotes concerning underlings who addressed him as "Guv." "I wonder who they can be?" said Mrs. Massie. "It takes a Wilkinson to find them." Mr. Cranefield was more indulgent; he had to be. A sardonic turn of mind would have been resented by E. C. Arden's readers. The blond-headed pair on his desk stood for a world of triumphant love, with which his readers felt easy kinship. The fair couple, though competent in any domain, whether restoring a toppling kingdom or taming a tiger, lived on the same plane as all human creatures except England's enemies. They raised the level of existence—raised it, and flattened it.

Mr. Cranefield—as is often and incorrectly said of children—lived in a world of his own, too, in which he kept everyone's identity clear. He did not confuse St. Damian with an Ethiopian, or Wilkinson with Raffles, or Barbara with a slut. This was partly out of the habit of neatness and partly because he could not make up his mind to live openly in the world he wanted, which was a homosexual one. He said about Wilkinson and Barbara and the blazing scandal at Lou Mas, "I am sure there is no harm in it. Barbara has too much to manage alone, and it is probably better for the children to have a man about the place."

When Wilkinson was not travelling, he stayed at Lou Mas. Until now his base had been a flat he'd shared with a friend who was a lawyer and who was also frequently away. Wilkinson left most of his luggage behind; there was barely enough of his presence to fill a room. For a reason no one understood Barbara had changed everyone's room around: she and Molly slept where Alec had been, the boys moved to Barbara's room, and Wilkinson was given Molly's bed. It seemed a small bed for so tall a man.

Molly had always slept alone, until now. Some nights, when Wilkinson was sleeping in her old room, she would waken just before dawn and find that her mother had disappeared. Her feeling at the sight of the empty bed was one of panic. She would get up, too, and go in to Will and shake him, saying, "She's disappeared."

"No, she hasn't. She's with Wilkinson." Nevertheless, he would rise and stumble, still nearly sleeping, down the passage—Alec's son, descendant of civil servants, off on a mission.

Barbara slept with her back against Wilkinson's chest. Outside, Mr. Cranefield's peacocks greeted first light by screaming murder. Years from now, Will would hear the first stirrings of dawn and dream of assassinations. Wilkinson never moved. Had he shown he was awake, he might have felt obliged to say a suitable one-liner—something like "I say, old chap, you are a bit of a trial, you know."

Will's mother picked up the nightgown and robe that lay white on the floor, pulled them on, flung her warm hair back, tied her sash—all without haste. In the passage, the door shut on the quiet Wilkinson, she said tenderly, "Were you worried?"

"Molly was."

Casual with her sons, she was modest before her daughter. Changing to a clean nightdress, she said, "Turn the other way." Turning, Molly saw her mother, white and gold, in the depths of Alec's mirror. Barbara had her arms raised, revealing the profile of a breast with at its tip the palest wash of rose, paler than the palest pink flower. (Like a Fragonard, Barbara had been told, like a Boucher—not by Alec.) What Molly felt now was immense relief. It was not the fate of every girl to turn into India rubber. But in no other way did she wish to resemble her mother.

Like the residue left by winter rains, awareness of Barbara and Wilkinson seeped through the house. There was a damp chill about it that crept to the bone. One of the children, Will, perceived it as torment. Because of the mother defiled, the source of all such knowledge became polluted, probably forever. The boys withdrew from Barbara, who had let the weather in. James imagined ways of killing Wilkinson, though he drew the line at killing Barbara. He did not want her dead, but different. The mother he wanted did not stand in public squares pointing crazily up to invisible saints, or begin sleeping in one bed and end up in another.

Barbara felt that they were leaving her; she put the blame on Molly, who had the makings of a prude, and who, at worst, might turn out to be something like Alec's sister. Barbara said to Molly, "I had three children before I was twenty-three, and I was alone, and there were all the air-raids. The life I've tried to give you and the boys has been so different, so happy, so free." Molly folded her arms, looked down at her shoes. Her height, her grave expression, her new figure gave her a bogus air of maturity: she was only thirteen, and she felt like a pony flicked by a crop. Barbara tried to draw near: "My closest friend is my own daughter," she wanted to be able to say. "I never do a thing without talking it over with Molly." So she would have said, laughing, her bright head against Molly's darker hair, if only Molly had given half an inch.

"What a cold creature you are," Barbara said, sadly. "You live in an ice palace. There is so little happiness in life unless you let it come near. I always at least had an *idea* about being happy." The girl's face stayed shut and locked. All that could cross it now was disappointment.

One night when Molly woke Will, he said, "I don't care where she is." Molly went back to bed. Fetching Barbara had become a habit. She was better off in her room alone.

When they stopped coming to claim her, Barbara perceived it as mortification. She gave up on Molly, for the moment, and turned to the boys, sat curled on the foot of their bed, sipping wine, telling stories, offering to share her cigarette, though James was still twelve. James said, "He told us it was dangerous to smoke in bed. People have died that way." "He" meant Alec. Was this all James would remember? That he had warned about smoking in bed?

James, who was embarrassed by this attempt of hers at making them equals, thought she had an odd smell, like a cat. To Will, at another kind of remove, she stank of folly. They stared at her, as if measuring everything she still had to mean in their lives. This expression she read as she could. Love for Wilkinson had blotted out the last of her dreams and erased her gift of second sight. She said unhappily to Wilkinson, "My children are prigs. But, then, they are only half mine."

Mademoiselle, whom the children now called by her name—Geneviève—still came to Lou Mas. Nobody paid her, but she corrected the children's French, which no longer needed correcting, and tried to help with their homework, which amounted to interference. They had always in some way spared her; only James, her favorite, sometimes said, "No, I'd rather work alone." She knew now that the Webbs were poor, which increased her affection: their descent to low water equalled her own. Sometimes she brought a packet of biscuits for their tea, which was a dull affair now the cook had gone. They ate the biscuits straight from the paper wrapping: nobody wanted to wash an extra plate. Wilkinson, playing at British something, asked about her aunt. He said "Madame la Comtesse." When he had gone, she cautioned the children not to say that but simply "your aunt." But as Geneviève's aunt did not receive foreigners, save for a few such as Mrs. Massie, they had no reason to ask how she was. When Geneviève realized from something said that Wilkinson more or less lived at Lou Mas, she stopped coming to see them. The Webbs had no further connection with Rivabella then except for their link with the hospital, where Alec still lay quietly, still alive.

Barbara went up every day. She asked the doctor, "Shouldn't he be having blood transfusions—something of that kind?" She had never been in a hospital except to be born and to have her children. She was remembering films she had seen, bottles dripping liquids, needles taped to the crook of an arm, nursing sisters wheeling oxygen tanks down white halls.

The doctor reminded her that this was Rivabella—a small town where half the population lived without employment. He had been so sympathetic at first, so slow to present a bill. She could not understand what had changed him; but she was hopeless at reading faces now. She could scarcely read her children's.

She bent down to Alec, so near that her eyes would have seemed enormous had he been paying attention. She told him the name of the scent she was wearing; it reminded her and perhaps Alec, too, of jasmine. Eric had brought it back from a dinner at Monte Carlo, given to promote this very perfume. He was often invited to these things, where he represented the best sort of Britishness. "Eric is being the greatest help," she said to Alec, who might have been listening. She added, for it had to be said some time, "Eric has very kindly offered to stay at Lou Mas."

Mr. Cranefield and Mrs. Massie continued to plod up the hill, she with increasing difficulty. They brought Alec what they thought he needed. But he had no addictions, no cravings, no use for anything now but his destination. The children were sent up evenings. They never knew what to say or what he could hear. They talked as if they were still eleven or twelve, when Alec had stopped seeing them grow.

To Mr. Cranefield they looked like imitations of English children —loud, humorless, dutiful, clear. "James couldn't come with us tonight," said Molly. "He was quite ill, for some reason. He brought his dinner up." All three spoke the high, thin English of expatriate children who, unknowingly, mimic their mothers. The light bulb hanging crooked left Alec's face in shadow. When the children had kissed Alec and departed, Mr. Cranefield could hear them taking the hospital stairs headlong, at a gallop. The children were young and alive, and Alec was forty-something and nearly always sleeping. Unequal chances, Mr. Cranefield thought. They can't really beat their breasts about it. When Mrs. Massie was present, she never failed to say, "Your father is tired," though nobody knew if Alec was tired or not.

The neighbors pitied the children. Meaning only kindness, Mr. Cranefield reminded Molly that one day she would type, Mrs. Massie said something more about helping in the garden. That was how everyone saw them now—grubbing, digging, lending a hand. They had become Wilkinson's second-hand kin but without his panache, his ease in adversity. They were Alec's offspring: stiff. Humiliated, they overheard and garnered for memory: "We've asked Wilkinson to come over and cook up a curry. He's hours in the kitchen, but I must say it's worth every penny." "We might get Wilkinson to drive us to Rome. He doesn't charge all that much, and he's such good company." Always Wilkinson, never Eric, though that was what Barbara had called him from their first meeting. To the children he was, and remained, "Mr. Wilkinson," friend of both parents, occasional guest in the house.

THE RAINS OF their third southern spring were still driving hard against the villa when Barbara's engineer brother wrote to say they were letting Lou Mas. Everything dripped wet as she stood near a window, with bougainvillea soaked and wild-looking on one side of the pane and steam forming on the other, to read this letter. The new tenants were a family of planters who had been forced to leave Malaya; it had a connection with political events, but Barbara's life was so full now that she never looked at the papers. They would be coming there in June, which gave Barbara plenty of time to find another home. He—her brother—had thought of giving her the Lou Mas cottage, but he wondered if it would suit her, inasmuch as it lacked electric light, running water, an indoor lavatory, most of its windows, and part of its roof. This was not to say it could not be fixed up for the Webbs in the future, when Lou Mas had started paying for itself. Half the rent obtained would be turned over to Barbara. She would have to look hard, he said, before finding brothers who were so considerate of a married sister. She and the children were not likely to suffer from the change, which might even turn out to their moral advantage. Barbara supposed this meant that Desmond—the richest, the best-educated, the most easily flabbergasted of her brothers—was still mulling over the description of Lou Mas Ron must have taken back.

With Wilkinson helping, the Webbs moved to the far side of the hospital, on a north-facing slope, away from the sea. Here the houses were tall and thin with narrow windows, set in gardens of raked gravel. Their neighbors included the mayor, the more prosperous shopkeepers, and the coach of the local football team. Barbara was enchanted to find industrial activity she had not suspected—a thriving ceramics factory that produced figurines of monks whose heads were mustard pots, dogs holding thermometers in their paws, and the patron saint of Rivabella wearing armor of pink, orange, mauve, or white. These were purchased by tourists who had trudged up to the town in the hope of seeing early Renaissance frescoes.

Barbara had never missed a day with Alec, not even the day of the move. She held his limp hand and told him stories. When he was not stunned by drugs, or too far lost in his past, he seemed to be listening. Sometimes he pressed her fingers. He seldom spoke more than a word at a time. Barbara described to him the pleasures of moving, and how pretty the houses were on the north side, with their gardens growing gnomes and shells and tinted bottles. Why make fun of such people, she asked his still face. They probably knew, by instinct, how to get the best out of life. She meant every word, for she was profoundly in love and knew that Wilkinson would never leave her except for a greater claim. She combed Alec's hair and bathed him; Wilkinson came whenever he could to shave Alec and cut his nails and help Barbara change the bedsheets; for it was not the custom of the hospital staff to do any of this.

Sometimes Alec whispered, "Diana," who might have been either his sister or Mrs. Massie. Barbara tried to remember her old prophetic dreams, from that time when, as compensation for absence of passion, she had been granted second sight. In none had she ever seen herself bending over a dying man, listening to him call her by another woman's name.

They lived, now, in four dark rooms stuffed with furniture, some of it useful. Upstairs resided the widow of the founder of the ceramics factory. She had been bought out at a loss at the end of the war, and disapproved of the new line of production, especially the monks. She never interfered, never asked questions—simply came down once a month to collect her rent, which was required in cash. She did tell the children that she had never seen the inside of an English villa, but did not seem to think her exclusion was a slight; she took her bearings from a very small span of the French middle-class compass.

Barbara and Wilkinson made jokes about the French widow-lady, but the children did not. To replace their lopped English roots they had grown the sensitive antennae essential to wanderers. They could have drawn the social staircase of Rivabella on a blackboard, and knew how low a step, now, had been assigned to them. Barbara would not have cared. Wherever she stood now seemed to suit her. On her way home from the hospital she saw two men, foreigners, stop and stare and exchange remarks about her. She could not understand the language they spoke, but she saw they had been struck by her beauty. One of them seemed to be asking the other, "Who can she be?" In their new home she took the only bedroom—an imposing matrimonial chamber. When Wilkinson was in residence he shared it as a matter of course. The boys slept on a pull-out sofa in the dining room, and Molly had a couch in a glassed-in verandah. The verandah contained their landlady's rubber plants, which Molly scrupulously tended. The boys had stopped quarrelling. They would never argue or ever say much to each other again. Alec's children seemed to have been collected under one roof by chance, like strays, or refugees. Their narrow faces, their gray eyes, their thinness and dryness, were similar, but not alike; a stranger would not necessarily have known they were of the same father and mother. The boys still wore second-hand clothes sent from England; this was their only connection with English life.

On market days Molly often saw their old housemaid or the laundress. They asked for news of Alec, which made Molly feel cold and shy. She was dressed very like them now, in a cotton frock and roped-soled shoes from a market stall. "Style is all you need to bring it off," Barbara had assured her, but she had none, at least not that kind. It was Molly who chose what the family would eat, who looked at prices and kept accounts and counted her change. Barbara was entirely busy with Alec at the hospital, and with Wilkinson at home.

With love, she had lost her craving for nursery breakfasts. She sat at table smoking, watching Wilkinson telling stories. When Wilkinson was there, he did much of the cooking. Molly was grateful for that.

The new people at Lou Mas had everyone's favor. If there had been times when the neighbors had wondered how Barbara and Alec could possibly have met, the Malayan planter and his jolly wife were an old novel known by heart. They told about jungle terrorists, and what the British ought to be doing, and they described the owner of Lou Mas—a Welshman who was planning to go into politics. Knowing Barbara to be Irish, no one could place the Welshman. The story started up that Barbara's family were bankrupt and had sold Lou Mas to a Welsh war profiteer.

Mrs. Massie presented the new people with *Flora's Gardening Encyclopaedia*. "It is by way of being a classic," she said. "Seventeen editions. I do all my typing myself."

"Ah, well, poor Barbara," everyone said now. What could you expect? Luckily for her, she had Wilkinson. Wilkinson's star was rising. "Don't underestimate Rommel" had been said to some effect —there was a mention in the *Sunday Telegraph*. "Wilkinson goes everywhere. He's invited to everything at Monte Carlo. He must positively live on lobster salad." "Good for old Wilkinson. Why shouldn't he?" Wilkinson had had a bad war, had been a prisoner somewhere.

Who imagined that story, Mr. Cranefield wondered. Some were mixing up Wilkinson with the dying Alec, others seemed to think Alec was already dead. By August it had become established that Wilkinson had been tortured by the Japanese and had spent the years since trying to leave the memory behind. He never mentioned what he'd been through, which was to his credit. Barbara and three kids must have been the last thing he wanted, but that was how it was with Wilkinson—too kind for his own good, all too ready to lend a hand, to solve a problem. Perhaps, rising, he would pull the Webbs with him. Have you seen that girl hanging about in the market? You can't tell her from the butcher's child.

From Alec's bedside Barbara wrote a long letter to her favorite brother, the pilot, Mike. She told about Alec, "sleeping so peacefully as I write," and described the bunch of daisies Molly had put in a jug on the windowsill, and how well Will had done in his finals ("He will be the family intellectual, a second Alec"), and finally she came round to the matter of Wilkinson: "You probably saw the rave notice in the *Telegraph*, but you had no way of knowing of course it was someone I knew. Well, here is the whole story. Please, Mike, do keep it to yourself for the moment, you know how Ron takes things sometimes." Meeting Eric had confirmed her belief there was something in the universe more reasonable than God—at any rate more logical. Eric had taken a good look at the Lou Mas cottage and thought something might be done with it after all. "You will adore Eric," she promised. "He is marvellous with the children and so kind to Alec," which was true.

"Are you awake, love?" She moistened a piece of cotton with mineral water from a bottle that stood on the floor (Alec had no table) and wet his lips with it, then took his hand, so light it seemed hollow, and held it in her own, telling him quietly about the Lou Mas cottage, where he would occupy a pleasant room overlooking the sea. He flexed his fingers; she bent close: "Yes, dear; what is it, dear?" For the first time since she'd known him he said, "Mother." She waited; but no, that was all. She saw herself on his balcony at Lou Mas in her white dressing gown, her hair in the sun, saw what the gardener would have been struck by if only he had looked up. She said to herself, "I gave Alec three beautiful children. That is what he is thanking me for now."

Her favorite brother had been away from England when her letter came, so that it was late in September when he answered to call her a bitch, a trollop, a crook, and a fool. He was taking up the question of her gigolo boyfriend with the others. They had been supporting Alec's family for three years. If she thought they intended to take on her lover (this written above a word scratched out); and here the letter ended. She went white, as her children did, easily. She said to Wilkinson, "Come and talk in the car, where we can be quiet," for they were seldom alone.

She let him finish reading, then said, in a voice that he had never heard before but that did not seem to surprise him—"I grew up blacking my brothers' boots. Alec was the first man who ever held a door open for me."

He said, "Your brothers all did well," without irony, meaning there was that much to admire.

"Oh," she said, "If you are comparing their chances with Alec's, if that's what you mean—the start Alec had. Well, poor Alec. Yes, a better start. I often thought, Well, there it is with him, that's the very trouble—a start too good."

This exchange, this double row of cards faceup, seemed all they intended to reveal. They instantly sat differently, she straighter, he more relaxed.

Wilkinson said, "Which one of them actually owns Lou Mas?"

"Equal shares, I think. Though Desmond has power of attorney and makes all the decisions. Alec and I *own* Lou Mas, but only legally. They put it in our name because we were emigrating. It made it easier for them, with all the taxes. We had three years, and not a penny in rent."

Wilkinson said, in a kind of anguish, "Oh, God bless my soul."

It was Wilkinson's English lawyer friend in Monte Carlo who drew up the papers with which Alec signed his share of Lou Mas over to Barbara and Alec and Barbara revoked her brother's power of attorney. Alec, his obedient hand around a pen and the hand firmly held in Barbara's, may have known what he was doing but not why. The documents were then put in the lawyer's safe to await Alec's death, which occurred not long after.

THE DOCTOR, who had sat all night at the bedside, turning Alec's head so that he would not strangle vomiting (for that was not the way he wished him to die), heard him breathing deeply and ever more deeply and then no longer. Alec's eyes were closed, but the doctor pressed the lids with his fingers. Believing in his own and perhaps Alec's damnation, he stood for a long time at the window while the roof and towers of the church became clear and flushed with rose; then the red rim of the sun emerged, and turned yellow, and it was as good as day.

There was only one nurse in the hospital, and a midwife on another floor. Summoning both, he told them to spread a rubber sheet under Alec, and wash him, and put clean linen on the bed.

At that time, in that part of France, scarcely anyone had a telephone. The doctor walked down the slope on the far side of Rivabella and presented himself unshaven to Barbara in her nightdress to say that Alec was dead. She dressed and came at once; there was no one yet in the streets to see her and to ask who she was. Eric followed, bringing the clothes in which Alec would be buried. All he could recall of his prayers, though he would not have said them around Barbara, were the first words of the Collect: "Almighty God, unto whom all hearts be open, all desires known, and from whom no secrets are hid."

Barbara had a new friend—her French widowed landlady. It was she who arranged to have part of Barbara's wardrobe dyed black within twenty-four hours, who lent her a black hat and gloves and a long crêpe veil. Barbara let the veil down over her face. Her friend, whose veil was tied round her hat and floated behind her, took Barbara by the arm, and they walked to the cemetery and stood side by side. The Webbs' former servants were there, and the doctor, and the local British colony. Some of the British thought the other woman in black must be Barbara's Irish mother: only the Irish poor or the Royal Family ever wore mourning of that kind.

The graveyard was so cramped and small, so crowded with dead from the time of Garibaldi and before, that no one else could be buried. The coffins of the recent dead were stored in cells in a thick concrete wall. The cells were then sealed, and a marble plaque affixed in lieu of a tombstone. Alec had to be lifted to shoulder level, which took the strength of several persons—the doctor, Mr. Cranefield, Barbara's brothers, and Alec's young sons. (Wilkinson would have helped, but he had already wrenched his shoulder quite badly carrying the coffin down the hospital steps.) Molly thrust her way into this crowd of male mourners. She said to her mother, "Not you—you never loved him."

God knows who might have heard that, Barbara thought.

Actually, no one had, except for Mrs. Massie. Believing it to be true, she dismissed it from memory. She was composing her own obituary: "Two generations of gardeners owed their . . ." "Two generations of readers owed their gardens . . ."

"Our Father," Alec's sister said, hoping no one would notice and

mistake her for a fraud. Nor did she wish to have a scrap of consideration removed from Barbara, whose hour this was. Her own loss was
beyond remedy, and so not worth a mention. There was no service
—nothing but whispering and silence. To his sister, it was as if Alec
had been left, stranded and alone, in a train stalled between stations.
She had not seen him since the day he left England, and had refused
to look at him dead. Barbara was aware of Diana, the mouse, praying
like a sewing machine somewhere behind her. She clutched the arm
of the older widow and thought, I know, I know, but she can get a
job, can't she? I was working when I met Alec, wasn't I? But what
Diana Webb meant by "work" was the fine stitching her own mother
had done to fill time, not for a living. In Diana's hotel room was a
box containing the most exquisite and impractical child's bonnet and
coat made from some of the white silk Alec had sent her from India,
before the war. Perhaps a luxury shop in Monte Carlo or one of
Barbara's wealthy neighbors would be interested. Perhaps there was
an Anglican clergyman with a prosperous parish. She opened her eyes
and saw that absolutely no one in the cemetery looked like Alec—
not even his sons.

The two boys seemed strange, even to each other, in their dark,
new suits. The word "father" had slipped out of their grasp just now.
A marble plaque on which their father's name was misspelled stood
propped against the wall. The boys looked at it helplessly.

Is that all? people began wondering. What happens now?

Barbara turned away from the wall and, still holding the arm of her
friend, led the mourners out past the gates.

It was I who knew what he wanted, the doctor believed. He had
told me long before. Asked me to promise, though I refused. I heard
his last words. The doctor kept telling himself this. "I heard his last
words"—though Alec had not said anything, had merely breathed,
then stopped.

"Her father was a late Victorian poet of some distinction," Mrs.
Massie's obituary went on.

Will, who was fifteen, was no longer a child, did not look like Alec,
spoke up in that high-pitched English of his: "Death is empty without God." Now where did that come from? Had he heard it? Read
it? Was he performing? No one knew. Later, he would swear that at

that moment a vocation had come to light, though it must have been born with him—bud within the bud, mind within the mind. I will buy back your death, he would become convinced he had said to Alec. Shall enrich it; shall refuse the southern glare, the southern void. I shall pay for your solitude, your humiliation. Shall demand for myself a stronger life, a firmer death. He thought, later, that he had said all this, but he had said and thought only five words.

As they shuffled out, all made very uncomfortable by Will, Mrs. Massie leaned half on her stick and half on James, observing, "You were such a little boy when I saw you for the first time at Lou Mas." Because his response was silence, she supposed he was waiting to hear more. "You three must stick together now. The Three Musketeers." But they were already apart.

Major Lamprey found himself walking beside the youngest of the Laceys. He told Mike what he told everyone now—why he had not moved to Malta. It was because he did not trust the Maltese. "Not that one can trust anyone here," he said. "Even the mayor belongs to an anarchist movement, I've been told. Whatever happens, I intend to die fighting on my own doorstep."

The party was filing down a steep incline. "You will want to be with your family," Mrs. Massie said, releasing James and leaning half her weight on Mr. Cranefield instead. They picked up with no trouble a conversation dropped the day before. It was about how Mr. Cranefield—rather, his other self, E. C. Arden—was likely to fare in the second half of the nineteen-fifties: "It is a question of your not being too modern and yet not slipping back," Mrs. Massie said. "I never have to worry. Gardens don't change."

"I am not worried about new ideas," he said. "Because there are none. But words, now. 'Permissive.' "

"What's that?"

"It was in the *Observer* last Sunday. I suppose it means something. Still. One musn't. One can't. There are limits."

Barbara met the mayor coming the other way, too late, carrying a wreath with a purple ribbon on which was written, in gold, "From the Municipality—Sincere Respects." Waiting for delivery of the wreath had made him tardy. "For a man who never went out, Alec made quite an impression," Mrs. Massie remarked.

"His funeral was an attraction," said Mr. Cranefield.

"Can one call that a funeral?" She was still thinking about her own.

Mike Lacey caught up to his sister. They had once been very close. As soon as she saw him she stood motionless, bringing the line behind her to a halt. He said he knew this was not the time or place, but he had to let her know she was not to worry. She would always have a roof over her head. They felt responsible for Alec's children. There were vague plans for fixing up the cottage. They would talk about it later on.

"Ah, Mike," she said. "That is so kind of you." Using both hands she lifted the veil so that he could see her clear gray eyes.

The procession wound past the hospital and came to the church square. Mr. Cranefield had arranged a small after-funeral party, as a favor to Barbara, who had no real home. Some were coming and some were not; the latter now began to say goodbye. Geneviève, whose face was like a pink sponge because she had been crying so hard, flung herself at James, who let her embrace him. Over his governess's dark shoulder he saw the faces of people who had given him second-hand clothes, thus (he believed) laying waste to his life. He smashed their faces to particles, left the particles dancing in the air like midges until they dissolved without a sound. Wait, he was thinking. Wait, wait.

Mr. Cranefield wondered if Molly was going to become her mother's hostage, her moral bail—if Barbara would hang on to her to show that Alec's progeny approved of her. He remembered Molly's small, anxious face, and how worried she had been about St. George. "You will grow up, you know," he said, which was an odd thing to say, since she was quite tall. They walked down the path Wilkinson had not been able to climb in his car. She stared at him. "I mean, when you grow up you will be free." She shook her head. She knew better than that now, at fourteen: there was no freedom except to cease to love. She would love her brothers when they had stopped thinking much about her: women's fidelity. This would not keep her from fighting them, inch by inch, over money, property, remnants of the past: women's insecurity. She would hound them and pester them about Alec's grave, and Barbara's old age, and where they were all to be buried: women's sense of order. They would by then be another James, an alien Will, a different Molly.

Mr. Cranefield's attention slipped from Molly to Alec to the funeral, to the extinction of one sort of Englishman and the emergence of another. Most people looked on Wilkinson as a prewar survival, what with his I say's and By Jove's, but he was really an English mutation, a new man, wearing the old protective coloring. Alec would have understood his language, probably, but not the person behind it. A landscape containing two male figures came into high relief in Mr. Cranefield's private image of the world, as if he had been lent trick spectacles. He allowed the vision to fade. Better to stick to the blond pair on his desk; so far they had never let him down. I am not impulsive, or arrogant, he explained to himself. No one would believe the truth about Wilkinson even if he were to describe it. I shall not insist, he decided, or try to have the last word. I am not that kind of fool. He breathed slowly, as one does when mortal danger has been averted.

The mourners attending Mr. Cranefield's party reached the motor road and began to straggle across: it was a point of honor for members of the British colony to pay absolutely no attention to cars. The two widows had fallen back, either so that Barbara could make an entrance, or because the older woman believed it would not be dignified for her to exhibit haste. A strong west wind flattened the black dresses against their breasts and lifted their thick veils.

How will he hear me, Molly wondered. You could speak to someone in a normal grave, for earth is porous and seems to be life, of a kind. But how to speak across marble? Even if she were to place her hands flat on the marble slab, it would not absorb a fraction of human warmth. She had to tell him what she had done—how it was she, Molly, who had led the intruder home, let him in, causing Alec, always courteous, to remove himself first to the hospital, then farther on. Disaster, the usual daily development, had to have a beginning. She would go back to the cemetery, alone, and say it, whether or not he could hear. The disaster began with two sentences: "Mummy, this is Mr. Wilkinson. Mr. Wilkinson wants to tell you how he happened to drive me home."

Barbara descended the steps to Mr. Cranefield's arm in arm with

her new friend, who was for the first time about to see the inside of
an English house. "Look at that," said the older widow. One of the
peacocks had taken shelter from the wind in Mr. Cranefield's electric
lift. A minute earlier Alec's sister had noticed, too, and had thought
something that seemed irrefutable: no power on earth would ever
induce her to eat a peacock.

Who is to say I never loved Alec, said Barbara, who loved Wilkinson. He was high-handed, yes, laying down the law as long as he was
able, but he was always polite. Of course I loved him. I still do. He
will have to be buried properly, where we can plant something—
white roses. The mayor told me that every once in a while they turn
one of the Russians out, to make room. There must be a waiting list.
We could put Alec's name on it. Alec gave me three children. Eric
gave me Lou Mas.

Entering Mr. Cranefield's, she removed her dark veil and hat and
revealed her lovely head, like the sun rising. Because the wind had
started blowing leaves and sand, Mr. Cranefield's party had to be
moved indoors from the loggia. This change occasioned some confusion, in which Barbara did not take part; neither did Wilkinson,
whose wrenched shoulder was making him feel ill. She noticed her
children helping, carrying plates of small sandwiches and silver buckets of ice. She approved of this; they were obviously well brought up.
The funeral had left Mr. Cranefield's guests feeling hungry and
thirsty and rather lonely, anxious to hold on to a glass and to talk to
someone. Presently their voices rose, overlapped, and created something like a thick woven fabric of blurred design, which Alec's sister
(who was not used to large social gatherings) likened to a flying
carpet. It was now, with Molly covertly watching her, that Barbara
began in the most natural way in the world to live happily ever after.
There was nothing willful about this: she was simply borne in a single
direction, though she did keep seeing for a time her black glove on
her widowed friend's black sleeve.

Escorting lame Mrs. Massie to a sofa, Mr. Cranefield said they
might as well look on the bright side. (He was still speaking about
the second half of the nineteen-fifties.) Wilkinson, sitting down
because he felt sick, and thinking the remark was intended for him,
assured Mr. Cranefield, truthfully, that he had never looked any-

where else. It then happened that every person in the room, at the same moment, spoke and thought of something other than Alec. This lapse, this inattention, lasting no longer than was needed to say "No, thank you" or "Oh, really?" or "Yes, I see," was enough to create the dark gap marking the end of Alec's span. He ceased to be, and it made absolutely no difference after that whether or not he was forgotten.

THE
LATEHOMECOMER

WHEN I CAME back to Berlin out of captivity in the spring of 1950, I discovered I had a stepfather. My mother had never mentioned him. I had been writing from Brittany to "Grete Bestermann," but the "Toeppler" engraved on a brass plate next to the bellpull at her new address turned out to be her name, too. As she slipped the key in the lock, she said quietly, "Listen, Thomas. I'm Frau Toeppler now. I married a kind man with a pension. This is his key, his name, and his apartment. He wants to make you welcome." From the moment she met me at the railway station that day, she must have been wondering how to break it.

I put my hand over the name, leaving a perfect palm print. I said, "I suppose there are no razor blades and no civilian shirts in Berlin. But some ass is already engraving nameplates."

Martin Toeppler was an old man who had been a tram conductor. He was lame in one arm as the result of a working accident and carried that shoulder higher than the other. His eyes had the milky look of the elderly, lighter round the rim than at the center of the iris, and he had an old woman's habit of sighing, "Ah, yes, yes." The sigh seemed to be his way of pleading, "It can't be helped." He must have been forty-nine, at the most, but aged was what he seemed to me, and more than aged—useless, lost. His mouth hung open much of the time, as though he had trouble breathing through his nose, but it was only because he was a chronic talker, always ready to bite down on a word. He came from Franconia, near the Czech border, close to where my grandparents had once lived.

"Grete and I can understand each other's dialects," he said—but we were not a dialect-speaking family. My brother and I had been made to say "bread" and "friend" and "tree" correctly. I turned my eyes to my mother, but she looked away.

Martin's one dream was to return to Franconia; it was almost the first thing he said to me. He had inherited two furnished apartments in a town close to an American military base. One of the two had been empty for years. The occupants had moved away, no one knew where—perhaps to Sweden. After their departure, which had taken place at five o'clock on a winter morning in 1943, the front door had been sealed with a government stamp depicting a swastika and an eagle. The vanished tenants must have died, perhaps in Sweden, and now no local person would live in the place, because a whole family of ghosts rattled about, opening and shutting drawers, banging on pipes, moving chairs and ladders. The ghosts were looking for a hoard of gold that had been left behind, Martin thought. The second apartment had been rented to a family who had disappeared during the confused migrations of the end of the war and were probably dead, too; at least they were dead officially, which was all that mattered. Martin intended to modernize the two flats, raise them up to American standards—he meant by this putting venetian blinds at the windows and gas-heated water tanks in the bathrooms—and let them to a good class of American officer, too foreign to care about a small-town story, too educated to be afraid of ghosts. But he would have to move quickly; otherwise his inheritance, his sole postwar capital, his only means of getting started again, might be snatched away from him for the sake of shiftless and illiterate refugees from the Soviet zone, or bombed-out families still huddled in barracks, or for latehomecomers. This last was a new category of persons, all one word. It was out of his mouth before he remembered that I was one, too. He stopped talking, and then he sighed and said, "Ah, yes, yes."

He could not keep still for long: he drew out his wallet and showed me a picture of himself on horseback. He may have wanted to substitute this country image for any idea I had of him on the deck of a tram. He held the snapshot at arm's length and squinted at it. "That was Martin Toeppler once," he said. "It will be Martin Toeppler again." His youth, and a new right shoulder and arm, and the hot, leafy summers everyone his age said had existed before the war were waiting for him in Franconia. He sounded like a born winner instead of a physically broken tram conductor on the losing side. He put the picture away in a cracked celluloid case, pocketed his wallet, and called to my mother, "The boy will want a bath."

My mother, who had been preparing a bath for minutes now, had been receiving orders all her life. As a girl she had worked like a slave in her mother's village guesthouse, and after my father died she became a servant again, this time in Berlin, to my powerful Uncle Gerhard and his fat wife. My brother and I spent our winters with her, all three sleeping in one bed sometimes, in a cold attic room, sharing bread and apples smuggled from Uncle Gerhard's larder. In the summer we were sent to help our grandmother. We washed the chairs and tables, cleaned the toilets of vomit, and carried glasses stinking with beer back to the kitchen. We were still so small we had to stand on stools to reach the taps.

"It was lucky you had two sons," Uncle Gerhard said to my mother once. "There will never be a shortage of strong backs in the family."

"No one will exploit my children," she is supposed to have replied, though how she expected to prevent it only God knows, for we had no roof of our own and no money and we ate such food as we were given. Our uniforms saved us. Once we had joined the Hitler Jugend, even Uncle Gerhard never dared ask, "Where are you going?" or "Where have you been?" My brother was quicker than I. By the time he was twelve he knew he had been trapped; I was sixteen and a prisoner before I understood. But from our mother's point of view we were free, delivered; we would not repeat her life. That was all she wanted.

In captivity I had longed for her and for the lost paradise of our poverty, where she had belonged entirely to my brother and to me and we had slept with her, one on each side. I had written letters to her full of remorse for past neglect and containing promises of future goodness: I would work hard and look after her forever. These letters, sent to blond, young, soft-voiced Grete Bestermann, had been read by Grete Toeppler, whose greying hair was pinned up in a sort of oval balloon, and who was anxious and thin, as afraid of things to come as she was of the past. I had not recognized her at the station, and when she said timidly, "Excuse me? Thomas?" I thought she was her own mother. I did not know then, or for another few minutes, that my grandmother had died or that my rich Uncle Gerhard, now officially de-Nazified by a court of law, was camped in two rooms carved out of a ruin, raising rabbits for a living and hoping that no one would notice him. She had last seen me when I was fifteen. We had been moving toward each other since early this morning, but I was exhausted and taciturn, and we were both shy, and we had not rushed into each other's arms, because we had each been afraid of embracing a stranger. I had one horrible memory of her, but it may have been only a dream. I was small, but I could speak and walk. I came into a room where she was nursing a baby. Two other women were with her. When they saw me they started to laugh, and one said to her, "Give some to Thomas." My mother leaned over and put her breast in my mouth. The taste was disgustingly sweet, and because of the two women I felt humiliated: I spat and backed off and began to cry. She said something to the women and they laughed harder than ever. It must have been a dream, for who could the baby have been? My brother was eleven months older than I.

She was cautious as an animal with me now, partly because of my reaction to the nameplate. She must have feared there was more to come. She had been raised to respect men, never to interrupt their conversation, to see that their plates were filled before hers—even, as a girl, to stand when they were sitting down. I was twenty-one, I had been twenty-one for three days, I had crossed over to the camp of the bullies and strangers. All the while Martin was talking and boasting and showing me himself on horseback, she crept in and out of the parlor, fetching wood and the briquettes they kept by the tile stove, carrying them down the passage to build a fire for me in the bathroom. She looked at me sidelong sometimes and smiled with her hand before her mouth—a new habit of hers—but she kept silent until it was time to say that the bath was ready.

M Y MOTHER spread a towel for me to stand on and showed me a chair where, she said, Martin always sat to dry his feet. There was a shelf with a mirror and comb but no washbasin. I supposed that he shaved and they cleaned their teeth in the kitchen. My mother said the soap was of poor quality and would not lather, but she asked me, again from behind the screen of her hand, not to leave it underwater where it might melt and be wasted. A stone underwater might have melted as easily. "There is a hook for your clothes," she said, though of course I had seen it. She hesitated still, but when I began to unbutton my shirt she slipped out.

The bath, into which a family could have fitted, was as rough as lava rock. The water was boiling hot. I sat with my knees drawn up as if I were in the tin tub I had been lent sometimes in France. The starfish scar of a grenade wound was livid on one knee, and that leg was misshapen, as though it had been pressed the wrong way while the bones were soft. Long underwear I took to be my stepfather's hung over a line. I sat looking at it, and at a stiff thin towel hanging next to it, and at the water condensing on the cement walls, until the skin of my hands and feet became as ridged and soft as corduroy.

There is a term for people caught on a street crossing after the light has changed: "pedestrian-traffic residue." I had been in a prisoner-of-war camp at Rennes when an order arrived to repatriate everyone who was under eighteen. For some reason, my name was never called. Five years after that, when I was in Saint-Malo, where I had been assigned to a druggist and his wife as a "free worker"—which did not mean free but simply not in a camp—the police sent for me and asked what I was doing in France with a large "PG," for *"prisonnier de guerre,"* on my back. Was I a deserter from the Foreign Legion? A spy? Nearly every other prisoner in France had been released at least ten months before, but the file concerning me had been lost or mislaid in Rennes, and I could not leave until it was found—I had no existence. By that time the French were sick of me, because they were sick of the war and its reminders, and the scheme of using the prisoners the Americans had taken to rebuild the roads and bridges of France had not worked out. The idea had never been followed by a plan, and so some of the prisoners became farm help, some became domestic servants, some went into the Foreign Legion because the food was better, some sat and did nothing for three or four years, because no one could discover anything for them to do. The police hinted to me that if I were to run away no one would mind. It would have cleared up the matter of the missing file. But I was afraid of putting myself in the wrong, in which case they might have an excuse to keep me forever. Besides, how far could I have run with a large "PG" painted on my jacket and trousers? Here, where it would not be necessary to wear a label, because "latehomecomer" was written all over me, I sensed that I was an embarrassment, too; my appearance, my survival, my bleeding gums and loose teeth, my chronic dysentery and anemia, my craving for sweets, my reticence with strangers, the cast-off rags I had worn on arrival, all said "war" when everyone wanted peace, "captivity" when the word was "freedom," and "dry bread" when everyone was thinking "jam and butter." I guessed that now, after five years of peace, most of the population must have elbowed onto the right step of the right staircase and that there was not much room left for pedestrian-traffic residue.

My mother came in to clean the tub after I was partly dressed. She used fine ash from the stove and a cloth so full of holes it had to be rolled into a ball. She said, "I called out to you but you didn't hear. I thought you had fallen asleep and drowned."

I was hard of hearing because of the anti-aircraft duty to which I'd been posted in Berlin while I was still in high school. After the boys were sent to the front, girls took our places. It was those girls, still in their adolescence, who defended the grown men in uniform down in the bunkers. I wondered if they had been deafened, too, and if we were a generation who would never hear anything under a shout. My mother knelt by the tub, and I sat on Martin's chair, like Martin, pulling on clean socks she had brought me. In a low voice, which I heard perfectly, she said that I had known Martin in my childhood. I said I had not. She said then that my father had known him. I stood up and waited until she rose from her knees, and I looked down at her face. I was afraid of touching her, in case we should both cry. She muttered that her family must surely have known him, for the Toepplers had a burial plot not far from the graveyard where my grandmother lay buried, and some thirty miles from where my father's father had a bakery once. She was looking for any kind of a link.

"I wanted you and Chris to have a place to stay when you came back," she said, but I believed she had not expected to see either of us again and that she had been afraid of being homeless and alone. My brother had vanished in Czechoslovakia with the Schörner army. All of that army had been given up for dead. My Uncle Gerhard, her only close relative, could not have helped her even if it had occurred to him; it had taken him four years to become officially and legally de-Nazified, and now, "as white as a white lilac," according to my mother, he had no opinions about anything and lived only for his rabbits.

"It is nice to have a companion at my age," my mother said. "Someone to talk to." Did the old need more than conversation? My mother must have been about forty-two then. I had heard the old men in prison camp comparing their wives and saying that no hen was ever too tough for boiling.

"Did you marry him before or after he had this apartment?"

"After." But she had hesitated, as if wondering what I wanted to hear.

The apartment was on the second floor of a large dark block—all that was left of a workers' housing project of the nineteen-twenties. Martin had once lived somewhere between the bathroom window and the street. Looking out, I could easily replace the back walls of the vanished houses, and the small balconies festooned with brooms and mops, and the moist oily courtyard. Winter twilight must have been the prevailing climate here until an air raid let the seasons in. Cinders and gravel had been raked evenly over the crushed masonry now; the broad concourse between the surviving house—ours—and the road beyond it that was edged with ruins looked solid and flat.

But no, it was all shaky and loose, my mother said. Someone ought to cause a cement walk to be laid down; the women were always twisting their ankles, and when it rained you walked in black mud, and there was a smell of burning. She had not lost her belief in an invisible but well-intentioned "someone." She then said, in a hushed and whispery voice, that Martin's first wife, Elke, was down there under the rubble and cinders. It had been impossible to get all the bodies out, and one day a bulldozer covered them over for all time. Martin had inherited those two apartments in a town in Franconia from Elke. The Toepplers were probably just as poor as the Bestermanns, but Martin had made a good marriage.

"She had a dog, too," said my mother. "When Martin married her she had a white spitz. She gave it a bath in the bathtub every Sunday." I thought of Martin Toeppler crossing this new wide treacherous front court and saying, "Elke's grave. Ah, yes, yes." I said it, and my mother suddenly laughed loudly and dropped her hand, and I saw that some of her front teeth were missing.

"The house looks like an old tooth when you see it from the street," she said, as though deliberately calling attention to the very misfortune she wanted to hide. She knew nothing about the people who had lived in this apartment, except that they had left in a hurry, forgetting to pack a large store of black-market food, some pretty ornaments in a china cabinet, and five bottles of wine. "They left without paying the rent," she said, which didn't sound like her.

It turned out to be a joke of Martin Toeppler's. He repeated it when I came back to the parlor wearing a shirt that I supposed must be his, and with my hair dark and wet and combed flat. He pointed to a bright rectangle on the brown wallpaper. "That is where they took Adolf's picture down," he said. "When they left in a hurry without paying the rent."

My father had been stabbed to death one night when he was caught tearing an election poster off the schoolhouse wall. He left my mother with no money, two children under the age of five, and a political reputation. After that she swam with the current. I had worn a uniform of one kind or another most of my life until now. I remembered wearing civilian clothes once, when I was fourteen, for my confirmation. I had felt disguised, and wondered what to do with my hands; from the age of seven I had stuck my thumbs in a leather belt. I had impressions, not memories, of my father. Pictures were frozen things; they told me nothing. But I knew that when my hair was wet I looked something like him. A quick flash would come back out of a mirror, like a secret message, and I would think, There, that is how he was. I sat with Martin at the table, where my mother had spread a lace cloth (the vanished tenants') and over which the April sun through lace curtains laid still another design. I placed my hands flat under lace shadows and wondered if they were like my father's, too.

She had put out everything she could find to eat and drink—a few sweet biscuits, cheese cut almost as thin as paper, dark bread, small whole tomatoes, radishes, slices of salami arranged in a floral design on a dish to make them seem more. We had a bottle of fizzy wine that Martin called champagne. It had a brown tint, like watered iodine, and a taste of molasses. Through this murk bubbles climbed. We raised our glasses without saying what we drank to, other than my return. Perhaps Martin drank to his destiny in Franconia with the two apartments. I had a plan, but it was my own secret. By a common accord, there was no mutual past. Then my mother spoke from behind the cupped hand and said she would like us to drink to her missing elder son. She looked at Martin as she said this, in case the survival of Chris might be a burden, too.

Toward the end of that afternoon, a neighbor came in with a bottle of brandy—a stout man with three locks of slick grey hair across his skull. All the fat men of comic stories and of literature were to be Willy Wehler to me, in the future. But he could not have been all that plump in Berlin in 1950; his chin probably showed the beginnings of softness, and his hair must have been dark still, and there must have been plenty of it. I can see the start of his baldness, the two deep peninsulas of polished skin running from the corners of his forehead to just above his ears. Willy Wehler was another Franconian. He and Martin began speaking in dialect almost at once. Willy was at a remove, however—he mispronounced words as though to be funny, and he would grin and look at me. This was to say that he knew better, and he knew that I knew. Martin and Willy hated Berlin. They sounded as if they had been dragged to Berlin against their will, like displaced persons. In their eyes the deepest failure of a certain political authority was that it had enticed peace-loving persons with false promises of work, homes, pensions, lives afloat like little boats at anchor; now these innocent provincials saw they had been tricked, and they were going back where they had started from.

It was as simple to them as that—the equivalent of an insurance company's no longer meeting its obligations. Willy even described the life he would lead now in a quiet town, where, in sight of a cobbled square with a fountain and an equestrian statue, he planned to open a perfume-and-cosmetics shop; people wanted beauty now. He would live above the shop—he was not too proud for that—and every morning he would look down on his blue store awnings, over window boxes stuffed with frilled petunias. My stepfather heard this with tears in his eyes, but perhaps he was thinking of his two apartments and of Elke and the spitz. Willy's future seemed so real, so close at hand, that it was almost as though he had dropped in to say goodbye. He sat with his daughter on his knees, a baby not yet three. This little girl, whose name was Gisela, became a part of my life from that afternoon, and so did fat Willy, though none of us knew it then. The secret to which I had drunk my silent toast was a girl in France, who would be a middle-aged woman, beyond my imagining now, if she had lived. She died by jumping or accidentally falling out of a fifth-floor window in Paris. Her parents had locked her in a room when they found out she was corresponding with me.

This was still an afternoon in April in Berlin, the first of my freedom. It was one day after old Adolf's birthday, but that was not mentioned, not even in dialect or in the form of a Berlin joke. I don't think they were avoiding it; they had simply forgotten. They would always be astonished when other people turned out to have more specific memories of time and events.

This was the afternoon about which I would always say to myself, "I should have known," and even "I knew"—knew that I would marry the baby whose movements were already so willful and quick that her father complained, "We can't take her anywhere," and sat holding both her small hands in his; otherwise she would have clutched at every glass within reach. Her winged brows reminded me of the girl I wanted to see again. Gisela's eyes were amber in color, and luminous, with the whites so pure they seemed blue. The girl in France had eyes that resembled dark petals, opaque and velvety, and slightly tilted. She had black hair from a Corsican grandmother, and long fine lashes. Gisela's lashes were stubby and thick. I found that I was staring at the child's small ears and her small perfect teeth, thinking all the while of the other girl, whose smile had been spoiled by the malnutrition and the poor dentistry of the Occupation. I should have realized then, as I looked at Willy and his daughter, that some people never go without milk and eggs and apples, whatever the landscape, and that the sparse feast on our table had more to do with my mother's long habit of poverty—a kind of fatalistic incompetence that came from never having had enough money—than with a real shortage of food. Willy had on a white nylon shirt, which was a luxury then. Later, Martin would say to me, "That Willy! Out of a black uniform and into the black market before you could say 'democracy,'" but I never knew whether it was a common Berlin joke or something Martin had made up or the truth about Willy.

Gisela, who was either slow to speak for her age or only lazy, looked at me and said, "Man"—all she had to declare. Her hair was so silky and fine that it reflected the day as a curve of mauve light. She was all light and sheen, and she was the first person—I can even say the first *thing*—I had ever seen that was unflawed, without shadow. She was as whole and as innocent as a drop of water, and she was without guilt.

Her hands, released when her father drank from his wineglass, patted the tablecloth, seized a radish, tried to stuff it in his mouth.

My mother sat with her chair pushed back a few respectful inches. "Do you like children, Thomas?" she said. She knew nothing about me now except that I was not a child.

The French girl was sixteen when she came to Brittany on a holiday with her father and mother. The next winter she sent me books so that I would not drop too far behind in my schooling, and the second summer she came to my room. The door to the room was in a bend of the staircase, halfway between the pharmacy on the ground floor and the flat where my employers lived. They were supposed to keep me locked in this room when I wasn't working, but the second summer they forgot or could not be bothered, and in any case I had made a key with a piece of wire by then. It was the first room I'd had to myself. I whitewashed the walls and boxed in the store of potatoes they kept on the floor in a corner. Bunches of wild plants and herbs the druggist used in prescriptions hung from hooks in the ceiling. One whole wall was taken up with shelves of drying leaves and roots—walnut leaves for treating anemia, camomile for fainting spells, thyme and rosemary for muscular cramps, and nettles and mint, sage and dandelions. The fragrance in the room and the view of the port from the window could have given me almost enough happiness for a lifetime, except that I was too young to find any happiness in that.

How she escaped from her parents the first afternoon I never knew, but she was a brave, careless girl and had already escaped from them often. They must have known what could happen when they locked that wild spirit into a place where the only way out was a window. Perhaps they were trying to see how far they could go with a margin of safety. She left a message for them: "To teach you a lesson." She must have thought she would be there and not there, lost to them and yet able to see the result. There was no message for me, except that it is a terrible thing to be alone; but I had already learned it. She must have knelt on the windowsill. The autumn rain must have caught her lashes and hair. She was already alien on the windowsill, beyond recognition.

I had made my room as neat for her as though I were expecting a military inspection. I wondered if she knew how serious it would be for both of us if we were caught. She glanced at the view, but only to see if anyone could look in on us, and she laughed, starting to take off her pullover, arms crossed; then stopped and said, "What is it— are you made of ice?" How could she know that I was retarded? I had known nothing except imagination and solitude, and the preying of old soldiers; and I was too old for one and repelled by the other. I thought she was about to commit the sacrifice of her person—her physical self and her immortal soul. I had heard the old men talking about women as if women were dirt, but needed for "that." One man said he would cut off an ear for "that." Another said he would swim the Atlantic. I thought she would lie in some way convenient to me and that she would feel nothing but a kind of sorrow, which would have made it a pure gift. But there was nothing to ask; it was not a gift. It was her decision and not a gift but an adventure. She hadn't come here to look at the harbor, she told me, when I hesitated. I may even have said, "No," and it might have been then that she smiled at me over crossed arms, pulling off her sweater, and said, "Are you made of ice?" For all her jauntiness, she thought she was deciding her life, though she continued to use the word "adventure." I think it was the only other word she knew for "love." But all we were settling was her death, and my life was decided in Berlin when Willy Wehler came in with a bottle of brandy and Gisela, who refused to say more than "Man." I can still see the lace curtains, the mark on the wallpaper, the china ornaments left by the people who had gone in such a hurry—the chimney sweep with his matchstick broom, the girl with bobbed orange hair sitting on a crescent moon, the dog with the ruff around his neck—and when I remember this I say to myself, "I must have known."

We finished two bottles of Martin's champagne, and then my mother jumped to her feet to remove the glasses and bring others so that we could taste Willy Wehler's brandy.

"The dirty Belgian is still hanging around," he said to Martin, gently rocking the child, who now had her thumb in her mouth.

"What does he want?" said my stepfather. He repeated the question; he was slow and he thought that other people, unless they reacted at once and with a show of feeling, could not hear him.

"He was in the Waffen-S.S.—he says. He complains that the girls here won't go out with him, though only five or six years ago they were like flies."

"They are afraid of him," came my mother's timid voice. "He stands in the court and stares . . ."

"I don't like men who look at pure young girls," said Willy Wehler. "He said to me, 'Help me; you owe me help.' He says he fought for us and nobody thanked him."

"He did? No wonder we lost," said Martin. I had already seen that the survivors of the war were divided into those who said they had always known how it would all turn out and those who said they had been indifferent. There are also those who like wars and those who do not. Martin had never been committed to winning or to losing or to anything—that explained his jokes. He had gained two apartments and one requisitioned flat in Berlin. He had lost a wife, but he often said to me later that people were better off out of this world.

"In·Belgium he was in jail," said Willy. "He says he fought for us and then he was in jail and now we won't help him and the girls won't speak to him."

"Why is he here?" my stepfather suddenly shouted. "Who let him in? All this is his own affair, not ours." He rocked in his chair in a peculiar way, perhaps only imitating the gentle motion Willy made to keep Gisela asleep and quiet. "Nobody owes him anything," cried my stepfather, striking the table so that the little girl started and shuddered. My mother touched his arm and made a sort of humming sound, with her lips pressed together, that I took to be a signal between them, for he at once switched to another topic. It was a theme of conversation I was to hear about for many years after that afternoon. It was what the old men had to say when they were not boasting about women or their own past, and it was this: What should the Schörner army have done in Czechoslovakia to avoid capture by the Russians, and why did General Eisenhower (the villain of the story) refuse to help?

Eisenhower was my stepfather's left hand, General Schörner was his right, and the Russians were a plate of radishes. I turned very slightly to look at my mother. She had that sad cast of feature women have when their eyes are fixed nowhere. Her hand still lay lightly on Martin Toeppler's sleeve. I supposed then that he really was her husband and that they slept in the same bed. I had seen one or two closed doors in the passage on my way to the bath. Of my first prison camp, where everyone had been under eighteen or over forty, I remembered the smell of the old men—how they stopped being clean when there were no women to make them wash—and I remembered their long boasting. And yet, that April afternoon, as the sunlight of my first hours of freedom moved over the table and up along the brown wall, I did my boasting, too. I told about a prisoner I had captured. It seemed to be the thing I had to say to two men I had never seen before.

"He landed in a field just outside my grandmother's village," I told them. "I was fourteen. Three of us saw him—three boys. We had French rifles captured in the 1870 war. He'd had time to fold his parachute and he was sitting on it. I knew only one thing in English; it was 'Hands up.'"

My stepfather's mouth was open, as it had been when I first walked into the flat that day. My mother stood just out of sight.

"We advanced, pointing our 1870 rifles," I went on, droning, just like the old prisoners of war. "We all now said, 'Hands up.' The prisoner just—" I made the gesture the American had made, of chasing a fly away, and I realized I was drunk. "He didn't stand up. He had put everything he had on the ground—a revolver, a wad of German money, a handkerchief with a map of Germany, and some smaller things we couldn't identify at once. He had on civilian shoes with thick soles. He very slowly undid his watch and handed it over, but we had no ruling about that, so we said no. He put the watch on the ground next to the revolver and the map. Then he slowly got up and strolled into the village, with his hands in his pockets. He was chewing gum. I saw he had kept his cigarettes, but I didn't know the rule about that, either. We kept our guns trained on him. The schoolmaster ran out of my grandmother's guesthouse—everyone ran to stare. He was excited and kept saying in English, 'How do you do? How do you do?' but then an officer came running, too, and he was screaming, 'Why are you interfering? You may ask only one thing: Is he English or American.' The teacher was glad to show off his English, and he asked, 'Are you English or American?' and the American seemed to move his tongue all round his mouth before he answered. He was the first foreigner any of us had ever seen, and they took him away from us. We never saw him again."

That seemed all there was to it, but Martin's mouth was still open. I tried to remember more. "There was hell because we had left the gun and the other things on the ground. By the time they got out to the field, someone had stolen the parachute—probably for the cloth. We were in trouble over that, and we never got credit for having taken a prisoner. I went back to the field alone later on. I wanted to cry, for some reason—because it was over. He was from an adventure story to me. The whole war was a Karl May adventure, when I was fourteen and running around in school holidays with a gun. I found some small things in the field that had been overlooked —pills for keeping awake, pills in transparent envelopes. I had never seen that before One envelope was called 'motion sickness.' It was a crime to keep anything, but I kept it anyway. I still had it when the Americans captured me, and they took it away. I had kept it because it was from another world. I would look at it and wonder. I kept it because of *The Last of the Mohicans,* because, because."

This was the longest story I had ever told in my life. I added, "My grandmother is dead now." My stepfather had finally shut his mouth. He looked at my mother as if to say that she had brought him a rival in the only domain that mattered—the right to talk everyone's ear off. My mother edged close to Willy Wehler and urged him to eat bread and cheese. She was still in the habit of wondering what the other person thought and how important he might be and how safe it was to speak. But Willy had not heard more than a sentence or two. That was plain from the way the expression on his face came slowly awake. He opened his eyes wide, as if to get sleep out of them, and —evidently imagining I had been talking about my life in France— said, "What were you paid as a prisoner?"

I had often wondered what the first question would be once I was home. Now I had it.

"Ha!" said my stepfather, giving the impression that he expected me to be caught out in a monstrous lie.

"One franc forty centimes a month for working here and there on a farm," I said. "But when I became a free worker with a druggist the official pay was three thousand francs a month, and that was what he gave me." I paused. "And of course I was fed and housed and had no laundry bills."

"Did you have bedsheets?" said my mother.

"With the druggist's family, always. I had one sheet folded in half. It was just right for a small cot."

"Was it the same sheet as the kind the family had?" she said, in the hesitant way that was part of her person now.

"They didn't buy sheets especially for me," I said. "I was treated fairly by the druggist, but not by the administration."

"Ah ha," said the two older men, almost together.

"The administration refused to pay my fare home," I said, looking down into my glass the way I had seen the men in prison camp stare at a fixed point when they were recounting a grievance.

"A prisoner of war has the right to be repatriated at administration expense. The administration would not pay my fare because I had stayed too long in France—but that was their mistake. I bought a ticket as far as Paris on the pay I had saved. The druggist sold me some old shoes and trousers and a jacket of his. My own things were in rags. In Paris I went to the Y.M.C.A. The Y.M.C.A. was supposed to be in charge of prisoners' rights. The man wouldn't listen to me. If I had been left behind, then I was not a prisoner, he said; I was a tourist. It was his duty to help me. Instead of that, he informed the police." For the first time my voice took on the coloration of resentment. I knew that this complaint about a niggling matter of train fare made my whole adventure seem small, but I had become an old soldier. I remembered the police commissioner, with his thin lips and dirty nails, who said, "You should have been repatriated years ago, when you were sixteen."

"It was a mistake," I told him.

"Your papers are full of strange mistakes," he said, bending over them. "There, one capital error. An omission, a grave omission. What is your mother's maiden name?"

"Wickler," I said.

I watched him writing "W-i-e-c-k-l-a-i-r," slowly, with the tip of his tongue sticking out of the corner of his mouth as he wrote. "You have been here for something like five years with an incomplete dossier. And what about this? Who crossed it out?"

"I did. My father was not a pastry cook."

"You could be fined or even jailed for this," he said.

"My father was not a pastry cook," I said. "He had tuberculosis. He was not allowed to handle food."

Willy Wehler did not say what he thought of my story. Perhaps not having any opinion about injustice, even the least important, had become a habit of his, like my mother's of speaking through her fingers. He was on the right step of that staircase I've spoken of. Even the name he had given his daughter was a sign of his sensitivity to the times. Nobody wanted to hear the pagan, Old Germanic names anymore—Sigrun and Brunhilde and Sieglinde. Willy had felt the change. He would have called any daughter something neutral and pretty—Gisela, Marianne, Elisabeth—any time after the battle of Stalingrad. All Willy ever had to do was sniff the air.

He pushed back his chair (in later years he would be able to push a table away with his stomach) and got to his feet. He had to tip his head to look up into my eyes. He said he wanted to give me advice that would be useful to me as a latehomecomer. His advice was to forget. "Forget everything," he said. "Forget, forget. That was what I said to my good neighbor Herr Silber when I bought his wife's topaz brooch and earrings before he emigrated to Palestine. I said, 'Dear Herr Silber, look forward, never back, and forget, forget, forget.' "

The child in Willy's arms was in the deepest of sleeps. Martin Toeppler followed his friend to the door, they whispered together; then the door closed behind both men.

"They have gone to have a glass of something at Herr Wehler's," said my mother. I saw now that she was crying quietly. She dried her eyes on her apron and began clearing the table of the homecoming feast. "Willy Wehler has been kind to us," she said. "Don't repeat that thing."

"About forgetting?"

"No, about the topaz brooch. It was a crime to buy anything from Jews."

"It doesn't matter now."

She lowered the tray she held and looked pensively out at the wrecked houses across the street. "If only people knew beforehand what was allowed," she said.

"My father is probably a hero now," I said.

"Oh, Thomas, don't travel too fast. We haven't seen the last of the changes. Yes, a hero. But too late for me. I've suffered too much."

"What does Martin think that he died of?"

"A working accident. He can understand that."

"You could have said consumption. He did have it." She shook her head. Probably she had not wanted Martin to imagine he could ever be saddled with two sickly stepsons. "Where do you and Martin sleep?"

"In the room next to the bathroom. Didn't you see it? You'll be comfortable here in the parlor. The couch pulls out. You can stay as long as you like. This is your home. A home for you and Chris." She said this so stubbornly that I knew some argument must have taken place between her and Martin.

I intended this room to be my home. There was no question about it in my mind. I had not yet finished high school; I had been taken out for anti-aircraft duty, then sent to the front. The role of adolescents in uniform had been to try to prevent the civilian population from surrendering. We were expected to die in the ruins together. When the women ran pillowcases up flagpoles, we shinnied up to drag them down. We were prepared to hold the line with our 1870 rifles until we saw the American tanks. There had not been tanks in our Karl May adventure stories, and the Americans, finally, were not out of *The Last of the Mohicans.* I told my mother that I had to go back to high school and then I would apply for a scholarship and take a degree in French. I would become a schoolmaster. French was all I had from my captivity; I might as well use it. I would earn money doing translations.

That cheered her up. She would not have to ask the ex-tram conductor too many favors. "Translations" and "scholarship" were an exalted form of language, to her. As a schoolmaster, I would have the most respectable job in the family, now that Uncle Gerhard was raising rabbits. "As long as it doesn't cost *him* too much," she said, as if she had to say it and yet was hoping I wouldn't hear.

It was not strictly true that all I had got out of my captivity was the ability to speak French. I had also learned to cook, iron, make beds, wait on table, wash floors, polish furniture, plant a vegetable garden, paint shutters. I wanted to help my mother in the kitchen now, but that shocked her. "Rest," she said, but I did not know what "rest" meant. "I've never seen a man drying a glass," she said, in apology. I wanted to tell her that while the roads and bridges of France were still waiting for someone to rebuild them I had been taught how to make a tomato salad by the druggist's wife; but I could not guess what the word "France" conveyed to her imagination. I began walking about the apartment. I looked in on a store cupboard, a water closet smelling of carbolic, the bathroom again, then a room containing a high bed, a brown wardrobe, and a table covered with newspapers bearing half a dozen of the flowerless spiky dull green plants my mother had always tended with so much devotion. I shut the door as if on a dark past, and I said to myself, "I am free. This is the beginning of life. It is also the start of the good half of a rotten century. Everything ugly and corrupt and vicious is behind us." My thoughts were not exactly in those words, but something like them. I said to myself, "This apartment has a musty smell, an old and dirty smell that sinks into clothes. After a time I shall probably smell like the dark parlor. The smell must be in the cushions, in the bed that pulls out, in the lace curtains. It is a smell that creeps into night-clothes. The blankets will be permeated." I thought, I shall get used to the smell, and the smell of burning in the stone outside. The view of ruins will be my view. Every day on my way home from school I shall walk over Elke. I shall get used to the wood staircase, the bellpull, the polished nameplate, the white enamel fuses in the hall —my mother had said, "When you want light in the parlor you give the center fuse in the lower row a half turn." I looked at a framed drawing of cartoon people with puffy hair. A strong wind had blown their umbrella inside out. They would be part of my view, like the ruins. I took in the ancient gas bracket in the kitchen and the stone sink. My mother, washing glasses without soap, smiled at me, forgetting to hide her teeth. I reëxamined the tiled stove in the parlor, the wood and the black briquettes that would be next to my head at night, and the glass-fronted cabinet full of the china ornaments God had selected to survive the Berlin air raids. These would be removed to make way for my books. For Martin Toeppler need not imagine he could count on my pride, or that I would prefer to starve rather than take his charity, or that I was too arrogant to sleep on his dusty sofa. I would wear out his soap, borrow his shirts, spread his butter on my bread. I would hang on Martin like an octopus. He had a dependent now—a ravenous, egocentric, latehomecoming high-school adolescent of twenty-one. The old men owed this much to me —the old men in my prison camp who would have sold mother and father for an extra ounce of soup, who had already sold their children for it; the old men who had fouled my idea of women; the old men in the bunkers who had let the girls defend them in Berlin; the old men who had dared to survive.

The bed that pulled out was sure to be all lumps. I had slept on worse. Would it be wide enough for Chris, too?

People in the habit of asking themselves silent useless questions look for answers in mirrors. My hair was blond again now that it had dried. I looked less like my idea of my father. I tried to see the reflection of the man who had gone out in the middle of the night and who never came back. You don't go out alone to tear down election posters in a village where nobody thinks as you do—not unless you *want* to be stabbed in the back. So the family had said.

"You were well out of it," I said to the shadow that floated on the glass panel of the china cabinet, though it would not be my father's again unless I could catch it unaware.

I said to myself, "It is quieter than France. They keep their radios low."

In captivity I had never suffered a pain except for the cramps of hunger the first years, which had been replaced by a scratching, morbid anxiety, and the pain of homesickness, which takes you in the stomach and the throat. Now I felt the first of the real pains that were to follow me like little dogs for the rest of my life, perhaps: the first compressed my knee, the second tangled the nerves at the back of my neck. I discovered that my eyes were sensitive and that it hurt to blink.

This was the hour when, in Brittany, I would begin peeling the potatoes for dinner. I had seen food my mother had never heard of —oysters, and artichokes. My mother had never seen a harbor or a sea.

My American prisoner had left his immediate life spread on an alien meadow—his parachute, his revolver, his German money. He had strolled into captivity with his hands in his pockets.

"I know what you are thinking," said my mother, who was standing behind me. "I know that you are judging me. If you could guess what my life has been—the whole story, not only the last few years—you wouldn't be hard on me."

I turned too slowly to meet her eyes. It was not what I had been thinking. I had forgotten about her, in that sense.

"No, no, nothing like that," I said. I still did not touch her. What I had been moving along to in my mind was: Why am I in this place? Who sent me here? Is it a form of justice or injustice? How long does it last?

"Now we can wait together for Chris," she said. She seemed young and happy all at once. "Look, Thomas. A new moon. Bow to it three times. Wait—you must have something silver in your hand." I saw that she was hurrying to finish with this piece of nonsense before Martin came back. She rummaged in the china cabinet and brought out a silver napkin ring—left behind by the vanished tenants, probably. The name on it was "Meta"—no one we knew. "Bow to the moon and hold it and make your wish," she said. "Quickly."

"You first."

She wished, I am sure, for my brother. As for me, I wished that I was a few hours younger, in the corridor of a packed train, clutching the top of the open window, my heart hammering as I strained to find the one beloved face.

BAUM, GABRIEL,
1935 – ( )

Uncle August

At the start of the nineteen-sixties Gabriel Baum's only surviving relative, his Uncle August, turned up in Paris. There was nothing accidental about this; the International Red Cross, responding to an appeal for search made on Gabriel's behalf many years before, had finally found Gabriel in Montparnasse and his uncle in the Argentine. Gabriel thought of his uncle as "the other Baum," because there were just the two of them. Unlike Gabriel's father and mother, Uncle August had got out of Europe in plenty of time. He owned garages in Rosario and Santa Fe and commercial real estate in Buenos Aires. He was as different from Gabriel as a tree is from the drawing of one; nevertheless Gabriel saw in him something of the old bachelor he too might become.

Gabriel was now twenty-five; he had recently been discharged from the French army after twenty months in Algeria. Notice of his uncle's arrival reached him at the theatre seating two hundred persons where he had a part in a play about J. K. Huysmans. The play explained

Huysmans' progress from sullen naturalism to mystical Christianity. Gabriel had to say, "But Joris Karl has written words of penetrating psychology," and four or five other things.

The two Baums dined at the Bristol, where Gabriel's uncle was staying. His uncle ordered for both, because Gabriel was taking too long to decide. Uncle August spoke German and Spanish and the pale scrupulous French and English that used to be heard at spas and in the public rooms of large, airy hotels. His clothes were old-fashioned British; watch and luggage were Swiss. His manners were German, prewar—pre-1914, that is. To Gabriel, his uncle seemed to conceal an obsolete social mystery; but a few Central Europeans, still living, would have placed him easily as a tight, unyielding remainder of the European shipwreck.

The old man observed Gabriel closely, watching to see how his orphaned nephew had been brought up, whether he broke his bread or cut it, with what degree of confidence he approached his asparagus. He was certainly pleased to have discovered a younger Baum and may even have seen Gabriel as part of God's subtle design, bringing a surrogate son to lighten his old age, one to whom he could leave Baum garages; on the other hand it was clear that he did not want just any Baum calling him "Uncle."

"I have a name," he said to Gabriel. "I have a respected name to protect. I owe it to my late father." He meant his own name: August Ernest Baum, b. Potsdam 1899– (   ).

After dinner they sat for a long time drinking brandy in the hushed dining room. His uncle was paying for everything.

He said, "But were your parents ever married, finally? Because we were never told he had actually *married* her."

Gabriel at that time seemed to himself enduringly healthy and calm. His hair, which was dark and abundant, fell in locks on a surprisingly serene forehead. He suffered from only two complaints, which he had never mentioned. The first had to do with his breathing, which did not proceed automatically, like other people's. Sometimes, feeling strange and ill, he would realize that heart and lungs were suspended on a stopped, held breath. Nothing disastrous had come of this. His second complaint was that he seemed to be haunted, or inhabited, by a child—a small, invisible version of himself, a Gabriel whose mauled pride he was called on to salve, whose claims against life he was forced to meet with whatever thin means time provided, whose scores he had rashly promised to settle before realizing that debt and payment never interlock. His uncle's amazing question and the remark that followed it awoke the wild child, who began to hammer on Gabriel's heart.

He fixed his attention on a bottle—one of the dark bottles whose labels bear facsimiles of gold medals earned at exhibitions no one has ever heard of, in cities whose names have been swept off the map: Breslau 1884, Dantzig 1897, St. Petersburg 1901.

"The only time I ever saw her, they certainly were not married," his uncle resumed. "It was during the very hot autumn of nineteen-thirty. He had left the university announcing that he would earn his living writing satirical poetry. My father sent me to Berlin to see what was going on. *She* was going on. Her dress had short sleeves. She wore no stockings. She had a clockwork bear she kept winding up and sending round the table. She was hopelessly young. 'Have you thought about the consequences?' I asked him. 'No degree. Low-grade employment all your life. Your father's door forever closed to you. And what about *her?* Is she an heiress? Will her father adopt you?' She was said to be taking singing lessons," he added, as if there were something wrong with that.

"Shut him up," ordered the younger Gabriel, but Gabriel was struggling for breath.

"I have lost everything and everyone but I still have a name," said his uncle. "I have a name to protect and defend. There is always the trace of a marriage certificate somewhere. Even when the registry office was bombed. Even when the papers had to be left behind. How old were you the last time you saw them?"

"Eight," said Gabriel, now in control.

"Were they together?"

"Oh, yes."

"Did they have time to say goodbye?"

"They left me with a neighbor. The neighbor said they'd be back."

"Where was this?"

"Marseilles. We were supposed to be from Alsace, but their French sounded wrong. People noticed I wasn't going to school. Someone reported them."

"Sounded wrong!" said his uncle. "Everything must have sounded wrong from the minute he left the university. It is a terrible story," he said, after a moment. "No worse than most, but terrible all the same. Why, why did he wait until the last minute? And once he had got to Marseilles what prevented him from getting on a boat?"

"He was a man of action," said Gabriel.

If his uncle wanted another Baum, he did not want a frivolous one. He said, "He was much younger than I was. I never saw him after nineteen-thirty. He went his own way. After the war I had the family traced. Everybody was dead—camps, suicide, old age. In his case, no one knew what had happened. He disappeared. Of course, it took place in a foreign country. Only the Germans kept accurate records. I wish you knew something about the marriage. I know that my late father would not have wanted a bastard in the family."

Uncle August visited Nice, Lugano, and Venice, which he found greatly changed, then he returned to South America. He sent long letters to Gabriel several times a year, undeterred by the fact that he seldom received an answer. He urged his nephew to take a strong, positive line with his life and above all to get out of Paris, which had never amounted to more than an émigré way station. Its moral climate invited apathy and rot.

Gabriel read his uncle's letters in La Méduse, a *bar-tabac* close to the old Montparnasse railway station. Actors and extras for television were often recruited there; no one remembered how or why this arrangement had come about. Gabriel usually sat with his back to the window, at a table to the right of the door facing the bar. He drank draught beer or coffee and looked at magazines other customers had left behind. Glancing up from one of his uncle's letters, he saw the misted window in the mirror behind the bar. In a polluted winter fog neon glowed warmly—the lights of home.

His uncle wrote that he had liquidated his holdings at a loss and was thinking of settling in South Africa. He must have changed his mind, for a subsequent letter described him retired and living near a golf course, looked after by the housekeeper he had often told

Gabriel about—his first mention of any such person. A heart attack made it tiring for him to write. The housekeeper sent news. Gabriel, who did not know Spanish, tried to get the drift. She signed "Anna Meléndes," then "Anna Baum."

Gabriel was playing a Brecht season in a suburban cultural center when word came that his uncle had died. *The Caucasian Chalk Circle* and *Mother Courage* alternated for an audience of schoolchildren and factory workers brought in by the busload, apparently against their will. Gabriel thought of Uncle August, his obstinacy and his pride, and truly mourned him. His uncle had left him an envelope he did not bother to open, being fairly certain it did not contain a check.

No Baum memorial existed, and so he invented one. Upon its marble surface he inscribed:

Various Baums:	Gone
Father:	1909 – 1943 (probably)
Mother:	1912 – 1943 (probably)
Uncle:	1899 – 1977
Gabriel B.:	1935 – ( )

Beneath the last name he drew a line, meaning to say this was the end. He saw, however, that the line, far from ending the Baum question, created a new difficulty: it left the onlooker feeling that these dates and names were factors awaiting a solution. He needed to add the dead to the living, or subtract the living from the dead —to come to some conclusion.

He thought of writing a zero, but the various Baums plus four others did not add up to nothing. His uncle by dying had not diminished the total number of Baums but had somehow increased it. Gabriel, with his feet on the finish line and with uncounted Baums behind him, was a variable quantity: for some years he had been the last of the Baums, then there had been two of them. Now he was unique again.

Someone else would have to work it out, he decided—someone unknown to him, perhaps unborn. In the meantime he had the memorial in his head, where it could not be lost or stolen.

Gabriel's Liselotte

Soon after Gabriel's uncle's visit, a generation of extremely pretty German girls suddenly blossomed in Paris. There would be just that one flowering—that one bright growth. They came because their fathers were dead or exiled under unremarkable names. Some of them were attracted to Gabriel—Gabriel as he was, with the dark locks, the serene brow—and he was drawn in turn, as to a blurred reflection, a face half-recalled.

Gabriel at that time still imagined that everyone's life must be about the same, something like a half-worked crossword puzzle. He was always on the lookout for definitions and new solutions. When he moved close to other people, however, he saw that their lives were not puzzles but problems set in code, no two of which ever matched.

The pretty girls went home, finally, whistled back by solemn young men with solemn jobs. They had two children apiece, were probably rinsing the gray out of their hair now. (Gabriel cut his own as short as possible as it grew scarce.) He remembered Freya, who had thrown herself in the Seine over a married man, but who could swim, and Barbara, whose abortion two or three of them had felt bound to pay for, and Marie, who had gone to Alsace and had nearly been crowned Miss Upper Rhine before they found out she was a foreigner. Gabriel's memory dodging behind one name after the other brought him face-to-face with his Liselotte. Daughter of a dead man and a whore of a mother (which seemed to be a standard biography then), embarked on the au-pair adventure, pursuing spiritual cleanness through culture, she could be seen afternoons in Parc Monceau reading books of verse whose close print and shoddy bindings seemed to assure a cultural warranty. There was something meek about the curve of her neck. She had heard once that if one were arrested and held without trial it was an aid to sanity to have an anthology of poems in one's head. Poor Liselotte, whose aid to sanity never got beyond "Le ciel est, par-dessus le toit, Si bleu, si calme!," held the book flat on her knees, following the words with her finger.

"Who would want to arrest you?" Gabriel asked.

"You never know."

Well, that was true. Thinking there might be a better career for her he gave her lines to try. She practiced, "Is it tonight that you DIE?" "Is it TONIGHT that YOU die?" Gabriel counted six, seven, eight shades of green around the place in Parc Monceau, where she sat asking this. He used to take the No. 84 bus to see her—he who never went out of Montparnasse unless he had to, who had never bothered to learn about bus routes or the names of streets. For the sake of Liselotte he crossed the Seine with prim, gloved women, with old men wearing slivers of ribbon to mark this or that war. Liselotte, now seeking improvement by way of love, made him speak French to her. She heard, memorized, and recited back to him without flaw his life's story. He had promised the child-Gabriel he would never marry a German, but it was not that simple; in an odd way she did not seem German *enough.*

She had learned her lines for nothing. The director he introduced her to also thought she did not look German. She was one of the brown-eyed Catholic girls from around Speyer. She prayed for Gabriel, but his life after the prayers was the same as before. She had a catch in her voice, almost a stammer; she tried to ask Gabriel if he wanted to marry her, but the word caught. He said to himself that she might not enjoy being Liselotte Baum after having been Liselotte Pfligge. Her stepfather, Wilhelm Pfligge—of Swiss origin, she said—had tried to rape her; still, she had his name. Gabriel thought that if the custom of name-changing had been reversed and he had been required, through marriage, to become Gabriel Pfligge, he might have done so without cringing, or at least with tact. Perhaps he would have been expected to call Wilhelm Pfligge "Papa." He saw Papa Pfligge with a mustache, strangely mottled ears, sporty shoes, a springy walk, speaking with his lips to Gabriel's ear: "We both love Liselotte so much, eh?"

While Gabriel continued to develop this, giving Papa Pfligge increasingly preposterous things to say, Liselotte gave up on love and culture and the au-pair adventure and went home. He accompanied her to the Gare de l'Est and lifted her two cases to the overhead rack. Then he got down and stood on the gray platform and watched her being borne away. The train was blurred, as if he were looking at it through Liselotte's tears.

For a time her letters were like the trail of a child going ever deeper into the woods. He could not decide whether or not to follow; while he was still deciding, and not deciding, the trail stopped and the path became overgrown behind her.

The Interview

UNTIL HE COULD no longer write letters, Gabriel's uncle nagged him with useless advice. Most of it was about money. Owing to Gabriel's inability to produce his father's marriage certificate (in fact, he never tried), his uncle could not in all conscience leave him Baum possessions. It was up to Gabriel, therefore, to look after his own future. He begged Gabriel to find a job with some large, benevolent international firm. It would give him the assurance of money coming in, would encourage French social-security bureaucrats to take an interest in him, and would put him in the way of receiving an annuity at the age of sixty-five.

"Sixty-five is your next step," his uncle warned, for Gabriel's thirtieth birthday.

He counselled Gabriel to lay claim to those revenues known as "German money," but Gabriel's parents had vanished without trace; there was no way of proving they had not taken ship for Tahiti. And it would not have been in Gabriel's power to equate banknotes to a child's despair. His uncle fell back on the Algerian war. Surely Gabriel was entitled to a pension? No, he was not. War had never been declared. What Gabriel had engaged in was a long tactical exercise for which there was no compensation except experience.

The Algerian-pension affair rankled with Gabriel. He had to fill out employment forms that demanded assurance that he had "fulfilled his military obligations." Sometimes it was taken for granted he had been rejected out of hand. There was no rational basis for this; he supposed it must be because of "Profession: Actor." After his return he continued to take an interest in the war. He was like someone who has played twenty minutes of a match and has to know the outcome. As far as he could make out, it had ended in a draw. The excitement died down, and then no one knew what to put in the magazines and political weeklies any more. Some journalists tried to interest Gabriel in Brittany, where there was an artichoke glut; others hinted that the new ecumenicity beginning to seep out of Rome was really an attack on French institutions. Gabriel doubted this. Looking for news about his pension, he learned about the Western European consumer society and the moral wounds that were being inflicted on France through full employment. Between jobs, he read articles about people who said they had been made unhappy by paper napkins and washing machines.

Most of the customers in La Méduse were waiting for a television call. The rest were refugees, poets' widows, and foreign students looking for work to supplement their scholarships. Up at the bar, where drinks were cheaper, were clustered the second-generation émigré actors Gabriel thought of as bachelor orphans. Unlike Gabriel, they had been everywhere—to Brazil, where they could not understand the language, and to New York, where they complained about the climate, and to Israel, where they were disappointed with the food. Now they were in Paris, where they disliked the police.

Sometimes Dieter Pohl shared Gabriel's table. He was a Bavarian Gabriel's age—thirty—who played in films about the Occupation. Dieter had begun as a private, had been promoted to lieutenant, and expected to become a captain soon. He had two good facial expressions, one for victory and one for defeat. Advancing, he gazed keenly upwards, as if following a hawk to the vanishing point. Sometimes he pressed binoculars to his eyes. Defeat found him staring at his boots. He could also be glimpsed marching off into captivity with a bandage around his head. The captivity scene took place in the last episode. Gabriel, enrolled as a victim, had generally been disposed of in the first. His rapid disappearance was supposed to establish the tone of the period for audiences too young to recall it.

It was around this time, when French editorial alarm about the morally destructive aspect of Western prosperity was at its most feverish, that a man calling himself Briseglace wandered into the bar and began asking all the aliens and strangers there if they were glad to be poor. He said that he was a journalist, that his wife had left him for a psychiatrist, and that his girlfriend took tickets in a cinema farther along the street. He said that the Montparnasse railway station was to be torn down and a dark tower built in its place; no one believed him. He wore a tie made of some yellow Oriental stuff. His

clothes looked as if they had been stitched by nuns on a convent
sewing machine. Gabriel and his generation had gone into black—
black pullovers, black leather jackets, soft black boots. Their haircuts
still spoke of military service and colonial wars. Briseglace's straggling,
grayish locks, his shapeless and shabby and oddly feminine-looking
overcoat, his stained fingers and cheap cigarettes, his pessimism and
his boldness and his belief in the moral advantages of penury all came
straight from the Latin Quarter of the nineteen-forties. He was the
Occupation; he was the Liberation, too. The films that Dieter and
Gabriel played in grew like common weeds from the heart of whatever young man he once had been. Gabriel's only feeling, seeing him,
was disgust at what it meant to grow old.

The dark garments worn in La Méduse gave the place the appearance of a camp full of armed militia into which Briseglace, outdated
civilian, had stumbled without cause. Actually, the leather jackets
covered only perpetual worry. Some people thought Briseglace was
with the CIA, others saw a K.G.B. agent with terrifying credentials.
The orphans were certain he was an inspector sent to see if their
residence permits were forgeries. But his questions led only to one
tame conclusion, which he begged them to ratify: it was that being
poor they were free, and being free they were happy.

Released from immediate danger, a few of the aliens sat and stood
straighter, looked nonchalant or offended, depending on how profound their first terrors had been. Dieter declared himself happy in
a profession that had brought him moral satisfaction and material
comfort, and that provided the general public with notions of history.
Some of those at the bar identified themselves as tourists, briefly in
Paris, staying at comfortable hotels. Someone mentioned the high
prices that had to be paid for soccer stars. Another recalled that on
the subject of personal riches Christ had been ambiguous yet reassuring. Briseglace wrote everything down. When he paid for his coffee
he asked for the check, which he had to turn in for expenses. Gabriel,
who had decided to have nothing to do with him, turned the pages
of *Paris-Match*.

Six weeks later Gabriel emerged in the pages of a left-wing weekly
as "Gabriel B., spokesman for the flotsam of Western Europe."

"His first language was German," Gabriel read. "Lacking the rudder of political motivation, his aimless wanderings have cast him up in Montparnasse, in the sad fragrance of coffee machines. Do you think he eats in the Jewish quarter, at Jo Goldenberg's, at La Rose d'Or? Never. You will find Gabriel B. gnawing veal cutlets at the Wienerwald, devouring potato dumplings at the Tannhaüser. For Gabriel B. this bizarre nourishment constitutes a primal memory, from infancy to age twelve." "Seven," Gabriel scrupulously corrected, but it was too late, the thing was in print. "This handsome Prince of Bohemia has reached the fatal age of thirty. What can he do? Where can he go? Conscience-money from the wealthy German republic keeps him in cigarettes. A holdover from bad times, he slips through the good times without seeing them. The Western European consumer society is not so much an economic condition as a state of mind."

Gabriel read the part about the Prince of Bohemia two or three times. He wondered where the Wienerwald was. In the picture accompanying the article was Dieter Pohl, with his eyes inked over so that he could not be identified and use the identification as an excuse for suing the magazine.

There was no explaining it; Dieter was sure he had not sat for a portrait; Gabriel was positive he had not opened his mouth. He thought of posting the article to Uncle August, but his uncle would take it to be a piece of downright nonsense, like the clockwork bear. Dieter bought half a dozen copies of the magazine for his relatives in Bavaria; it was the first time that a picture of him had ever been published anywhere.

Gabriel's escape from annihilation in two real wars (even though one had been called something else) had left him with reverence for unknown forces. Perhaps Briseglace had been sent to nudge him in some new direction. Perhaps the man would turn up again, confessing he had never been a journalist and had been feigning not in order to harm Gabriel but to ensure his ultimate safety.

Nothing of the kind ever happened, of course. Briseglace was never seen again in La Méduse. The only reaction to the interview came from a cousin of Dieter's called Helga. She did not read French easily and had understood some of it to mean that Dieter was not eating enough. She sent him a quantity of very good gingerbread in a tin box and begged him, not for the first time, to pack his things and come home and let a woman look after his life.

Unsettling Rumors

As he grew older and balder, stouter, and more reflective, Gabriel found himself at odds with the few bachelors he still saw in Montparnasse. They tended to cast back to the nineteen-sixties as the springtime of life, though none of them had been all that young. Probably because they had outlived their parents and were without children, they had no way of measuring time. To Gabriel the decade now seemed to have been like a south wind making everyone fretful and jumpy. The colder their prospects, the steadier his friends had become. They slept well, cashed their unemployment checks without grumbling, strolled along the boulevards through a surf of fallen leaves, and discarded calls to revolution, stood in peaceful queues in front of those cinemas that still charged no more than eleven francs. Inside, the seats and carpets were moldering slowly. Half the line shuffling up to the ticket office was probably out of work. His friends preferred films in which women presented no obstacles and created no problems and were shown either naked or in evening dress.

Much of Gabriel's waking time was now spent like this, too—not idly, but immersed in the present moment.

Soon after the Yom Kippur War, a notice had been posted in La Méduse: "Owing to the economic situation no one may sit for more than thirty minutes over a single order." The management had no legal means of enforcing this; still the notice hung there, a symptom of a new harshness, the sourness engendered by the decline.

"That sign was the end of life as we knew it in the sixties," said Dieter Pohl. He was a colonel now, and as fussy as a monarch at a review about a badge misplaced or a button undone. Gabriel had no equivalent staircase to climb; who ever has heard of a victim's being promoted? Still, he had acquired a variety of victim experiences. Gabriel had been shot, stoned, drowned, suffocated, and marked off for hanging; had been insulted and betrayed; had been shoved aboard trains and dragged out of them; had been flung from the back of a truck with such accidental violence that he had broken his collarbone.

His demise, seen by millions of people, some eating their dinner, was still needed in order to give a push to the old dishonorable plot—told ever more simply now, like a fable—while Dieter's fate was still part of its moral.

On this repeated game of death and consequences Dieter's seniority depended. He told Gabriel that the French would be bored with entertainment based on the Occupation by about 1982; by that time he would have been made a general at least once, and would have saved up enough money to buy a business of some kind in his native town.

He often spoke as if the parting were imminent, though he was still only a colonel: "Our biographies are not the same, and you are a real actor, who took lessons, and a real soldier, who fought in a real war. But look at the result—we ended up in the same place, doing the same work, sitting at the same table. Years and years without a disagreement. It is a male situation. Women would never be capable of such a thing."

Gabriel supposed Dieter to mean that women, inclined by nature to quick offense and unending grudges, were not gifted for loyal friendship. Perhaps it was true, but it seemed incomplete. Even the most solitary of the women he could observe—the poets' widows, for instance, with their crocheted berets, their mysterious shopping bags, their fat, waddling dogs—did not cluster together like anxious pigeons on the pretext of friendship. Each one came in alone and sat by herself, reading whatever fascinating stuff she could root out of the shopping bag, staring at strangers with ever-fresh interest, sometimes making comments about them aloud.

A woman can always get some practical use from a torn-up life, Gabriel decided. She likes mending and patching it, making sure the edges are straight. She spreads the last shred out and takes its measure: "What can I do with this remnant? How long does it need to last?" A man puts on his life ready-made. If it doesn't fit, he will try to exchange it for another. Only a fool of a man will try to adjust the sleeves or move the buttons; he doesn't know how.

Some of the older customers were now prey to unsettling rumors. La Méduse was said to have been sold by its owner, a dour Breton with very small eyes. It would soon be converted to a dry-cleaner's establishment, as part of the smartening-up of Montparnasse. The chairs, the glasses, the thick, grayish cups and saucers, the zinc-covered bar, the neon tubes on the ceiling—sociological artifacts—had been purchased at roaring prices for a museum in Stockholm. It seemed farfetched to Gabriel but not impossible; the Montparnasse station had been torn down, and a dark ugly tower had been put in its place. He remembered how Briseglace had predicted this.

Gabriel had noticed lately that he was not seeing Paris as it was but the way it had stayed in his mind; he still saw butchers and grocers and pastry shops, when in reality they had become garages and banks. There was a new smell in the air now, metallic and hot. He was changing too. Hunger was drawn to his attention by a feeling of sadness and loss. He breathed without effort. The child-Gabriel had grown still. Occupation films had fallen off a little, but Gabriel had more resources than Dieter. He wore a checked cap and sang the "Internationale;" he was one of a committee bringing bad news to Seneca. He had a summer season playing Flavius in *Julius Caesar*, and another playing Aston in *The Caretaker* and the zoo director in *The Bedbug*. These festivals were staged in working-class sub-urbs the inhabitants of which had left for the Côte d'Azur. During one of those summers La Méduse changed hands, shut for three months, and opened with rows of booths, automobile seats made of imitation leather, orange glass lampshades, and British First World War recruiting posters plastered on the walls. The notice about not sitting for more than thirty minutes had vanished, replaced by an announcement that ice cream and hamburgers could be obtained. Washrooms and telephones were one flight up instead of in the basement; there was someone on hand to receive tips and take mes-sages. At each table was a bill of fare four pages long and a postcard advertising the café, which customers could send to their friends if they wanted to. The card showed a Medusa jellyfish with long eyelashes and a ribbon on its head, smiling out of a tiny screen. Beneath this one could read:

PUB LA MÉDUSE
THE OLDEST AND MOST CELEBRATED
MEETING-PLACE FOR TELEVISION
STARS IN PARIS

Gabriel tried a number of booths before finding one that suited him. Between the automobile seat and a radiator was a space where he could keep magazines. The draught beer was of somewhat lower quality than before. The main difference between the old place and the new one was its smell. For a time he could not identify it. It turned out to be the reek of a chicory drink, the color of boot polish, invented to fight inflation. The addition of sugar made it nauseating, and it was twice as expensive as coffee had ever been.

The Surrender

Dieter heard that a thirteen-hour television project about the Occupation was to be launched in the spring; he had seen the outline.

He said, "For the moment they just need a few people to be deported and to jump off the train."

Some old-timers heard Dieter say, "They want to deport the Poles," and some heard, "They are rounding up the foreign-born Socialists," and others swore he had asked for twelve Jews to be run over by a locomotive.

Dieter wore a new civilian winter costume, a light-brown fur-lined winter coat and a Russian cap. He ate roasted chestnuts, which he peeled with his fingernails. They were in a cornucopia made of half a page of *Le Quotidien de Paris*. In the old Méduse eating out of newspaper would have meant instant expulsion. Dieter spread the paper on Gabriel's table, sat down, and told him about the film. It would begin with a group of Resistance fighters who were being deported jumping out of a train. Their group would include a coal miner, an anti-Semitic aristocrat, a Communist militant, a peasant with a droll Provençal accent, a long-faced Protestant intellectual, and a priest in doubt about his vocation. Three Jews will be discovered to have jumped or fallen with them: one aged rabbi, one black-market operator, and one anything.

The one anything will be me, Gabriel decided, helping himself to chestnuts. He saw, without Dieter's needing to describe them, the glaring lights, the dogs straining at their leads, the guards running and blowing whistles, the stalled train, a rainstorm, perhaps.

The aristo will be against taking the extra three men along, Dieter said, but the priest will intercede for them. The miner, or perhaps the black-market man, will stay behind to act as decoy for the dogs while the others all get in a rowboat and make for the maquis. The peasant will turn out to be a British intelligence agent named Scott. The Protestant will fall out of the rowboat; the priest will drown trying to save him; the Communist . . .

"We know all that," Gabriel interrupted. "Who's there at the end?"

The aristo, said Dieter. The aristo and the aged rabbi will survive twelve episodes and make their way together back to Paris for the Liberation. There they will discover Dieter and his men holed up in the Palais du Luxembourg, standing fast against the local Resistance and a few policemen. The rabbi will die next to the Medici fountain, in the arms of the aristo.

Gabriel thought this did not bode well for the future, but Dieter reassured him: the aristo will now be a changed man. He will storm the Palais and be seen at the end writing "MY FRIENDS REMEMBERED" on the wall while Dieter and the others file by with their hands up.

"What about the one anything?" said Gabriel. "How long does he last?"

"Dear friend and old comrade," said Dieter, "don't take offense at this. Ten years ago you would have been the first man chosen. But now you are at the wrong age. Who cares what happens to a man of forty-three? You aren't old enough or young enough to make anyone cry. The fact is—forgive me for saying so—but you are the wrong age to play a Jew. A uniform has no age," he added, because he was also forty-three. "And no one is expected to cry at the end, but just to be thoughtful and satisfied."

While Gabriel sat mulling this over, Dieter told him about the helmets the Germans were going to wear. Some were heavy metal, museum pieces; they gave their wearers headaches and left red marks on the brow. A certain number of light plastic helmets would be distributed, but only to officers. The higher one's rank, the lighter the helmet. What Dieter was getting around to was this: he wondered if Gabriel might not care to bridge this stage of his Occupation career by becoming a surrendering officer, seen in the last episode instead of vanishing after the first. He would be a colonel in the Wehrmacht (humane, idealistic, opposed to extreme measures) while Dieter would have to be the S.S. one (not so good). He and Dieter would both have weightless helmets and comfortable, well-cut uniforms.

Gabriel supposed that Dieter was right, in a way. Certainly, he was at a bad age for dangerous antics. It was time for younger men to take their turn at jumping off moving vehicles, diving into ice-cold streams, and dodging blank shot; nor had he reached that time of life when he could die blessing and inspiring those the script had chosen to survive him. As an officer, doomed to defeat, he would at least be sure of his rank and his role and of being in one piece at the end.

Two weeks later Dieter announced to the old-timers that the whole first scene had been changed; there would now be a mass escape from a convoy of lorries, with dozens of men gunned down on the spot. The original cast was reduced, with the Protestant, the Communist, and the miner eliminated completely. This new position caused some argument and recrimination, in which Gabriel did not take part. All he had to wait for now was the right helmet and good weather.

The usual working delays occurred, so that it was not until May that the last of the Baums tried on his new uniform. Dieter adjusted the shoulders of the tunic and set the plastic helmet at a jaunty angle. Gabriel looked at himself. He removed the helmet and put it back on straight. Dieter spoke encouragingly; he seemed to think that Gabriel was troubled about seeming too stout, too bald, too old for his rank.

"There is nothing like a uniform for revealing a man's real age to him," said Dieter. "But from a distance everyone in uniform looks the same."

Gabriel in his new uniform seemed not just to be looking at himself in a glass but actually to be walking through it. He moved through a liquid mirror, back and forth. With each crossing his breath came a little shorter.

Dieter said generously, "A lot of soldiers went bald prematurely because the helmets rubbed their hair."

The surrender was again delayed, this time on account of bad weather. One sodden afternoon, after hanging about in the Luxembourg Gardens for hours, Dieter and Gabriel borrowed capes from a couple of actors who were playing policemen and, their uniforms concealed, went to a post office so that Dieter could make a phone call. His cousin, Helga, destined by both their families to be his bride, had waited a long time; just when it was beginning to look as if she had waited too long for anything, a widower proposed. She was being married the next day. Dieter had to call and explain why he could not be at the wedding; he was held up waiting for the surrender.

Helga talked to Dieter without drawing breath. He listened for a while then handed the receiver to Gabriel. Helga continued telling Dieter, or Gabriel, that her husband-to-be had a grandchild who could play the accordion. The child was to perform at the wedding party. The accordion was almost as large as the little girl, and twice as heavy.

"You ought to see her fingers on the keyboard," Helga yelled. "They fly—fast, fast."

Gabriel gave the telephone to Dieter, who assumed a look of blank concentration. When he had heard enough he beckoned to Gabriel. Gabriel pressed the receiver to his ear and learned that Helga was worried. She had dreamed that she was married and that her husband would not make room for her in his apartment. When she wanted to try the washing machine, he was already washing his own clothes. "What do you think of the dream?" she said to Gabriel. "Can you hear me? I still love you." Gabriel placed the receiver softly on a shelf under the telephone and waved Dieter in so that he could say goodbye.

They came out of the post office to a drenching rain. Dieter wondered what shape their uniforms would be in by the time they surrendered. Gabriel argued that after the siege of the Palais du Luxembourg the original uniforms must have shown wear. Dieter answered that it was not up to him or Gabriel to decide such things.

RAIN FELL FOR another fortnight, but, at last, on a cool shining June day, they were able to surrender. During one of the long periods of inextricable confusion, Dieter and Gabriel walked as far as the Delacroix monument and sat on its rim. Dieter was disappointed in his men. There were no real Germans among them, but Yugoslavs,

Turks, North Africans, Portuguese, and some unemployed French. The Resistance forces were not much better, he said. There had been complaints. Gabriel had to agree that they were a bedraggled-looking lot. Dieter recalled how in the sixties there used to be real Frenchmen, real Germans, authentic Jews. The Jews had played deportation the way they had seen it in films, and the Germans had surrendered according to film tradition, too, but there had been this difference: They had at least been doing something their parents had done before them. They had not only the folklore of movies to guide them but—in many cases—first-hand accounts. Now, even if one could assemble a true cast of players, they would be trying to imitate their grandfathers. They were at one remove too many. There was no assurance that a real German, a real Frenchman would be any more plausible now than a Turk.

Dieter sighed, and glanced up at the houses on the other side of the street edging the park. "It wouldn't be bad to live up there," he said. "At the top, with one of those long terraces. They grow real trees on them—poplars, birches."

"What would it cost?"

"Around a hundred and fifty million francs," said Dieter. "Without the furniture."

"Anyone can have a place like that with money," said Gabriel. "The interesting thing would be to live up there without it."

"How?"

Gabriel took off his helmet and looked deeply inside it. He said, "I don't know."

Dieter showed him the snapshots of his cousin's wedding. Helga and the groom wore rimless spectacles. In one picture they cut a cake together; in another they tried to drink out of the same champagne glass. Eyeglasses very like theirs, reduced in size, were worn by a plain little girl. On her head was a wreath of daisies. She was dressed in a long, stiff yellow gown. Gabriel could see just the hem of the dress and the small shoes, and her bashful anxious face and slightly crossed eyes. Her wrists were encircled by daisies, too. Most of her person was behind an accordion. The accordion seemed to be falling apart; she had all she could do to keep it together.

"My cousin's husband's granddaughter," said Dieter. He read

Helga's letter: " 'She can play anything—fast, fast. Her fingers simply fly over the keyboard.' "

Gabriel examined every detail of the picture. The child was dazzled and alarmed, and the accordion was far too heavy. "What is her name?" he said.

Dieter read more of the letter and said, "Erna."

"Erna," Colonel Baum repeated. He looked again at the button of a face, the flower bracelets, the feet with the heels together—they must have told her to stand that way. He gave the snapshot back without saying anything.

A crowd had collected in the meantime, drawn by the lights and the equipment and the sight of the soldiers in German uniform. Some asked if they might be photographed with them; this often happened when a film of that kind was made in the streets.

An elderly couple edged up to the two officers. The woman said, in German, in a low voice, "What are you doing here?"

"Waiting to surrender," said Dieter.

"I can see that, but what are you *doing?*"

"I don't know," said Dieter. "I've been sitting on the edge of this monument for thirty-five years. I'm still waiting for orders."

The man tried to give them cigarettes, but neither colonel smoked. The couple took pictures of each other standing between Dieter and Gabriel, and went away.

Why is it, said Gabriel to himself, that when I was playing a wretched, desperate victim no one ever asked to have his picture taken with me? The question troubled him, seeming to proceed from the younger Gabriel, who had been absent for some time now. He hoped his unruly tenant was not on his way back, screaming for a child's version of justice, for an impossible world.

Some of the men put their helmets upside-down on the ground and tried to make the visitors pay for taking their pictures. Dieter was disturbed by this. "Of course, you were a real soldier," he said to Gabriel unhappily. "All this must seem inferior." They sat without saying anything for a time and then Dieter began to talk about ecology. Because of ecology, there was a demand in Bavaria for fresh bread made of authentic flour, salt, water, and yeast. Because of unemployment, there were people willing to return to the old, forgotten trades, at which one earned practically nothing and had to work all night. The fact was that he had finally saved up enough money and had bought a bakery in his native town. He was through with the war, the Occupation, the Liberation, and captivity. He was going home.

This caused the most extraordinary view in Gabriel's view of the park. All the greens in it became one dull color, as if thunderous clouds had gathered low in the sky.

"You will always be welcome," said Dieter. "Your room will be ready, a bed made up, flowers in a vase. I intend to marry someone in the village—someone young."

Gabriel said, "If you have four or five children, how can you keep a spare room?"

Still, it was an attractive thought. The greens emerged again, fresh and bright. He saw the room that could be his. Imagine being wakened in a clean room by birds singing and the smell of freshly baked bread. Flowers in a vase—Gabriel hardly knew one from the other, only the caged flowers of parks. He saw, in a linen press, sheets strewn with lavender. His clothes hung up or folded. His breakfast on a white tablecloth, under a lime tree. A basket of warm bread, another of boiled eggs. Dieter's wife putting her hand on the white coffee pot to see if it was still hot enough for Gabriel. A jug of milk, another of cream. Dieter's obedient children drinking from mugs, their chins on the rim of the table. Yes, and the younger Gabriel, revived and outraged and jealous, thrashing around in his heart, saying, "Think about empty rooms, letters left behind, cold railway stations washed down with disinfectant, dark glaciers of time." And, then, Gabriel knew nothing about the country. He could not see himself actually *in* it. He had never been to the country except to jump out of trains. It was only in films that he had seen mist lifting or paths lost in ferns.

They surrendered all the rest of the afternoon. The aristo wrote "MY FRIENDS REMEMBERED" on the wall while Dieter and Gabriel led some Turks and Yugoslavs and some unemployed Frenchmen into captivity. The aristo did not even bother to turn around and look. Gabriel was breathing at a good rhythm—not too shallow, not too fast. An infinity of surrenders had preceded this one, in color and in black-and-white, with music and without. A long trail of application forms and employment questionnaires had led Gabriel here: "Baum, Gabriel, b. 1935, Germany, nat. French, mil. serv. obl. fulf." (Actually, for some years now his date of birth had rendered the assurance about military service unnecessary.) Country words ran meanwhile in Gabriel's head. He thought, Dense thickets, lizards and snakes, a thrush's egg, a bee, lichen, wild berries, dark thorny leaves, pale mushrooms. Each word carried its own fragrance.

At the end of the day Dieter's face was white and tired and perfectly blank. He might have been listening to Helga. The aristo came over, smoking a cigarette. About twenty-three years before this, he and Gabriel had performed before a jury in a one-act play of Jules Renard's. The aristo had received an honorable mention, Gabriel a first. The aristo hadn't recognized Gabriel until now because of the uniform. He said, "What's the matter with him?"

Dieter sat slumped in an iron chair belonging to the park administration, staring at his boots. He jerked his head up and looked around, crying, "Why? Where?" and something else Gabriel didn't catch.

Gabriel hoped Dieter was not going to snap now, with the bakery and the flowers and the children in sight. "Well, well, old friend!" said Dieter, clutching Gabriel and trying to get to his feet. "Save your strength! Don't take things to heart! You'll dance at my wedding!"

"Exhaustion," said the aristo.

Gabriel and Dieter slowly made their way to the street, where Volkswagen buses full of actors were waiting. The actors made signs meaning to tell them to hurry up; they were all tired and impatient and anxious to change into their own clothes and get home. Dieter leaned on his old friend. Every few steps he stopped to talk excitedly, as people put to a great strain will do, all in a rush, like the long babbling of dreams.

"You'll have to walk faster," said Gabriel, beginning to feel irritated. "The buses won't wait forever, and we can be arrested for wearing these uniforms without a reason."

"There's a very good reason," said Dieter, but he seemed all at once to recover.

That night at La Méduse Dieter drew the plan of the bakery and the large apartment above it, with an X marking Gabriel's room. He said that Gabriel would spend his summers and holidays there, and would teach Dieter's children to pronounce French correctly. The light shining out of the orange glass lampshade made the drawing seem attractive and warm. It turned out that Dieter hadn't actually bought the bakery but had made a down payment and was negotiating for a bank loan.

The proprietor of La Méduse now came over to their table, accompanied by a young couple—younger than Dieter and Gabriel, that is—to whom he had just sold the place. He introduced them, saying, "My oldest customers. You know their faces, of course. Television."

The new owners shook hands with Gabriel and Dieter, assuring them that they did not intend to tamper with the atmosphere of the old place; not for anything in the world would they touch the recruiting posters or the automobile seats.

After they had gone Dieter seemed to lose interest in his drawing; he folded it in half, then in half again, and finally put his glass down on it. "They are a pair of crooks, you know," he said. "They had to get out of Bastia because they had swindled so many people they were afraid of being murdered. Apparently they're going to turn La Méduse into a front for the Corsican Mafia." Having said this, Dieter gave a great sigh and fell silent. Seeing that he had given up talking about the bakery and Gabriel's room, Gabriel drew a magazine out from behind the radiator and began to read. Dieter let him go on reading for quite a while before he sighed again. Gabriel did not look up. Dieter unfolded the drawing and smoothed it flat. He examined it, made a change or two with a pencil, and said something indistinct.

Gabriel said, "What?" without raising his head. Dieter answered, "My father lived to be ninety."

FROM
THE FIFTEENTH
DISTRICT

ALTHOUGH an epidemic of haunting, widely reported, spread through the Fifteenth District of our city last summer, only three acceptable complaints were lodged with the police.

Major Emery Travella, 31st Infantry, 1914–18, Order of the Leopard, Military Beech Leaf, Cross of St. Lambert First Class, killed while defusing a bomb in a civilian area 9 June, 1941, Medal of Danzig (posthumous), claims he is haunted by the entire congregation of St. Michael and All Angels on Bartholomew Street. Every year on the Sunday falling nearest the anniversary of his death, Major Travella attends Holy Communion service at St. Michael's, the church from which he was buried. He stands at the back, close to the doors, waiting until all the communicants have returned to their places, before he approaches the altar rail. His intention is to avoid a mixed queue of dead and living, the thought of which is disgusting to him. The congregation sits, hushed and expectant, straining to hear the Major's footsteps (he drags one foot a little). After receiving the Host, the Major leaves at once, without waiting for the Blessing. For the past several years, the Major has noticed that the congrega-

tion doubles in size as 9 June approaches. Some of these strangers
bring cameras and tape recorders with them; others burn incense
under the pews and wave amulets and trinkets in what they imagine
to be his direction, muttering pagan gibberish all the while. References he is sure must be meant for him are worked into the sermons:
"And he that was dead sat up, and began to speak" (Luke 7:15), or
"So Job died, being old and full of days" (Job 42:17). The Major
points out that he never speaks and never opens his mouth except to
receive Holy Communion. He lived about sixteen thousand and sixty
days, many of which he does not remember. On 23 September, 1914,
as a young private, he was crucified to a cart wheel for five hours for
having failed to salute an equally young lieutenant. One ankle was left
permanently impaired.

The Major wishes the congregation to leave him in peace. The
opacity of the living, their heaviness and dullness, the moisture of
their skin, and the dustiness of their hair are repellent to a man of
feeling. It was always his habit to avoid civilian crowds. He lived for
six years on the fourth floor in Block E, Stoneflower Gardens, without
saying a word to his neighbors or even attempting to learn their
names. An affidavit can easily be obtained from the former porter at
the Gardens, now residing at the Institute for Victims of Senile
Trauma, Fifteenth District.

M RS. IBRAHIM, aged thirty-seven, mother of twelve children, complains about being haunted by Dr. L. Chalmeton of Regius Hospital,
Seventh District, and by Miss Alicia Fohrenbach, social investigator
from the Welfare Bureau, Fifteenth District. These two haunt Mrs.
Ibrahim without respite, presenting for her ratification and approval
conflicting and unpleasant versions of her own death.

According to Dr. Chalmeton's account, soon after Mrs. Ibrahim
was discharged as incurable from Regius Hospital he paid his patient
a professional call. He arrived at a quarter past four on the first
Tuesday of April, expecting to find the social investigator, with whom
he had a firm appointment. Mrs. Ibrahim was discovered alone, in
a windowless room, the walls of which were coated with whitish
fungus a quarter of an inch thick, which rose to a height of about forty

inches from the floor. Dr. Chalmeton inquired, "Where is the social investigator?" Mrs. Ibrahim pointed to her throat, reminding him that she could not reply. Several dark-eyed children peeped into the room and ran away. "How many are yours?" the Doctor asked. Mrs. Ibrahim indicated six twice with her fingers. "Where do they sleep?" said the Doctor. Mrs. Ibrahim indicated the floor. Dr. Chalmeton said, "What does your husband do for a living?" Mrs. Ibrahim pointed to a workbench on which the Doctor saw several pieces of finely wrought jewelry; he thought it a waste that skilled work had been lavished on what seemed to be plastics and base metals. Dr. Chalmeton made the patient as comfortable as he could, explaining that he could not administer drugs for the relief of pain until the social investigator had signed a receipt for them. Miss Fohrenbach arrived at five o'clock. It had taken her forty minutes to find a suitable parking space: the street appeared to be poor, but everyone living on it owned one or two cars. Dr. Chalmeton, who was angry at having been kept waiting, declared he would not be responsible for the safety of his patient in a room filled with mold. Miss Fohrenbach retorted that the District could not resettle a family of fourteen persons who were foreign-born when there was a long list of native citizens waiting for accommodation. Mrs. Ibrahim had in any case relinquished her right to a domicile in the Fifteenth District the day she lost consciousness in the road and allowed an ambulance to transport her to a hospital in the Seventh. It was up to the hospital to look after her now. Dr. Chalmeton pointed out that housing of patients is not the business of hospitals. It was well known that the foreign poor preferred to crowd together in the Fifteenth, where they could sing and dance in the streets and attend one another's weddings. Miss Fohrenbach declared that Mrs. Ibrahim could easily have moved her bed into the kitchen, which was somewhat warmer and which boasted a window. When Mrs. Ibrahim died, the children would be placed in foster homes, eliminating the need for a larger apartment. Dr. Chalmeton remembers Miss Fohrenbach's then crying, "Oh, why do all these people come here, where nobody wants them?" While he was trying to think of an answer, Mrs. Ibrahim died.

In her testimony, Miss Fohrenbach recalls that she had to beg and plead with Dr. Chalmeton to visit Mrs. Ibrahim, who had been discharged from Regius Hospital without medicines or prescriptions or advice or instructions. Miss Fohrenbach had returned several times that April day to see if the Doctor had arrived. The first thing Dr. Chalmeton said on entering the room was "There is no way of helping these people. Even the simplest rules of hygiene are too complicated for them to follow. Wherever they settle, they spread disease and vermin. They have been responsible for outbreaks of aphthous stomatitis, hereditary hypoxia, coccidioidomycosis, gonorrheal arthritis, and scleroderma. Their eating habits are filthy. They never wash their hands. The virus that attacks them breeds in dirt. We took in the patient against all rules, after the ambulance drivers left her lying in the courtyard and drove off without asking for a receipt. Regius Hospital was built and endowed for ailing Greek scholars. Now it is crammed with unteachable persons who cannot read or write." His cheeks and forehead were flushed, his speech incoherent and blurred. According to the social investigator, he was the epitome of the broken-down, irresponsible old rascals the Seventh District employs in its public services. Wondering at the effect this ranting of his might have on the patient, Miss Fohrenbach glanced at Mrs. Ibrahim and noticed she had died.

Mrs. Ibrahim's version of her death has the social investigator arriving first, bringing Mrs. Ibrahim a present of a wine-colored dressing gown made of soft, quilted silk. Miss Fohrenbach explained that the gown was part of a donation of garments to the needy. Large plastic bags, decorated with a moss rose, the emblem of the Fifteenth District, and bearing the words "Clean Clothes for the Foreign-Born," had been distributed by volunteer workers in the more prosperous streets of the District. A few citizens kept the bags as souvenirs, but most had turned them in to the Welfare Bureau filled with attractive clothing, washed, ironed, and mended, and with missing buttons replaced. Mrs. Ibrahim sat up and put on the dressing gown, and the social investigator helped her button it. Then Miss Fohrenbach changed the bed linen and pulled the bed away from the wall. She sat down and took Mrs. Ibrahim's hand in hers and spoke about a new, sunny flat containing five warm rooms which would soon be available. Miss Fohrenbach said that arrangements had been made to send the twelve Ibrahim children to the mountains for special winter classes. They would be taught history and languages and would learn to ski.

The Doctor arrived soon after. He stopped and spoke to Mr. Ibrahim, who was sitting at his workbench making an emerald patch box. The Doctor said to him, "If you give me your social-security papers, I can attend to the medical insurance. It will save you a great deal of trouble." Mr. Ibrahim answered, "What is social security?" The Doctor examined the patch box and asked Mr. Ibrahim what he earned. Mr. Ibrahim told him, and the Doctor said, "But that is less than the minimum wage." Mr. Ibrahim said, "What is a minimum wage?" The Doctor turned to Miss Fohrenbach, saying, "We really must try and help them." Mrs. Ibrahim died. Mr. Ibrahim, when he understood that nothing could be done, lay face down on the floor, weeping loudly. Then he remembered the rules of hospitality and got up and gave each of the guests a present—for Miss Fohrenbach a belt made of Syriac coins, a copy of which is in the Cairo Museum, and for the Doctor a bracelet of precious metal engraved with pomegranates, about sixteen pomegranates in all, that has lifesaving properties.

Mrs. Ibrahim asks that her account of the afternoon be registered with the police as the true version and that copies be sent to the Doctor and the social investigator, with a courteous request for peace and silence.

MRS. CARLOTTE ESSLING, née Holmquist, complains of being haunted by her husband, Professor Augustus Essling, the philosopher and historian. When they were married, the former Miss Holmquist was seventeen. Professor Essling, a widower, had four small children. He explained to Miss Holmquist why he wanted to marry again. He said, "I must have one person, preferably female, on whom I can depend absolutely, who will never betray me even in her thoughts. A disloyal thought revealed, a betrayal even in fantasy, would be enough to destroy me. Knowing that I may rely upon some one person will leave me free to continue my work without anxiety or distraction." The work was the Professor's lifelong examination of the philosopher Nicolas de Malebranche, for whom he had named his eldest child. "If I cannot have the unfailing loyalty I have described, I would as soon not marry at all," the Professor added. He had just begun work on *Malebranche and Materialism*.

Mrs. Essling recalls that at seventeen this seemed entirely within her possibilities, and she replied something like "Yes, I see," or "I quite understand," or "You needn't mention it again."

Mrs. Essling brought up her husband's four children and had two more of her own, and died after thirty-six years of marriage at the age of fifty-three. Her husband haunts her with proof of her goodness. He tells people that Mrs. Essling was born an angel, lived like an angel, and is an angel in eternity. Mrs. Essling would like relief from this charge. "Angel" is a loose way of speaking. She is astonished that the Professor cannot be more precise. Angels are created, not born. Nowhere in any written testimony will you find a scrap of proof that angels are "good." Some are merely messengers; others have a paramilitary function. All are stupid.

After her death, Mrs. Essling remained in the Fifteenth District. She says she can go nowhere without being accosted by the Professor, who, having completed the last phase of his work *Malebranche and Mysticism*, roams the streets, looking in shopwindows, eating lunch twice, in two different restaurants, telling his life story to waiters and bus drivers. When he sees Mrs. Essling, he calls out, "There you are!" and "What have you been sent to tell me?" and "Is there a message?" In July, catching sight of her at the open-air fruit market on Dulac Street, the Professor jumped off a bus, upsetting barrows of plums and apricots, waving an umbrella as he ran. Mrs. Essling had to take refuge in the cold-storage room of the central market, where, years ago, after she had ordered twenty pounds of raspberries and currants for making jelly, she was invited by the wholesale fruit dealer, Mr. Lobrano, aged twenty-nine, to spend a holiday with him in a charming southern city whose Mediterranean Baroque churches he described with much delicacy of feeling. Mrs. Essling was too startled to reply. Mistaking her silence, Mr. Lobrano then mentioned a northern city containing a Gothic cathedral. Mrs. Essling said that such a holiday was impossible. Mr. Lobrano asked for one good reason. Mrs. Essling was at that moment four months pregnant with her second child. Three stepchildren waited for her out in the street. A fourth stepchild was at home looking after the baby. Professor Essling, working on his *Malebranche and Money*, was at home, too, expecting his lunch. Mrs. Essling realized she could not give Mr. Lobrano one good reason. She left the cold-storage room without another word and did not return to it in her lifetime.

Mrs. Essling would like to be relieved of the Professor's gratitude. Having lived an exemplary life is one thing; to have it thrown up at one is another. She would like the police to send for Professor Essling and tell him so. She suggests that the police find some method of keeping him off the streets. The police ought to threaten him; frighten him; put the fear of the Devil into him. Philosophy has made him afraid of dying. Remind him about how he avoided writing his *Malebranche and Mortality*. He is an old man. It should be easy.

POTTER

Piotr was almost forty-one when he fell in love with Laurie Bennett. She lived in Paris, for no particular reason he knew; that is, she had not been drawn by work or by any one person. She seemed young to him, about half his age. Her idea of history began with the Vietnam war; Genesis was her own Canadian childhood. She was spending a legacy of careless freedom with an abandon Piotr found thrilling to watch, for he had long considered himself to be bankrupt—of belief, of love, of license to choose. Here in Paris he was shackled, held, tied to a visa, then to the system of mysterious favors on which his Polish passport depended. His hands were attached with a slack rope and a slipknot. If he moved abruptly, the knot tightened. He had a narrow span of gestures, a prudent range. His new world of love seemed too wide for comfort sometimes, though Laurie occupied it easily.

He called his beloved "Lah-ow-rie," which made her laugh. She could not pronounce "Piotr" and never tried; she said Peter, Prater, Potter, and Otter, and he answered to all. Why not? He loved her. If she took some forms of injustice for granted, it was because she did not know they were unjust. Piotr was supposed to know *by instinct* every shade of difference between Victoria, British Columbia, and Charlottetown, Prince Edward Island, whereas he, poor Potter, came out of a cloudy Eastern plain bereft of roads, schools, buses, elevators, perhaps even frontiers—this because she could not have found Warsaw on a map. She knew he was a poet and a teacher, but must have considered him a radical exception. She had been touchingly pleased when he showed her poems of his in an American university quarterly. Three pages of English were all he had needed to get past her cultural customs barrier. She kept a copy of the review in a plastic bag, and so far as he knew had never read more than his name on the cover. None of this disturbed him. It was not as a poet that Laurie had wanted Piotr but as a lover—thank God. The surprise to him after their first conversations was that there were any roads, schools, etc., in Canada, though she talked often of an Anglican boarding school where she had been "left" and "abandoned" and which she likened to a concentration camp. "You've really never heard of it, Potter?" It seemed incredible that a man of his education knew nothing about Bishop Purse School or its famous headmistress, Miss Ellen Jones. Bishop Purse, whatever its advantages, had not darkened Laurie's sunny intelligence with anything like geography, history, or simple arithmetic. She had the handwriting of a small boy and could not spell even in her own language. For a long time Piotr treasured a letter in which he was described as "a really sensative person," and Laurie herself as "mixed-up in some ways but on the whole pretty chearfull."

Her good nature made her entirely exotic. Piotr was accustomed to people who could not look at a letter without saying eagerly, "Bad news?" He had known women who set aside a little bit of each day for spells of soft, muted weeping. The problem with Polish women, as Piotr saw it, was that they had always just been or were just about to be deserted by their men. At the first rumor of rejection (a fragment of gossip overheard, some offhand evidence of a lover's neglect) they gave way at once, stopped combing their hair, stopped making their beds. They lay like starfish, smoking in the strewn, scattered way of the downhearted. He saw them, collectively, wet-cheeked and feverish, heard a chorus of broken voices gasping out the dreadful story of male treachery. Out of the fear of losing the man at hand would grow a moist determination to find another to take his place. Piotr was separated from his wife, he was irresolute, and he never had quite what he wanted. What he did not want was a feather bed of sadness. He knew that unhappiness is catching and wondered if happiness might not be infectious, too. All that he needed was to love a happy person and get her to love him.

"Am I too cheerful?" Laurie asked. "They say I am sometimes. I've been told. It puts people off. You know, like 'It's nothing to laugh about.'" *I've been told.* There, at the beginning, she had given him the raw material of future anguish, if only he had been alert. But it had come linked with another statement, which was that if Potter was not exactly her first lover he was certainly among the first, and the first ever to please her—a preposterous declaration he accepted on the spot.

Piotr met Laurie through a cousin he had in Paris, an émigré bachelor who worked at a travel agency. Piotr had never seen Marek's office. Meeting Piotr for lunch in one of the smoky café-bars around the Place de l'Opéra, Marek would look at his watch and whisper, "I have to meet someone very high up in Swiss television," or "the editor of the most important newspaper, the most politically powerful man south of the Loire," or "a countess who controls absolutely everything at the Quai d'Orsay." Although he did not say so, it sounded to Piotr very much like social survival in Warsaw. By means of his affability, his ease with languages, and a certain amount of cultural soft-soaping, Marek had acquired a French circle of acquaintance, of which he was extremely proud. But it was a fragile affair, like a child with a constant chest cold. He lavished great amounts of time, care, and worry on keeping it alive, which did not prevent him from knowing every name, event, scandal, and political maneuver in the local Polish colony. He knew so much, in fact, that he was widely believed to be working for the French police. Like most informers —should that have been his story—he was often hard up and often had unexpected money to spend. He lived in the run-down area east of the Hôtel de Ville. The street seemed drab and gritty to Piotr, but his cousin assured him that it was thought fashionable in the highest reaches of bohemia. His rooms were next door to a synagogue and one flight up from an undertaker's. When, as it sometimes happened, nighttime outbursts of anti-Semitism caused swastikas to be chalked on the synagogue, a few usually spilled along to the undertaker's sombre window and over the door and staircase leading to Marek's. The swastikas gave rise to another legend: Marek had been a double agent in the French Resistance. Actually, he had been nowhere near France, and had been barely thirteen by the end of the war. Rumor also had him working for Israel (possibly because of the proximity of the synagogue) and for the C.I.A. His quarters contained large soft lumps of furniture, gray in color, considered "modern," and "American," which had undoubtedly been shipped by airfreight from Washington in exchange for information about Mr. X, who had bought a controlling interest in a toy shop, or little Miss Y, who had triumphantly terminated another school year. The chairs and sofas had in fact been the gift of a Swiss decorator from Bern, who owed Marek money or favors or help of some kind—the explanation always faded out. Although he was far more interested in men than in girls, there were usually more girls than men at his parties. The most beautiful young women Piotr had ever seen climbed the unlighted staircase, undaunted by the matter-of-fact trappings of death on the ground floor or the occasional swastika. Piotr marvelled at his cousin's ease with women, at the casual embracing and hand-holding. It was as though the girls, having nothing to fear, or much to hope for, enjoyed trying out the lesser ornaments of seduction. The girls were Danish, German, French, and American. They were students, models, hostesses at trade fairs, hesitant fiancées, restless daughters. Their uniform the year Piotr met Laurie was bluejeans and velvet blazers. They were nothing like the scuffed, frayed girls he saw in the Latin Quarter, so downcast of face, so dejected of hair and hem that he had to be convinced by Marek they were well-fed children of the middle classes and not the rejects of a failing economy. Marek's girls kept their hair long and glossy, their figures trim. They discussed their thoughts, but not their feelings, with a solemn hauteur Piotr found endlessly touching. But he did not find them lighthearted. They were simply less natively given to despair than Polish women. He was looking for someone, though no one could have told. Perhaps his cousin knew. Why else did he keep on inviting Piotr with all those pretty women? One scowling French girl almost won Piotr when he noticed that the freckles across her nose were spots of russet paint. She was severe, and held her cigarette like a ruler, but she must have been very humble alone with her mirror. "Help me," she must have implored the glass. "Help me to be suitable, wanted." She remarked to Piotr, "How can anyone write poetry today? Personally, I reject the absolute." Piotr had no idea what she meant. He had never asked her, or any woman, to accept the absolute. He had been toying with the hope that she might accept him. Before he could even conceive of an answer, Laurie Bennett intervened. She simply came up to Piotr and told him her name. She had blue eyes, fair hair down to her shoulders, and a gap between her upper front teeth.

"I've never wanted to have it fixed," she told Piotr. "It's supposed to be lucky."

"Are you lucky?" said Piotr.

"Naturally. Who isn't? Aren't you?"

They sat down, Piotr in a Swiss armchair, the girl on the floor. Remarks in a foreign language often left him facing an imaginary brick wall. Lucky? Before he could answer she said, "You're the famous cousin? From there?"—with a wave that indicated a world of bad train connections and terrible food. "Do you know Solzhenitsyn? If Solzhenitsyn were to walk in here, I'd get right down on my knees and thank him."

"What for?" said Piotr.

"*I* don't know. I thought you might."

"He isn't likely to come in," said Piotr. "So you won't have to make a fool of yourself."

She was already kneeling, as it happened, sitting on her heels at Piotr's feet. She slid nearer, placed her glass of rosy wine on the arm of his chair, her elbow on his knee: "I was just trying to show you I sympathized." He wanted to touch her hair but clasped his hands instead. His cousin had told him he looked like a failed priest sometimes. He did, in fact, inspire confessions rather than passion from women.

In his later memories he thought it must have been then that Laurie began to tell about her neglected childhood and her school. She did not sound in the least mournful, though the story was as dismaying as the smiling girl could make it. After Bishop Purse, what she had hated most was someone called "my brother Ken." "My brother Ken" was so neurotically snobbish that he'd had a breakdown trying to decide between a golden and a Labrador. His wife, whose name sounded like "Bobber Ann," took the case to a psychotherapist, who advised buying one of each. Piotr did not know Laurie was talking about dogs, and after she explained he found the incident even more mystifying. What he loved at once was her built-up excitement. She was ignited by her own stories and at the end could scarcely finish for laughing. Yes, her brother's wife was Bobber Ann. Barbara, that is—she had been imitating Bobber Ann's Toronto accent. "Actually, my brother Ken's a mean sort of bugger," said Laurie, happily. "And she, Bobber Ann, she wears white gloves all the time, cleans 'em with bread crumbs—it's true. How long are you in Paris for, Otter, Potter, I can't pronounce it. Would you come to a party, if I gave one?"

She was living then in a borrowed apartment on Avenue Mozart. The name of this street remained incantatory to Piotr long after he knew he would never see Laurie again. He remembered of the strange rooms their stern blue walls, a plant that looked like a heap of lettuce leaves, which Laurie kept forgetting to water, and rows and rows of grim sepia views of bridges and rivers.

"My friends are well printed, eh?" said Laurie. Her friends worked at UNESCO "or some kind of culture racket like it." As the last English-speaking stragglers left her party, having finished off the last of the absent hosts' duty-free gin, Laurie said, with no particular emphasis, "No, you, Potter, you stay."

THE PLACE on Avenue Mozart was one of so many that in time Piotr stopped counting. Her home was never her own but rooms she camped in while the owners were away. Sometimes she had a dog to walk or a budgerigar to feed, but mostly just the run of the house. She told Piotr she moved on because she wanted peace and could never find it. He supposed, not unkindly, that she had heard some such statement at one of Marek's parties. A year after Avenue Mozart, the "B" page of his address book was such a hedgehog of scratched-out directions that he bought a book for Laurie alone. He recorded in it the enchanting names of her Paris streets, and mysterious Poste Restante or American Express directions for Cannes, Crans-sur-Sierre, Munich, Portugal, Normandy, Gstaad, Madrid. She sent him bright scraps of news about eccentric living quarters, funny little jobs that never lasted for long, and she sent Piotr all, yes, all of her love. Word came from sunny beaches that Laurie was eating too much, she was lazy and brown and drinking delicious wine. Often she sounded alone. If she wrote "we," there seemed to be three of them; she travelled with couples, never the same pair twice. "You and I will come here together," she would promise, of places he would never see in his lifetime. He had told her about the passport and how having it for even three weeks was an erratic favor, because once, twenty years ago now, he had been arrested for political lèse-majesté. He explained, but she kept forgetting. She had no memory, except of her school days; she was like a blackboard wiped clean every week or so. Laurie could not recall restaurants where their most important conversations had taken place. Her life seemed to him fragile and silvery, like a Christmas bauble. When he and Laurie were apart, which was to say nearly always, her life reflected a female, Western mystery: it reflected hotel rooms and crouched skiers and glasses of wine and distorted faces. He could hear her voice and remembered her light hair. He was exiled from Laurie—never Laurie from Piotr. She simply picked up her world and took it with her. He resented his exile. He wanted to take her world, compress it, make sparkling dust of it. He could almost have made himself hate her, because of her unthinking, pointless freedom, her casual way with frontiers. She went from place to place without noticing where she was—he could tell that. What was she doing? Eating, drinking, loving probably, being silly. But even her silliness was a tie, a conspiracy. It had drawn him, made him share private jokes that stayed alive, compelled him to send drawings, pictures, reminders, whatever would strengthen the bond. But by the time these arrived Laurie had usually forgotten the joke and was on to another.

She was not always silly. He saw a face of true unhappiness sometimes, and always because of him—because she loved him and there was half a continent between them; because he had children; because the wife he no longer lived with, had admired but never loved, was like a book he could neither read nor shut. It seemed to him then that he bore a disease that might infect the confident girl and cripple her. He saw the self-doubt on her face, and the puzzled wretchedness. When she said, "There must be something wrong with me," he heard his wife, too.

T͟HEY PARTED twice; they had to. Piotr had to go back. Laurie picked up her life and never wondered about his; at least, she never asked. In Warsaw he woke up each morning with the same question: Is there a letter? Her letters were funny, friendly, loving, misspelled. They were not a substitute for Laurie; they were like medicine that can quiet a symptom but not the root of the malady. She phoned sometimes but he preferred the voice in his mind, and the calls left him empty.

The second time he came to Paris, it was at the end of a hot summer. He found her over an art gallery on Boulevard Malesherbes. She told him that Proust had lived somewhere near, perhaps in the next house. She was unsure who Proust was. Like the Solzhenitsyn remark, it was made to please; it was Laurie's way of paying a compliment to someone she considered clever.

They lived behind closed shutters because of the heat, and came out to the still steaming streets after dark. He noticed that she was wearing a new watch with a white strap. The watch was transparent, with a multitude of stars spinning inside.

"I've always had it," she said when he asked where such a marvel was to be found. She wore it for sleep and in love—that was how he happened to see it. He observed Laurie (she did not see him looking) removing the watch and kissing it before taking a bath. A little later she said, "I picked it up in Zurich once," and then, such was her capacity for forgetting, "It was a birthday present." When the time came to accompany Piotr to the airport she suddenly produced a car. To Piotr, who did not know one automobile from another, it was merely cream-colored and small. "It belongs to the girl who owns the apartment," she said, though until now she had spoken of the owners as "they." At the airport, at the last minute, she said she and Piotr had better forget each other. These separations were killing her inch by inch. She could not look at him, did not want him to touch her. It was a shifting, evasive misery, like a dying animal's. She said, "I'm taking the car and driving somewhere. I don't know where. I don't even know where I'll be sleeping tonight. I can't go back and sleep alone in that apartment."

"Will you write?" said Piotr.

She turned, weeping, and ran.

For weeks he was stunned by her absence, her silence, her grief, his own guilt. Out of need, out of vanity, he had tampered with a young life. He had not expected this gift of deep sentiment. Perhaps he did not know what to do with it. He knew nothing about women; he had been in jail at the age when he should have been learning. Perhaps Laurie, so lighthearted and careless, had a capacity for passion that overshot Piotr. He had learned in prison that fasting, like any deprivation, made fullness impossible. He had been sick after eating an apple; it was like eating a wet stone. The solitude of prison made anyone else's presence exhausting, and the absence of love in his life now made love the transformed apple—the wet stone he could not taste or digest.

Three days after returning to Warsaw he broke an ankle—just like that, stupidly, stepping off a curb. He wrote into the silence of Paris that he was handicapped, in pain, but the pain was nothing to his longing for Laurie. Weeks later, she answered that she still loved him and no one else. She seemed upset about the ankle; in some way she blamed herself. They were now as they had been, in love, miles apart, with no hope of meeting. He was flattered that she recalled enough of him to say she still loved him—she who had no memory.

Piotr became forty-three. After delayed, drawn-out, finger-crossed, and breath-holding negotiations he obtained a new passport and a three-month visa for France, where he had been invited to give a series of lectures. A young woman was coming to Warsaw, in exchange, to instruct Polish students on tendencies in French poetry since 1950. Piotr silently wished her luck. His departure date had been twice postponed, so he was in a state of tension, dizziness, and unbearable control when he boarded the Air France plane on a cold day of autumn. Until the plane lifted he expected to be recalled because they had all changed their minds. The steward's unintelligible welcome over the intercom seemed for a sickening moment to be meant for him—the plane was going to land so that Professor S— could be removed. Among a dozen gifts for his love in Piotr's luggage were two she had asked for: Polish birth-control pills, superior to any on the Western market (they prevented conception and also made you lose weight), and a soporific potion that was excitingly habit-forming and provided its addicts with the vivid, colorful dreams of opium sleep. In this way, wrote Laurie, sleep was less boring.

Marek met him in Paris, and wept as they embraced. He had taken a hotel room without a bath for his cousin in order to spare his limited funds. He gave Piotr confusing instructions about a locked bathroom down the hall, advice about the French franc exchange (Piotr had in his possession the allowed one hundred dollars and nothing more), and all the local Polish gossip. Piotr, who had never lied to Marek except over Laurie, invented a university dinner. Fifteen minutes after Marek departed, Piotr, carrying the smaller of his two suitcases, took a taxi to Laurie's new address. The names of her streets were to haunt him all his life: Avenue Mozart, Boulevard Malesherbes, Impasse Adrienne, Place Louis-Marin, Rue de l'Yvette, Rue Sisley, Rue du Regard. This year she occupied a studio-and-bath on the top floor of a new house in Rue Guynemer.

"It's my own, Potter. It isn't borrowed" was the first thing she said to him. "It costs the earth." Then, incoherently, "I'm not always here. Sometimes I go away."

The studio was bright, as neat and almost as bare as a cell, and smelled of fresh paint. So that was what Laurie was like, too. He found her face a shade thinner, her figure a trace fuller; but the hair, the eyes, the voice—no change. Now he recalled her perfume, and the smell beneath the fragrance. She laughed at his suitcase, because, suddenly embarrassed, he tried to conceal it behind the door; laughed at a beret he wore; laughed because she loved him but still she would not make love: "I can't, not yet, not just like that." Their evening fitted his memory of older evenings—Laurie greedy with a menu, telling Piotr in a suddenly prim voice all about wines. She was certainly repeating a lesson, but Piotr felt immeasurably secure, and tolerant of the men she might be quoting. Laurie said, "Isn't this marvellous?"—taking his happiness for granted simply because she was so entirely alive. He remembered how, once out, she hated to go home. "But it's a children's hour," she protested when he said at midnight that he was tired. Four hours later, as they sat in a harsh café, she said, "Potter, I'm so glad I was born," lifting her straight soft hair away from her neck in a ritual gesture of gladness. He took this to be a tribute to his presence. Piotr did not love being alive, but he absolutely did not want to die, which was another thing. At their table a drunk slept deeply with his head on his arms. The day behind Piotr lay in shreds, like the old Métro tickets and strips of smudged paper on the café floor. Laurie said that the papers were receipts— the café was an offtrack betting shop. Like the old story about the golden and the Labrador, this information contained an insoluble mystery. All he knew was that in a hell of urban rubbish Laurie was glad she'd been born. Exhaustion gave Piotr hallucinations; he saw doors yawning in blank walls, dark flights of steps, nuns hovering, but still he did not lose track of the night. The night had to end, and even Laurie would be bound to admit that it was time to go home.

THEY HAD the next day, a night, a day of sun and long walks, and a night again. From Laurie's window he looked across to the Luxembourg Gardens, which were golden, rust brown, and the darkest green, like a profound shade of night. Each morning he walked to his hotel, unmade his bed, and asked for mail and messages. On the third morning the porter handed Piotr an envelope from his cousin containing a loan in French money, an advance on his university fees. He counted out fifteen hundred francs. The last barrier between Piotr and peace of mind dissolved.

On his way back to Laurie he bought croissants, a morning paper, and cigarettes. He knew that he would never be as happy again. He found Laurie dressed in jeans and a Russian tunic, packing a suitcase. The bed was made, the sheets they had slept in were folded on a chair; through the doorway he could see their damp towels hanging side by side on the shower rail. She looked up, smiled, and said she was going to Venice.

"When?"

"Today. In a couple of hours. I'm meeting this friend of mine." He suddenly imagined the girl with the painted freckles. "You'll be busy for the next few days anyway," she went on. "You put off coming to Paris twice, remember. I couldn't put off my friend anymore. I didn't tell you before, because I didn't want to spoil things when you arrived."

He carried her suitcase to the Gare Saint-Lazare. At the station she put coins in a machine that distributed second-class tickets. He looked around and said, "Do you go to Venice from here?"

"No, they're local trains. We're meeting at a station out of town. It saves driving through Paris, with the traffic and all."

An enormous hope was contained in "we're meeting." He understood, at last, that Laurie was going to Venice with a man. Laurie seemed unaware that he had not taken it in until now, or unaware that it mattered. She was hungry; she had missed her breakfast. "Café de la Passerelle" gleamed in green neon at the end of a dark buffet. Laurie chose from among twenty empty tables as if her choice could make any difference. Piotr, sleepwalking now, ordered and ate apricot pie. The café was shaped like a corridor, with dusty windows on either wall. He and Laurie had exchanged climates, seasons, places—for the windows looked out on slanting rain and deserted streets. Laurie slid back her cuff so that she could keep an eye on her watch. Piotr was silent. She said—sulking, almost—Now, why? What harm was there in her taking a few days off with an old friend while he had so many other things to do?

"It's an old story, you know," she said. "Hardly worth the trouble of breaking off. He always takes me somewhere for my birthday." She stopped, as if wondering how to explain what the old friendship was based on. She said, simply, "You know how it is. He got me young."

"Do you love him?"

"No, nothing like that. I love you. But we planned this trip ages ago. I couldn't be sure you would ever get to Paris. I don't want to hurt his feelings. You'd like him, Potter. Honestly you would. He speaks three different languages. He's independent—enjoys running his own business. I don't even make a dent in his life."

"Does he love you?"

"I keep telling you, it isn't like that. We aren't really lovers. I mean, not as you and I are. We sleep together—well, if we find ourselves in the same bed."

"Try not to find yourself," said Piotr.

"What?" She seemed as candid, as confident, as tender as always. Her eyes were as clear as a child's. Her hand shook suddenly. What was coming now? The unloved childhood? The day her mother left her at Bishop Purse School? The school must have provided clean sheets and warm rooms and regular meals, but she was of a world that took these remarkable gifts for granted. His wife, younger then than Laurie was now, had stolen food for Piotr when he lay in a prison infirmary absolutely certain he was about to die. She had been a prisoner, too, dispatched as medical aide and cleaner. She stopped at the foot of his cot. When she started talking she couldn't stop. He saw that her amber eyes focussed nowhere—her "in-looking eyes" he was to call them. Because of the eyes and the mad rush of words and the danger she was calling down on them he had thought, The girl is insane. Then sanely, quietly, she said, "I have some bread for you." You could not compare Laurie Bennett with a person of that quality. All the same, Piotr had guessed: his wife was insane, but only with him. Danger had reached him after he seemed well out of it, only to be caught on the danger a couple create for each other.

"Look, Potter," said Laurie. "If you mind all that much, I won't go. I'll talk to him."

"When?"

"Now; soon. But I'd be sad. He's a good friend. Why would he want to take me to Venice, except out of friendship? He doesn't need *me*. He knows all kinds of interesting people. I'd be poorer without him—really alone." She was already making women's gestures of leaving, straightening the spoon in its saucer, gathering in whatever belonged to her, bringing her affairs close—protecting herself. "Don't come to the train," she said. "Drink your coffee, read the paper. Look, I've even brought it along. Keep the key to my room. You'll stay there, won't you? As we arranged? If you mind about the concierge seeing you—not that she cares—just use the garage instead of the front door. That's how the married ladies in the building meet their lovers. I'll write," she said. "I'll write to your hotel."

He pushed his chair back. As he got to his feet his ankle gave way. "Oh, Potter, your poor ankle!" Laurie said. "I was on a sailing holiday when you broke it. I was at Lake Constance and I wasn't getting my mail. I wasn't seeing newspapers or anything, and when I finally got back to Paris someone told me there'd been this war on in the Middle East. All those dead and it was already over and I hadn't known a thing—not about your ankle, not anything." She smiled, kissed him, picked up her suitcase, and walked away. Without knowing why, he touched his forehead. He was wearing his beret, which Marek had implored him not to do in Paris; the beret made Piotr look like an out-of-town intellectual, like a teacher from the provinces, like a priest from a working-class parish. What did it matter? Any disguise would do to hide the shame of being Piotr.

Only a few men now were left in the café—Algerians reading want ads, middle-aged stragglers clearly hating Piotr because he was alone and demented, like half the universe. Later, he had no memory of having taken the Métro, only that when he came back up to daylight the rain had stopped. He walked on wet leaves. Like the married women's lovers he entered Laurie's building by way of the garage, slipping and sliding because the slope was abrupt and the soles of his shoes had grown damp. Her room was airless now, with sun newly ablaze on the shut window. He was starting a new day, the third day since this morning. His croissants were still on the table. He picked them up, thinking that it was better to leave nothing. Then he saw there was nothing much he could leave, because Laurie had packed his things. Piotr's suitcase stood locked, buckled, next to the chair on which were folded the sheets they had slept in. Her neatness erased him. The extra towel on the shower rail might have been anyone's. He was wiped out by her clothes' hanging just so, by her sweaters and shirts in plastic boxes, by the prim order of the bouillon cubes and Nescafé and yellow bowls on a shelf, by the books—presents, probably—lined up by size beneath the window. He saw the review containing his poems, still honored by its dustproof bag. What he had never noticed before was that the bag also held a thin yellow book

of verse, the Insel-Bücherei edition of Christian Morgenstern's
Palmström poems. Piotr had once translated some of these, entirely
for pleasure. When he was arrested he had had scraps of paper in his
pocket covered with choppy phrases in Polish and German that
became entirely sinister when read by the police. "Well, you see,"
said a blond, solemn Piotr of twenty years ago, "Morgenstern was not
much understood and finally he was mad, but the poems in their way
are funny."

"Why a German?" The sarcasm of the illiterate. "Aren't there
enough mad Poles?"

"There soon will be," said Piotr, to his own detriment.

Now, in Laurie's room, even the yellow binding seemed to speak
to him. Where had it come from? Someone, another doting Potter,
had offered it to her, thinking, Love something I love and you are
sure to love me. Who? The flyleaf said nothing. He turned the pages
slowly and, on the same page as a poem called "The Dreamer," came
upon a color snapshot of two people in an unknown room. Piotr
recognized Laurie but not the man. The man was fair, like Piotr, but
somewhat younger. His hair was brushed. He wore a respectable suit
and a dark-red tie. What Piotr saw at once about his face was that
it was genuinely cheerful. Here, at last, caught by chance, was the
bon naturel Piotr had hopelessly been seeking from woman to
woman. Laurie, naked except for her wristwatch, sat on the arm of
his chair, with her legs curled like the tail of a mermaid. One hand
was slipped behind the man's neck. She held a white shower cap,
probably the very cap now hanging on a tap in the next room.

A casual happiness suffused this picture. Piotr was looking at people who did not know or really understand how lucky they were. A
sun risen for the lovers alone shone in at the window behind them
and made Laurie's hair white and sparkling, like light seen through
an icicle. Those were Piotr's immediate, orderly thoughts. He sensed
the particular eroticism of the clothed man and the naked girl and
only then felt the shock, like a door battered in. The door collapsed,
and Piotr saw whatever he had been dreading since he had dared to
fall in love—solitude, cruelty, the loneliness of dying: all of that.

Laurie had deliberately left the picture for him to find. She had
gone to a foreign bookshop, perhaps the place in the Rue du Dragon

that she had pointed out to him, saying she once worked there for a week before they realized she spoke nothing but English, and chose the very book that was bound to catch his eye. She had then staged the picture. Piotr's wife, in *her* calculated dementia, had recorded her own lovemaking with another man on a tape on which Piotr had been assembling the elements of a course in Russian poetry. Recalling this, he remembered that where his wife had been frantic Laurie was only heedless. The book and the picture were part of the blithe indifference of the two lovers, no more.

He was suddenly overcome with a need to shut his eyes, to be blessed by darkness. He lay flat on the bed and said to himself, What can I give her? I am never here. When he rose and looked at the picture again, it seemed to him it was not where he had left it. Also, in the neat row of clothing he saw a hanger askew. Where there had been only Piotr's croissants on the table there was now, as well, an enamel four-leaf-clover pin, open, as if it had parted from its wearer unnoticed. The door had to be locked from within; he tested the handle and saw he had forgotten to turn the key. Anyone might have entered while Piotr had his eyes shut and examined the snapshot and put it in the wrong place. Laurie, he now saw, had a coarse face, small, calculating blue eyes, and a greedy, vacuous expression. What he had mistaken for gaiety had been nothing but guile. The man seemed more sympathetic somehow. For one thing, he was decently dressed. He looked sane. There was nothing *wrong* with that man, really, except for the peculiar business of having set up a camera in the first place. He was a Western European by dress, haircut, expression. He was not a Latin. Nor was this an English face. Piotr sensed a blunt sureness about him. He would be sure before, during, and after any encounter. He would not feel any of Piotr's anxiousness over pleasing Laurie and pleasing himself. He might have been a young officer of solid yeoman origins, risen from the ranks, in the old Imperial Army—a character in a pre-1914 Viennese novel, say. He became then, and for all time, "the Austrian" in Piotr's mind.

Piotr replaced the picture where he now thought it must have been, next to a poem called "Korf in Berlin." No one had entered the room—he knew that. The clover pin had fallen from Laurie's

tunic. It was normal for a hanger to be askew when someone even
as neat as Laurie had packed in a hurry.

He went out the front door this time, brave enough to confront
the concierge and give up Laurie's key.

"Bennett," he said, and on receiving no answer said it again.

"I heard you." She seemed blurred and hostile. He had to narrow
his eyes to keep her in focus. The trees in the Luxembourg Gardens
were indistinct, as if seen through tears. He found himself caught in
a crocodile of schoolboys. A harridan in a polo coat screamed at them,
at Piotr, too, "Watch your step, keep together!" Piotr began to search
for something that could protect him—trees in a magic ring around
a monument might be suitable. As soon as he had selected a metal
chair not too close to anyone the sun vanished. A north wind came
at him. Leaves rolled over and over along the damp path. He sat on
the edge of a forbidden grass plot, staring at a bust he at first took
to be Lenin's. He still wore his reading glasses—the reason the concierge had seemed undefined. The bust was in fact a monument to
Paul Verlaine.

The grass had kept its midsummer green; when the sun came out
briefly the tree shadows were still summer's shadows. But the season
was autumn, and he saw a gleaming chestnut lying among the split
casings. He would have picked it up, but someone might have seen.

Laurie had escaped from her locked room. It was not her face, not
her hair, but her voice and her voice in her letters that pursued Piotr.
He. We. I. "*He* always takes me somewhere for my birthday." "*We*
took the tellypherique and walked down from the reservoir." "*I* was
on a sailing holiday at Lake Constance." It had been *we* in the Italian
Tyrol—"We take lovely picnics up behind the hotel, you can hear
bells from the other valley." *We* turned up again in Rome, at Crans-
sur-Sierre, at a hotel in Normandy. *We* were old friends—James and
Nancy, Mike and Sylvia, Hans and Heidi. *We* existed in a few letters,
long enough to spin out a holiday, then fell over Laurie's horizon.
Piotr's only balm was that *he* was wiped out. There was a big X over
his ugly face. Laurie, or *I,* had been alone for at least the time it took
to remember Piotr and write him an eager, loving letter full of
spelling mistakes. Piotr had been with her in Portugal, in Switzerland;
she had generously included him by making herself, for a few min-

utes, alone and available. Perhaps Laurie had been alone in her mind, truly loyal to Piotr—*he* meanwhile in the bar of the hotel? In the shower? Off on some disloyal pretext of his own so that he could slip an *I* message to his wife?

She was a good girl, all the same, for she had always taken care to give Piotr a story so plausible he could believe it without despising himself. Now that she had told him the truth, he was as bitter as if she had deceived him. Why shouldn't Laurie be taken for holidays? Did he want her alone, crabbed, dishevelled, soured? The only shadow over her life that Piotr knew of had been Piotr himself. Her voice resumed: "I am taking the car and driving . . ." Whose car, by the way? Piotr moved his feet and struck his suitcase. His ankle made a snapping sound. There was no pain, but the noise was disconcerting, as if the bones were speaking to him. She had left him at the airport; she had not known where she would be sleeping that night. "That time you broke your ankle . . . I was on a sailing holiday at Lake Constance." Yes, and something else, about a war in the Middle East. The fragments were like smooth-grained panels of wood. The panels slid together, touched, fitted. Her wild journey to forget Piotr had only one direction: to Lake Constance, where someone was waiting.

There were aspects of Laurie's behavior that, for the sake of his sanity, Piotr had refused to consider. Now, sitting on a cold metal chair, eyes fixed on a chestnut he was too self-conscious to pick up, he could not keep free of his knowledge; it was like the dark wind that struck through the circle of trees. She had used him, made an audience of him, played on his feelings, and she was at this moment driving to Venice with—the element of farce in every iniquity—Piotr's Polish birth-control pills. Moreover, she had entirely forgotten Piotr. His grief was so beyond jealousy that he seemed truly beside himself; there was a Piotr in a public park, trying hard to look like other people, and a Piotr divorced from that person. His work, his childhood, his imprisonment, his marriage, his still mysterious death were rolled in a compact ball, spinning along the grass, away from whatever was left of him. Then, just as it seemed about to disappear, the two Piotrs came together again. The shock of the joining put him to sleep. His head fell forward; he pulled it up with a start. He may have slept for a second, no more. No one had noticed—he looked for that. The brief death had cleansed him. His only thought now was that his memory was better than hers and so he knew what they were losing. As for Laurie's abuse of him, it was simply that she did not know the meaning of words, their precision, their power—why, she could not even spell them. She did not realize when she was lying, because she did not know what words were about. This new, gentle tolerance made Piotr wonder: what if his feeling for Laurie was no more than tenderness, and what if Piotr was incapable of love other than the kind he could give his children? His wife had said this—had screamed it. She did not want his friendship, his loyalty, his affection, his devotion, his companionship. She wanted what he had finally bestowed on Laurie; at least, he thought he had.

H E GAVE HIS first lecture and poetry reading in an amphitheatre that was usually used by an institute of Polish civilization for showing films and for talks by visiting art historians. Most of the audience was made up of the Polish colony. A few had come to hear him read, but most of them were there to see what he looked like. The colony was divided that night not into its usual social or political splinters but over the issue of how Piotr was supposed to have treated his wife. All were agreed on the first paragraphs of Piotr's story: there were clues and traces in his early poems concerning the girl who saved his life. He and the girl had married, had lived for years on his earnings as an anonymous translator. Here came the first split in public opinion, for some said that it was really his wife who had done all the work, while Piotr, idle, served a joyous apprenticeship for his later career of pursuing girl students. Others maintained that his wife was ignorant of foreign languages; also, only Piotr could have made something readable out of the translated works.

Next came the matter of his wife's lovers: no one denied them, but what about Piotr's affairs? Also, what about his impotence? For he was held to be satyr and eunuch and in some ineffable way to be both at once. Perhaps he was merely impotent. Who, then, had fathered his wife's two—or four, or six—children? Names were offered, of men powerful in political and cultural circles.

Piotr had tried to kill his wife—some said by flinging her down a flight of stone steps, others said by defenestration. He had rushed at her with a knife, and to save herself she had jumped through a window, landing easily, but scarring her face on the broken panes. A pro-Piotr faction had the wife a heavy drinker who had stumbled while carrying a bottle and glass. The symmetry of the rumors had all factions agreed on the beginning (the couple meeting in prison) and on the end—Piotr collecting his wife's clothes in a bundle and leaving them on the doorstep of her latest lover.

Before starting his lecture Piotr looked at the expectant faces and wondered which story was current now. After the lecture, strangers crowded up to congratulate him. He was pleased to see one of them, an old sculptress his parents had known before the war. When she smiled her face became as flat and Oriental and as wrinkled as tissue paper. Maria, as virginal as her name, had once been a militant; quite often such women automatically became civil servants, referred to by a younger generation as "the aunts of the Revolution." Her reward had been of a different order: Summoned to Moscow by someone she trusted, arrested casually, released at random, she had lived in Paris for years. She never mentioned her past, and yet she was in it still, for her knowledge of Paris was only knowledge about bus stops. Her mind, ardent and young, moved in the direction of dazzling changes, but these were old changes now—from 1934 to 1935, say. Piotr recalled her spinster's flat, with the shaky, useless tables, the dull, green, beloved plants, the books in faded jackets, the lumpy chairs, the divans covered in odd lengths of homespun materials in orchard colors—greengage, grape, plum. Her references had been strict, dialectical, until they became soft and forgiving, with examples drawn from novels got by heart. He did not know of any experience of passion, other than politics, in Maria's life. Her work as a sculptress had been faithful and scrupulous and sentimental; seeing it, years before, one should have been able to tell her future. She had never asked him questions. Few women had mattered; she was one: a discreet, mistaken old woman he had seen twice since his childhood, with whom he talked of nothing but politics and art. These were subjects so important to him that their conversations seemed deeply personal. Maria did not praise Piotr's lecture but said only, "I heard

every word," meaning, "I was listening." There were too many people; they could not speak. They agreed to meet, and just at that
moment another woman, with dry red hair and a wide, nervous grin,
pushed her way past Maria and said to Piotr, "My husband and I
would think it an honor if you came to stay with us. We have a large
flat, we are both out all day, and you would be private. We admire
your work." She had something Piotr considered a handicap in a
woman, which was that she showed her gums. "You are probably in
a hotel," she said, "but just come to us when your money runs out."

Piotr kept the card she gave him, and later Marek examined it and
said, "I know who they are. She is a doctor. No, no, they are not
political, nothing like that. You would be all right there."

W AS IT BECAUSE of the lecture? Because of seeing Maria? Because
he had been invited by the doctor? Piotr now considered Laurie's
absence with a sense of deliverance, as if a foreign object had been
removed from his life. She had always lied. He recalled how she could
tremble at will—how she had once spilled a cup of coffee, explaining
later that she was attracted to him at that moment but felt too
diffident to say so. She had let him think she was inexperienced in
order to torture him, had kept him in her bed for hours of hesitation
and monologue, insisting that she was afraid of a relationship that
might be too binding, that she was afraid of falling in love with him
—this after the party where she had said, "You, Potter, you stay."
Afterward she told Piotr that she'd had her first lover at fifteen. Old
family friend, she said, with children about her age. He used to take
her home for holidays from Bishop Purse. She was his substitute for
a forbidden daughter, said Laurie, calmly, drinking coffee without
spilling it this time. Piotr should have smacked her, kicked her, cut
up her clothes with scissors and hung the rags all over the lamps and
furniture. He should have followed her around Paris, calling insults,
making a fool of her in restaurants. As he was incapable of doing
anything even remotely violent, it was just as well she had gone.
Relief made him generous: he reminded himself that she had added
to his life. She had given Piotr whatever love was left over from her
love for herself. You could cut across any number of lies and reach

the person you wanted, he decided, but no one could get past narcissism. It was like the crust of the earth.

He slept soundly that night and part of the next afternoon. Marek had left books at his hotel, the new novels of the autumn season. Nothing in them gave Piotr a clue to the people he saw in the streets, but the fresh appearance of the volumes, their clean covers, the smooth paper and fanciful titles put still more distance between himself and his foolish love affair. After dark his cousin arrived to take him to a French dinner party. Piotr had been accepted by a celebrated, beautiful hostess named Eliane, renowned for her wit, her lovers, and her dislike of foreigners. She had been to Piotr's lecture. At the dinner party she planned to place Piotr on her right. Marek was afraid that Piotr did not take in what this signified in terms of glory. Any of the people at that lecture would have given an arm and a leg if the sacrifice had meant getting past Eliane's front door.

Piotr asked, "What does she do?"

They travelled across Paris by taxi. Marek continued his long instructions, telling Piotr what Eliane was likely to talk about and what she thought about poetry and Poland. Piotr was not to contradict anything, even if he knew it to be inaccurate; above all, he was not to imagine that anything said to him was ever meant to be funny. Marek and Piotr would be the only foreign guests. He begged Piotr not to address any remark to him in Polish in anyone's hearing. Answering Piotr's question finally, he said that Eliane did not "do" anything. "You must get over the habit of defining women in terms of employment," he concluded.

During the preliminary drink—a thimble of sweet port—Marek did not leave his cousin's side. The hostess was the smallest woman Piotr had ever seen, just over dwarf size. She wore a long pink dress and had rings on every finger. To Piotr's right, at table, sat a pregnant girl with soft dark hair and a meek profile. He smiled at her. She stared at a point between his eyes. His smile had been like a sentence uttered too soon. Marek's expression signalled that Piotr was to turn and look at his hostess. Eliane said to him gravely, "Have you ever eaten salmon before?" She next said, "I heard your lecture." Piotr, still bemused by the salmon question, made no reply. She continued, "The poetry you recited was not in French, and I could not understand it." She waited; he waited, too. "Were you *greatly* influenced by Paul Valéry?" Piotr considered this. His hostess turned smoothly to the man on her left, who wore a red ribbon and a rosette on his lapel.

"Cézanne was a Freemason," Piotr heard him saying. "So was Braque. So was Juan Gris. So was Soutine. No one who was not a Freemason has ever had his work shown in a national museum."

The pregnant girl's social clockwork gave her Piotr along with the next course. "Is this your first visit to Paris?" she said. Her eyes danced, rolled almost. She tossed her head, as a nervous pony might. Where the rest of the table was concerned, she and Piotr were telling each other something deliciously amusing and private.

"It is my third trip as an adult. I came once with my parents when I was a child." He wondered if his discovery of chestnut meringues at Rumpelmayer's tearoom in 1938 was of the slightest interest.

"The rest of the time you were always in your pretty Poland?" The laugh that accompanied this was bewildering to him. "What could have been keeping you there all this time?" In another context, in a world more familiar, the look on the girl's face would have been an invitation. But what Piotr could see, and the others could not, was that she was not really looking at him at all.

"Well, at one time I was in prison," he said, "and sometimes translating books, and sometimes teaching at a university. Sometimes the progression goes in reverse, and your poet begins at the university and ends in jail."

"Have you ever had veal cooked this way before?" she said, after a quick glance to see if their hostess was ready to take on Piotr again. "It is typically French. But not typically Parisian. No, it is typically provincial. Eliane likes doing these funny provincial things." She paused again. Piotr was still hers. "And where did you learn your good French and your charming manners?" she said. "In Poland?"

"The hardest thing to learn was not to spit on the table," said Piotr.

After that both women left him in peace. But of course he was not in peace, for Marek was watching. He did not reproach Piotr, but Piotr knew he would not be invited to a French evening again.

PERHAPS BECAUSE he had slept too much in the afternoon, he found that night long and full of dark misery. He awoke at the worst possible hour, at four, when it was too late to read—his eyes watered and would not focus—and too early to get up. He heard the chimes of the hotel clock downstairs striking five, then six. He slept lightly and woke on the stroke of seven. His body had taken over and was trying to show him that the nonchalance about Laurie had been a false truce. Feeling dull and sick, he shaved at the basin in his room, and asked the maid to unlock the door down the hall so that he could have a bath. He entered the steamy room, with its cold walls and opaque windows, reminding himself that Laurie was a foreign object, that he had a life of his own, that he had a center of gravity. His body reacted to this show of independence with stomach cramps and violent nausea. His mouth went dry when he returned to his room to find a breakfast tray waiting. The skin around his mouth felt attacked by small stinging insects. A headache along his hairline prevented him from unfolding the morning paper or reading a letter from home. The day was sunny, and he saw now that the commonplace sayings about crossed love were all true: the weather mocked him; he craved darkness and rain. His unhappiness was a disease. Strangers would see signs of it, and would despise him.

He loved her. For more than two years now his waking thought had been Is there a letter? He wanted to reach across to her, straight to Venice, but she had to want him—otherwise he was a demand, a claim, a dead weight on her life; he was like the soft, curled-up, dejected women who seemed to make an equal mess of love and cigarette ash. Laurie was in Venice, on a snowy beach. (The Venice of his imagining was all blue and white.) She lay immodestly close to a cloudy man. Piotr could not really see him. Perhaps he was placid, like the Austrian, or thin and worried, like Piotr. Perhaps he was a disgusting boulevardier with cheeks like boiled shrimp. "He speaks three languages . . . enjoys running his own business." Oh, inferior, callous, stupid!

Piotr told his diminished self, My poems are translated into . . . I have corresponded with . . . been invited by . . . I can lecture in Polish, Russian, Lithuanian, German, English, French, and I can also . . .

Laurie had assured Piotr that no one, ever, had been like him. She had said, "To think that until now I thought I was just one more frigid North American!" Piotr had believed. He wanted to compose a scream of a letter: Where are you? Why don't you send me a telegram, give me a sign? I haunt the hotel office where mail is kept. I mistake the hotel bill for a message saying you have come back. They say that mail from Italy is slow, but I see other people receiving letters with Italian stamps. I wake at dawn wondering if today will be the day of the letter.

His torment was intensified by the number of mail deliveries; there were three a day, with a fourth for parcels (should she show she remembered him by sending a book). The porter, sorting letters, would see Piotr hovering and call, "Nothing!" and Piotr would scurry away as if he had been caught in some shameful voyeur posture. He now heard and saw "Venice" everywhere: When he bought fruit he found it stamped on an orange. He even said, "God," though until now he had thought there was no God to hear him.

PIOTR HAD still not received any money from the university. He was used to administrative languor, but the francs his cousin had advanced him were melting fast and Piotr did not want to ask Marek for more. The day came when he decided to leave his hotel and move in with the doctor and her husband. Marek approved of the address, which was close to the École Militaire; he had unearthed what he thought of as useful information: the doctor and her husband had emigrated to France, separately, before the war. They had met in a Polish Resistance network operating out of Grenoble. The marriage was not a happy one. The husband had a mistress and an illegitimate daughter, with whom he spent every Sunday. The doctor was certain to fall in love with Piotr, Marek said.

Piotr did not care for the street, which seemed to him frozen and hostile. There was a desperate, respectable shabbiness about the house. Laurie would never have lived there. In the icy stairwell an elevator creaked on swaying cables. The halls were dim. Tenants rode in the lift and crossed in passageways without speaking, staring flatly. He imagined each high-ceilinged apartment occupied by one person, living alone, working in a ministry, eating ready-made food on the edge of a table at night. His hostess welcomed him as an old acquaintance and made up his bed in the room she had once used for private consultations. Vestiges of the old regime remained—the powerful lights overhead, the washbasin in a corner, a leather folding screen. Under his bed he discovered a case of books. None were newer than the early nineteen-fifties; probably it was then that the couple's marriage had broken down. The French bindings had gone from white to yellow. There were a number of volumes about the war. Piotr, a decade or so younger than the heroic generation, had always been faintly irritated by them.

The doctor was on the staff of a clinic in the Thirteenth Arrondissement, where she now had an office and received her private patients. She gave Piotr a ring of house keys and the key to a letter box downstairs in the court. This led Piotr to new hauntings. He could not bring himself to cross the courtyard without peering through the slot of the box, even if he had looked only half an hour before. He expected word from Laurie at any time: his old hotel might easily receive a special-delivery letter and send it around by messenger. Sometimes a gleam of light on the metal lining of the box could have been a letter, and the hope he felt almost made up for the disappointment. He also had a new worry: a lump, like a large black stone, filled his chest. He felt it when he woke up in the morning. The first thing he heard was an alarm clock in the doctor's bedroom shortly before six, and then he would become aware of the stone. He would hear the doctor's husband getting up and listening to the six-o'clock news in the bathroom. He was small and bald and polite to Piotr. He did not really have to get up before six. He simply did not want to be alone with his wife more than he had to. The doctor actually said so to Piotr, staring at him craftily and boldly, obviously hoping for some oblique, similar confidence about his wife. Piotr noticed that when the pair were alone they argued in French. It was their language for reproach and for justification. He would remember how he had parted from his wife and given up his children so that the children would not have to hear adult violence from their dark bedroom. Often in the night Piotr heard the doctor's singsong complaint, which had an almost poetical rhythm to it. She said that her husband was a miser who did not love her. He deprived her of money; he deprived her of warmth. If the husband replied—a low grumble of words in which Piotr caught "never" and "idea"—her voice became discordant, choppy, like a child banging crazily on piano keys. He heard, "Some men are cruel, but at least they are intelligent. How you must be gloating. You think *you* have come out of this safely. Well, you may not have a chance to gloat for long."

Sometimes the doctor had breakfast with Piotr. She told him how she had studied medicine in France, and about the war and the Resistance, adding, inevitably, "You are too young to remember." She said, "My husband was brave in that war. But he does not understand an educated woman and should never have married one." What she really wanted to talk about was Piotr and his wife. She looked, she stared, she hoped, she waited. Piotr was used to that.

He gave his second lecture, in French, in a basement classroom. This time he had a row of well-dressed, perfumed Frenchwomen— the inevitable *femmes du monde* attracted by the foreign poet— including, to his surprise, the pregnant girl from the fatal dinner party. A number of students, lowering as though Piotr intended in some way to mislead them, slumped at the back of the room. After the lecture a young man wearing a military-service haircut got up to ask if Piotr considered himself right-wing. Piotr said no.

"I heard they only let Fascists out."

"I have not been let out like a dog," said Piotr amiably. "I am here like any ordinary lecturer."

A girl applauded. One of the well-dressed women called him *"Maître."* Piotr pulled his beret down to his ears and scuttled out to the street. The students had been suspicious, the women distant and puzzled. What did they expect? He remembered Laurie's smile, her light voice, how suddenly her expression could alter as one quick wave of feeling followed another. He remembered that she had loved him and tried to make him happy, and that he was on his way to the doctor's silent flat. The stone in his chest expanded and pressed on his lungs. All that prevented him from weeping in the street was the thought that he had never seen a man doing that. In his room, he was overtaken. He was surprised at how warm tears were—surely warmer than blood. He said to himself, "Well, at least I am crying over something real," and that was odd, for he believed that he lived in reality, that he had to. The stone dissolved, and he understood now about crying. But the feverish convalescence that followed the tears was unpleasant, and after a few hours the stone came back.

Aɴᴅ ꜱᴏ ᴄᴏɴᴛɪɴᴜᴇᴅ the most glorious autumn anyone in Paris could remember. The rainy morning of Laurie's departure had given way to blue and gold. And yet when Piotr, a haunter of anonymous parks now, sat with his back in shade, he felt a chill, as if the earth were tipping him into the dark. Marek, forgiving him for his French dinner fiasco, invited him to a new restaurant in the Latin Quarter. Piotr had the habit of eating anything put before him without tasting or noticing much. He could hear Laurie's voice mockingly describing their meal: "Mushrooms in diesel oil, steak broiled over moldy straw, Beaujolais like last year's vinegar." The other diners were plain-looking couples in their thirties and forties with *Le Monde* or *Le Nouvel Observateur* folded next to their plates. He noticed all this as if he were saving up facts to tell Laurie. The cousins' conversation was quiet gossip about Poles. They recalled a writer who had once been such a power in Warsaw that his objection to a student newspaper had sent Piotr to jail and Marek into exile. Now this man was teaching in America, where he was profoundly respected as someone who had been under the whip and survived to tell. He still had his sparse black teeth, said Marek, whose knowledge of such details was endless, and the university at which he taught had offered to have them replaced by something white and splendid. But the fact was that the writer who had broken other men's lives in the nineteen-fifties was afraid of the dentist.

Marek ordered a second bottle of wine and said, "Every day I wonder what I am doing in Paris. I have no real friends. I have enemies who chalk swastikas on my staircase. I speak seven languages. My maternal grandmother was the daughter of a princess. Who cares about that here? Perhaps I should go back to Poland." This was a normal émigré monologue; Piotr did not attempt to reply. They walked in the mild night, along bright streets, threading their way past beggars and guitar players, stopping to look at North African pastry shops. Piotr was troubled by the beggars—the bedraggled whining mothers with drugged, dozing babies, the maimed men exhibiting their blindness and the stumps of arms and legs for cash. "Yugoslav gangs," said Marek, shrugging. He reminded Piotr that begging was part of freedom. Men and women, here, were at liberty to beg their rent, their drink, their children's food. Piotr looked at him but could see no clue, no double meaning. Marek had settled for something, once and for all, just as Piotr had done in an entirely other existence. As they neared the Seine he had a childlike Christmas feeling of expectancy, knowing that the lighted flank of Notre Dame church would be reflected, trembling, on the dark water. He was forgetting Laurie—oh, surely he was! He decided that he would write about their story, fact on fact. Writing would remove the last trace of Laurie from his mind and heart. He was not a writer of prose and only an intermittent keeper of diaries, but he began then and there taking the cool historical measure of Laurie and love. He felt bold enough to say something about Laurie Bennett, and something else about Venice.

"Oh, Laurie—Laurie is in Florence," said Marek. "I had a card." Between Piotr's ribs the stone grew twice its size. "She travels," Marek went on. "An older man gives her money." He dropped the only important subject in the world to go on talking about himself.

"The older man," said Piotr. "Is he her lover?"

"She has never produced him," said Marek. "You always see Laurie alone. I have known her for years. You can never look at Laurie and look at another man and say 'sleeping with.' But this man—she was so innocent when she first came to Paris that she tried to declare him to the police as her source of income and nearly got herself kicked out of the country. That was years ago now."

Years ago? Piotr had never questioned her real age. Laurie looked young, and she talked about her school days as if they were just behind her. Perhaps she was someone who refused to have anything to do with time. In that case her youthfulness implied a lack of understanding: Just as she spelled words wrong because she did not know what words meant, she could not be changed by time because she did not know what change was about.

Piotr awoke the next morning with a flaming throat and a pain in his left shoulder. He could scarcely get his clothes on or swallow or speak. His hostess sat wearing a wrapper, hunched over a pot of strong tea. Today was Sunday.

"Mass in the morning, horse races in the afternoon," she said, referring to her husband, who had vanished. Piotr remembered what Marek had said about the illegitimate child. The doctor gave Piotr dark bread, cream cheese, and plum jam, and waited to hear—about his wife, of course. She never stopped waiting. From the kitchen he could see the room he had just left. He thought of his bed and wished he were in it, but then he would be her prisoner and she might talk to him all morning long.

Outside, above the courtyard, thin autumn clouds slid over the sun. He could hear the cold sound of water slopped on the cobblestones and traffic like a dimmed helicopter. His life seemed to have solidified overnight. Its substance was translucid, like jasper. He was contained in everything he had ever said and done. As for his pain, it was an anxious mystery. My shoulder, my throat, my ribs: Is it a fatal angina? Cancer of the trachea? Of the lungs? The left side of his body was rotting with illness within the jasper shell of his life.

He said to the doctor, "I may have caught a chill." He heard himself describing every one of his symptoms, as if each were a special grievance.

The doctor heard him out. "I think it is just something I call bachelor's ailment," she said. "You ought to have a mistress, if only to give you something real to worry about." Perhaps she meant this kindly, but even a doctor can have curious motives, especially one who shows her gums when she laughs, and whose husband gets up early to avoid being alone with her. "Do you want to see someone at my clinic?"

"No. It will go away."

"Suit yourself."

H E DELIVERED his third lecture through a tight, cindery throat. The room was filled with students this time, smoking, fidgeting, reading, whispering. He wondered what they were doing indoors on a glowing day. They showed little interest and asked only a few of their puzzling questions. After the lecture a plump man who introduced himself as a journalist invited Piotr to the terrace of the Brasserie Balzar. He wore a nylon turtleneck pullover and blazer and a large chrome-plated watch. Piotr supposed that he must have been sent by Marek—one of his cousin's significant connections. The reporter drank beer. Piotr, whose vitals rejected even its smell now, had weak tea, and even his tea seemed aggressive.

The reporter had a long gulp of his beer and said, "Are you one of those rebel poets?"

"Not for a second," said Piotr fervently.

"What about the letter you sent to *Pravda* and that *Pravda* refused to print?"

"I have never written to *Pravda,*" said Piotr.

The reporter scribbled away, using many more words than Piotr had. Piotr remarked, "I am not a Soviet poet. I am a Polish lecturer, officially invited by a French university."

At this the reporter wrote harder than ever, and then asked Piotr about the Warsaw Legia—which Piotr, after a moment of brick wall, was able to recognize as the name of a football team—and about its great star, Robert Gadocha, whom Piotr had never heard of at all. The reporter shook Piotr's hand and departed. Piotr meant to make a note of the strange meeting and to ask Marek about the man, but as he opened his pocket diary he saw something of far greater importance—today was the sixteenth of October, the feast day of St. Jadwiga. His hostess, whose name this was, had particularly wanted him to be there for dinner. He went to a Swiss film about a girl in love with a married dentist, slept comfortably until the renunciation scene, and remembered when he came out that he would have to bring his hostess a present. Buying flowers, he glanced across the shop and saw the Austrian. He was with an old woman—his mother, perhaps. She moved back and forth, pointing and laughing in a way Piotr took to be senile. As she bent her topknot over calla lilies Piotr saw the Austrian clearly. Oh, it was the same man, with the wide forehead and slight smile. He gave the babbling old woman all his attention and charm. But when he and Piotr stood side by side, each of them paying—one for lilies, one for roses—Piotr saw that he was older than the Austrian in the picture, and that his arms and shoulders were stiff, slightly paralyzed. The senile old mother was efficient and brisk; it was she who carried the flowers. The Austrian was back in Venice, where he belonged. Is that where I want him, Piotr wondered.

The entire apartment, even Piotr's part of it, smelled of food cooking. The doctor had waved and tinted her hair and darkened her lashes. Her husband was dressed in a dark suit and sombre tie. His gift to his wife, a pair of coral earrings, reposed on a velvet cushion on the dining-room table. The guests, remnants of the couple's old, happy days in the Resistance, sat stiffly, drinking French apéritifs. They were "little" Poles; Marek would not have known their names, or wished to. Their wives were French, so that the conversation was in French and merely polite. No one came in unexpectedly, as friends usually did for a name day. St. Jadwiga, incarnated in Paris, seemed to Piotr prim and middle-class. From Heaven his mind moved naturally to Venice, where he saw a white table and white chairs on the edge of a blue square. But perhaps Venice was quite other—perhaps it was all dark stone.

He had trouble swallowing his drink. A demon holding a pitchfork sat in his throat. Sometimes the pitchfork grazed his ear. The three men and Jadwiga soon slipped into Polish and reminiscences of the war. The French wives chatted to each other, and then the doctor drew their chairs close to the television set. She had been one of a delegation of doctors who that day had called on the Minister of Health; if they looked hard they might see a glimpse of her. All seven stared silently at the clockface now occupying the screen. The seconds ticked over. As soon as the news began, the doctor's husband began closing the shutters and drawing the curtains. It was a noisy performance, and Piotr saw that the doctor had tears in her eyes. Piotr thought of how this sniping went on night after night, with guests or without. He stared at lights reflected on the glassy screen, like fragments of a planet. A clock on the marble mantel had hands that never moved. The mirror behind the clock was tipped at an angle, so that Piotr could see himself. His hostess, following her most important guest's gaze, cried that the clock worked perfectly; her husband kept forgetting to wind it! At this everyone smiled at Piotr, as if to say, "So that is what poets wonder about!"

Dinner was further delayed because of a television feuilleton everyone in the room except Piotr had been following for seventeen weeks.
A girl named Vanessa had been accused of euthanasia on the person
of her aunt, named Ingrid, who had left Vanessa a large fortune.
Anthony, a police detective from the Sûreté whose role it was to bully
Vanessa into a hysterical confession, was suspected by all in the room
(save Piotr). Anthony was a widower. His young daughter, Samantha,
had left home because she wanted to be a championship swimmer.
Anthony was afraid Samantha would die of heart failure as her
mother, Pamela, had. Samantha did not know that at the time of her
mother's death there had been whispers about euthanasia. The detective's concern for Samantha's inherited weakness was proof to everyone (except Piotr) that he had been innocent of Pamela's death. The
dead aunt's adopted son, Flavien, who had been contesting the will,
and who had been the cause of poor Vanessa's incarceration in the
Santé prison, now said he would not testify against her after all.
Piotr's France, almost entirely out of literature, had given him people
sensibly called Albertine, Berthe, Marcel, and Colette. This flowering
of exotic names bewildered him, but he did not think it worth
mentioning. He had a more precise thought, which was that if his
throat infection turned out to be cancer it would remove the need
for wondering about anything. He invented advice he would leave his
children: "Never try to make an unhappy person happy. It is a waste
of life, and you will defeat your own natural goodness." In the looking
glass behind the stopped clock Piotr was ugly and old.

Before going to sleep that night he read the account he had
written of his love for Laurie. It had turned into a long wail, something for the ear, a babbling complaint. Describing Laurie, he had
inevitably made two persons of her. Behind one girl—unbreakably
jaunty, lacking only in imagination—came a smaller young woman
who was fragile and untruthful and who loved out of fear. He had
never sensed any fear in Laurie. He decided he would never write in
that way about his life again.

He was pulled out of a long dream about airports by his own
choked coughing. His left lung was on fire and a new pain, like an

electric wire, ran along his arm to the tip of his little finger. He tried to suppress the coughing because another burst would kill him, and as he held his breath he felt a chain being forged, link by link, around his chest. The last two links met; the chain began to tighten. Before he could suffocate, a cough broke from him and severed the chain. He was shaking, covered in icy sweat. Panting, unable to raise himself on an elbow because of the pain, he gasped, "Help me." He may have fainted. The room was bright, the doctor bent over him. She swabbed his arm—he felt the cold liquid but not the injection. He wanted to stay alive. That overrode everything.

Piotr awoke fresh and rested, as though nothing had happened in the night. Nevertheless he let his hostess make an appointment at her clinic. "I still think it is bachelor's ailment," she grumbled, but she spoke with a false gruffness that meant she might be unsure.

"It is a chill in the throat," he said. Oh, to be told there were only six weeks to live! To settle scores; leave nothing straggling; to go quietly. Everything had failed him: his work (because it inevitably fell short of his vision), his marriage, politics, and now, because of Laurie, he had learned something final about love. He had been to jail for nothing, a poet for nothing, in love for nothing. And yet, in the night, how desperately he had craved his life—his own life, not another's. Also, how shamefully frightened he had felt. Laurie had told him once that he was a coward.

"All married men of your kind are scared," she had said, calmly. This took place at the small table of one of the drugstores she favored. Piotr said he was not married, not really. "I'll tell you if you're married *and* scared," she said. She looked at him over a steaming coffee cup. "Supposing I bought a Matisse and gave it to you."

"How could you?"

"We're imagining. Say I went without a winter coat to buy you a Matisse."

"A Matisse what?"

"Anything. Signed."

"For a winter coat?"

"Can't you imagine anything, Potter? Your lovely Matisse arrives in Warsaw. You unwrap it. It is a present from me. You know that it comes with my love. It's the sign of love and of going without."

The trouble was that he *could* see it. He could see himself unrolling the picture. It was the head of a woman. "Would you hang it up on the wall?"

"Of course."

"And tell people where it came from?"

"What people?"

"If your wife came to see you, what would you say?"

"That it came from Paris."

"From someone who loved you?"

"It isn't her business," said Piotr.

"You see?" said Laurie. "You'd never dare. You're just a married man, and a frightened one. As frightened as any. You're even scared of an *ex*-wife. The day you can tell her where your Matisse came from, the day you say, 'I'm proud that any girl ever could have loved me that much,' then you'll know you've stopped being a scared little guy."

The Matisse was as real to him now as the car in which she had rushed away from the airport. Laurie could never in a lifetime have bought a Matisse. "Matisse" was only a name, the symbol of something famous and costly. She could accuse Piotr of fear because she was not certain what fear was; at least, she had never been frightened. Piotr thought this over coolly. Her voice, which had sung in his mind since her departure, suddenly left him. It had died on the last words, "scared little guy."

"How silent my life will be now," Piotr said to himself. Yet it seemed to him that his anguish was diminishing, leaving behind it only the faint, daily anxiety any man can endure. A few days later he actually felt slow happiness, like water rising, like a tide edging in. He sat drinking black tea with Maria in her cramped little flat full of bric-a-brac and sagging divans. He saw sun on a window box and felt the slow tide. Maria was talking about men and women. She used books for her examples and the names of characters in novels as if they were friends: "Anna lived on such a level of idiocy, really." "If Natasha had not had all those children . . ." "Lavretsky was too resigned." Piotr decided this might be the soundest way of getting at the truth. Experience had never brought him near to the truth about anything. If he had fled Warsaw, forsaken his children, tried to live with Laurie, been abandoned by her, he would have been washed up in rooms like Maria's. He would have remembered to put clean sheets on the bed when he had a new girl in the offing, given tea to visitors from the home country, quoted from authors, spoken comic-sounding French and increasingly old-fashioned Polish until everyone but a handful of other émigrés had left him behind.

At ten in the morning, by appointment, Piotr arrived at the clinic where his hostess had her office. She had drawn a map and had repeated her instructions in every form except Braille. The clinic was a nineteenth-century brick house, miles from a Métro stop and unknown to buses. He approached it through streets of condemned houses with empty windows. A nurse directed him out to a mossy yard that smelled of mushrooms, and across to a low, shabby building, where the dim light, the atmosphere of dread and of waiting, the smell of ether and of carbolic were like any prison infirmary on inspection day. He joined a dozen women and one other man sitting around the four sides of a room. A kitchen table, dead center, held last winter's magazines. No one looked at these except Piotr, who tiptoed to the table and back. The room was so silent that he could hear one of the women swallowing saliva. Then from next door came the sound of thuds and iron locks. His prison memories, reviving easily, said, Someone is dying. They have gone out, all of them, and left a prisoner to die alone.

"My throat," he rehearsed. "I have no fever, no other symptoms, nothing seriously the matter, nothing but an incurable cancer of the throat."

A few mornings later his hostess knocked at the bedroom door and came in without waiting. His pajama jacket was undone. He groped for his glasses and put them on, as if they dressed him. The doctor placed a small glass tube filled with pink tablets on the night table.

"I still think it is bachelor's ailment," she said. "But if the pain should leave your throat, where you seem to want it to be, and you feel something here," placing an impudent hand on his chest, "take two of these half an hour apart. As soon as you get back to Warsaw, go into hospital for serious tests. I'll give you your dossier before you leave, with a letter for your doctor."

"What is it?"

"Just do as I tell you. It isn't serious."

"I'll imagine the worst," said Piotr.

"Imagining the worst protects you from it."

The worst was not a final illness; it was still a Venice built of white stone, with white bridges and statues. On a snowy street Laurie studied the menu outside a restaurant. Hand in hand with the Austrian, she said, "I'd rather go home and make love." Piotr's hand closed around the vial of pills. He guessed that the medicine was a placebo, but it could be a remedy for the worst. A placebo might accidentally attack the secret enemy that, unknown to the most alert and intelligent doctors in Paris, was slowly killing Piotr.

THE WORST, as always, turned out to be something simple. The French teacher sent to Poland in exchange for Piotr had wandered from her subject. Finding her students materialistic and coarsely bourgeois, she had tried to fire them with revolutionary ideals and had been expelled from the country. In retaliation, Piotr was banished from France. Marek accompanied his cousin to police headquarters. He seemed as helpless as Piotr and for once had no solutions. Piotr received a five-day reprieve to wind up his affairs. He would not give another lecture, and unless Laurie came back he would never see her again. Marek questioned him—grilled him, in fact: Who was the reporter he had talked to at the Balzar? Could Piotr describe him? Was he a Pole, an American? What about the pregnant girl—had Piotr offended her, had he made foolish and untranslatable jokes during that day's lecture? Piotr answered patiently, but Marek was not satisfied. There must have been Someone, he said, meaning the shadowy Someone who dogged their lives, who fed émigré fears and fantasies. In Marek's experience Someone always turned out to have a name, to be traceable. When, barely two days later, Someone informed Piotr that he had violated his agreement (that is, he was leaving) and therefore would not receive any money, he gazed at the unreadable signature and knew for certain that no human brain could be behind this; it was entirely the work of some bureaucratic machine performing on its own. Marek continued to grumble and to speculate about Someone, while Piotr settled for the machine. It was a restful solution and one he had learned to live with.

Except for his debt to Marek, which he now had no means of repaying, Piotr had no regrets about leaving. He seemed to have been sleeping in the doctor's old office forever, hearing her wounded voice in the night, assaulted by the strident news broadcast at six, measuring the size of today's stone in his chest, opening the shutters to a merciless sky, thinking of the mailbox and the key and the message from Laurie. Piotr suddenly realized that he had gone in and out of the house twice that day without looking for a letter. That was freedom! It was like the return to life after a long illness, like his wife feeding him smuggled soup out of a jar and saying, "You *will* get better." When he called Maria to say goodbye, she took the news of his leaving calmly. Piotr was only another novel. She turned the pages slowly. Sometimes in novels there is bound to be a shock. She invited him to tea, as though he had just arrived and their best conversations were yet to come. On his way to this last visit Piotr forced himself to look in the letter box, out of distant sympathy for the victim he had once been. Inside, propped at an angle, was a view of San Pietro in Venice and a message in Laurie's childish hand, with the inevitable spelling mistake:

> It is over.
> My friend and I seperating forever.
> It is you I love.
> Back Monday 8 PM. Please meet chez moi.

"Love" was underlined three times.

Piotr had been condemned to death by hanging but now the blindfold was removed. He descended the gallows steps to perfect safety. The hangman untied his hands, lit his cigarette. He was given a passport good for all countries and for eternity. His first poems had just been published. He had fallen in love and she loved him, she was "really chearfull," and love, love, love was underlined three times. Today was Monday; there were still four hours to wait. The courtyard and the dull street beyond it became as white as Piotr's imagined Venice. He stood in the transformed street and said to himself that he was forty-three and that at last, for the first time, a woman had

given something up for him. Laurie had turned from the person who
provided travel, friendship, warmth, material help (somebody was
certainly paying for the seventh-floor studio) for the sake of Piotr. She
had done it without asking him to underwrite her risk, without a
guarantee. Now he understood the fable about the Matisse, about
loving and doing without.

He began to walk slowly toward a bus stop. Now, think about this,
he told himself. She is alone except for that one brother who never
writes. She has no training, no real education to speak of, and no
money, and money is oxygen here in the West. Well, she has me,
he thought. She has only me, and she could have anyone. The feeling
that her silvery world depended on him now made it all the more
mysterious and desirable. Now, be practical, he said. Now, be practical. . . . But he did not know what to be practical about; it was part
of his new, thrilling role as Laurie's protector. What next? Piotr was
separated, not divorced. He would return to Warsaw, divorce his
wife, come back to France, and marry Laurie. He wondered how he
had been so obtuse until now, why he had not thought of this sooner.
Laurie had never mentioned any such arrangement—another proof
of her generosity. He would apply for a post in France, perhaps at
a provincial university. He would read poetry aloud to the wives of
doctors and notaries and they would imagine he had escaped from
Siberia and it was Russian they were hearing.

Piotr had forgotten that he was expelled, might never be allowed
out of Poland or back into France in his lifetime, that he owed money
to Marek, that he was entangled, hobbled, bound. His children became remote and silent, as if they had never existed outside their
father's imagination.

Piotr, who never discussed his private affairs, told Maria about
Laurie. His account of the long journey leading up to the arrival of
the postcard, and Maria's reaction to it, created a third person in the
room. She was a quiet, noble girl who without a trace of moral
blackmail had traded safety for love. "She is the wonderful woman
you deserve," said Maria, listening intently. Before bliss submerged
him completely Piotr was able to see Maria and himself as two figures
bobbing in the wake of a wreck. Their hopefulness about love had
survived prisons. And yet every word he was saying seemed to him

like part of a long truth. His new Laurie resembled the imaginary Matisse she had sent to Warsaw, which he had unrolled with wonder and admiration: she was motionless, mute, she was black-on-white, and she never looked at him.

"Promise me one thing," said Maria. "That you will not ask her any questions. Promise." He promised. Leaning forward, she took Piotr's face in her hands and kissed him. "I wish you so much happiness," she said.

Hɪs ᴜɴᴘᴀᴄᴋᴇᴅ suitcase at his feet, Piotr sat on the edge of the bed. Laurie lay on her side, her head on her arm. The ashtray between them did not prevent her from sprinkling the white coverlet with ash. She had been under the shower when he arrived and she still wore a towelling bathrobe. Her hair, damp and darkened, lay flat on her neck and cheek and gave her a tight, sleek, unknown quality.

"Oh, it was all right when we were tramping around looking at those damned churches," she said. "But right from the beginning I knew it was going wrong. I felt something in him—a sort of disapproval of me. Everything he'd liked until now he started to criticize. Those Catholics—they always go back to what they were. Sex was wrong, living was wrong. Only God was O.K. He said why didn't I work, why didn't I start training to be a nurse. He said there was a world shortage of nurses. 'You could be having a useful life,' he said. It was horrible, Potter. I just don't know what went wrong. I thought maybe he'd met a girl he liked better than me. I kept fishing, but he wouldn't say. He was comparing—I could tell that. He said, 'All *you* ever think about is your lunch and your breakfast'—something like that."

Piotr said, "What is the business he so enjoys running?"

"Watch straps."

"Watch straps?"

"That's what he was doing in Italy. Buying them. We were in Florence, Milan. Venice was the holiday part. You should have seen the currency he smuggled in—Swiss, American. The stuff was falling out of his pockets like oak leaves. His mind was somewhere else the whole time. We weren't really together. We were just two travellers who happened to be sharing a room."

"You didn't happen to find yourself in the same bed?" said Piotr. He moved the ashtray out of the way and edged a box of paper handkerchiefs into its place. Although her face did not crumple or her voice change, tears were forming and spilling along her cheek and nose.

"Oh, sometimes, after a good dinner. He said a horrible thing. He said, 'Sometimes I can't bear to touch you.' No, no, we were just two travellers," she said, blowing her nose. "We each had our own toothpaste, he had his cake of soap. I didn't bring any soap and when we were moving around, changing hotels, he'd pack his before I'd even had my bath. I'd be there in the bathtub and he'd already packed his soap. He'd always been nice before. I just don't know. I'll never understand it. Potter, I can't face going out. I haven't eaten all day, but I still can't face it. Could you just heat some water and pour it over a soup cube for me?"

"Watch straps," said Piotr in a language she could not understand. He turned on the little electric plate. "Watch straps."

"He pretended he was doing it for me," said Laurie, lying flat on her back now. "Letting me go so I could create my own life. Those Catholics. He just wanted to be free for some other reason. To create his, I suppose."

"Is he still young enough for that?" said Piotr. "To create a whole life?"

"He's younger than you are, if that's young."

"I thought it might have been a much older person," said Piotr. "Your first friend of all. He took you home for holidays, out of Bishop Purse."

"*That* one. No-o-o. What finally happened with *him* was, his wife got sick. She got this awful facial neuralgia. It made a saint out of him. Believe me, Potter, when you get mixed up with a married man you're mixed up with his wife, too. They work as a team. Even when she doesn't know, she knows. It's an inside job. They went all over the place seeing new doctors. She used to scream with pain in hotel rooms. It's the sickness of unhappy wives—did you know?"

"I know about the ailment of bachelors. I thought you said it was the Venice person"—he was about to say "the Austrian"—"who knew you when you were young."

"Everybody got me young, when it comes to that. Oh," she said, suddenly alert, sitting up, dry-eyed, "don't sit there looking superior."

"I am standing," said Piotr. "I am here like a dog on its hind legs with a bowl of soup."

She took the bowl, with a scowl that would have meant ingratitude had its source been anything but mortification. "Well," she said abruptly, "I couldn't count on you, could I? You come and go and you've got those children. Who do they live with?"

"Their mother."

A tremor, like a chill, ran over her, and he recalled how she had trembled and spilled her coffee long ago. "How old are they?"

"Twelve and six."

"Why did you have the second one?" (Her first sensible observation.) "Girls?"

"Two boys."

"I hope they die."

"I don't," said Piotr.

"Do they love you?"

He hesitated; where love was concerned he had lost his bearings. He said, "They seem to eat up love and wait for more."

"Is there always more?"

"So far."

"They're like me, then," said Laurie.

"No, for children it is real food. It adds to their bones."

"Then it's not like me. I soak it up and it disappears and I feel undernourished. Do they like you?"

"They are excited and happy when they see me but hardly notice when I go."

"That's because you bring them presents." She began to cry, hard this time. "They won't need you much longer. They've got their mother. I really need you. I need you more than they do. I need any man more than his children do."

Piotr found sheets in the wardrobe and made the bed; he found pajamas in one of her plastic boxes, and the Polish sleeping potion in the bathroom. He counted out the magic drops. "Now sleep," he said. Something was missing: "Where is your white watch?"

"I don't know. I must have lost it. I lost it ages ago," she said, and turned on her side.

Piotr hung up Laurie's bathrobe and emptied the ashtray. He rinsed the yellow bowl and put it back on the shelf. He still had to break the news of his going; he did not feel banished but rather as if it were he who had decided to leave, who had established his own fate. Who gave you the "Palmstroem" poems, said Piotr silently. Another Potter? The man who had you at fifteen and then shipped you to Europe when you started getting in his way? Was it the Austrian? The man in Venice who suddenly feels he is sinning and can't bear to touch you? At the back of his mind was a small, anxious, jealous Piotr, for whom he felt little sympathy.

Laurie, though fresh from a shower, had about her a slightly sour smell, the scent that shock and terror produce on the skin. She was young, so that it was no worse than fresh yeast, or the odor of bread rising—the aura of the living, not yet of the dead. He remembered his wife and how her skin, then her voice, then her mind had become acid. "Am I plain?" she had said. "Am I diseased? Don't you consider me a normal woman?" You are good, you are brave, you are an impeccable mother to your children, but I don't want you, at least not the way you want me to, had been his answer. And so she became ugly, ill, haunted—all that he dreaded in women. It seemed to him that he saw the first trace of this change in the sleeping Laurie. She had lost her credentials, her seal of aristocracy. She had dropped to a lower division inhabited by Piotr's wife and Piotr himself; they were inferiors, unable to command loyalty or fidelity or even consideration in exchange for passion. Her silvery world, which had reflected nothing but Piotr's desperate inventions, floated and sank in Venice. This is what people like Maria and me are up against, he thought—our inventions. We belong either in books or in prison, out of the way. Romantic people are a threat to civilization. That man in Venice who wanted to make a nurse of poor Laurie was a romantic, too, a dangerous lunatic.

Laurie lay breathing deeply and slowly, in a sleep full of colored dreams—dreams of an imaginary Matisse, a real Lake Constance, a real Venice, dark and sad. "On a sailing holiday at Lake Constance . . ." Even now, when it no longer mattered, the truth of this particular dream clamped on Piotr's chest like the ghost of an old pain. Quietly, in order not to disturb her, he took one of his pink placebos. He thought of how frightened she would be if she woke to find him in the grip of an attack—she would be frightened of nearly everything now. He could still see the car hurtling all over the map as Laurie tried to run away from him and what she called "the situation." He could see it even though the journey had been only in her imagination, then in his. She had flown to Zurich, probably, and been met by, certainly, the man whose business was watch straps, or even . . . It doesn't matter now, he said. She had been telling the truth, because her mind had been in flight.

He lay down beside her and, reaching out, switched off the light. The pattern of reflected street lights that sprang to life on the ceiling had, for three nights long ago, been like the vault of heaven. After tonight Laurie would watch it alone—at any rate, without Piotr. Poor Laurie, he thought. Poor, poor Laurie. He felt affection, kindness—less than he could feel for his children, less than the obligation he still owed his wife. Out of compassion he stroked her darkened hair. No one but Piotr himself could have taken the measure of his disappointment as he said, So there really was nothing in it, was there? So this was all it ever was—only tenderness. An immense weight of blame crushed him, flattened him, and by so doing cleansed and absolved him. I was incapable of any more feeling than this. I never felt more than kindness. There was nothing in it from the beginning. It was only tenderness, after all.

HIS MOTHER

HIS MOTHER had come of age in a war and then seemed to live a long grayness like a spun-out November. "Are you all right?" she used to ask him at breakfast. What she really meant was: Ask me how I am, but she was his mother and so he would not. He leaned two fists against his temples and read a book about photography, waiting for her to cut bread and put it on a plate for him. He seldom looked up, never truly saw her—a stately, careless widow with unbrushed red hair, wearing an old fur coat over her nightgown; her last dressing gown had been worn to ribbons and she said she had no money for another. It seemed that nothing could stop her from telling him how she felt or from pestering him with questions. She muttered and smoked and drank such a lot of strong coffee that it made her bilious, and then she would moan, "God, God, my liver! My poor head!" In those days in Budapest you had to know the black market to find the sort of coffee she drank, and of course she would not have any but the finest smuggled Virginia cigarettes. "Quality," she said to him— or to his profile, rather. "Remember after I have died that quality was important to me. I held out for the best."

She had known what it was to take excellence for granted. That was the difference between them. Out of her youth she could not recall a door slammed or a voice raised except in laughter. People had floated like golden dust; whole streets of people buoyed up by optimism, a feeling for life.

He sat reading, waiting for her to serve him. He was a stone out of a stony generation. Talking to him was like lifting a stone out of water. He never resisted, but if you let go for even a second he sank and came to rest on a dark sea floor. More than one of her soft-tempered lovers had tried to make a friend of him, but they had always given up, as they did with everything. How could she give up? She loved him. She felt shamed because it had not been in her to control armies, history, his stony watery world. From the moment he appeared in the kitchen doorway, passive, vacant, starting to live again only because this was morning, she began all over: "Don't you feel well?" "Are you all right?" "Why can't you smile?"—though the loudest sentence was in silence: Ask me how I am.

After he left Budapest (got his first passport, flew to Glasgow with a soccer team, never came back) she became another sort of person, an émigré's mother. She shed the last of her unimportant lovers and with the money her son was soon able to send she bought a white blouse, combs that would pin her hair away from her face, and a blue kimono. She remembered long, tender conversations they had had together, and she got up early in the morning to see if a letter had come from him and then to write one of her own describing everything she thought and did. His letters to his mother said, Tell me about your headaches, are you still drinking too strong coffee, tell me the weather, the names of streets, if you still bake poppy-seed cakes.

She had never been any sort of a cook, but it seemed to her that, yes, she had baked for him, perhaps in their early years together, which she looked back upon as golden, and lighter than thistledown.

On Saturday afternoons she put on a hat and soft gray gloves and went to the Vörösmarty Café. It had once had a French name, Gerbeaud, and the circle of émigrés' mothers who met to exchange news and pictures of grandchildren still called it that. "Gerbeaud" was a sign of caste and the mark of a generation, too. Like herself, the women wore hats and sometimes scarves of fur, and each carried a stuffed handbag she would not have left behind on a tabletop for even a second. Their sons' letters looked overstamped, like those he sent her now. She had not been so certain of her rank before, or felt so quietly sure, so well thought of. A social order prevailed, as it does everywhere. The aristocrats were those whose children had never left Europe; the poorest of the poor were not likely ever to see their sons again, for they had gone to Chile and South Africa. Switzerland was superior to California. A city earned more points than a town. There was no mistaking her precedence here; she was a grand duchess. If Glasgow was unfamiliar, the very sound of it somehow rang with merit. She always had a new letter to show, which was another symbol of one's station, and they were warm messages, concerned about her health, praising her remembered skill with pies and cakes. Some mothers were condemned to a lowly status only because their children forgot to write. Others had to be satisfied with notes from foreign daughters-in-law, which were often sent from table to table before an adequate reading could be obtained. Here again she was in demand, for she read three foreign languages, which suggested a background of governesses and careful schools. She might have left it at that, but her trump credentials were in plain sight. These were the gifts he bestowed—the scarves and pastel sweaters, the earrings and gloves.

What she could not do was bring the émigré ritual to its final celebration; it required a passport, a plane ticket, and a visit to the absent son. She would never deliver into his hands the three immutable presents, which were family jewelry, family photographs, and a cake. Any mother travelling to within even a few miles of another woman's son was commissioned to take all three. The cake was a bother to carry, for the traveller usually had one of her own, but who could say no? They all knew the cake's true value. Look at the way her own son claimed his share of nourishment from a mother whose cooking had always been a joke.

No one had ever been close to Scotland, and if she had not applied for her own passport or looked up flight schedules it was for a good reason: her son had never suggested she come. And yet, denied even the bliss of sewing a garnet clip into a brassière to be smuggled to an unknown daughter-in-law, she still knew she was blessed. Other ismissed, forgotten. More than one had confided, "My ⸻ ⸺ vell be dead." She did not think of him as dead—how could she?—but as a coin that had dropped unheard, had rolled crazily, lay still. She knew the name of his car, of his street, she had seen pictures of them, but what did she know?

AFTER HE disappeared, as soon as she had made certain he was safe and alive, she rented his room to a student, who stayed with her for three years in conditions of some discomfort, for she had refused, at first, to remove anything belonging to her son. His books were sacred. His records were not to be played. The records had been quite valuable at one time; they were early American rock slipped in by way of Vienna and sold at a murderous rate of exchange. These collected dust now, like his albums of pictures—like the tenant student's things too, for although she pinned her hair up with combs and wore a spotless blouse, she was still no better a housekeeper. Her tenant studied forestry. He was a bumpkin, and somewhat afraid of her. She could never have mistaken him for a son. He crept in and out and brought her flowers. One day she played a record for him, to which he listened with deference rather than interest, and she remembered herself, at eighteen, hearing with the same anxious boredom a warped scene from "Die Walküre," both singers now long dead. Having a student in the flat did not make her feel she was in touch with her son, or even with his generation. His room changed meanwhile; even its smell was no longer the same. She began to wonder what his voice had been like. She could see him, she dreamed of him often, but her dreams and memories were like films with the sound track removed.

The bumpkin departed, and she took in his place a future art historian—the regime produced these in awesome numbers now—who gave way, in turn, to the neurasthenic widow of a poet. The poet's widow was taken over in time by her children, and replaced by a couple of young librarians. And then came two persons not quite chosen by herself. She could have refused them, but thought it wiser not to. They were an old man and his pregnant granddaughter. They seemed to be brokenly poor; the granddaughter almost to the end of her term worked long hours in a plasma laboratory. And yet they appeared endowed with dark, important connections: no sooner were they installed than she was granted a telephone, which her tenants never used without asking, and only for laconic messages—the grandfather to state that his granddaughter was not yet at home, or the girl to take down the day and hour of a meeting somewhere. After the granddaughter had her baby they became four in a flat that had barely been comfortable for two. She cleared out the last of her son's records and his remaining books (the rest had long ago been sold or stolen), and she tried to establish a set of rules. For one, she made it a point to remain in the kitchen when her tenants took their meals. This was her home; it was not strictly a shared and still less a communal Russian apartment. But she could go only so far: it was at Gerbeaud's that she ranked as a grand duchess. These people reckoned differently, and on their terms she was, if not at the foot of the ladder, then dangerously to one side of it; she had an émigré son, she received gifts and money from abroad, and she led in terms of the common good a parasitic existence. They were careful, even polite, but they were installed. She was inhabited by them, as by an illness one must learn to endure.

It was around this time—when her careless, undusted, but somehow pure rooms became a slum, festooned with washing, reeking of boiling milk, where she was seldom alone or quiet—that she began to drift away from an idea she had held about her age and time. Where, exactly, was the youth she recalled as happy? What had been its shape, its color? All that golden dust had not belonged to her—it had been part of her mother. It was her mother who had floated like thistledown, smiled, lived with three servants on call, stood with a false charming gaucherie, an arm behind her, an elbow grasped. That simulated awkwardness took suppleness and training; it required something her generation had not been granted, which was time. Her mother had let her coat fall on the floor because coats were replaceable then, not only because there had been someone to pick it up. She had carried a little curling iron in her handbag. When she quarrelled with her husband, she went to the station and climbed into a train marked "Budapest-Vienna-Rome," and her husband had thought it no more than amusing to have to fetch her back. Slowly, as "eighteen" came to mean an age much younger than her son's, as he grew older in Scotland, married, had a child, began slipping English words into his letters, went on about fictitious apple or poppy-seed cakes, she parted without pain from a soft, troubled memory, from an old gray film about porters wheeling steamer trunks, white fur wraps, bunches of violets, champagne. It was gone: it had never been. She and her son were both mistaken, and yet they had never been closer. Now that she had the telephone, he called her on Easter Sunday, and on Christmas Eve, and on her birthday. His wife had spoken to her in English:

"It's snowing here. Is it snowing in Budapest?"

"It quite often snows."

"I hope we can meet soon."

"That would be pleasant."

His wife's parents sent her Christmas greetings with stern Biblical messages, as if they judged her, by way of her son, to be frivolous, without a proper God. At least they knew now that she spoke correct English; on the other hand, perhaps they were simple souls unable to imagine that anything but English could ever be.

They were not out of touch; nor did he neglect her. No one could say that he had. He had never missed a monthly transfer of money, he was faithful about sending his overstamped letters and the colored snapshots of his wife, his child, their Christmas tree, and his wife's parents side by side upon a modern-looking sofa. One unposed picture had him up a ladder pasting sheets of plastic tiles on a kitchen wall. She could not understand the meaning of this photograph, in which he wore jeans and a sweater that might have been knitted by an untalented child. His hair had grown long, it straggled in brown mouse-tails over the collar of the lamentable pullover. He stood in profile, so that she could see just half of a new and abundant mustache. Also—and this might have been owing to the way he stood, because he had to sway to hold his balance—he looked as if he might have become, well, a trifle stout. This was a picture she never showed anyone at Vörösmarty Place, though she examined it often, by several kinds of light. What did it mean, what was its secret expression? She looked for the invisible ink that might describe her son as a husband and father. He was twenty-eight, he had a mustache, he worked in his own home as a common laborer.

She said to herself, I never let him lift a finger. I waited on him from the time he opened his eyes.

In response to the ladder picture she employed a photographer, a former schoolfriend of her son's, to take a fiercely lighted portrait of her sitting on her divan-bed with a volume of Impressionist reproductions opened on her lap. She wore a string of garnets and turned her head proudly, without gaping or grinning. From the background wall she had removed a picture of clouds taken by her son, then a talented amateur, and hung in its stead a framed parchment that proved her mother's family had been ennobled. Actually a whole town had been ennobled at a stroke, but the parchment was legal and real. Normally it would not have been in her to display the skin of the dog, as these things were named, but perhaps her son's wife, looking at the new proud picture of his mother, might inquire, "What is that, there on the wall?"

She wrote him almost every morning—she had for years, now. At night her thoughts were morbid, unchecked, and she might have been likely to tell about her dreams or to describe the insignificant sadness of a lifetime, or to recall the mornings when he had eaten breakfast in silence, when talking to him had been like lifting a stone. Her letters held none of those things. She wrote wearing her blue, clean, now elderly kimono, sitting at the end of her kitchen table, while her tenants ate and quarrelled endlessly.

She had a long back-slanting hand she had once been told was the hand of a liar. Upside down the letter looked like a shower of rain. It was strange, mysterious, she wrote, to be here in the kitchen with the winter sun on the sparkling window (it was grimy, in fact; but she was seeing quite another window as she wrote) and the tenant granddaughter, whose name was Ilona, home late on a weekday. Ilona and the baby and the grandfather were all three going to a funeral this morning. It seemed a joyous sort of excursion because someone was fetching them by car; that in itself was an indication of their sombre connections. It explained, in shorthand, why she had not squarely refused to take them in. She wrote that the neighbors' radios could be heard faintly like the sounds of life breaking into a fever, and about Ilona preparing a boiled egg for the baby, drawing a face on the shell to make it interesting, and the baby opening his mouth, patting the table in a broken rhythm, patting crumbs with a spread-out hand. Here in the old kitchen she shared a wintry, secret, morning life with strangers.

Grandfather wore a hearing aid, but he had taken it apart, and it lay now on the table like parts of a doll's skull. Wearing it at breakfast kept him from enjoying his food. Spectacles bothered him, too. He made a noise eating, because he could not hear himself; nor did he see the mess around his cup and plate.

"Worse than an infant!" his granddaughter cried. She had a cross-looking little Tartar face. She tore squares of newspaper, one to go on the floor, another for underneath his plate. He scattered sugar and pipe ash and crusts and the pieces of his hearing aid. At the same time he was trying to attend to a crossword puzzle, which he looked at with a magnifying glass. But he still would not put his spectacles on, because they interfered with his food. Being deaf, he travelled alone in his memories and sometimes came out with just anything. His mind plodded back and forth. Looking up from the puzzle he said loudly, "My granddaughter has a diploma. Indeed she has. She worked in a hospital. Yes, she did. Some people think too much of themselves when they have a diploma. They begin to speak pure Hungarian. They try to speak like educated people. Not Ilona! You will never hear one word of good Hungarian from *her.*"

His granddaughter had just untied a towel she used as a bib for the child. She grimaced and buried her Tartar's grimace in the towel. Only her brown hair was seen, and her shaking shoulders. She might have been laughing. Her grandfather wore a benign and rather a foolish smile until she looked up and screamed, "I hate you." She reminded him of all that she had done to make him happy. She described the last place they'd lived in, the water gurgling in the pipes, the smell of bedbugs. She had found this splendid apartment; she was paying their rent. His little pension scarcely covered the coffee he drank. "You thought your son was too good for my mother," she said. "You made her miserable, too."

The old man could not hear any of this. His shaking freckled hands had been assembling the hearing aid. He adjusted it in time to hear Ilona say, "It is hard to be given lessons in correct speech by someone who eats like a pig."

He sighed and said only, "Children," as one might sound resigned to any natural enemy.

The émigré's mother, their landlady, had stopped writing. She looked up, not at them, but of course they believed they could be seen. They began to talk about their past family history, as they did when they became tense and excited, and it all went into the letter. Ilona had lost her father, her mother, and her little sister in a road accident when, with Grandfather, they had been on their way to a funeral in the suburbs in a bus.

Funerals seemed to be the only outing they ever enjoyed. The old man listened to Ilona telling it again, but presently he got up and left them, as if the death of his son allowed him no relief even so many years later. When he came back he had his hat and coat on. For some reason, he had misunderstood and thought they had to leave at once for the new excursion. He took his landlady's hand and pumped it up and down, saying, "From the bottom of my heart . . . ," though all he was leading up to was "Goodbye." He did not let her hand go until he inadvertently brought it down hard on a thick cup.

"He has always embarrassed us in public," said Ilona, clearing away. "What could we do? He was my father's father."

That other time, said the old man—calmed now, sitting down in his overcoat—the day of the *fatal* funeral, there had been time to spare, out in a suburb, where they had to change from one bus to another. They had walked once around a frozen duckpond. He had been amazed, the old man remembered, at how many people were free on a working weekday. His son carried one of the children; little Ilona walked.

"Of course I walked! I was twelve!" she screamed from the sink.

He had been afraid that Ilona would never learn to speak, because her mother said everything for her. When Ilona pointed with her woolly fist, her mother crooned, "Skaters." Or else she announced, "You are cold," and pulled a scarf up over Ilona's apple cheeks.

"That was my sister," Ilona said. "I was twelve."

"Now, a governess might have made the child speak, say words correctly," said the old man. "Mothers are helpless. They can only say yes, yes, and try to repeat what the child seems to be thinking."

"He has always embarrassed us," Ilona said. "My mother hated going anywhere in his company."

Once around the duckpond, and then an old bus rattled up and they got in. The driver was late, and to make up for time he drove fast. At the bottom of a hill, on a wide sheet of black ice, the bus turned like a balky horse, rocked, steadied, and the driver threw himself over the wheel as if to protect it. An army lorry came down the hill, the first of two. Ilona's mother pulled the baby against her and pulled Ilona's head on her lap.

"Eight killed, including the two drivers," Ilona said.

Here was their folklore, their richness; how many persons have lost their families on a bus and survived to describe the holocaust? No wonder she and Grandfather were still together. If she had not married her child's father, it was because he had not wanted Grandfather to live with them. "You, yes," he had said to Ilona. "Relatives, no." Grandfather nodded, for he was used to hearing this. Her cold sacrifice always came on top of his disapproval.

Well, that was not quite the truth of it, the émigré's mother went on writing. The man who had interceded for them, whom she had felt it was wiser not to refuse, who might be the child's father, had been married for quite a long time.

The old man looked blank and strained. His eyes had become small. He looked Chinese. "Where we lived then was a good place to live with children," he said, perhaps speaking of a quarter fading like the edge of a watercolor into gray apartment blocks. Something had frightened him. He took out a clean pocket handkerchief and held it to his lips.

"Another army lorry took us to the hospital," said Ilona. "Do you know what you were saying?"

He remembered an ambulance. He and his grandchild had been wrapped in blankets, had lain on two stretchers, side by side, fingers locked together. That was what he remembered.

"You said, '*My mother, my mother,*'" she told him.

"I don't think I said that."

Now they are having their usual disagreement, she wrote her son. Lorry or ambulance?

"I heard," said Ilona. "I was conscious."

"I had no reason. If I said, 'My mother,' I was thinking, 'My children.'"

The rainstorm would cover pages more. Her letter had veered off and resembled her thoughts at night. She began to tell him she had trouble sleeping. She had been given a wonderful new drug, but unfortunately it was habit-forming and the doctor would not renew it. The drug gave her a deep sleep, from which she emerged fresh and enlivened, as if she had been swimming. During the sleep she was allowed exact and colored dreams in which she was a young girl again and men long dead came to visit. They sat amiably discussing their deaths. Her first fiancé, killed in 1943, opened his shirt to show the chest wound. He apologized for having died without warning. He did not know that less than a year later she had married another man. The dead had no knowledge of love beyond the span of their own lives. The next night, she found herself with her son's father. They were standing together buying tickets for a play when she realized he was dead. He stood in his postwar shabbiness, discreet, hidden mind, camouflaged face, and he had ceased to be with the living. Her grief was so cruel that, lest she perish in sleep from the shock of it, someone unseen but conciliating suggested that she trade any person she knew in order to keep him with her. He would never have the misery of knowing that he was dead.

What would her son say to all this? My mother is now at an age when women dream of dead men, he might tell himself; when they begin to choose quite carelessly between the dead and the living. Women are crafty even in their sleep. They know they will survive. Why weep? Why discuss? Why let things annoy you? For a long time she believed he had left because he could not look at her life. Perhaps his going had been as artless, as simple, as he still insisted: he had got his first passport, flown out with a football team, never come back. He was between the dead and the living, a voice on the telephone, an affectionate letter full of English words, a coin rolled and lying somewhere in secret. And she, she was the revered and respected mother of a generous, an attentive, a camouflaged stranger.

Tell me the weather, he still wrote. Tell me the names of streets. She began a new page: Vörösmarty Place, if you remember, is at the beginning of Váci Street, the oldest street in the Old City. In the middle of the Place stands a little park. Our great poet, for whom the Place is named, sits carved in marble. Sculptured figures look gratefully up to him. They are grateful because he is the author of the national anthem. There are plane trees full of sparrows, and there are bus stops, and even a little Métro, the oldest in Europe, perhaps old-fashioned, but practical—it goes to the Zoo, the Fine Arts Museum, the Museum of Decorative Art, the Academy of Music, and the Opera. The old redoubt is there, too, at least one wall of it, backed up to a new building where you go to book seats for concerts. The real face of the redoubt has been in ruins since the end of the war. It used to be Moorish-romantic. The old part, which gave on the Danube, had in her day—no, in her mother's day—been a large concert hall, the reconstruction of which created grave problems because of modern acoustics. At Gerbeaud's the pastries are still the best in Europe, she wrote, and so are the prices. There are five or six little rooms, little marble tables, comfortable chairs. Between the stiff lace curtains and the windowpanes are quite valuable pieces of china. In summer one can sit on the pavement. There is enough space between the plane trees, and the ladies with their elegant hats are not in too much danger from the sparrows. If you come there, you will see younger people, too, and foreigners, and women who wait for foreigners, but most of the customers, yes, most, belong to the magic circle of mothers whose children have gone away. The café opens at ten and closes at nine. It is always crowded. "You can often find me there," she went on, "and without fail every Saturday," as if she might look up and see him draw near, transformed, amnesiac, not knowing her. I hope that I am not in your dreams, she said, because dreams are populated by the silent and the dead, and I still speak, I am alive. I wear a hat with a brim and soft gray gloves. I read their letters in three foreign languages. Thanks to you, I can order an endless succession of little cakes, I can even sip cognac. Will you still know me? I was your mother.

IRINA

O<small>NE OF</small> <small>IRINA</small>'s grandsons, nicknamed Riri, was sent to her at Christmas. His mother was going into hospital, but nobody told him that. The real cause of his visit was that since Irina had become a widow her children worried about her being alone. The children, as Irina would call them forever, were married and in their thirties and forties. They did not think they were like other people, because their father had been a powerful old man. He was a Swiss writer, Richard Notte. They carried his reputation and the memory of his puritan equity like an immense jar filled with water of which they had been told not to spill a drop. They loved their mother, but they had never needed to think about her until now. They had never fretted about which way her shadow might fall, and whether to stay in the shade or get out by being eccentric and bold. There were two sons and three daughters, with fourteen children among them. Only Riri was an only child. The girls had married an industrial designer, a Lutheran minister (perhaps an insolent move, after all, for the daughter of a militant atheist), and an art historian in Paris. One boy had become a banker and the other a lecturer on Germanic musical tradition. These were the crushed sons and loyal daughters to whom Irina had been faithful, whose pictures had travelled with her and lived beside her bed.

Few of Notte's obituaries had even mentioned a family. Some of his literary acquaintances were surprised to learn there had been any children at all, though everyone paid homage to the soft, quiet wife to whom he had dedicated his books, the subject of his first rapturous poems. These poems, conventional verse for the most part, seldom translated out of German except by unpoetical research scholars, were thought to be the work of his youth. Actually, Notte was forty when he finally married, and Irina barely nineteen. The obituaries called Notte the last of a breed, the end of a Tolstoyan line of moral lightning rods—an extinction which was probably hard on those writers who came after him, and still harder on his children. However, even to his family the old man had appeared to be the very archetype of a respected European novelist—prophet, dissuader, despairingly opposed to evil, crack-voiced after having made so many pronouncements. Otherwise, he was not all that typical as a Swiss or as a Western, liberal, Protestant European, for he neither saved, nor invested, nor hid, nor disguised his material returns.

"What good is money, except to give away?" he often said. He had a wife, five children, and an old secretary who had turned into a dependent. It was true that he claimed next to nothing for himself. He rented shabby, ramshackle houses impossible to heat or even to clean. Owning was against his convictions, and he did not want to be tied to a gate called home. His room was furnished with a cot, a lamp, a desk, two chairs, a map of the world, a small bookshelf—no more, not even carpets or curtains. Like his family, he wore thick sweaters indoors as out, and crouched over inadequate electric fires. He seldom ate meat—though he did not deprive his children—and drank water with his meals. He had married once—once and for all. He could on occasion enjoy wine and praise and restaurants and good-looking women, but these festive outbreaks were on the rim of his real life, as remote from his children—as strange and as distorted to them—as some other country's colonial wars. He grew old early, as if he expected old age to suit him. By sixty, his eyes were sunk in pockets of lizard skin. His hair became bleached and lustrous, like the scrap of wedding dress Irina kept in a jeweller's box. He was photographed wearing a dark suit and a woman's plaid shawl—he was always cold by then, even in summer—and with a rakish felt hat shading half his face. His wife still let a few photographers in, at the end—but not many. Her murmured "He is working" had for decades been a double lock. He was as strong as Rasputin, his enemies said; he went on writing and talking and travelling until he positively could not focus his eyes or be helped aboard a train. Nearly to the last, he and Irina swung off on their seasonal cycle of journeys to Venice, to Rome, to cities where their married children lived, to Liège and Oxford for awards and honors. His place in a hotel dining room was recognizable from the door because of the pills, drops, and powders lined up to the width of a dinner plate. Notte's hypochondria had been known and gently caricatured for years. His sons, between them, had now bought up most of the original drawings: Notte, in infant's clothing, downing his medicine like a man (he had missed the Nobel); Notte quarrelling with Aragon and throwing up Surrealism; a grim female figure called "Existentialism" taking his pulse; Notte catching Asian flu on a cultural trip to Peking. During the final months of his life his children noticed that their mother had begun acquiring medicines of her own, as if hoping by means of mirror-magic to draw his ailments into herself.

If illness became him, it was only because he was fond of ritual, the children thought—even the hideous ceremonial of pain. But Irina had not been intended for sickness and suffering; she was meant to be burned dry and consumed by the ritual of him. The children believed that the end of his life would surely be the death of their mother. They did not really expect Irina to turn her face to the wall and die, but an exclusive, even a selfish, alliance with Notte had seemed her reason for being. As their father grew old, then truly old, then old in mind, and querulous, and unjust, they observed the patient tenderness with which she heeded his sulks and caprices, his almost insane commands. They supposed this ardent submission of hers had to do with love, but it was not a sort of love they had ever experienced or tried to provoke. One of his sons saw Notte crying because Irina had buttered toast for him when he wanted it dry. She stroked the old man's silky hair, smiling. The son hated this. Irina was diminishing a strong, proud man, making a senile child of him, just as Notte was enslaving and debasing her. At the same time the son felt a secret between the two, a mystery. He wondered then, but at no other time, if the secret might not be Irina's invention and property.

Notte left a careful will for such an unworldly person. His wife was to be secure in her lifetime. Upon her death the residue of income from his work would be shared among the sons and daughters. There were no gifts or bequests. The will was accompanied by a testament which the children had photocopied for the beauty of the handwriting and the charm of the text. Irina, it began, belonged to a generation of women shielded from decisions, allowed to grow in the sun and shade of male protection. This flower, his flower, he wrote, was to be cherished now as if she were her children's child.

"In plain words," said Irina, at the first reading, in a Zurich lawyer's office, "I am the heir." She was wearing dark glasses because her eyes were tired, and a tight hat. She looked tense and foreign.

Well, yes, that was it, although Notte had put it more gracefully. His favorite daughter was his literary executor, entrusted with the unfinished manuscripts and the journals he had kept for sixty-five years. But it soon became evident that Irina had no intention of giving these up. The children adored their mother, but even without love as a factor would not have made a case of it; Notte's lawyer had already told them about disputes ending in mazelike litigation, families sundered, contents of a desk sequestered, diaries rotting in bank vaults while the inheritors thrashed it out. Besides, editing Notte's papers would keep Irina busy and an occupation was essential now. In loving and unloving families alike, the same problem arises after a death: What to do about the widow?

Irina settled some of it by purchasing an apartment in a small Alpine town. She chose a tall, glassy, urban-looking building of the kind that made conservationist groups send round-robin letters, accompanied by incriminating photographs, to newspapers in Lausanne. The apartment had a hall, an up-to-date kitchen, a bedroom for Irina, a spare room with a narrow bed in it, one bathroom, and a living room containing a couch. There was a glassed-in cube of a balcony where in a pinch an extra cot might have fitted, but Irina used the space for a table and chairs. She ordered red lampshades and thick curtains and the pale furniture that is usually sold to young couples. She seemed to come into her own in that tight, neutral flat, the children thought. They read some of the interviews she gave, and approved: she said, in English and Italian, in German and French, that she would not be a literary widow, detested by critics, resented by Notte's readers. Her firm diffidence made the children smile, and they were proud to read about her dignified beauty. But as for her intelligence—well, they supposed that the interviewers had confused fluency with wit. Irina's views and her way of expressing them were all camouflage, simply part of a ladylike undereducation, long on languages and bearing, short on history and arithmetic. Her origins were Russian and Swiss and probably pious; the children had not been drawn to that side of the family. Their father's legendary peasant childhood, his isolated valley-village had filled their imaginations and their collective past. There was a sudden April lightness in her letters now that relieved and yet troubled them. They knew it was a sham happiness, Nature's way of protecting the survivor from immediate grief. The crisis would come later, when her most secret instincts had built a seawall. They took turns invading her at Easter and in the summer, one couple at a time, bringing a child apiece— there was no room for more. Winter was a problem, however, for the skiing was not good just there, and none of them liked to break up their families at Christmastime. Not only was Irina's apartment lacking in beds but there was absolutely no space for a tree. Finally, she offered to visit them, in regular order. That was how they settled it. She went to Bern, to Munich, to Zurich, and then came the inevitable Christmas when it was not that no one wanted her but just that they were all doing different things.

She had written in November of that year that a friend, whom she described, with some quaintness, as "a person," had come for a long stay. They liked that. A visit meant winter company, lamps on at four, China tea, conversation, the peppery smell of carnations (her favorite flower) in a warm room. For a week or two of the visit her letters were blithe, but presently they noticed that "the person" seemed to be having a depressing effect on their mother. She wrote that she had been working on Notte's journals for three years now. Who would want to read them except old men and women? His moral and political patterns were fossils of liberalism. He had seen the cracks in the Weimar Republic. He had understood from the beginning what Hitler meant. If at first he had been wrong about Mussolini, he had changed his mind even before Croce changed his, and had been safely back on the side of democracy in time to denounce Pirandello. He had given all he could, short of his life, to the Spanish Republicans. His measure of Stalin had been so wise and unshakably just that he had never been put on the Communist index—something rare for a Western Socialist. No one could say, ever, that Notte had hedged or retreated or kept silent when a voice was needed. Well, said Irina, what of it? He had written, pledged, warned, signed, declared. And what had he changed, diverted, or stopped? She suddenly sent the same letter to all five children: "This Christmas I don't want to go anywhere. I intend to stay here, in my own home."

They knew this was the crisis and that they must not leave her to face it alone, but that was the very winter when all their plans ran down, when one daughter was going into hospital, another moving to a different city, the third probably divorcing. The elder son was committed to a Christmas with his wife's parents, the younger lecturing in South Africa—a country where Irina, as Notte's constant reflection, would certainly not wish to set foot. They wrote and called and cabled one another: What shall we do? Can you? Will you? I can't.

Irina had no favorites among her children, except possibly one son who had been ill with rheumatic fever as a child and required long nursing. To him she now confided that she longed for her own childhood sometimes, in order to avoid having to judge herself. She was homesick for a time when nothing had crystallized and mistakes were allowed. Now, in old age, she had no excuse for errors. Every thought had a long meaning; every motive had angles and corners, and could be measured. And yet whatever she saw and thought and attempted was still fluid and vague. The shape of a table against afternoon light still held a mystery, awaited a final explanation. You looked for clarity, she wrote, and the answer you had was paleness, the flat white cast that a snowy sky throws across a room.

Part of this son knew about death and dying, but the rest of him was a banker and thoroughly active. He believed that, given an ideal situation, one should be able to walk through a table, which would save time and roundabout decisions. However, like all of Notte's children he had been raised with every awareness of solid matter too. His mother's youthful, yearning, and probably religious letter made him feel bland and old. He told his wife what he thought it contained, and she told a sister-in-law what she thought he had said. Irina was tired. Her eyesight was poor, perhaps as a result of prolonged work on those diaries. Irina did not need adult company, which might lead to morbid conversation; what she craved now was a symbol of innocent, continuing life. An animal might do it. Better still, a child.

Riri did not know that his mother would be in hospital the minute his back was turned. Balanced against a tame Christmas with a grandmother was a midterm holiday, later, of high-altitude skiing with his father. There was also some further blackmail involving his holiday homework, and then the vague state of behavior called "being reasonable"—that was all anyone asked. They celebrated a token Christmas on the twenty-third, and the next day he packed his presents (a watch and a tape recorder) and was put on a plane at Orly West. He flew from Paris to Geneva, where he spent the real Christmas Eve in a strange, bare apartment into which an aunt and a large family of cousins had just moved. In the morning he was wakened when it was dark and taken to a six-o'clock train. He said goodbye to his aunt at the station, and added, "If you ask the conductor or anyone to look after me, I'll—" Whatever threat was in his mind he seemed ready to carry out. He wore an R.A.F. badge on his jacket and carried a Waffen-S.S. emblem in his pocket. He knew better than to keep it in sight. At home they had already taken one away but he had acquired another at school. He had Astérix comic books for reading, chocolate-covered hazelnuts for support, and his personal belongings in a fairly large knapsack. He made a second train on his own and got down at the right station.

He had been told that he knew this place, but his memory, if it was a memory, had to do with fields and a picnic. No one met him. He shared a taxi through soft snow with two women, and paid his share—actually more than his share, which annoyed the women; they could not give less than a child in the way of a tip. The taxi let him off at a dark, shiny tower on stilts with granite steps. In the lobby a marble panel, looking like the list of names of war dead in his school, gave him his grandmother on the eighth floor. The lift, like the façade of the building, was made of dark mirrors into which he gazed seriously. A dense, thoughtful person looked back. He took off his glasses and the blurred face became even more remarkable. His grandmother had both a bell and a knocker at her door. He tried both. For quite a long time nothing happened. He knocked and rang again. It was not nervousness that he felt but a new sensation that had to do with a shut, foreign door.

His grandmother opened the door a crack. She had short white hair and a pale face and blue eyes. She held a dressing gown gripped at the collar. She flung the door back and cried, "Darling Richard, I thought you were arriving much later. Oh," she said, "I must look dreadful to you. Imagine finding me like this, in my dressing gown!" She tipped her head away and talked between her fingers, as he had been told never to do, because only liars cover their mouths. He saw a dark hall and a bright kitchen that was in some disorder, and a large dark, curtained room opposite the kitchen. This room smelled stuffy, of old cigarettes and of adults. But then his grandmother pushed the draperies apart and wound up the slatted shutters, and what had been dark, moundlike objects turned into a couch and a bamboo screen and a round table and a number of chairs. On a bookshelf stood a painting of three tulips that must have fallen out of their vase. Behind them was a sky that was all black except for a rainbow. He unpacked a portion of the things in his knapsack—wrapped presents for his grandmother, his new tape recorder, two school textbooks, a note-book, a Bic pen. The start of this Christmas lay hours behind him and his breakfast had died long ago.

"Are you hungry?" said his grandmother. He heard a telephone ringing as she brought him a cup of hot milk with a little coffee in it and two fresh croissants on a plate. She was obviously someone who never rushed to answer any bell. "My friend, who is an early riser, even on Christmas Day, went out and got these croissants. Very bravely, I thought." He ate his new breakfast, dipping the croissants in the milk, and heard his grandmother saying, "Well, I must have misunderstood. But he managed. . . . He didn't bring his skis. Why not? . . . I see." By the time she came back he had a book open. She watched him for a second and said, "Do you read at meals at home?"

"Sometimes."

"That's not the way I brought up your mother."

He put his nose nearer the page without replying. He read aloud from the page in a soft schoolroom plain-chant: " 'Go, went, gone. Stand, stood, stood. Take, took, taken.' "

"Richard," said his grandmother. When he did not look up at once, she said, "I know what they call you at home, but what are you called in school?"

"Riri."

"I have three Richard grandsons," she said, "and not one is called Richard exactly."

"I have an Uncle Richard," he said.

"Yes, well, he happens to be a son of mine. I never allowed nicknames. Have you finished your breakfast?"

"Yes."

"Yes who? Yes what? What is your best language, by the way?"

"I am French," he said, with a sharp, sudden, hard hostility, the first tense bud of it, that made her murmur, "So soon?" She was about to tell him that he was not French—at least, not really—when an old man came into the room. He was thin and walked with a cane.

"Alec, this is my grandson," she said. "Riri, say how do you do to Mr. Aiken, who was kind enough to go out in this morning's snow to buy croissants for us all."

"I knew he would be here early," said the old man, in a stiff French that sounded extremely comical to the boy. "Irina has an odd ear for times and trains." He sat down next to Riri and clasped his hands on his cane; his hands at once began to tremble violently. "What does that interesting-looking book tell you?" he asked.

" 'The swallow flew away,' " answered Irina, reading over the child's head. " 'The swallow flew away with my hopes.' "

"Good God, let me look at that!" said the old man in his funny French. Sure enough, those were the words, and there was a swallow of a very strange blue, or at least a sapphire-and-turquoise creature with a swallow's tail. Riri's grandmother took her spectacles out of her dressing-gown pocket and brought the book up close and said in a loud, solemn way, " 'The swallows will have flown away.' " Then she picked up the tape recorder, which was the size of a glasses case, and after snapping the wrong button on and off, causing agonizing confusion and wastage, she said with her mouth against it, " 'When shall the swallows have flown away?' "

"No," said Riri, reaching, snatching almost. As if she had always given in to men, even to male children, she put the book down and the recorder too, saying, "Mr. Aiken can help with your English. He has the best possible accent. When he says 'the girl' you will think he is saying 'de Gaulle.' "

"Irina has an odd ear for English," said the old man calmly. He got up slowly and went to the kitchen, and she did too, and Riri could hear them whispering and laughing at something. Mr. Aiken came back alone carrying a small glass of clear liquid. "The morning heart-starter," he said. "Try it." Riri took a sip. It lay in his stomach like a warm stone. "No more effect on you than a gulp of milk," said the old man, marvelling, sitting down close to Riri again. "You could probably do with pints of this stuff. I can tell by looking at you you'll be a drinking man." His hands on the walking stick began to tremble anew. "I'm not the man I was," he said. "Not by any means." Because he did not speak English with a French or any foreign accent, Riri could not really understand him. He went on, "Fell down the staircase at the Trouville casino. Trouville, or that other place. Shock gave me amnesia. Hole in the stair carpet—must have been. I went there for years," he said. "Never saw a damned hole in anything. Now my hands shake."

"When you lift your glass to drink they don't shake," called Riri's grandmother from the kitchen. She repeated this in French, for good measure.

"She's got an ear like a radar unit," said Mr. Aiken.

Riri took up his tape recorder. In a measured chant, as if demonstrating to his grandmother how these things should be done, he said, " 'The swallows would not fly away if the season is fine.' "

"Do you know what any of it means?" said Mr. Aiken.

"He doesn't need to know what it means," Riri's grandmother answered for him. "He just needs to know it by heart."

T HEY WERE GLASSED in on the balcony. The only sound they could hear was of their own voices. The sun on them was so hot that Riri wanted to take off his sweater. Looking down, he saw a chalet crushed in the shadows of two white blocks, not so tall as their own. A large, spared spruce tree suddenly seemed to retract its branches and allow a great weight of snow to slip off. Cars went by, dogs barked, children called—all in total silence. His grandmother talked English to the old man. Riri, when he was not actually eating, read *Astérix in Brittany* without attracting her disapproval.

"If people can be given numbers, like marks in school," she said, "then children are zero." She was enveloped in a fur cloak, out of which her hands and arms emerged as if the fur had dissolved in certain places. She was pink with wine and sun. The old man's blue eyes were paler than hers. "Zero." She held up thumb and forefinger in an O. "I was there with my five darling zeros while he . . . You are probably wondering if I was *ever* happy. At the beginning, in the first days, when I thought he would give me interesting books to read, books that would change all my life. Riri," she said, shading her eyes, "the cake and the ice cream were, I am afraid, the end of things for the moment. Could I ask you to clear the table for me?"

"I don't at home." Nevertheless he made a wobbly pile of dishes and took them away and did not come back. They heard him, indoors, starting all over: " 'Go, went, gone.' "

"I have only half a memory for dates," she said. "I forget my children's birthdays until the last minute and have to send them telegrams. But I know *that* day. . . ."

"The twenty-sixth of May," he said. "What I forget is the year."

"I know that I felt young."

"You were. You *are* young," he said.

"Except that I was forty if a day." She glanced at the hands and wrists emerging from her cloak as if pleased at their whiteness. "The river was so sluggish, I remember. And the willows trailed in the river."

"Actually, there was a swift current after the spring rains."

"But no wind. The clouds were heavy."

"It was late in the afternoon," he said. "We sat on the grass."

"On a raincoat. You had thought in the morning those clouds meant rain."

"A young man drowned," he said. "Fell out of a boat. Funny, he didn't try to swim. So people kept saying."

"We saw three firemen in gleaming metal helmets. They fished for him so languidly—the whole day was like that. They had a grappling hook. None of them knew what to do with it. They kept pulling it up and taking the rope from each other."

"They might have been after water lilies, from the look of them."

"One of them bailed out the boat with a blue saucepan. I remember that. They'd got that saucepan from the restaurant."

"Where we had lunch," he said. "Trout, and a coffee cream pudding. You left yours."

"It was soggy cake. But the trout was perfection. So was the wine. The bridge over the river filled up slowly with holiday people. The three firemen rowed to shore."

"Yes, and one of them went off on a shaky bicycle and came back with a coil of frayed rope on his shoulders."

"The railway station was just behind us. All those people on the bridge were waiting for a train. When the firemen's boat slipped off down the river, they moved without speaking from one side of the bridge to the other, just to watch the boat. The silence of it."

"Like the silence here."

"This is planned silence," she said.

Riri played back his own voice. A tinny, squeaky Riri said, " 'Go, went, gone. Eat, ate, eaten. See, saw, sen.' "

" 'Seen'!" called his grandmother from the balcony. " 'Seen,' not 'sen.' His mother made exactly that mistake," she said to the old man. "Oh, stop that," she said. He was crying. "Please, please stop that. How could I have left five children?"

"Three were grown," he gasped, wiping his eyes.

"But they didn't know it. They didn't know they were grown. They still don't know it. And it made six children, counting him."

"The secretary mothered him," he said. "All he needed."

"I know, but you see she wasn't his wife, and he liked saying to strangers 'my wife,' 'my wife this,' 'my wife that.' What is it, Riri? Have you come to finish doing the thing I asked?"

He moved close to the table. His round glasses made him look desperate and stern. He said, "Which room is mine!" Darkness had gathered round him in spite of the sparkling sky and a row of icicles gleaming and melting in the most dazzling possible light. Outrage, a feeling that consideration had been wanting—that was how homesickness had overtaken him. She held his hand (he did not resist—another sign of his misery) and together they explored the apartment. He saw it all—every picture and cupboard and doorway—and in the end it was he who decided that Mr. Aiken must keep the spare room and he, Riri, would be happy on the living-room couch.

The old man passed them in the hall; he was obviously about to rest on the very bed he had just been within an inch of losing. He carried a plastic bottle of Evian. "Do you like the bland taste of water?" he said.

Riri looked boldly at his grandmother and said, "Yes," bursting into unexplained and endless-seeming laughter. He seemed to feel a relief at this substitute for impertinence. The old man laughed too, but broke off, coughing.

At half past four, when the windows were as black as the sky in the painting of tulips and began to reflect the lamps in a disturbing sort of way, they drew the curtains and had tea around the table. They pushed Riri's books and belongings to one side and spread a cross-stitched tablecloth. Riri had hot chocolate, a croissant left from breakfast and warmed in the oven, which made it deliciously greasy and soft, a slice of lemon sponge cake, and a banana. This time he helped clear away and even remained in the kitchen, talking, while his grandmother rinsed the cups and plates and stacked them in the machine.

The old man sat on a chair in the hall struggling with snow boots. He was going out alone in the dark to post some letters and to buy a newspaper and to bring back whatever provisions he thought were required for the evening meal.

"Riri, do you want to go with Mr. Aiken? Perhaps you should have a walk."

"At home I don't have to."

His grandmother looked cross; no, she looked worried. She was biting something back. The old man had finished the contention with his boots and now he put on a scarf, a fur-lined coat, a fur hat with earflaps, woollen gloves, and he took a list and a shopping bag and a different walking stick, which looked something like a ski pole. His grandmother stood still, as if dreaming, and then (addressing Riri) decided to wash all her amber necklaces. She fetched a wicker basket from her bedroom. It was lined with orange silk and filled with strings of beads. Riri followed her to the bathroom and sat on the end of the tub. She rolled up her soft sleeves and scrubbed the amber with laundry soap and a stiff brush. She scrubbed and rinsed and then began all over again.

"I am good at things like this," she said. "Now, unless you hate to discuss it, tell me something about your school."

At first he had nothing to say, but then he told her how stupid the younger boys were and what they were allowed to get away with.

"The younger boys would be seven, eight?" Yes, about that. "A hopeless generation?"

He wasn't sure; he knew that his class had been better.

She reached down and fetched a bottle of something from behind the bathtub and they went back to the sitting room together. They put a lamp between them, and Irina began to polish the amber with cotton soaked in turpentine. After a time the amber began to shine. The smell made him homesick, but not unpleasantly. He carefully selected a necklace when she told him he might take one for his mother, and he rubbed it with a soft cloth. She showed him how to make the beads magnetic by rolling them in his palms.

"You can do that even with plastic," he said.

"Can you? How very sad. It is dead matter."

"Amber is too," he said politely.

"What do you want to be later on? A scientist?"

"A ski instructor." He looked all round the room, at the shelves and curtains and at the bamboo folding screen, and said, "If you didn't live here, who would?"

She replied, "If you see anything that pleases you, you may keep it. I want you to choose your own present. If you don't see anything, we'll go out tomorrow and look in the shops. Does that suit you?" He did not reply. She held the necklace he had picked and said, "Your mother will remember seeing this as I bent down to kiss her

good night. Do you like old coins? One of my sons was a collector."
In the wicker basket was a lacquered box that contained his uncle's
coin collection. He took a coin but it meant nothing to him; he let
it fall. It clinked, and he said, "We have a dog now." The dog wore
a metal tag that rang when the dog drank out of a china bowl.
Through a sudden rainy blur of new homesickness he saw that she
had something else, another lacquered box, full of old cancelled
stamps. She showed him a stamp with Hitler and one with an Italian
king. "I've kept funny things," she said. "Like this beautiful Russian
box. It belonged to my grandmother, but after I have died I expect
it will be thrown out. I gave whatever jewelry I had left to my
daughters. We never had furniture, so I became attached to strange
little baskets and boxes of useless things. My poor daughters—I had
precious little to give. But they won't be able to wear rings any more
than I could. We all come into our inherited arthritis, these knotted-
up hands. Our true heritage. When I was your age, about, my mother
was dying of . . . I wasn't told. She took a ring from under her pillow
and folded my hand on it. She said that I could always sell it if I had
to, and no one need know. You see, in those days women had nothing
of their own. They were like brown paper parcels tied with string.
They were handed like parcels from their fathers to their husbands.
To make the parcel look attractive it was decked with curls and piano
lessons, and rings and gold coins and banknotes and shares. After
appraising all the decoration, the new owner would undo the knots."

"Where is that ring?" he said. The blur of tears was forgotten.

"I tried to sell it when I needed money. The decoration on the
brown paper parcel was disposed of by then. Everything thrown,
given away. Not by me. My pearl necklace was sold for Spanish
refugees. Victims, flotsam, the injured, the weak—they were important. I wasn't. The children weren't. I had my ring. I took it to a
municipal pawnshop. It is a place where you take things and they give
you money. I wore dark glasses and turned up my coat collar, like a
spy." He looked as though he understood that. "The man behind the
counter said that I was a married woman and I needed my husband's
written consent. I said the ring was mine. He said nothing could be
mine, or something to that effect. Then he said he might have given
me something for the gold in the band of the ring but the stones were

worthless. He said this happened in the finest of families. Someone had pried the real stones out of their setting."

"Who did that?"

"A husband. Who else would? Someone's husband—mine, or my mother's, or my mother's mother's, when it comes to that."

"With a knife?" said Riri. He said, "The man might have been pretending. Maybe he took out the stones and put in glass."

"There wasn't time. And they were perfect imitations—the right shapes and sizes."

"He might have had glass stones all different sizes."

"The women in the family never wondered if men were lying," she said. "They never questioned being dispossessed. They were taught to think that lies were a joke on the liar. That was why they lost out. He gave me the price of the gold in the band, as a favor, and I left the ring there. I never went back."

He put the lid on the box of stamps, and it fitted; he removed it, put it back, and said, "What time do you turn on your TV?"

"Sometimes never. Why?"

"At home I have it from six o'clock."

THE OLD MAN came in with a pink-and-white face, bearing about him a smell of cold and of snow. He put down his shopping bag and took things out—chocolate and bottles and newspapers. He said, "I had to go all the way to the station for the papers. There is only one shop open, and even then I had to go round to the back door."

"I warned you that today was Christmas," Irina said.

Mr. Aiken said to Riri, "When I was still a drinking man this was the best hour of the day. If I had a glass now, I could put ice in it. Then I might add water. Then if I had water I could add whiskey. I know it is all the wrong way around, but at least I've started with a glass."

"You had wine with your lunch and gin instead of tea and I believe you had straight gin before lunch," she said, gathering up the beads and coins and the turpentine and making the table Riri's domain again.

"Riri drank that," he said. It was so obviously a joke that she turned her head and put the basket down and covered her laugh with her fingers, as she had when she'd opened the door to him—oh, a long time ago now.

"I haven't a drop of anything left in the house," she said. That didn't matter, the old man said, for he had found what he needed. Riri watched and saw that when he lifted his glass his hand did not tremble at all. What his grandmother had said about that was true.

They had early supper and then Riri, after a courageous try at keeping awake, gave up even on television and let her make his bed of scented sheets, deep pillows, a feather quilt. The two others sat for a long time at the table, with just one lamp, talking in low voices. She had a pile of notebooks from which she read aloud and sometimes she showed Mr. Aiken things. He could see them through the chinks in the bamboo screen. He watched the lamp shadows for a while and then it was as if the lamp had gone out and he slept deeply.

THE ROOM was full of mound shapes, as it had been that morning when he arrived. He had not heard them leave the room. His Christmas watch had hands that glowed in the dark. He put on his glasses. It was half past ten. His grandmother was being just a bit loud at the telephone; that was what had woken him up. He rose, put on his slippers, and stumbled out to the bathroom.

"Just answer yes or no," she was saying. "No, he can't. He has been asleep for an hour, two hours, at least. . . . Don't lie to me—I am bound to find the truth out. Was it a tumor? An extrauterine pregnancy? . . . Well, look. . . . Was she or was she not pregnant? What can you mean by 'not exactly'? If you don't know, who will?" She happened to turn her head, and saw him and said without a change of tone, "Your son is here, in his pajamas; he wants to say good night to you."

She gave up the telephone and immediately went away so that the child could talk privately. She heard him say, "I drank some kind of alcohol."

So that was the important part of the day: not the journey, not the necklace, not even the strange old guest with the comic accent. She could tell from the sound of the child's voice that he was smiling. She picked up his bathrobe, went back to the hall, and put it over his shoulders. He scarcely saw her: he was concentrated on the distant voice. He said, in a matter-of-fact way, "All right, goodbye," and hung up.

"What a lot of things you have pulled out of that knapsack," she said.

"It's a large one. My father had it for military service."

Now, why should that make him suddenly homesick when his father's voice had not? "You are good at looking after yourself," she said. "Independent. No one has to tell you what to do. Of course, your mother had sound training. Once when I was looking for a nurse for your mother and her sisters, a great peasant woman came to see me, wearing a black apron and black buttoned boots. I said, 'What can you teach children?' And she said, 'To be clean and polite.' Your grandfather said, 'Hire her,' and stamped out of the room."

His mother interested, his grandfather bored him. He had the Christian name of a dead old man.

"You will sleep well," his grandmother promised, pulling the feather quilt over him. "You will dream short dreams at first, and by morning they will be longer and longer. The last one of all just before you wake up will be like a film. You will wake up wondering where you are, and then you will hear Mr. Aiken. First he will go round shutting all the windows, then you will hear his bath. He will start the coffee in an electric machine that makes a noise like a door rattling. He will pull on his snow boots with a lot of cursing and swearing and go out to fetch our croissants and the morning papers. Do you know what day it will be? The day after Christmas." He was almost asleep. Next to his watch and his glasses on a table close to the couch was an Astérix book and Irina's Russian box with old stamps in it. "Have you decided you want the stamps?"

"The box. Not the stamps."

He had taken, by instinct, the only object she wanted to keep. "For a special reason?" she said. "Of course, the box is yours. I am only wondering."

"The cover fits," he said.

She knew that the next morning he would have been here forever and that at parting time, four days later, she would have to remind him that leaving was the other half of arriving. She smiled, knowing how sorry he would be to go and how soon he would leave her behind. "This time yesterday . . ." he might say, but no more than once. He was asleep. His mouth opened slightly and the hair on his forehead became dark and damp. A doubled-up arm looked uncomfortable but Irina did not interfere; his sunken mind, his unconscious movements, had to be independent, of her or anyone, particularly of her. She did not love him more or less than any of her grandchildren. You see, it all worked out, she was telling him. You, and your mother, and the children being so worried, and my old friend. Anything can be settled for a few days at a time, though not for longer. She put out the light, for which his body was grateful. His mind, at that moment, in a sunny icicle brightness, was not only skiing but flying.